Burn, Black Wall Street, Burn

by Dennis "Mitch" Maley

A novel based on real events

Author's photo by Virginia Hoffman Photography

For all of the people on the margins of society whose stories have been erased by the more powerful forces that canonize our history.

"Ignorance, allied with power, is the most ferocious enemy justice can have."

James Baldwin

Chapter 1

Greenwood District, Tulsa, Oklahoma: 1921

Dick Rowland wasn't an early riser. In fact, his Aunt Damie would sometimes take to throwing a pitcher of water at him on the occasions she had to climb the stairs a third time to chase him out of bed.

Most mornings, the tall, slender 17 year old would practically sleepwalk through breakfast, little more than a mumble to the boarders at the big table in his aunt's kitchen, at least until he'd had a second cup of her notoriously strong coffee in his system, a third if he was out late drinking gin with the neighborhood boys the night before.

But once he hit Greenwood Avenue, the rhythm of its hustle bustle ran through Dick's feet, and you could practically see the energy move up his thin, gangly body and out to his lanky limbs. Dick loved the frenetic pace, the sounds of the motor cars scooting by and the hum from the throngs of Greenwood's Black citizens who weaved between one another on their way to work, school or some manner of commerce.

On Friday, Aunt Damie would walk with him, at least until they got to the streetcar stop on 1st Street where she would catch a ride to the bank in order to make the weekly deposit. Dick didn't like the streetcar. He found it claustrophobic and grew impatient as it made the stops on the way to downtown Tulsa. He preferred to walk to the shine stand where he and the other young men from Greenwood who'd dropped out of high school to stake their claim in Tulsa's bounty would polish the shoes of oil tycoons, often collecting more money than some of the doctors and lawyers back across the Frisco tracks.

"There he is, Diamond Dick, right there," said a young boy who was standing next to a friend that was hustling newspapers on a busy corner before school.

"Diamond Dick, you want a paper?" asked the other boy.

Neither of them looked older than eight. Dick smiled, happy to be recognized, which caused Aunt Damie to frown.

"Nah, but let me get one for my Auntie," said Dick.

He flicked a coin to the boy and winked as both craned their necks for a peek at Dick's shiny, diamond pinky ring, which caught the sun as he rolled the paper, putting it under the arm that Aunt Damie would take, though not before shooting him a dirty look.

"You know the good book says that pride is the beginning of sin," said Damie.

"Come on, Aunt Damie, a man's gotta look good to earn his place in this world. I don't think they was meaning it's a sin to put a little shine to yourself from time to time. If so, wouldn't be so many church-going women keeping the hat shops in business."

Dick smirked as he cleaned the ring against his shirt.

"I just don't know why you bought that flashy thing, is all," said Damie. "It don't do nothing but draw attention, and attention be the last thing a young Black man ought want to draw to himself in this world. Only thing you'll end up earning is your final reward."

Just then, two teenaged girls around Dick's age walked by and smiled. He tipped his hat and grinned.

"Seems some kinds of attention are much better than others in this world, Aunt Damie," he said while sneaking a peek over his shoulder.

Damie gave him a playful smack on the arm with her handbag.

"That's the kind of attention that's gonna be quickest to send you outta this world if you're not careful," she said in an even sterner voice. "You keep that up and you can go meet your maker and ask him what he meant your own foolish self."

They arrived at the 1st Street streetcar stop, where Dick was to depart and Damie would to board. 1st Street had long been the de facto border between the Black and white sections, and the crowd began to become one of mixed races. A white prostitute from one of the nearby brothels smiled at Dick as she passed.

"Good morning, Dick."

Dick tipped his hat and smiled back.

"Ma'am."

Aunt Damie hit him with her handbag again, this time in earnest.

"Boy, if I didn't raise you smart enough to know that you're not to even look at a white woman, even *that* sort a one, then you ain't got a thought worth having!"

Dick sighed.

"Aunt Damie, that's just Ellie from around the way. We just friendly, that's all."

Damie stiffened and pointed toward the boy's face.

"Don't give me no lip, young man, and don't act as though I'm a fool. If you think that just because we in Greenwood a man can't get hung for breaking certain rules, you got less sense than a mule! Mind yourself, Dick Rowland. Mind yourself."

Dick bowed his head.

"Yes, Aunt Damie."

Her posture softened.

"You got anything you want me to put in the bank, have less help getting yourself in trouble?"

Dick pulled out a thick wad of bills and peeled off several, giving them to his aunt, whose eyes widened at the sight.

"For the bank," said Dick, handing her the money before peeling off a crisp five. "And for you to treat yourself to a new church hat."

Damie's jaw dropped.

"Boy, where you keep getting all this money from? I know you're not bringing that much in just shining shoes for those wildcatters."

"Wha'chu mean?"

"I mean I'd best not find out you're running liquor, or numbers, or anything else illegal with Freddy and those troublemakers you be associating with!"

"Aunt Damie, I swear, I don't need to do nothing illegal in this here town," said Dick. "These oil tycoons have so much money they tip you five dollars for a shine just to show up they friend who just tipped you four. And I got regulars who'll wait on line to get me to polish they wingtips when there's two seats open, just 'cause they know my shines are the brightest in Tulsa. Them white men across town know who got they shoes shined by Dick Rowland that morning and who didn't, and that's the truth."

Damie stared at him, shaking her head until she finally broke down and gave him a smile.

"I gotta get to that bank before it's 10 deep in the colored folks line," said Damie. "You keep your head down on that side of the tracks, young man, and you get back home for dinner straight after work. No gin on your breath neither, you hear?"

Dick smiled.

"I love you, Aunt Damie," he said, bending down to kiss the crown of her head.

"Mmm-hmmm," said Damie, flashing him the evil eye.

****

A loud whistle blew as a train rolled slowly to a stop next to a platform, where a sizable crowd had assembled outside of the Tulsa Union Depot station. When the door was opened, passengers immediately began to spill onto the platform and down the steps. A reasonably well-dressed, Black teenaged boy near the platform seemed to be looking for someone specific to step out. A well-dressed Black man finally emerged, pausing for a moment to take in the sight. Recognizing him, the young man quickly started off in his direction.

"Mr. Franklin, over here," cried the boy. "Mr Franklin."

The man's face registered surprise. The boy waved as he began to trot. When he arrived, he quickly picked up the two suitcases next to the man.

"Excuse me, were you perhaps sent by Mr. Spears?" asked the man.

"No sir, Mr. O.W. Gurley sent me over here to receive you," said the boy. "My name's Cecil."

The two men shook hands.

"Buck Franklin," said the man. "Pleased to meet you, Cecil."

"Mr. Gurley want me to give you a ride into Greenwood and offer you accommodations at his hotel," said Cecil.

At this, Buck looked even more perplexed.

"And how did you, or rather Mr. Gurley, know that I would be arriving today?"

Cecil looked to be confused by the question.

"Why it's big news in Greenwood, sir. Mr. Smitherman even wrote about the Amazing B.C. Franklin, the famous Negro attorney, in the Tulsa Star—that's our own Black newspaper—and how you was coming to town today on the train."

Buck remained surprised.

"All right then, Cecil," said Buck. "It's a pleasure to make your acquaintance. I suppose we should go and see your Mr. Gurley."

"Yes sir, Mr. Franklin, sir. Right this way to the motor car."

"Motor car?" asked Buck with an air of disbelief.

"Yes sir, Mr. Franklin," said Cecil. "We got our own jitney service in Greenwood, Negro owned by Mr. Franklin Berry, too. Mr. Gurley had Mr. Berry send over a private motor car just for you, sir."

Buck shook his head and smiled as they walked off.

****

On 1st Street, prostitutes were leaning over a porch railing trying to lure johns. Every door seemed to lead to either a saloon or a cat house, and no one was making much of an effort to keep a low profile for such illicit trade. The nation was under prohibition, but 1st Street was the quasi-legal red-light district of Tulsa, on which the pillars of the community had decided to concentrate vice, a significantly more manageable undertaking than trying to eliminate it, as efforts to do the latter had proven futile.

"Choctaw beer, gin, brown, strongest cheapest drinks in town," cried a barker in front of one of the speakeasies as a couple of roughnecks who hadn't made it back to the oil camps walked by the street, which seemed quite busy for mid-morning.

On the opposite corner, three Black men were conducting business with some Indians who'd pulled up on a covered Ford flatbed. The younger two wheeled kegs of

Choctaw beer toward a side door under the direction of the third, a man known as King Henry, a short but stout fellow of 32, whose powerful build remained noticeable under his dapper clothing.

"Mooch, get that choc into the back and then run the last two kegs over to the chink's place," said Henry to one of his boys. "He gonna have an envelope for you."

In the middle of the street, a mountainous mulatto man was riding a horse that seemed to be sauntering down the road the same way it looked as though the man himself might, were he on foot. The giant wore an Army Calvary jacket, and a leather satchel hung over his shoulder. It was quite clear that the man moved at his own pace, holding no fear of errant motorcars as he made his way, dead center, bisecting the street. This was a man for whom people got out of the way, instinctively eager to distance themselves from him, even if they did not suspect bad intentions.

Freddy was a thin and wiry boy of 16 who'd left school to work for King Henry the year before. He was the sort of young man who saw himself the way other slightly-built and unassuming men often do—harmless to the point of being invisible to the strong, a target only for the less weak. While the others looked to the ground or pretended to busy themselves, Freddy looked on. Henry wanted badly to seem above looking away from the giant but fell into that middle ground. Whereas he was surely no threat to the big man, his station in the hierarchy meant that he could more easily provoke him. Still, he couldn't allow Freddy or Mooch to see him cower, so he busied himself counting out money for the squat Indian man waiting by the truck.

"How much money you figure Obie got in that satchel, King?" asked Freddy.

"If it's one dime less than all the money in the whole damned world, it ain't worth thinking about," Henry answered.

"I bet he got a thousand at least, all the business Mann Brothers be doing," said Freddy, seemingly oblivious to Henry's tone. "Makes that run from they market to the bank every week, same day, same time, same streets, no heater or nothin'."

Henry stopped counting money out to the Indian and turned to Freddy, glancing out of the corner of his eye to ensure that the man was not yet close enough to possibly hear him speak.

"So wha'chu sayin', Freddy?"

"I'm just sayin' that's a lot of scratch to be wandering around with like that," said Freddy. "It's a wonder no one ever tried to jack him is all."

Henry gave him a light slap on the cheek, drawing his eye contact away from the street. Freddy put his hand to the spot that stung and looked at Henry, half offended, half confused.

"It's a wonder you manage to get your shoes tied in the morning, Freddy," said Henry in a hushed but purposeful tone. "Obie Mann don't carry no heater 'cause that man ain't gotta worry about gettin' jacked. Not by no white man, not by no Negroes, not even by no damned Martians. That giant killed more Krauts over in Germany than they could count. He damn sure ain't afraid of nothin' in Greenwood, believe dat."

The men hushed as Obie passed the intersection, giving a mean stare in both directions. Henry tipped his hat, but the giant offered no response.

"Yeah, I'm just sayin' though," said Freddy, just above a whisper.

"Well, don't be sayin', and don't be thinkin'," said Henry. "And if you even catch yourself dreaming about it, you best wake up and smack yourself in your own stupid, nappy head. Now y'all best get that other keg down to the chink's place like I told you to."

****

The lobby of O.W. Gurley's hotel was deliberately neutral, curated in such a way as to suggest that the well-appointed trappings were costly for the sake of quality and durability with the appropriate amount of ornate decorative flair, but without drawing the sort of attention to his holdings that he still didn't feel it safe for a very wealthy Black man to receive, even in Greenwood.

In Gurley's estimate, it was okay to be thought of as *well off* but dangerous to be perceived as eager to let white men know such a thing, especially those whose own possessions might leave them feeling vastly inferior to a Negro. Everything about him seemed designed with just such an effect in mind, from his clothes to his personal possessions. Anything that was not in a vault had strategic show value above all else.

Presently, Gurley was sorting through slips at the front desk with his employee.

"What room did you put Mr. Franklin in, Cecil?"

"Number four, Mr. Gurley, sir," said Cecil. "Had Charmaine clean it up extra good this morning, too. Put two mints under the pillow and the fruit soaps in the washroom."

"That a boy," said Gurley. "He doesn't strike me as a man ostentatious enough to feel comfortable in that grand palace of Stradford's, especially before his family has joined him."

"Osten ..." began Cecil, struggling with the word.

Gurley sighed.

"Ostentatious, son; flamboyant; given to gaudy displays of opulence."

Cecil gave him a blank look, to which Gurley wagged his finger.

"See, this is exactly why I've encouraged you to go back to school," said Gurley.

"Why I need to know all those white man words when I work here in Greenwood?" asked Cecil.

Gurley bristled before he'd even finished the sentence.

"Dammit, Cecil, they're not white words! It's the language of an educated man in America. You're only fluent in two things, the language of the street and the submissive language of servitude, and they will indeed suffice where you presently live and work, but they will never allow for you to rise above either."

"Why I want to go anywhere else, Mr. Gurley?" asked Cecil. "There's no place in this country where colored folks got it so good. You say so yourself all the time."

At this, Gurley softened just a bit.

"And there won't be anyplace else in this country where colored folk have it so good until we think bigger than the borders of our own neighborhood," said Gurley. "Greenwood isn't big enough for every Negro in America to come here, and the last thing the Black man needs to do is put himself all in one place anyway. It'd make it all too easy for these peckerwoods out here to exterminate us all at once! Lord, just look at what they did to the Indians."

Cecil shook his head and exhaled.

"You prolly right about that, Mr. Gurley. Whooee, you prolly right. Anyway, I think Mr. Franklin be real happy in our place, sir. He don't seem to me to be one of them dandies that go looking to flap they gums about how fancy everything they got is. He dapper for sure, but not showy about it, you know what I mean?"

Gurley shook his head and smiled at the irony.

"I believe you make a fine point, Cecil. However, renting a room to Mr. Franklin is not my primary interest."

"I don't understand?" said Cecil.

"Buck Franklin is going to be a prominent man in this town, you just wait and see," explained Gurley. "He has a reputation as one of the finest Negro lawyers in these parts. He's going to do a lot of business in Greenwood, and someday he'll likely have a lot of influence. The last thing I need is Stradford filling his head with all of those radical notions he likes to spout off about, but you keep that close to your vest, son, you hear?"

Cecil picked up a broom and began sweeping the floor in front of the desk.

"Mum's the word, Mr. Gurley, sir. Mum's the word."

****

Dick Rowland was hard at work on the shoes of a well-dressed white businessman who was reading the paper while seated next to three other men in suits doing the same as other bootblacks shined their wingtips. The speed at which the young man was able to bring the towel back and forth was stunning, and the man looked over his copy of the Tulsa Tribune with a grin as Dick's thin but muscled forearms blurred from the brisk movement. As Dick finished the shine, he snapped the towel hard enough to make a crack audible along the entire street. He sprung back like a cat, landing four feet from where he'd been squatting, admiring his work the entire time. He wiped the sweat from his brow with his forearm and looked at his customer.

"Hot damn, Mr. Reynolds, sir, that's it. That there's the diamond shine. Yes siree, you'll be the envy of your fellow tycoons today for sure."

Mr. Reynolds stepped off the stool, smiled, folded his paper and dug out a coin from his pocket, flipping it to Dick, who looked down to see that it was a shiny $5 Indian head.

"And now you'll be the envy of all your fellow *regular coons* today for sure," said the man, tipping his fedora as he let off a good-natured chuckle.

Dick tucked the coin into his pocket and looked at Bump, the old man at the box next to his. Bump raised his eyebrows and sighed, but Dick just jingled his pocket and smiled, turning to the street to look for his next fare.

"Diamond shine, get that diamond shine right over here."

Bump concluded his business before ambling over toward Dick, who was standing a few feet from the boxes. Just then, Sarah Page, a young white girl who worked as an elevator operator at a nearby office building and often passed through on her lunch break, walked by the two men. The attractive young lady smiled at Dick, who returned the gesture subtly, while adding a wink as he dropped his head, lest anyone notice.

"Boy, you'd best let them thoughts go right out your head," said Bump, "lest you wanna feel that noose around the neck that leads up to it."

Dick went on looking toward the ground, but with his eyes raised up toward his flat cap for cover as he refocused his gaze on Sarah.

"She sure is a fine one though, ain't she, Bump? Hotter than that July jam."

Bump shook his head and busied himself nervously.

"I done told you to stick with the brown sugar, son. Ain't no white kind worth the trouble it'll bring you, and that's the dang truth. All feels the same on the inside, anyway."

"Now how the hell would you know about that?" asked Dick playfully.

"Wouldn't make sense for the lord to make 'em any different," said Bump.

Dick shrugged. "Still, she fine though."

****

Gurley was alone at the desk when Buck entered the lobby from his room.

"Mr. Franklin, I trust you've found your accommodations satisfactory?" asked Gurley.

"Please, call me Buck, and yes, you have a lovely hotel, Mr. Gurley. As fine as any I've ever seen, in fact."

Buck picked up a newspaper sitting on a table next to a couch in the lobby.

"I'm glad it's to your liking," said Gurley. "There aren't too many places in this country, in my experience anyway, where a Black man can rent a dignified room from another Black man for a fair rate. Commercial enterprise among honest Negroes, you'll find this town is choc full of it."

Gurley smiled as Buck looked up from the paper.

"Speaking of such, I was hoping you might point me in the direction of a good lunch counter nearby."

"I can, indeed," said Gurley, as he came out from behind the desk. "You can hardly throw a stone in Greenwood without hitting a Black-owned eatery. Hamburger Kelly's is a good place this time of day. Come on, I'll walk

22

you over. I can give you a little tour of the neighborhood along the way."

"I'd be obliged," said Buck.

The two men made their way into the streets of the crowded Greenwood business district, which seemed to Buck to be bustling at all hours, whereas most towns he'd lived in seemed perpetually dormant during all but the lunch hour within the business day.

"I expect your family will be following on at some point, Buck?" asked Gurley as they began to turn onto the sidewalk.

"Yes, sir, our daughter just started her first semester at Lane College, but my wife and two sons are still down in Rentiesville. They'll be coming up as soon as I manage to get settled. I plan to practice with Mr. Spears and Mr. Chappelle."

"I heard as much," said Gurley, clasping his hands behind him as he walked. "Fine lawyers, indeed. Howard educated too. Of course, I've heard you're no slouch in a courtroom yourself. You've made quite a name for yourself down in Rentiesville."

"Well, I was the only Black lawyer in an all-Black town," said Buck with a chuckle.

"So, why leave, if you don't mind me asking?"

"Truth?" asked Buck.

"Always."

"I didn't see a future there. There wasn't much enterprise to speak of, and every time some of us tried to pull the town into modernity we'd get bogged down by silly old feuds and religious divisions."

Gurley nodded in agreement.

"I suspect that, being a Black town, the churches held much sway?"

"Hah, that's one way to put it," said Buck. "Not being a member of the right one could certainly handicap your ambitions and, as luck would have it, I didn't belong to the right one."

Both men chuckled before Gurley's tone shifted toward the serious.

"I also hear it told you're a Jeffersonian Democrat, Buck. Was that a problem for you?"

"Word travels fast," said Buck with a cautious look. "Well, it certainly did me no favors in Rentiesville, where the thought of a Black man being *any* kind of Democrat was considered heresy. You think it will be a problem for me here?"

"Hasn't been for me," said Gurley, studying Buck's response, which appeared to be one of shock.

"You? Really?"

"One might say that I too march to my own beat," Gurley said as he turned his head forward again. "Most of

Greenwood is Baptist, I started the first African Methodist Episcopal Church, Vernon AME over on North Greenwood. Near all of it is Republican, party of Lincoln and all, but I believe that Jefferson's ideals were the ones our nation should aspire to."

"Are there many others?" asked Buck.

"Not nearly as many as there are Republicans, but in a town of ten thousand Negroes, many of them educated, you'll find a lot more than anywhere else, I suspect."

Buck was clearly happy to have heard this and nodded accordingly.

"What brought you to Greenwood, Mr. Gurley, if you don't mind my asking?"

"Not at all. I came to Oklahoma from Arkansas for the land run back in '89," said Gurley, as they continued to walk at a very leisurely pace.

"That's where your people are from, sir?"

"Mostly. My father had come out to Pine Bluff from Alabama when he was emancipated."

"You were born free?" asked Buck with some surprise evident in his voice.

Gurley nodded.

"First member of my family—Christmas Day, 1868," he said, shaking his head wistfully. "We sharecropped, but I was able to go to school, even taught for a spell when I finished up. My daddy taught me that a free man's currency was land, though, and I bought every little tiny, unfarmable scrap I could get a deed on, put up some small, modest houses, rented to the Black folks there, did okay. But when I heard they were *giving* away land down here? I ran as fast as my short, skinny, Black legs would carry me."

Both men laughed.

"Wound up in Perry," said Gurley, "where I was principal of the Black school—damn near got myself elected county treasurer, too."

This stopped Buck in his tracks.

"Seriously?"

"I kid you not," said Gurley. "But when they hit that gusher up here in '05, the Ida Glenn, I just knew Tulsa would be the place where a Black man could really stake a claim for himself. And now, just look," he said, waving his arm at the expanse of commerce and industry before them.

"So you started all this here, Greenwood that is?"

Gurley considered the question for a moment.

"All this?" he asked rhetorically, with a shorter wave of his hand toward the immediate business district. "Yes. JB Stradford, man that owns that garish hotel over yonder—lawyer like yourself I might add—he was the first to start building houses in Greenwood. Still has thousands on a tract on the north side of town where it started. I put up my first building right over there 15 years back, a boarding house, then started building and renting more commercial space."

"Why so close to the tracks?" asked Buck.

"Center of our universe," answered Gurley with a smile. "Half the Blacks live in servant quarters on that side, rest live out there. You see, Buck, I understood the fatal error the white men of Tulsa had made very early on."

"And what was that?" asked Buck.

Gurley gave another pause before responding, which Buck, being a lawyer, recognized along with the measured pace of Gurley's words as the speaking techniques of a savvy communicator. He was not surprised that the man he was talking to was rumored to be a millionaire.

"Well, they all wanted cheap Negro help doing the labor they saw as beneath themselves, and they wanted Negro servants for their homes—again much cheaper than European immigrants and still possessing a slave's mentality. Only they wouldn't dream of allowing these Negroes into their stores or allowing landlords to rent them homes on their side of the tracks. But they had to shop somewhere. They had to live someplace."

"Not their problem, let the Negroes figure it out?" asked Buck.

Gurley smiled.

"Exactly."

"And you all did just that, I can see," said Buck.

"We did indeed. Without a thought to the consequences, they gave us the one thing we were never allowed—Black enterprise. With a self-contained market, Black entrepreneurs finally had the chance to flourish, to prove that given the same opportunities and education, we could pull ourselves up just like the white man always said we should, even if they never really wanted us to."

"No doubt," said Buck, interest heavy in his voice.

"And look at us now," said Gurley. "We got 21 restaurants, 30 grocery stores, a first-class theater, 2 hotels, 2 schools, a hospital, a whole mess of candy and soda shops, and enough law offices and medical practices to service the whole community. All Negro-owned, Buck."

"Impressive, to say the least."

"Blacks buying and selling with other Blacks, and the white man doesn't catch a dime of it— aside from the bankers. Haven't been able to get a charter yet, but we're working on that too," said Gurley, as he nodded confidently.

"Booker T. Washington came through here last year, and you know what he called it?" asked Gurley.

Buck smiled, anticipating his answer.

"Black Wall Street," Gurley said with a chuckle. "Can you imagine?"

"It's a beautiful thing, to be sure, Mr. Gurley," said Buck. "I'm privileged to be here."

"Of course it is a tenuous situation, to say the least," said Gurley, his tone having tightened noticeably.

"I imagine there are those who are less than enthused with the scope of its success?" asked Buck.

"Indeed there are. Especially now that the war's over, and the call for gasoline has subsided a bit. Don't get me wrong, they're still filling their pockets with both hands across town, but it's just enough for those giant masses at the bottom to feel a little pinch, and it's those at the bottom, those who like to think that no matter how tight things get, at least they don't have to be Negroes, that we need to worry about most."

Buck nodded in agreement. As the two men passed the Stradford Hotel, an extremely well-dressed man walked out, chest held high as he wiped his brow, putting the handkerchief back in his breast pocket with one hand as he re-affixed his fedora with the other. Despite looking to be in his sixties, the man carried himself with the physical confidence of a young man. The size of his hands and what one could only assume were age-atrophied shoulders, suggested he had once been a force to reckon with, physically. The rest of him suggested he still was, in at least every other regard. When he caught sight of Gurley, the man stopped and flashed a broad smile.

"O.W.!" bellowed the man. "Let me guess, that fine looking, young Negro businessman walked into your hotel and—dapper as he is—you just couldn't help but walk him straight up here to get a room at the Stradford."

The man laughed heartily, slapping his knee. Gurley approached, shaking his head and sporting a restrained smile, and the two men shook hands, Gurley patting the bigger man's shoulder.

"Well, when W.E.B. Du Bois came through not two weeks ago—and stayed at the Gurley—I told him as much, but he said, 'O.W., a real Negro gentleman prefers understated elegance to lavish and grandiose trimmings.'"

Both men laughed.

"It takes all kinds, I suppose," the man said, still smiling.

"Buck, this is John the Baptist Stradford," said Gurley. "That is his given Christian name too, I swear it. He is my chief competition in all regards—excepting for looks, of course."

Again, both men laughed.

"JB, this is Buck Franklin," said Gurley. "He's gonna be joining Isaiah Spears' and Philip Chappelle's firm."

Stradford nodded as he sized up Buck.

"Of course, of course. I read all about it in Smitherman's column. He called you the *Amazing Buck*

Franklin, couldn't go on enough about what a talented attorney you are."

Buck was embarrassed by the praise.

"That's some generous hyperbole to be sure," he told Stradford. "Mr. Gurley tells me you're an attorney as well?"

"He did?" asked Stradford. "Well, I suppose that's true, but I gave up practicing in pursuit of commerce when I came here. I figure we finally got enough young Black lawyers that I could take a break."

"Amen to that," said Buck.

Stradford withdrew a pocket watch from inside his jacket and studied it.

"I do hate to run off so quickly, gentlemen, but I have a meeting to attend," he told the two men. "I hope to see you again soon, Buck. Perhaps you'll be at Mt. Zion tonight? I'm sure O.W. will tell you all about it if he hasn't already."

Stradford stepped into the passenger seat of a motor car that had apparently been waiting for him at the curb and tipped his hat to Buck with a wink as it zipped off.

"Mt. Zion?" asked Buck.

"Community meeting at one of the churches tonight," said Gurley. "Since we can't exactly govern ourselves in an official capacity, it sort of serves as our council, you might say. All of Greenwood's elders attend, there's a speaker and, invariably, issues are debated. You should definitely come.

Captain Townsend Jackson will be the speaker tonight. I trust you've heard of him?"

"I sure have," said Buck. "His son, as well. I read where the Mayo brothers called him the finest Black surgeon in the country."

Gurley snorted.

"And if he was white, they'd just have called him the finest surgeon in the country."

"I know it," said Buck.

"Nevertheless, it should prove interesting," said Gurley. "The captain has got a reputation to be sure—all that lawman stuff in Memphis and such. But I know him personally, and I don't think Stradford's crowd is gonna hear what they are hoping to."

"Which would be?" asked Buck.

Gurley turned his mustache as he contemplated Buck.

"Suffice it to say there's been some disagreement on certain postures and positions in terms of how Greenwood should interact with Tulsa," said Gurley, carefully monitoring for any response Buck's face might register.

"Race relations?"

"Precisely," said Gurley as he turned and began walking again. "You see, Stradford has some rather radical notions as to how progress should be sought, particularly for a man his age. As we discussed, there's already considerable white resentment in Tulsa. Then he goes and builds that flashy hotel, almost as if to rub it in their faces."

Buck nodded. "I could see where that would chafe some of them."

"Plus we've got a lot of Negro war veterans who've just come back from Europe," said Gurley. "They went and got it in their heads that they'd be welcomed back as heroes, you know, parades in the streets and whatnot, be able to walk in the front doors of downtown businesses just because they were wearing a uniform."

"Didn't quite work out the way, I suspect?"

Gurley snorted again.

"No, not quite," said Gurley. "Then you've got men like Stradford who stoke their angst. Smitherman's another one, which you'll get a sense of if you read the Star."

"You're worried they'll push it too far?" asked Buck.

"Look, I'm all for the advancement of Negro rights and eventual equality, don't get me wrong," said Gurley. "But take another good hard look at what we've managed to build here, Buck, something that doesn't exist anywhere else in this country. You mark my words, that bunch gets too bold, starts making the white folks on the other side of those Frisco tracks nervous, and it will all come crashing down in a heap just like Chicago, Atlanta, Washington. How many dozen race riots has this nation seen in the last two years alone? And when have the Negroes ever come out better than they went in?"

"Not once that I know of," said Buck.

"Exactly. The hoodlums riot, and the Black men who've managed to make something for themselves lose everything—every single time. And Stradford? That man's got more to lose than anyone, myself included."

"Why do you reckon he's so bold?" asked Buck.

Gurley shrugged.

"He's just one of those stubborn Negroes that came into this world spoiling for a fight, I guess," said Gurley, pausing to regard Buck's facial reaction, again twirling his mustache.

"Years back, when this was still Indian territory," continued Gurley, "a white delivery man comes into one of Stradford's concerns and calls one of his workers a nigger. JB goes and stomps him within an inch of the man's life. Somehow manages not to hang for it. I think he got it in his head for good that he's got some sort of impunity. But there's no impunity for the Negro, not in this country and damn sure not in Oklahoma."

Buck sighed. "I can attest to that."

The two men turned and resumed their walk. After a few steps, Gurley pointed to a storefront with his walking cane.

"This is Hamburger Kelly's. Fine luncheon and something of a hub, especially for newcomers. Mr. Kelly is sort of a broker between new arrivals and the companies that hire Negro labor in Tulsa. Not a bad man to know if you plan on having family or acquaintances come to town who aren't of a professional stature—tradesmen, laborers, housemaids and such."

Gurley extended his hand and gave a warm smile as the two men shook.

"Now, if you'll excuse me, Buck, commerce calls. Come by the desk at 6:30 if you'd like to accompany me to the meeting tonight."

"I would like that very much," said Buck. "Thank you. I'll see you then."

Inside, a row of four Black men in work clothes were seated at the counter speaking to Mr. Kelly, a tall, older Black man wearing an apron and holding a spatula, who was stationed behind it. Buck walked past them and took a seat a few stools down.

"What about work in the oil fields?" said one of the young Black men. "I hear a man can make $100 a week out there."

Mr. Kelly waved him off.

"Sheeyit, boy, they don't let Negroes work in no oil fields, Jews neither. Some of them won't even take on Catholics. But that don't mean there ain't good money to be had. Any of you got trades or even construction experience?"

A good-sized and fit-looking man in his thirties named Ernie Wash was first to speak up.

"I worked on a crew building houses on Indian reservations for a little while," he said. "I can frame some."

Mr. Kelly nodded. "Good, good," he said, handing the man a calling card. "You go see Wilfred Dickinson. He's a good man, a Brit, ain't got no qualms with colored folks. Show up on time, do good, honest work, and he'll treat you straight."

At the other end of the counter, an old waitress was sleeping on a stool across from where Buck was seated. Mr. Kelly noticed Buck and gave a yell.

"Ida, wake up, baby. You got a customer."

The woman jerked her head forward, noticed Buck, and steadied herself after trying to rise too quickly.

"Sorry, baby." she said. "We usually slow after the lunch rush. I sometimes nod off after a busy one, and lord was we busy today!"

"That's quite alright, ma'am," said Buck with a smile.

"What'cha have, sugar?"

Buck pointed to a slate wall where a menu was scrawled in chalk.

"How's the hamburger plate?" he asked.

"Well, they don't call him Hamburger Kelly for nothin'," said the old woman.

"Hamburger plate it is then, and a cup of coffee if you don't mind."

"I used to work on cars back in Fayetville, motorbikes too," said Horace Frank, a skinny teenaged boy sitting down at the other end. At this, Mr. Kelly took out another calling card and handed it to him.

"You're a mechanic? You go see John Williams over at his garage. He needs all the help he can get. Every damn white man with a motor car in Tulsa—which is damn near every last white man these days—bring they wheels to good old John. Ain't a damn thing that man can't fix, but he's busy as a bee. I know he can use the help."

****

Obie Mann was sitting in the back room of the Mann Brothers Grocery cutting the heads off of chickens while three women pluck the feathers when another man walked in and handed him two more birds. With his giant hands, he effortlessly broke their necks before setting them next to the others.

"We're down to three yard birds out front," said the other man, who while not nearly as big as Obie, was still quite the physical presence. "Gonna have to call Smitty and see if he can run more out, I suppose."

"Gonna have to raise the price on Fitz is what we gonna have to do," said Obie.

"Raise the price? All the birds he be buyin'? That's the busiest restaurant in Tulsa."

Obi stopped working and regarded the man for a moment.

"And the most expensive, McKinley," he told him. "Has his man come all the way over here to buy our birds so he can save a nickel a pound? All secretive about it too. I can't tell if it's because he's embarrassed to be buying them over here or he's afraid of what his people might think if they find out they eatin' nigger chicken from Greenwood."

McKinley laughed, sighed, and shook his head.

"Man pay cash on the barrel every time, Obie. His money green like all the rest of it."

Obie stopped working and looked at him, tilting his head and softening his voice just a bit.

"I just don't like when we run out of birds for the people in our neighborhood 'cause they filling up the plate at some place where all parties involved got plenty a scratch to afford the perfectly good birds they got over that way."

"Well, once we get that refrigeration unit we been talking about, it won't matter none," said McKinley, eying a corner of the room where he imagined it would go. "We can sell as many birds as we can get our hands on."

"I told you, McKinley, people want fresh birds that they can see when they get here," Obie said. "Birds they know just been plucked before they go in the pot."

"Where you think Fitz's birds go, Obi?" asked McKinley. "He got a whole row of new Kelvinators in the back. He be happy to take his across town cold, and our people can pick theirs from out front—everybody will be happy."

"Everybody?" asked Obi, returning to his work.

"Everybody except you, my little brother. You're the one motherfucker I know that's *never* happy."

Obi gave McKinley a broad grin as he chopped off the last of the heads.

"You close up so I can get over to Mt. Zion on time?" asked Obie.

"Long as you don't plan on stirrin' up no trouble," said McKinley with a knowing smile.

"I don't stir trouble, my brother, I *am* trouble," Obie said with a smile of his own. "And you *know* this."

McKinley laughed, as he shook his head and walked back to the front room of the store.

****

As they left the law office, Buck was shaking hands with his associates, Isaiah Spears, a short man in his early thirties, and Philip Chappelle, a rotund man of fifty and the senior partner at the firm. Buck and Isaiah exited into the street while Philip remained in the doorway. Greenwood Avenue was even far more crowded than earlier in the day and had a festive atmosphere.

"Glory be," said Buck, surveying the crowd, "and I thought these streets were packed at lunch hour."

"Thursday—maid's night out," said Isaiah.

Buck gave him a quizzical look.

"All the white folk in Tulsa, they give the live-in help Thursday night off," explained Isaiah. "Get out early, come back to Greenwood, spend the night with their families. Makes it the most lively night of the week around here, not even Saturday night can top it. You can hardly get a ticket if there's a good picture show at the Dreamland."

"I imagine it's payday too?" asked Buck.

"No chance," sneered Isaiah. "Payday is on Friday. That way if any of them get ideas about not going back, they lose a full week's wages."

Buck gave him a knowing smirk, and both men shook their heads.

"You going to that community meeting at Mt. Zion church tonight?" asked Buck.

"Not me," said Isaiah. "I avoid the politics around here whenever possible."

"You think I should do the same?" asked Buck.

"I got no qualms either way," said Isaiah. "Word to the wise, though? It pays to be liked by that crowd. I mean Gurley and Stradford got more juice than anybody around here. Smitherman's not far behind. You just don't want to be liked too much by one side, because it usually means you're liked very little by the other, which could be bad for your business. They all seem to like you well enough, that's for sure, but that also might mean they'll be competing for your loyalties, so to speak."

Buck nodded knowingly.

"I figured there would be some pitfalls to avoid. Got any advice?"

"You going with Gurley?" asked Isaiah.

"Yes, he invited me after Stradford mentioned it when we ran into him on the street earlier today."

Isaiah nodded.

"Just make sure you make your way over to Stradford on your own at some point and say hello. Don't let nobody peg you as *Gurley's boy*, just his guest. Get me?"

"I do," said Buck. "Thanks for the heads up."

Isaiah patted Buck on the back.

"I gotta run. Promised the wife I'd take her and the kids to a picture tonight. I'll see you tomorrow, Buck. Thanks again for getting up here so quickly. We sure can use the help."

"Please, I'm happy for the work," said Buck, tipping his hat as both men walked off in opposite directions.

****

People were still jockeying for what little space remained in the pews of the recently-completed Mount Zion Church when Reverend Whitaker, a stout man in his mid-fifties, took to the lectern. He paused for a moment, taking in the sight of his house of worship filled with not only the bulk of his congregation but the people that anyone familiar with Greenwood might call the pillars of society. The audience was completely Black and dressed in their Sunday best.

"Thank you all for attending tonight's civic meeting," said the reverend, with a smile still on his face. "I might remind you that it does not count for your weekly spiritual trip to Mt. Zion, so I expect to see you all here again on Sunday. I'll now turn the floor over to Andrew Smitherman, editor of our Tulsa Daily Star, who will introduce this week's esteemed guest speaker."

Smitherman, who was seated next Stradford in the second row, rose and shuffled to the end of the aisle. A short man in his late thirties, he walked with energy, every movement exuding purpose. He shook the reverend's hand and placed a note card on the lectern.

"Tonight's guest really needs no introduction at all," said Smitherman. "Nonetheless, it is a great honor indeed to welcome one of the true heroes of the Black race, a legendary lawman who was born a slave but won his freedom for his heroic efforts at the Battle of Mount Lookout while just 10 years old—already a war veteran of three years by that point. He went on to achieve mythical status as a deputy in Memphis and later came to Oklahoma where he was elected Justice of the Peace in Guthrie. We are lucky to have him as our guest speaker and on a timely topic indeed: the proper course of action for the Negro race in our efforts to fully assimilate into free American society. I give you the legendary Captain Townsend Jackson."

A few rows back, Gurley leaned in and whispered to Buck, "Always a flair for the dramatic, that one."

The audience gave generous applause as a large, light-skinned Black man rose from the first row, struggling a bit to get to his feet. Sixty-eight years-old and carrying some obvious physical impairments, Captain Jackson still cut an impressive figure. He remained powerfully-built, barrel-chested, his stocky form complimented by the long duster that seemed part of some nondescript uniform. The lectern, which neared the clavicles of the previous two men, barely cleared his belly.

"Thank you, Andrew, for that generous introduction, and thank you all for having me as your honored speaker this evening," said Captain Jackson. "These are changing times, to be sure. As Mr. Smitherman noted, I was born a slave. I've seen the emancipation of our people and, by the grace of God, I have brought free children into this world. Most of you know my son, Dr. A.C. Jackson, who's here with me tonight along with his beautiful wife Julia, who I'm sure has taught some of your children over at Booker T. Washington."

Heads turned toward a handsome young man and the beautiful woman seated next to him in the front row.

"To see all that my son has accomplished, things I would have sworn to be impossible just decades ago, warms my heart with pride and fills me with hope for our peoples' continued progress," the captain continued. "Regarding our path forward, which I'm told many people here would like to hear my thoughts on, I don't pretend to speak for anyone but myself. However, I can say that I was surely reckless in my youth. Many of you have heard the stories of my stubborn tendency to resist the reality of our predicament, and while many have taken heart in my boldness, the truth is that it came at great expense and left me with very little beyond the stories people tell. I never saw that more clearly than when I lost my dear wife, Sophronia, a few years back, just before moving here to Greenwood. We raised our children to understand the foolishness of insubordination, the power of discipline and deference, and the value of earned respect through education and competence. As a result, they have prospered in this great nation."

Smitherman was leaning forward, writing furiously in a notepad, while Stradford wore a look of obvious disappointment. Gurley, however, looked to Buck with a satisfied grin.

Captain Jackson's speech continued to surprise most of the audience, many of whom had come to hear fire and brimstone from a mythical man who'd been called "the most brazenly-defiant Black man to ever wear a badge." Instead, they got what sounded like a lecture on servility as the captain went on and on about pragmatic methods of seeking social change until he'd lost near everyone's attention by the time he cleared his throat to conclude his speech.

"And that is why I believe that producing more young negro men like my son, men who prove with their minds, with their learned skills, that any negro given the same opportunity as his white counterpart in this world can thrive equally, is the best strategy for our people," Captain Jackson said, not seeming to realize that he'd long ago lost the crowd. "That is what I believe will lead to equality for the Negro race—creating a reality over a few generations that cannot be denied, as opposed to trying to impose a reality today that simply will not be accepted by the more empowered race."

There was polite applause as the captain nodded his head and picked up his notes to signal he was finished. Smitherman continued writing furiously in his notebook while shaking his head in what could only be disapproval. Gurley, however, was sitting so far upright he looked like he was leaning back, sporting a large grin as he clapped much louder and for longer than anyone else in the audience.

At the lectern, Reverend Whitaker had returned. Standing next to him was Obie Mann, whose tremendous physicality made even the captain seem small as they passed each other with a respectful nod exchanged between them.

"Thank you, Captain Jackson," said the Reverend. "It was a pleasure indeed, and we hope you'll continue to grace our meetings with your presence. We'll conclude with an announcement from Obie Mann, who you all know from the Mann Brothers Grocery. Obie is a veteran of World War I, where he fought in Germany with the 92nd Infantry Division, better known as the Buffalo Soldiers."

The crowd clapped as Obie took the lectern.

"Thank you, Reverend Whitaker," said Obie. "I'm not much for speaking at these things, but I come to you today representing those of us in this community who are veterans of the Great War, men who fought to defend this nation against the Kaiser, who fought for freedom and against oppression. On Monday, we again plan to march, in uniform, amongst the other vets in the Tulsa Memorial Day parade. As many of you know, we met with some resistance last year and, in the end, were not allowed to participate. However, we will not be deterred, and we hope that as many members of the Greenwood community as possible will show up to support our cause."

Reverend Whitaker, who'd remained next to the lectern this time, stepped forward.

"At this time, we'll open the subject to the floor for commentary."

Gurley's hand shot up and waved insistently, like a child who couldn't wait to show his teacher he knew the answer to a question she'd posed.

"Yes, Otto," said Reverend Whitaker.

"Obie, can I say first that I commend your service to our nation, and I can certainly appreciate your position and don't disagree that you and the other Negro soldiers have, without a doubt, earned the right to stand tall and march proud, but I would implore you to consider the words of another veteran that we heard this very evening. Captain Jackson so eloquently spoke of the power of deference, the wisdom in patience. Now you and your brother have built an impressive enterprise—biggest grocers in all of Greenwood. I bet half the chickens in town pass through your shop."

The crowd laughed.

"As you grow and expand your industries, however," continued Gurley, "I truly believe that is the path to the respect you seek. Please, I beg of you, consider Shakespeare's notion that discretion is the better part of valor, my brother. Why do you want to march in the white man's parade anyway?"

At that, Stradford, who had risen to his feet, broke in.

"Fuck that, let the vets march."

The crowd let out a collective gasp with some cheers. Reverend Whitaker cleared his throat forcefully and Stradford momentarily looked chastened.

"Pardon my language, everyone, Reverend, I do apologize," said Stradford. "My passions got the best of me. But these men fought for this country—including every pecker wood across those tracks. Why should they be shut out from a parade celebrating such service just because they have brown skin?"

Smitherman jumped to his feet.

"I couldn't agree more, and tomorrow's edition of the Star will feature an editorial expressing that exact sentiment!"

The room grew noisy as people talked amongst themselves in the crowd. Obie put his giant hands on the front of the lectern, leaning forward in a soldier's subtle way of expressing both seriousness and physical superiority.

"With all due respect, Mr. Gurley, and to Capt. Jackson—one of the men in this room who *does* know what combat feels like—deference was not an option in Germany. And I didn't see nothin' advertising Monday's event as a *white man's* parade. Now we gonna show up to march, and if they send us home peacefully, we'll go home peacefully, but every person there will see us in our uniforms and be reminded of what our people gave to the war effort. They will have to look us in the eyes and disrespect our service to our faces, and they'll have to do it every year until we are allowed to take our rightful place. So if any of y'all can make it, we'd be much obliged."

As Obie exited the lectern, the assembled crowd gave him the most generous applause of the evening. In fact, most of the people in attendance were distracted enough in watching the giant man walk back to his seat to miss most of what Reverend Whitaker said in his brief conclusion of the meeting, though they came to when he raised his voice just a tad to invite them to join him in prayer. When the reverend finished, the crowd began slowly moving toward the front doors, stopping to exchange pleasantries with those around them.

"Ain't that some shit?" said Gurley to Buck as they shuffled sideways down the aisle of their pew. "Captain Jackson goes and gives a speech like that, and then the only man in the room bigger than him has to go and kick the hornet's nest."

"That Obie Mann fellow is a specimen," said Buck. "I wouldn't want him cross with me."

"Indeed you wouldn't," Gurley agreed. "His grandfather was something of a mythical figure. Big white rancher down in Texas. Seven feet tall, I kid you not. His wife dies, and the rancher commences breeding with his prettiest Negress slave, who was said to be a tall drink of water herself. He sired three generations of giants, but I doubt any of them are as big and fearless as that damned Obie Mann."

"I believe that," said Buck.

"And then you have Stradford winding him up?" continued Gurley. "I tell you, no good will come of it. He ought to stick to that grocery store. His brother, McKinley? Much smarter that way. Older brother too, but even big as he is, he's no match for Obie."

"What man would be?" asked Buck.

Gurley stopped moving and raised his eyebrows as he regarded Buck for a moment before speaking.

"You don't need one, son," he said. "They'll get 40, dressed in hoods and sheets, and if there isn't an oak tree big enough for him to swing from, they'll hang him from that big standpipe up on the hill."

Buck nodded solemnly as they continued down the center aisle toward the door. Just then he caught sight of Stradford and motioned to him.

"Excuse me," Buck said to Gurley. "I'm gonna go say hello."

"Mr. Stradford," he called out with his hand raised. Stradford noticed Buck and smiled. Gurley tried to hide his disappointment but frowned, nevertheless.

On the church steps, Reverend Whitaker was glad-handing with the people as they exited. Aunt Damie approached, Dick, standing somewhat shyly behind her.

"Damie, my dear, it is good to see you, but who is this fine-looking young man?" asked the Reverend in a facetious tone. "I know it can't be Dick Rowland, because even though he's managed to avoid Sunday service for quite some time, I don't think it could have been long enough for him to have grown *that* much... or has it?"

Reverend Whitaker smirked at Dick, who bowed his head bashfully.

"Reverend Whitaker, you are right as rain," said Damie. "Dick here was raised to be a church-going man, but he been slacking for some time, not wanting to get his lazy bones out of bed after he been out late with his fool buddies on a Saturday night."

"Mmmm hmmm," said the reverend, eying Dick suspiciously. "Well, I hope he isn't picking up the sort of Saturday night habits that can land a young Black man in a world of trouble. You know the kind I mean, young man."

"No, sir, Reverend Whitaker," said Dick. "We just be acting up a little bit, you know, kid's stuff. But I been working real hard, saving up my money and taking real good care of my auntie, I promise."

At this, the reverend finally cracked a smile and softened his voice a bit.

"Well, that's good to hear, but you get your narrow behind outta bed and down to Sunday service once in a while. Get straight with the Lord. Drop a few of those oil tycoon coins into the offering too, so we can do his work for some of the less fortunate in this community."

Reverend Whitaker turned to Damie.

"And if he doesn't, I think you should make him give you double to drop in on his behalf, a *sin tax* we can call it."

Aunt Damie regarded Dick with a satisfied look, holding her stare as she answered.

"I think that's a *fine* idea, Reverend Whitaker. Better that money go to the church than to more sinnin'."

Damie soon relaxed her posture, however, and smiled.

"But he did buy me this new church hat just this morning," said Damie, unable to hide her affection for the young man any longer.

Reverend Whitaker smiled.

"Now that's a good boy. The queens do need their crowns."

Aunt Damie walked off, still smiling, with Dick trailing behind her. Reverend Whitaker grabbed the young man's arm as he passed.

"In all seriousness, son," he whispered. "You be careful out there. It may seem like all fun and games right now, especially in these high times, but there is an evil that lurks on that side of the tracks that would make the devil proud. Now you mind yourself, you hear?"

Reverend Whitaker held his intensive stare.

"Yes, sir, I'll mind myself good," Dick answered in a hushed tone.

****

In a large field on the outskirts of Tulsa and not far from the northern border of the Greenwood community, the green hillside was flooded by a sea of men dressed in stark white robes, their faces covered by pointy cloth headpieces with slits at the eyes and mouth. Many carried lit torches and. at the front of the massive congregation, three wooden crosses had been erected. The center one was a good 30 feet high, while the outer two stood nearly 20. In front of the crosses stood Bill Rodgers, a powerful man in the Tulsa political and business communities, and while he too was costumed—though in a robe and hood made of fine red satin—there were few men in attendance who couldn't name him.

"My brethren, you'd best believe that God almighty himself has chosen Tulsa as the theater for the staging of the white man's stand," bellowed Rodgers with the fervor of a Baptist preacher. "He's brought us to a land where Catholics and dagos and kikes lay with filthy squaw whores; where even a nigger can buy a white woman by the hour and inseminate her with the devil's own seed; a place where heathen Indians, chinks, and other dirt worshipers can do business out in the open, and he's challenged *us*, his one and only chosen race to come to his aid and defend his earthly paradise. He's asked whether we accept this vile miscegenation, or whether we will uphold his law. My brothers, we light these crosses as a symbol of the fire of God's endless wrath which will fall upon the wicked as a symbol that we shall prevail and that the dirty, filthy beasts among us shall fall! They shall be consumed with the fire of the righteous, and they shall burn!"

On cue, a number of Klansmen who had been busy pouring gasoline on the wood of the crosses managed to light them nearly in sync. The entire hillside was suddenly lit up brighter than if there had been a full moon on the clearest of nights. The congregation immediately began to chant in unison, "Burn! Burn! Burn!"

Toward the back of the hillside, from a vantage point that allowed them to look down on the spectacle from higher ground, stood a large group of younger Klansmen, most of whom were veterans of the Great War and had recently returned to Tulsa after being discharged, only to find that the war's end had slowed the boom just enough to ensure that there were not enough spaces at the trough for them to muscle their snoots in and feed. Indeed, many of them had found the very will to make it through the worst of times on the front lines by holding onto stories of their hometown having been turned into a sea of financial opportunity in their absence and dreams of staking a claim among the bounty upon their return.

Rodgers had proven himself quite skilled at helping them misdirect their frustration and these men seemed to chant the loudest, jutting their torches to the sky with a youthful passion stirred by manufactured hatred and man's innately tribal nature. Give some young men a place to point their economic anxiety, angst, and insecurities, and they'll stab forward without thinking much as to whether any sense can be made of the cause. Ironically, it was the same qualities that had made them good soldiers that also made them good pawns in the game that Rodgers and his cohorts were milking to their own enrichment.

These ignorant young men who'd had a lifetime of bigoted orientation could no longer discern right from wrong. They only saw winning or losing. In the latter, it could be argued that they were no different than the town's upper crust. The real difference was that the powerful didn't even need hate to conjure evil, for they had greed, and that had proven to be an even more inexhaustible source of fuel. They wanted it *all* to themselves and sewing such turmoil was useful in terms of supporting a status quo in which they would remain the unchallenged force at the top of the pecking order. Exploiting the will to hate in others who had not been allowed to profit enough to even understand the lure of greed was just a useful tool and means to their ends. *Who's keeping you down? They are.* Say it long enough and loud enough, and they won't even look up to see whose boot is actually on their neck.

The young man at the center of the vets was 25-ear-old Lawton Mercer, a ne'er-do-well around town who'd enlisted in the Marines only because a judge had given him the option in lieu of jail time after one of his frequent run-ins with the law over some matter of petty larceny. Coming home in uniform had served to cleanse him just enough so that while he was still far from respectable, he could nonetheless show his face in certain circles that had once been off-limits to him. Lawton was never going to be a socialite or date the daughter of a Tulsa swell, of course, but they noticed the young man enough to allow him to prove his skill-set useful from time to time.

They were of course unaware that it was only the chaotic disorganization following the Armistice of Compiègne that had spared he and many other soldiers from being charged in the looting that occurred at the war's end. It was rumored that Lawton had been arrested by British MPs on charges that he'd raped a young German girl in a village his unit had been patrolling, but they ultimately found it easier to just release him to American authorities who proved far too busy to investigate. In truth, it likely would not have mattered to people like Rodgers even if he had known. To the greedy, being useful usually proved paramount above all transgressions, so long as they weren't committed against them and theirs.

As the blaze rose from the crosses, the crackling of the flames could be heard all the way back at their position. Much to the surprise of his entourage, Lawton lifted his hood to get a better look, revealing a long, thick scar given to him by a German soldier's bayonet that ran from above his left ear, down the entire side of his face. His black eyes reflected the flames from the crosses, but that only added to what had already been a burning intensity, complemented by a sneer that suggested intentions that were at least sinister, if not downright evil.

"Burn! Burn! Burn!" screamed Lawton with a zealot's fervor.

The men around him also raised the volume of their chants, half out of inspiration, half out of fear of appearing unsatisfactorily inspired to the leader of their clique.

Chapter 2

Downtown Tulsa

It took three sheriff's deputies to subdue the giant oil field worker they were trying to get into the holding cell at the county jail, and even then they couldn't manage to get him any closer to the cell door.

Mike Evers, the youngest and best-conditioned deputy on the squad and a former high school wrestler, had a good armbar locked in on the much larger man, while Deputy Shoemaker, who was pretty fit himself at 32 but had an even greater disadvantage in size, wrapped himself around one of the man's legs, which looked like oak tree trunks. Together they were able to at least prevent any sort of earnest forward movement. Barney Clever, the department's only Black deputy, tried his best to contend with the man's free arm, which he had been swatting vigorously in his direction. As Evers reached back to open the cell's door, the roughneck, now partially free of the armbar, was able to gain some forward momentum and lurched toward Deputy Clever.

"Get your filthy nigger hands off me," the big Texan screamed.

At this, Sheriff William McCullough, who had just reentered the building and had been in the hallway when he heard the scuffle, ran into the room.

Evers, still holding one arm, pulled the giant man in the other direction, which momentarily squared him up directly with the oncoming sheriff. McCullough, who was in superb shape despite nearing 50, removed a blackjack from his belt as he moved toward the man with great purpose until he was within an arm's distance. Without hesitation, the sheriff delivered a short, powerful left hook to the gut, followed by a lightning-quick shot to the head from the blackjack in his right hand. The large man fell to a heap as if shot by an elephant gun, and the deputies were finally able to drag him into the cell.

"Christ almighty that's a big son of a bitch," said the sheriff. "What's he doing here?"

"Smacked a girl up real good in a brothel over on First," said Deputy Clever. "Drug her out in the street by the hair. It was hell getting him in the wagon."

"Is it just me, or do these roughnecks keep getting bigger and surlier?" asked the sheriff.

"Used to be they'd only cause trouble on the weekends," said Deputy Clever, still breathing heavily from the effort. "Get their pay and come down from the camps to spend their jack. Now they come down during the week, get too drunk to make it back up in the morning, and then start right in again once they've slept it off."

"How the hell you manage to bring him in?" asked the sheriff.

"Had to hold him at gunpoint *and* fire a warning shot," said Deputy Evers.

The sheriff shook his head.

"I wish to hell that damned Glen Pool would go on and dry up already," said Deputy Shoemaker.

"Careful what you wish for, deputy," said the sheriff. "You think it's bad now, wait and see what a city of 100,000 folks looks like once half of them lose their livelihood."

Deputy Shoemaker winced as he rolled a sore shoulder.

"They just ain't got no respect for nothing, sheriff."

"About the same percentage of troublemakers as the general population, I suspect," said the sheriff. "Just so many of them up there these days is all. No different than a town near an Army installation."

"I suppose," said Shoemaker.

The sheriff patted him on the back.

"Good work. Go on and write it up."

****

When Chip Bennett arrived at the Tulsa Tribune, he took a moment to take in the sight. It was an impressive building, to be sure. Not as big as his last paper but given the circumstances, it was much loftier than he had expected.

When he entered the crowded, second floor newsroom, Chip found it filled with just as much energy and buzz as that of any big city daily, again a bit of a surprise, given that it was Tulsa, which until just a few years prior had remained something of an overpopulated frontier town. Chip eventually managed to get the attention of an attractive young woman who had been walking in the opposite direction.

"Excuse me, ma'am, I'm looking for Tucker Johnson," he told her. "He's expecting me."

The woman smiled and pointed toward a balding, potbellied man of middle age who was adjusting his eyeglasses as he bent over a desk examining dummy sheets with a junior editor.

"That's him, right over there," said the woman, who upon closer examination Chip found to be even more attractive than at first glance.

"Thanks, I'm Chip Bennett," he said while extending his hand. "It's my first day."

The woman smiled again and extended her hand to meet his.

"Amy Comstock."

As she walked off, Chip took one more look before heading toward his new editor's desk, clearing his throat to get his attention when he arrived.

Tucker looked up and extended his hand.

"Mr. Johnson?" asked Chip. "Chip Bennett. I just got in from St. Louis on the night train."

"Chip Bennett, right, our new metro reporter," said Tucker. "Welcome to Tulsa. We're just getting these set for the proof. This is- "

Both men suddenly straightened up, looking past Chip, where another man, clearly their superior, was now standing, his arms outstretched, shirtsleeves rolled and necktie loosened. The man's voice boomed as he began to speak.

"This must be my new metro reporter, fresh in from that great gateway to the West, St. Louis, Missouri! I'm Richard Lloyd Jones. Welcome to the Tribune, the very beating heart of Tulsa."

The two men shook hands and Richard gave him a hearty pat on the back.

"Chip Bennett, sir. It's a pleasure to finally meet you. I'm familiar with your work from back when you wrote for Colliers."

"Ah yes, Colliers," said Richard, clearly impressed. "Weren't those the good old days? Truth be told, I'd give anything to be back down in the muckety muck again. But alas, I had to go and become a publisher. Now all my time is taken up by bankers, businessmen. and shit-heel politicians."

He shook his head wistfully as he sized up Chip.

"Come on back to my office so I can give you a proper welcome."

The two men headed into a makeshift office, which had been framed along the wall of the otherwise open newsroom. Once inside, Richard closed the frosted door and poured some Canadian whiskey from a pint bottle into two coffee cups, a small splash in each. Chip looked at a photo on the wall, which was lined with pictures and other memorabilia.

"We keep a dry newsroom, generally, as a matter of principle," said Richard, handing Chip one of the cups. "Certain, shall we say ... *elements* of Tulsa society look upon imbibing, well, less than favorably—more so since last January."

"Thanks," said Chip, taking the cup.

"My pleasure. You see, I like to welcome new reporters with a snort of whiskey, a bit of which I happened to procure *before* prohibition went into effect, of course," said Richard with a wink. "I mean, what kind of land would we be living in if two gentlemen couldn't toast their enterprise?"

Chip smiled. "You make a good point."

The two men raised their glasses in a toast.

"To the fourth estate?" asked Richard.

Chip nodded, toasted Richard's glass and both men threw back the shot with Chip wincing a bit as it went down. Richard looked up at the picture Chip had been examining.

"Ah, good old Robert Collier, himself," said Richard. "Taught me everything I know about this business. Would you believe that way back when he and I actually managed to marshal the resources to purchase the birth home of the great Abraham Lincoln?"

Chip's jaw dropped.

"Get out, really?"

"Now how could I tell tales when it comes to old Honest Abe?" said Richard with a smile, as he looked back at the picture and shook his head.

"Yes, sir, 100 acres in Hodgenville, Kentucky—about to be foreclosed upon. We bought it at courthouse auction right before it would have been demolished."

"I'd read it had been made into a museum, but-"

"Damn right," said Richard. "First time in the history of these United States that we've marked the birthplace of a great man."

"Look here," said Richard as he led him to another photo on the opposite wall.

"That's President Teddy Roosevelt on the day of its dedication. He laid the cornerstone for the monument. Oh and that's President Taft, who was in office at the time. He gave the dedication."

Chip was clearly impressed.

"That's you, in a picture, with two different Presidents?"

Richard gave him a coy smile.

"At the birthplace of a third."

"That's quite an accomplishment, sir. The museum and all."

Richard waved him off modestly.

"Accomplishment? Hell, that was the greatest pleasure of my entire life. That man had the wit of a philosopher, the courage of a soldier, and the heart of a mother. Did you know he inspired more books than any other man who's ever walked this Earth? Hell, Jesus Christ himself only got four."

"He was a great man, that's for sure," said Chip, who was beginning to worry he was coming off as a kiss ass, even though he was genuinely impressed.

"Saved the republic and ended the scourge of slavery," said Richard, again shaking his head. "What president could ever top that? I tell you, he is the symbol of all that is good and holy in this country."

"I'd been aware that you were a skilled writer, Mr. Jones, but no one warned me of your oratory prowess," said Chip, immediately regretting that he now *definitely* looked like a kiss ass.

Richard continued to drink it in, however.

"Oh that probably trickles down from my daddy," he said. "He was a minister. Me, I have always made my publication my pulpit."

He picked up a newspaper from the desk and waved it.

"And I *do preach*."

Chip spotted another picture over Richard's shoulder.

"Is that Mark Twain?"

"Ah yes, Mark's a dear friend. Hell of a writer too.

Chip then noticed another picture close by and pointed to it with just as much awe.

"And that's Frank Lloyd Wright, the architect."

Richard was much less enthused this time.

"Indeed, good old cousin Frank, the toast of all towns. Personally, I never did go in for all that newfangled *organic architecture* stuff of his. He is family though. I suppose there's no accounting for that."

****

The luncheonette was close enough to both the courthouse and city hall, as well as two of Tulsa's biggest banks and a number of law offices, to draw a good crowd of movers and shakers on any weekday morning and an even bigger crowd for lunch, when it often took 15 minutes to get a table if you could get one at all. In fact, being deemed important enough to skip the wait was a good measure of one's social significance. Sheriff McCullough, a widower, nearly always took his meals at the counter, where the seat closest to the kitchen door was generally left available for him even when there wasn't another seat in the house, which had been the case when he arrived that morning.

As he entered, the door bell clanged and he was met immediately by Mayor Thaddeus Evans, who was leaving with Bill Rodgers and two of the most important men in the Tulsa business community, Wash Hudson and Horton McGuire.

"Well look here, fellas," said Mayor Evans in his usual loud and gregarious voice. "If it ain't my fellow Republican, our former, present, former, and recently-elected-again sheriff. I only hope I have as many political lives as good old Bill, here. What's the good word, sheriff?"

"I suppose it's justice, Thaddeus," said the sheriff, "but coffee will suffice this early in the day."

"Sheriff, I take it you know Horton McGuire here, President of both the National Bank and our Chamber of Commerce?" asked the mayor, rhetorically. "Of course you must know Wash Hudson, Chair of the Tulsa Benevolent Society? And if you don't know Bill Rodgers, he surely knows you, having just beaten his man on the Democratic slate. But Bill don't hold grudges, now do you, Bill?"

"None at all," said Rodgers. "As you well know, any Republican that can manage to get himself elected in my city can't help but leave me impressed."

The mayor gave a goodhearted laugh.

"Your city? I thought I was the mayor?"

Rodgers barely smiled.

"You are, Thaddeus. Mayor of *my* city ... presently, anyway."

The mayor let out another guffaw and looked to the sheriff.

"What do you say, sheriff, will you shoot him for me?" laughed the mayor, while slapping his knee. "Favor from one Republican to another?"

"I never shoot anyone before I've had my coffee," said the sheriff, "not even Democrats."

At this, the sheriff tipped his hat and turned toward the lunch counter where his empty seat awaited.

"Come on now fellas, considering the coffee in this place, we'd best make ourselves scarce," said the mayor, continuing to amuse himself with his own laughter as the group made their exit.

When the sheriff took his seat, a pretty brunette waitress with milky skin named Annie Shepton greeted him with a big smile, turned over the mug at his place setting and filled it from a percolator.

"Morning, sheriff," she said softly.

"How many times have I got to tell you to call me Bill?"

"Sorry, Bill," she said, broadening her smile.

The sheriff returned the smile and took a sip of his coffee.

"Thaddeus must be out of his wits again. The only thing better than this coffee is that pretty smile."

"Wait 'til you have the bacon," she said with a wink.

The sheriff winked back as he took another sip from the mug.

"What's a Republican mayor doing with Bill Rodgers, anyway?" Annie asked. "Isn't he the party boss for the Democrats?"

"He is, but he's also a greedy lawyer who's got his fingers in every juicy pie in town. I suppose a Republican mayor could do worse than to stay on his good side, especially one as plum simple as old Thaddeus."

"What about you?" she asked, more serious in tone.

"What about me?"

"Are you on his good side, Bill?"

The sheriff took another sip as he contemplated the question.

"Truth be told, I don't expect he has much of a good side," he finally told her. "The rest of that lot's not much better, either. I'd just as soon avoid them all at every turn, but not if it means missing out on this here coffee and that pretty smile."

This brought a grin back to Annie's face and her cheeks blushed a bit, which was all the more noticeable owed to her pale complexion.

"Like I said, wait until you have the bacon," she said in a coy voice.

****

The small and faded sign above the door of the storefront read, *Dixie Social Club*. Beneath it, in smaller print: *Members Only*. Drab and unwelcoming, it wasn't exactly the sort of place someone was likely to wander into out of curiosity or to approach for solicitation, even after hearing the music and conversation that reverberated into the street.

The building's inside was everything its facade seemed to foretell: unfinished wood floors covered with a layer of sawdust, old and mismatched pieces of furniture scattered around a makeshift bar, a tattered pool table near the storefront window, dim light provided by a few unshaded bulbs hanging between the wooden rafters of the unfinished ceilings.

Lawton Mercer was standing at the bar across from two other vets who were seated on old, rickety stools. Red was a lean and sinister-looking man in his mid-twenties, and Willie, a 19-year-old simpleton, was equally thin but sported a kind-looking face that set him apart from the other two men, every detail of which suggested both hardness and desperation. Around them, there were half a dozen other men throwing darts, drinking, and playing cards.

"I swear, I don't even recognize this town no more," said Lawton between swigs from a brown pint bottle. "A man goes off to war, spills blood for his country, gets fuckin' maimed while he's at it (points to the scar running down the side of his face), then he comes back and it's as if the damned Earth got knocked off its axis or something. Can't even get a job in the oil fields, because they got all those roughnecks in from Texas doing the work."

"Half of them ain't even real Americans, neither," sneered Red. "They got wops workin' out there, bohunks, prolly some kikes too."

"I'm surprised they ain't got niggers working on the rigs," said Willie, who had a way of punctuating his statements with nervous laughter and an uneasy look, as though he was never quite sure if he'd said the right thing.

"It's not funny," yelled Lawton as he pounded the bar. "The niggers ain't gotta work out there, 'cause they got everything else. You go over to Little Africa and they're wearing suits and smoking cigars for Christ's sake, even drivin' motor cars."

"Not to mention walking around in uniform," said Red.

"Thank the fuckin' Frenchies for that," said Lawton. "We had them peeling potatoes and cleaning toilets where they belonged until those nigger-loving frogs invited them to cuddle in their foxholes."

Lawton took another pull from the bottle and grimaced at the taste.

"And don't even get me started on this fucking bathtub gin we gotta drink," he continued. "We're fighting a war halfway across the world and teetotalers back home go and turn the country dry while we're gone? Gotta pay top dollar to get this scrap iron?"

"Meanwhile the redskins and niggers are getting tight on choc for two pennies a glass and making it with the white whores on 1st Avenue," said Red. "The world's gone to shit, fellas. When I was a kid, the darkies knew their place. My old man used to say, look, there's Negroes and there's niggers. Maybe you tolerate the first if he knows his place, but the second are like roaches. You let one hang around and get even a little bit bold, next thing you know, they've ruined your goddamn house."

"And you gotta deal with them the same way, Red," said Lawton, staring off into space as he lightly fingered the scar on his face. "You gotta burn them out. Every last dirty, filthy fuckin' one."

****

Gary Kale, a young photographer for the Tribune was helping Chip get settled at his desk, unloading supplies from a box as Chip looked for the right drawer to put them in.

"That should get you started," said Gary. "The supply room is right over there whenever you run out of pencils or notepads. The break room is two doors down. If you finish off the coffee, make sure you put more on, but if you've worked in newsrooms before I don't need to tell you that."

They both chuckled.

"Thanks, I really appreciate you helping me get squared away," said Chip.

"No problem. Mind if I ask you something though?"

"Shoot," Chip said with a shrug.

"What brings you from St. Louis all the way out to Oakie country? Weren't you at the Post-Dispatch? I mean that's practically the New York Times."

Chip laughed. "That was sort of the problem. Try and get noticed at a paper that big."

"Tough climb, eh?"

Chip nodded.

"It took me two years to get off obits and onto a police beat, and I tried for three more to get on the metro desk or out to the Washington bureau, but I couldn't get any play."

"Okay, but why Tulsa?" asked Gary.

"Are you kidding me?" said Chip. "This place is the future, and you can still get in on the ground floor. Outside of this territory, Tulsa is like another planet, this oil boom town that sprung up from nowhere. And I don't need to tell you that some pretty crazy stories have come out of here."

"So you thought it'd be a good stepping stone, or are you looking to dig in your heels?" asked Gary.

"I dunno," said Chip with a shrug. "I figured I'd give it a go and if it didn't work out, maybe I could strike it rich in oil or marry some tycoon's widow and make off with the dough."

Gary laughed. "You and every other guy in town."

"Right?" said Chip with a smile. "I mean I had nothing going back home. The only thing I was making progress at was embarrassing my old man by way of my occupation."

"He's not a newspaper man?"

"Reads three a day," said Chip. "He just likes to think the tuition he sprung for at Yale should have landed me someplace north of cub reporter, you know? Probably thinks I should be Ring Lardner by now."

"Yale, eh? Nice."

"Not all it's cracked up to be," said Chip.

Gary looked around their immediate area and then leaned in close enough to be heard just above a whisper.

"So, what did you think of our fearless publisher?" he asked.

"He seemed great," Chip said with a shrug. "I mean I don't wanna act like some big city reporter coming out to the sticks, but I thought you'd need to go to New York or Washington before you saw those kinds of pictures on the boss's wall."

Gary gave him a smug chuckle.

"Let me guess, he gave you the mighty Lincoln speech? Told you about the museum, and how Lincoln is the symbol of all that is good and holy in this country, *the man who ended the scourge of slavery?*"

"Well, yeah, something like that, but I mean, again, no offense," said Chip, "but I wasn't exactly expecting the most progressive atmosphere out here either. Tulsa's got a bit of a reputation when it comes to... well, social progress."

"Heh, that's one way to put it," said Gary. "But don't get too wrapped up in Jones' spiel. For a Lincoln devotee, he's got a lot to say about our colored population and none of it is, shall we say, *progressive*."

Chip gave him a confused look.

****

The morning sun was shining down on Mayor Evans as he held court before a congregation of a half dozen bankers in front of the Brady Hotel. It was the kind of picture-perfect May morning that suggested optimism. But with Horton McGuire and Tate Brady beaming on his flanks, the mayor was offering more than suggestions to the men in expensive suits who were standing before him.

"Welcome to Tulsa, gentleman, the oil capital of the world. Black gold is our business and business is booming. There are 120,000 barrels a day coming out of the Ida Glenn Pool, and the amount of commerce such activity supports means that the time is ripe for investment. Ain't that right, Horton?"

"Oh it's plum ripe, Mayor, plum ripe, indeed," said McGuire.

"Over 400 gas and oil companies are active this very day," the mayor continued, "and that activity has spawned department stores, half a dozen new banks, hundreds of restaurants, while providing funding for such amenities as our new, state of the art convention hall, and of course we've got several world-class luxury hotels like this one right here."

The mayor swept his arm outward toward the grand facade of the Brady Hotel.

The group was then escorted inside the hotel to an ornate banquet room where they assembled at a long table where an impressive feast had been spread out for breakfast.

"Mr. Brady, this is as fine a hotel as I'd be likely to find on Park Avenue, back home," said one of the bankers.

"Thank you, sir," replied Tate. "We figure that if Tulsa's gonna be a first-rate city, it wouldn't do to be without first-rate accommodations."

"Mayor, I just cannot believe my eyes," said another banker. "They say Rome wasn't built in a day, but I'll be damned if this here city of yours didn't spring up in no time flat. I've never seen anything quite like it."

"You're not alone, there," said the mayor. "Folks started calling it the Magic City a while back, as though it just appeared out of thin air, poof," he said with a laugh. "Damn near did, too. In the five years after they hit that gusher, the population of this town went from just 10,000 to more than 100,000 people."

"You see our oil isn't only plentiful, boys, but it's the lightest and sweetest the geologists have ever seen," said Horton, "much faster and cheaper to refine than that thick, sour crud down in Texas where you've got most of your money. The future is in oil, gentlemen, you know that already, but *oil's* future is right here in Tulsa."

"Tell us more about this refinery, Horton," asked another banker.

"Well, like I was saying, we need more ability to refine locally if we're to leverage Tulsa's full potential. Texaco's pipeline down to the gulf coast is at full flow, and Standard Oil's piping crude up to their operation in Indiana just as fast. Every refinery we have nearby is at full capacity already."

"This is a growing nation, gentlemen," said the mayor, "and this postwar boom is gonna prove thirsty for oil."

"You don't think we might be a little late to the dance, so to speak?" asked the first banker. "Some people got burned real bad down in Beaumont by getting in late on the Spindletop."

"Yeah, that was a mighty gusher too," said another banker, "but it played out in just a few years."

"No sir," said Horton. "I assure you, you're still on the ground floor. Read the geological report in that prospectus. The Ida Glenn is shallow, true, that's what makes it so easy to extract. But it's as broad as an ocean, boys. We'll be financing two or three more of these by this time next year, and whoever is with us now will have first bite at the apple each time out."

Tate Brady raised a hand.

"Horton, if I may?"

"Of course, Tate."

"Gentlemen, there's not only the matter of the prudence of this investment, which is assured, but consider that Tulsa is presently a vital spoke in the wheel of this great nation," said Tate. "I kid you not when I say that I consider it my Christian duty as a patriotic American to do everything I can to assist in its development and the growth of my country."

Horton smiled.

"And if anyone were to say, make a bundle while doing so, all the better."

The mayor laughed.

"I know I wouldn't hold such good fortune against them," he said, "regardless of how embarrassing the bounty of their riches may prove to be."

The other men joined the mayor for a chuckle.

"Well, I'm sold, gentlemen," said the second banker. "And I think I can safely say that our people back in New York are going to be just as eager to be a part of your project."

"If you'll have your people at the bank draw up the paperwork this afternoon, Horton, we can make the evening train and still get to enjoy some of the holiday weekend," said the first banker.

"Far be it from me to stand between another man and his bank holiday," said Horton.

Both men let out a laugh as they shook hands.

As the bankers were chauffeured away in a limousine, Horton, the mayor, and Tate were standing on the sidewalk just outside the hotel.

Horton McGuire gave a broad smile and watched the car pull off into the distance as he spoke.

"Well, gentlemen, business is indeed good for he who has the goose that lays the golden eggs."

"Sure was easy," said Tate. "Like shootin' fish in a barrel, eh, Thaddeus?"

"Happy to do my part, gentlemen," said the mayor.

"Well, you did real good, Thaddeus," said Horton, "and I'll make sure all the right people know it."

After a handshake, Horton stood staring at the mayor with a fixed smile, as though to suggest he was dismissed. Thaddeus quickly looked at his wristwatch.

"Well, if you gentlemen will excuse me, I really must get back to City Hall."

"Of course," said Horton. "Thanks, again, mayor."

Tate tipped his hat as the mayor walked off toward his motor car.

Once he was out of earshot, Horton turned to Tate.

"See? And you were acting as though it were the end of the world when he got elected. Didn't I tell you a Republican mayor could serve certain purposes in a town like this?"

"I will admit," said Tate, while shaking his head, "I always thought he was about as useless as tits on a bull when he was a judge, but he's the right guy for the job when it comes to putting them northern bankers at ease."

"He'll be just fine, provided the job never gets any harder than that," said Horton, rolling his eyes as he chuckled.

****

Deputy Evers was standing in front of the sheriff's desk, telling him about a problem with one of the squad cars when an old Black man wandered in, flushed and short of breath.

"Can I help you find someone, friend?" asked the sheriff, not accustomed to having Blacks enter his office on their own accord.

"Yes, sir, sheriff, sir, I need to know where I can report a crime," said the old man, holding his cap in his hands, against his chest, and doing his best to appear deferential, as he was no more accustomed to entering a police station on his own accord than the sheriff had been in receiving him.

"Well, generally, that'd be over at the police station," the sheriff told him. "What did you see?"

"That's the thing, sheriff, I can't be reportin' it there," said the man. "I'll get my head cracked fo' sho'."

The sheriff's neck stiffened a bit.

"How's that?"

"It'd be a police officer who did the crime, robbed me right in the middle of the street," said the man. "Broad daylight."

"You were robbed by a city police officer?" asked the sheriff.

"I sho' was, sheriff, took five dollars I had to go all the way down Detroit Avenue—nearly to 13th—just to get. Took a streetcar far as I could but prolly walked 20 blocks by the time he stopped me on my ways back."

"What's your name, partner?"

"Ben Smith, sheriff."

"What were you doing over in that part of town, Ben, if you don't mind me asking?"

"No, sir. You ask me anything you want, and lord as my witness, you'll get the truth."

"I believe I will, Ben," the sheriff told him. "Go on now."

"Well, see my people live over in Greenwood, been there since there was nothing but shacks on the north end. My daughter Anita though, she work as help over in Tulsa, for the Parker family. You see, my wife, she got the whooping cough, sir, got it real bad, too. This morning, she had a fit. Knocked over the medicine bottle and it spilled right out. I just paid the gas bill and the rent, too. Anita won't be home till next Thursday, so I gotta go over and see if she can front me the money to get more medicine"

"I'm with you, go on," said the sheriff.

"Well, I get over there and she only got a five-dollar bill, so she tell me to take it and get the medicine, but get it from the druggist near our house back Greenwood where it's cheaper, and then save the change for her 'til she come back next Thursday. But I'm walking back to where I can get the streetcar again, and this copper come up to me axing about what I'm doin' in that part of town."

"You sass him at all, Ben?" asked the sheriff.

"No, sir, sheriff, God as my witness. I'm an old man, and I done learned enough to know a Black man in that part a town just outta keep his head down and mind his self in that situation."

"So, what happens next?"

"I tell him my story, and he axes to see the money she gave me," said Ben. "I show it to him, but he snatches it. Says any nigger with five dollars in his pocket gotta be up to no good. Then he asks if I got any identification or other money, and I say no. So he says that's enough to bring me up on vagrancy charges. I tell him I ain't no vagrant, that my people got roots here, that I was a porter on the railways for 47 years."

"What's he say to that?" asked the sheriff.

"He just say, he be collecting the five dollar fine now, and then we can forget about it. Otherwise, he gonna run me in. I axe him, what about my wife? She sick. He tells me the world's full of problems, and how am I gonna be any good to her if I'm locked up. Took out his billy club and tell me he better not catch me in that part of town again or I'll have *real* trouble."

"You get the officer's name?" asked the sheriff.

"Yes, sir, Clayton's what his tag said. I can read real good, sheriff, and I remember that fo' sho'."

The sheriff looked to Deputy Evers and then back to Ben.

"Sheriff, I can't go home without no medicine," said the old man with a look of fierce desperation. "My wife is good and sick with that whoopin' cough. Lord knows how many fits she had today while I was gone."

"Mike, take Ben here into the back room," said the sheriff. "Mr. Smith, I'm gonna need you to just sit tight for a little while, alright? If what you told me is true, I'll get your money back for you, but I need you out of sight for just a bit while I sort it out. Don't worry, you're not in any kind of trouble."

"Yes, sir, I do what you tell me," said Ben, "and it's true, every last word of it. God as my witness."

The sheriff nodded.

"Deputy Shoemaker, come back here for a minute please."

Deputy Evers took Ben out through the office door, and Deputy Shoemaker passed them as he entered.

"Yes, sheriff?" asked the deputy.

"I'm gonna need you to head over to the police station and tell Chief Gustafson that as much as I hate to interrupt his day, it is imperative that he and Officer Tim Clayton come down the street and see me as soon as possible."

"And if he asks what it's about?" asked Shoemaker.

"Tell him the truth, deputy."

"The truth, sheriff?"

"Yes, Harold," said the sheriff, clearly annoyed. "That you don't know because I didn't tell you."

"Yes, sir, sheriff."

****

Bill Rodgers was sitting in Richard Lloyd Jones' office, looking quite at ease. One foot was kicked up on a knee as he spun his fedora on his finger. The door to the office had been left open and, like every other employee within earshot, Chip and Gary were doing their best to listen in on what had sounded like a tense conversation.

"We may have political differences, Bill, no doubt about that, but where the rubber meets the road, I do not believe you'll find we differ much at all in terms of the core values this community should aspire to," said Richard. "I mean, what if anything in the pages of the Tribune, especially my editorials, could possibly give the chamber, and the uh ... Benevolence Association, pause?"

Bill remained silent, giving the hat one more spin before speaking. He enjoyed being so at ease when people around him tensed up at any comment that even suggested a negative disposition on his part.

"Oh, I wasn't suggesting there was anything of the kind, Richard," he finally said. "Don't be so sensitive. Hell, you've probably been tougher on old Thaddeus than any Democratic publisher would have been. I mean, that business with the Spavinaw Water Project? You've been brutal! I've almost felt bad for the poor sap."

Richard tried to manage a confident laugh, while Rodgers only smiled, keeping his mouth closed as he did.

"It's just that there are some bigger issues that are coming down the pike, and the chamber, along with the association—which is to say, most of your current and potential advertisers—would like to make sure you remember where *they* stand before deciding where *you* do."

Richard snapped his suspenders and leaned back in his chair, genuinely more at ease now that he knew what Rodgers had come over to talk about.

"You're talking about all that business over in Niggertown?" asked Richard.

"You've been appropriately hard on those union pinkos, and we appreciate your candor on uppity niggers not knowing their place," said Rodgers. "It seems, however, that in our righteous desire to keep them out of our shops and our stores—preventing them from patronizing good, proper white-owned businesses—we've unintentionally created a sizable commercial vacuum."

Richard wasn't sure what the man was getting at.

"And?"

"And?" asked Rodgers with some indignation. "And a few big-word talking, enterprising darkies have gone and filled it. I hear it told they even got themselves a couple of *millionaires* in Greenwood. Can you imagine? Nigger millionaires."

"I wouldn't be surprised by it," said Richard with a sigh. "Hell, that Stradford character owns tract after tract of tenements. What he don't got, that greedy bastard Gurley does. Wouldn't surprise me a bit if they were each worth a million dollars by now. Just scooping up all that nigger money white folks pass on to the ones who'll actually do an honest day's work."

"Money and property are the basis of influence, Richard," said Rodgers. "I don't need to tell you that. And the more of the first two that such niggers accumulate, the more of the third they are likely to find. We let this go on and before you know it they'll be sitting next to us in our restaurants, our churches, trying on the same suits at our haberdasheries."

At this, Richard let out an authentic laugh.

"Oh, I doubt they'll find any that are gaudy enough for their liking on this side of the tracks, Bill."

Rodgers rolled his eyes.

"Laugh if you want, but how long after that until they're going to our schools, holding public office even? Eventually, they're dating our damn daughters, Richard, making themselves an army of little half-breeds. At the rate those animals procreate, they'd outnumber the white man in a generation or so, at most. The purity of the white race is at stake here, my good man. I trust you can see that?"

Out in the newsroom, Chip, having heard nearly every word of the conversation, looked to Gary in shock.

"Bill Rodgers runs the Tulsa Benevolent Association, which is pretty much the social arm of the local Klan chapter," explained Gary. "He's also their leader, the uh, Exalted Cyclops, it's called."

Both men leaned back in their chair to get a better listen.

"Oh I see it, Bill, I do indeed," said Richard. "You know I abhorred slavery, and on that point we may differ, but it is vital that the Negro know his place in this society and not forget who gave him that freedom or what he was meant by God to do with it."

"Only good nigger's a dead one far as I'm concerned, Richard."

"Oh come on now, that's a bit extreme, Bill, even for you. Hell, you go into any household in Tulsa, my own included, and you'll find fine Negro help, servants who are grateful for the decent lives the white families have given them, lifting them out of squalor to clean our homes, look after our children, cook our meals, and tend to our gardens— not as slaves, mind you, but as a free people. They are a deferential, respectful, and god-fearing lot."

"I'm not talking about servants," said Rodgers, more tersely this time.

"I know who you're talking about, Bill, those fancy suit-wearing, slick-talking jigaboos you'll find by the dozen cross those tracks, spouting off all kinda talk about integration and equality. Now, if those ones get out of line and the noose happens to find a few of their necks, be it in front of the courthouse by way of the law, or up on the hill by way of those defending the righteous purity of this great Republic, well then I'll call it justice, either way, you be sure of that."

Rodgers paused to consider Richard with a giant grin, then smiled, stood up and shook his hand.

"I had a feeling we'd see eye to eye on that point, Richard, I really did. I tell people all the time, you know, if every Republican were as reasonable as Richard Lloyd Jones, us Democrats would be in a heap of trouble. Hell, I might even be inclined to switch parties!"

Outside, Chip was slack-jawed and wide-eyed in disbelief as Rodgers passed through the office door and into the newsroom behind them.

"Not exactly *progressive*, eh, Yale?" asked Gary.

Richard emerged from the office just moments later, as though nothing out of the usual had happened.

"Tucker, I'll be at lunch for the next hour," he said to his editor. "When I get back, I expect I can see the proofs?"

"Yes, sir, just about there," said Tucker.

"Miss Comstock, will you please join me," said Richard as he walked on. "I'll need to dictate some while I eat."

The young lady gave him a warm smile.

"Of course, Mr. Jones. Let me just grab my pocketbook."

****

Sheriff McCullough was sitting at his desk going over paperwork when Deputy Shoemaker returned with Chief Gustafson and Officer Clayton following behind him. The sheriff stood when the three men entered.

"What's this about, Bill? Don't tell me you need backup serving a warrant?" said the chief with something between a smirk and a smile.

"You excuse us, deputy?" the sheriff said to Shoemaker

"Yes, sir," he answered, exiting quickly.

"You mind if I ask your boy a few questions, John?" asked the sheriff as he nodded toward Clayton.

"By all means," said the chief.

"You have a problem with an old colored man today, over off of Detroit?" the sheriff asked the young patrolman, who looked a bit nervous.

"Came across a vagrant over there, wandering around a nice neighborhood," said Clayton. "Ran him off. Why, what gives?"

"You impose a *fine* on this... vagrant?"

Clayton looked to the chief, confused.

"What the hell's this about, Bill?" Gustafson asked.

"It's about an honest old man needing to go see his daughter to spot him some dough for her momma's cough medicine and getting pilfered for it on his way home."

Officer Clayton leaned forward, somewhat aggressively.

"You takin' some nigger's word over a cop's?"

Chief Gustafson put his arm in front of Clayton's chest.

"You watch your tone, officer," warned the chief.

Clayton looked at Gustafson, who gave him a stern look, then back at the sheriff.

"Sorry, sheriff," said Clayton.

The chief nodded.

"Now what is this about, Bill? I came over here as a courtesy, but I got more important things to do than listen to stories about what some old nigger says about five dollars he probably never had in the first place."

McCullough clasped his hands, elbows on the desk, and leaned in.

"I'm not stupid, fellas. I know there are certain liberties certain law officers take and certain justifications about the job and what it pays that they think square such business. And

I'm aware that they think that by taking those liberties against a certain class of people, it matters, well, *less*. But this ain't about to become the kind of town where an honest old man's biggest fear is gonna be someone dressed in blue."

The chief's eyes widened and he puffed out his chest at the younger and more fit sheriff.

"You might want to be careful what you're suggesting, sheriff."

McCullough kicked back in his chair, clasping his hands behind his head.

"What I'm suggesting is that your boy reaches into his pocket, pulls out a five-dollar bill, and puts it on my desk as a donation to the sheriff's fund for dumb ass decisions. And then I'm suggesting we forget what we'll call a *misunderstanding*. That seem reasonable enough to you, John?"

The chief paused, then nodded to Officer Clayton, who pulled a wad of crumpled bills from his pocket and put them on the desk.

"You see I only got four ones, 'cause I didn't take no five-dollar bill from no one, but I'll be happy to donate it to your a ... *fund*, sheriff."

The chief, embarrassed, shook his head at Officer Clayton.

"That'll have to do, I suppose," said McCullough. "I thank you for your donation, officer, and I sincerely hope it'll be the last one we ever need to discuss."

The chief looked at his officer and shook his head.

"Get the hell back to the station."

Officer Clayton rose quickly and exited the room. Chief Gustafson watched him leave and then turned to the sheriff and shrugged.

"What are you gonna do, right?" he said with a hopeful look.

"Maybe start by telling your boys that colored folks are not only subject to but protected by the same laws as the rest of us?"

The chief rolled his eyes.

"Sure, Bill, I'll make it the theme of my next shift meeting. It ought to go over real good, raise morale and give us a boom in recruiting."

The sheriff smirked and tipped his hat. The chief sighed and shook his head as he exited. Once he was gone, the sheriff called Deputy Evers back into the room, reached into his wallet, and pulled out a five-dollar bill, replacing it with the four ones, while handing Evers the five.

"Go get Mr. Smith. Give him this, and then walk him to the streetcar. Be sure you see him leave on it without being harassed."

"Yes, sir," said the deputy, taking the bill.

"Sheriff?"

The sheriff looked up at him in silence.

"I just want to say that that was a real nice thing you did, sir. I mean for that old guy."

The sheriff sighed.

"No, son, nice had nothing to do with it. It was just the right thing, and even that's a hard thing to do around here sometimes."

"Yes, sir," said the deputy, holding up the bill as he left.

****

Richard Lloyd Jones and his wife Georgia lived in a large Victorian-style home in one of Tulsa's more prestigious neighborhoods along with their three children: Richard Jr., who was 12; Jenkin, who was 10; and their little sister Florence, who'd just turned 7. The house had been built by a wealthy farmer a decade before the family moved to Tulsa and had been put up for sale after the man who built it passed on, which, as fate would have it, was just weeks before the Jones family would move to town.

It was richly-appointed with fine woodwork, heavy wallpaper, quality furniture and large, ornate rugs across most of the rooms' mahogany floors. Georgia handled the home decorating but in keeping with her husband's overall presentation, the home spoke to sophistication and an appreciation of history, without seeming as though the man was trying to show off his wealth—even if he was, at least a little bit.

The family typically dined later than most, owed to the head of household's late hours at the paper, and it was after seven before they'd finally sat down that evening. Richard was scooping mashed potatoes onto his own plate, as his wife drizzled gravy atop of the mound on their daughter's.

"So I said, 'Look, Bill, I'm sorry, but I'm just not against the niggers in the same way you are'," Richard told his wife. "'I do, however, agree that there is a profound difference from say, Mammy, who has taken care of our children and cooked our meals and is home right now enjoying a fine time with her own family as she does every Thursday I'm sure, and those animals who live over in Little Africa'."

Georgia gave him a displeased look, nodding toward the kids.

"What?" asked Richard.

"I'm just not certain this is a suitable topic for the children," she said.

Richard shook his head forcefully.

"Quite the contrary, Georgia, they need to hear this sort of talk so that they'll recognize the hateful bigotry of men like him from the truth of the matter. I will not have our children growing up thinking that all niggers are lowly creatures. Yes, there are some, the lowest of the low, who are a stain on our society, but those who live on this side of the Frisco tracks, in servant quarters with good, Christian, white families that teach them to live in cleanliness and to understand deference and gratuity are another thing altogether."

"I think most people would agree, I'm only suggesting that-"

"Not Bill Rodgers," he said, cutting her off. "He'd rather see them back in chains, or hanging from a rope, every last one. It's a battle, my dear, and if we don't win, if we don't stem the rise of these arrogant types, we really will have a nigger problem of the sort Bill and his crowd already sees."

"Well aren't you the progressive?" she said with a warm grin.

"What's a progressive, father?" asked his eldest son.

"A progressive is a forward thinker, Junior, a champion of progress who is not bound by the backward thinking of the past. And your mother is right indeed, I *am* a progressive."

"Mammy is good" said Florence. "I love her."

"As you should, buttercup, as you should," he told her. "That's my point. Do you know where Booker T. Washington, the great Negro educator stayed when no hotel back in Madison would rent him a room?"

"Where?" asked Richard Jr.

"Our house, that's where," said his father.

"I don't remember him," said Jenkin.

"Well it was before you were born, son, but you best believe he did," he told him, giving a wink and smile to his wife, before taking another bite. "Progressive indeed."

****

Sheriff McCullough entered the luncheonette just as Chief Gustafson was leaving cash on his table, preparing to exit. He looked up at the sheriff and grinned.

"Evening, sheriff."

The sheriff tipped his cowboy hat.

"Chief."

"Working late tonight?" the chief asked.

"We don't got banker hours like the city police, John, you know that," said the sheriff with a smile.

"Sheeyit," said Gustafson. "If they let me leave at noon I surely would, but I'm headed back to the office now myself. Idle hands being the devil's playthings and all."

The sheriff looked at him with an arched brow and grinned.

"Have a good night, Bill."

The sheriff tipped his hat, grateful that the chief hadn't brought up that afternoon's events, though his demeanor seemed to signal there were no hard feelings, no more than usual anyway. Technically, the sheriff, holding an elected position that covered the entire county, was above him in the pecking order, even if they were under completely different chains of command. But Gustafson had job security and more of the kind of power that mattered. For his part, he resented the sheriff's squeaky clean reputation and the holier-than-thou way he seemed to look down at he and the other law enforcement officers who played the game as it had been played for the 14 years since Oklahoma had achieved statehood.

In truth, McCullough only disliked the chief so much because he was in a position of authority and therefore, he suspected, was capable of setting a better example that might clean up the culture of the city police department, which had enjoyed a reputation for spectacular corruption from its inception. Then again, he did make allowances for the fact that their department was much larger than his and its ranks were filled with the sort of men who joined the force precisely so they could get in on such spoils. It'd be a tough job for any man to change that, and he figured the chief didn't have it in him, even if he had been inclined to do so.

Gustafson was probably doing the best he could with what he was working with both internally and externally, and the sheriff knew full well that the department could do even worse in terms of a chief.

The sheriff had arrived a little later than usual and, much to his liking, he noticed that the dinner crowd had thinned considerably as he took his usual seat at the counter where Annie was waiting with a smile as she turned over his mug and poured hot coffee into it.

"Can't make no promises on the coffee," she told him. "I'd have made a fresh batch if I knew you were still gonna make it in."

"I'm sure it'll be just fine," said the sheriff.

She smiled.

"Now is it just me, or did it take all the will you could muster to be even half nice to the chief?" she asked, arching an eyebrow as he took his first sip of coffee.

"Now why would you say a thing like that?"

"Because you're a good man, Bill McCullough, and that there son of a bitch is not."

"Bill does his best, I suppose. I've certainly seen worse."

She shook her head and began wiping the counter.

"I haven't."

The sheriff leaned back in his chair and smiled, shaking his head in appreciation of the woman's grit.

"How's the meatloaf tonight?" he asked her.

"Gone," she told him. "Wasn't as good as the fried chicken, anyway. Still got some of that left, though it's only thighs and drumsticks."

"Then yard bird it is."

Annie leaned in toward him, her elbows resting on the Formica. As she stared into his eyes, he could feel his breath shorten and his heart rate pick up.

"When you gonna take this war widow out for a drink, old man?" she asked, finally taking the lead in this dance of theirs, which he'd been carrying on for a month with no progression. "You know it ain't proper for no lady to go into a speakeasy by herself."

The sheriff gave her a broad, closed-mouth grin.

"And you know it ain't proper for no law officer to be seen in no speakeasy."

"The way I hear it, you'd likely bump elbows with a few while you were there, politicians too."

"All the more reason to stay away," said the sheriff with a smile.

Annie stood back up and resumed wiping the counter.

"I suppose I'll have to wait until they get rid of this prohibition then," she said wistfully.

"Nah, this county has a habit of voting me out of office with great frequency. Soon as I turn in the star, you and I will howl at the moon. How's that?"

"You best not wait that long, cowboy" she told him with a coy smile. "Somebody else might come along and make an honest woman of me yet."

****

Outside the luncheonette, Bill Rodgers stood on the corner of a nearby side street with Lawton Mercer. Lawton was under a streetlamp, leaning against its post, but Bill made sure he was closer to the brick wall as to not be so easily seen. It irked Lawton that Bill could call on him so often, yet had to make such obvious efforts to reduce the chance of anyone seeing them together. He liked to tell himself that it was for both of their protection but, deep down, he knew better. People had been taking such pains since long before he'd met Bill Rodgers, and he hated each one of them for it.

"Times are tough, I know it," said Rodgers.

"Do you?" asked Lawton, his voice dripping with cynicism as he looked at him from foot to head, assessing the polished leather shoes, his fine tailored suit, and the crisp, shiny fedora.

"Tougher for some than others, that may be true," said Rodgers, puffing his chest a bit to show he wasn't intimidated.

"But what have I ever been but a friend to you, Lawton? I told you, my people out in the oil fields have assured me it's vets first."

"Only they just laid off and ain't hiring," said Lawton, testily. "What good is being first in a line that ain't movin'?"

Rodgers softened his stance and tone, adopting a more fatherly demeanor.

"That's just the business cycle, kid. It over-expands, then it contracts a bit to correct itself. There was a glut that built up right after the armistice. But now the economy is starting to hum and demand will spike. You and your boys will be on soon enough."

Lawton kept his posture but retrained his angst away from Rodgers.

"Meanwhile, they got all them Texas roughnecks on up there," he complained. "Wops and even krauts getting top dollar while we gotta starve?"

"Hey now!" said Rodgers. "Who's starving? You know good old Uncle Bill would never let that happen."

Rodgers peeled some money from his billfold and handed it to him.

"There, that ought to hold you over for a bit. And you're not wrong about that trash floatin' up from Texas, either. Makes me sick to my stomach, those filthy roughnecks coming down from the camps every Friday and Saturday night and turning our fair town into a veritable den of iniquity. Hell they even stand out among the filth over on First Street."

Lawton surmised the wad of cash approvingly.

"They're as bad as the niggers, Bill. It's enough to make you wanna retch."

"I couldn't agree more, young man," said Rodgers. "Someone really ought to do something about that one of these days. Maybe make an example out of one of them?"

He gave Lawton a pat on the back and began walking away. Lawton looked down at the cash in his hand, only then realizing the transactional nature of the encounter.

"You have a good night now, Lawton," said Rodgers as he walked off. "Stay out of trouble."

When Rodgers got to his car, Lawton Stuffed the wad of bills into his pocket and shook his head as he watched him drive off.

****

Back inside the luncheonette, the sheriff was picking at a piece of lemon meringue pie, while the only other customers—a young man and his pregnant wife—settled up with Annie at the cash register. She smiled, looking back at him as the couple exited.

"You sure have been taking your time picking at that pie, sheriff. You don't like it?"

"You in a hurry to get me out of here?" he asked.

"No, sir, I'm grateful for the company of a handsome stranger," she said with her most flirtatious smile of the evening.

"Stranger?" he asked, arching an eyebrow.

"Well, I've never once even seen you outside of this place. How well can a woman know a man if he's never even taken her for a Sunday stroll?"

The sheriff smiled.

"Pie's fine, ma'am. It's just that it's only the second sweetest thing before me, and my attentions have been diverted by the first."

Annie, her elbows on the counter at this point, began to lean in toward him and he may have kissed her had the saloon doors from the kitchen not swung open. Evie, a stout woman in her fifties who managed the luncheonette, passed through with a tray of clean coffee mugs and saucers. Annie and the sheriff jumped back and tried to compose themselves.

"Oh hell, like you two are foolin' anyone anyhow," said Evie. "Why don't you just kiss her, Bill, and get the damn thing over with? This thing between you two is the longest bit of foreplay I ever saw."

The sheriff and Annie smiled at each other while Evie shook her head. The sheriff reached into his pocket, withdrew some money and put it on the table as he stood up.

"I do have to run," he told the two women, though his gaze never left Annie. "Evening, ladies."

The sheriff winked at Annie and then tipped his hat to Evie as he headed to the door.

"He is a handsome devil, isn't he?" asked Evie, as the bell from the door jingled upon his exit.

"As handsome as the day is long," said Annie, "but as slow to proceed as molasses in January. I fear I'll be through the change by the time he works up the will to take me on a first date."

Both women laughed.

"Be patient, darlin'," said Evie. "It's only been two years since he lost that wife of his. He's got it for you good, that's clear as can be. He just needs to go at his own pace."

****

Inside the 1st Street speakeasy, Dick Rowland was drinking a milky looking mug of what the locals called choc beer, which was made on reservations by Choctaw Indians and was a staple in any of Tulsa's underground bars, themselves often referred to as choc houses as a result. There was a modest crowd of prostitutes and drinkers mingling as a man played jazz music at a well-weathered upright piano, accompanied by a trumpet player. Freddy, who was known for his sense of humor, was regaling his friends with a joke. He always gesticulated the action wildly with his hands, which seemed to make his humor even more effective.

"She say, nuh-uh, I got a tight pussy," said Freddy. "Look here, put your finger in me. He do, and she start moanin'. Then she say, put two fingers in me, and he do, and now she moanin' good. She say, put your whole hand in me, and he like, okay. She moan even more. Then she say, put both hands in me. So now he got both hands in there real good, and she say, now clap your hands. He tries and says, I can't do it. The girl look at him and say, See, I told you I had a tight pussy!"

Dick and Mooch laughed hard, pounding the bar with their hands. Shaking his head, Dick took out a wad of money, held it high and waved it around.

"Another round for us, and a drink for every lady in here," Dick told the old man behind the bar.

"Even the ugly ones!" laughed Mooch.

A Black, heavyset prostitute slyly inched up to Dick's arm and punched Mooch's shoulder playfully.

"Man, look at Mr. Money Bags," said Freddy. "He actin' like he the new king of Black Wall Street."

Mooch, clearly drunk, grabbed Dick's wrist with one hand and held up his ringed finger with the other.

"Diamond Dick Rowland, baby!" screamed Mooch. "He big time."

"Quit foolin' around, Mooch," said Dick, feigning embarrassment as he drew back his arm. "I'm just trying to share the wealth with my friends, that's all."

Dick turned and caressed the face of a pretty second prostitute who'd since eased up along his other arm.

"Man, had I known you could make that kind of coin shining shoes, I'd a got me a shine box a long time ago," said Freddy.

"Forget that, man, we gonna be gangsters," said Mooch. "King Henry be comin' up, and we goin' with him."

Mooch raised his glass to toast Freddy.

"I hear that," said Freddy. "First thing I'm gonna do is get me a ring just like that, bigger maybe."

"Man, you remember when he used to be *Slick Dick Rowland*, cutting up the field at Booker T.?" asked Mooch.

"I surely do," said Freddy.

"I do miss football, that's for sure," said Dick, "but a man gotta have money in this world."

"Money get a man all kind of things," said the second prostitute, now caressing the side of Dick's face with the back of her hand.

Dick smiled and drew the girl closer.

"Like what, baby?"

"Like a slick dick, Mr. Rowland, bahahahaha!" laughed Freddy.

At this, Freddy and Mooch doubled over in laughter. Dick flashed a broad smile to the prostitute who smiled back, seductively.

****

The alleys that connected to the south side of 1st Street were known for rough trade, and those who knew their way around the red light district knew to stick the well-lit confines of the main thoroughfare, even if they were only moderately less dangerous. Lawton, Red, and Willie were standing on a dark corner of one of those alleys, just out of the light that was shining down on 1st Street when the person they had been waiting for arrived.

The man they called Horse was a fellow veteran, and anyone who took one look at him didn't ask how he'd gotten the nickname. He stood nearly six and a half feet tall and had the sort of mountainous frame that could have supported much more than even his 250 pounds. With thick joints and broad shoulders, his otherwise enormous head looked right at home atop of his 19 inch neck. He ambled along with his hands in his pocket, a man clearly comfortable in this or any other environment, and nodded to his friends when he approached the spot where they were waiting.

"Kept us waitin' long enough," said Lawton.

"I told you I'd be downright after dinner," said Horse, indifferently.

"I guess we forgot how long it took a guy your size to eat," sneered Lawton.

Horse shrugged.

"Maw made meatloaf and mashed potatoes," he said. "I stuck around for a second helping."

Horse posted up against the brick wall with the other three men, as they watched drunks, prostitutes, and other revelers amble along in every direction. Some were Black, some were white, some were Native American.

"Look at this fucking mess," said Lawton. "Have you ever seen anything like it? Three years fighting the Jerries to come back to see Tulsa turn into a shithole like this?"

"Yeah, and how long until it spreads past 1st Street?" asked Red.

"No fucking chance, pal," said Lawton

"What d'ya wanna do, Lawton?" asked Willie.

"Send a message, Willie. Send a message loud and clear."

****

Dick and Freddy were good and drunk, still talking to the same prostitutes. Mooch was passed out, face first on the bar, when King Henry walked in and approached Dick from behind, sticking his finger into his back as if it were a gun.

"Gimme your money and that shiny ring, fool!" said Henry in a deep, gruff voice.

Dick, alarmed but slowed by the booze, raised his arms clumsily. Freddy broke out in laughter and a confused Dick finally turned around to see Henry, who was also laughing hysterically by that point.

"Man, you was scared with a capital S!" said Mooch, still laughing.

"For real, I thought I was gonna get my card punched, King," said Dick, a smile finally materializing on his face.

"What'chu doing here, King?" asked Freddy.

"Looking for you fools," said Henry. "How'd I know that on your night off you'd be chocked up in some juke joint on 1st? Only the second bucket I had to poke my head into. Started with the nastiest one and figured I'd work my way up the ladder."

The bartender looked up from wiping glasses.

"At least we wash the glasses in our joint, not like that rat-trap alley dive you run," he said to Henry.

"You'd better wash 'em extra good too, some of the crusty-lipped Negroes I seen drinking in this place," said Henry with a laugh.

"Ain't no crust on these lips, baby?" said the heavyset prostitute.

"Which ones, sugar?" asked Henry.

"Not on the ones you can see for free, nor the ones you can see for a fee," said the woman, inching closer to Henry's face with a seductive smile.

"Is that right?" asked Henry. "What we hanging around here for then? Let's take this party back to the king's castle."

"Oh yeah?" asked the woman.

"Yeah, and maybe I'll let you sit on the throne when we get there," said Henry, pulling a thick billfold from his pocket and smiling back at her. Then he motioned toward Mooch. "What's wrong with that fool? Man, wake his ass up, and let's get out of here before I get flea bites on my ass from this bar stool."

Freddy roused Mooch and the six of them staggered out to the street, Mooch slung over Freddy's shoulder. King Henry had his arm around the first prostitute and Dick had his around the other. Meanwhile, a crew of four large, drunk roughnecks strolled down the middle of the street, whooping loudly. Their faces were stained with grease and their overalls and shirts were covered with dark stains from the fields.

"You niggers had better make way," said one of the roughnecks as they careened toward Henry and his crew. "This is the white side of the street you're all on."

King put his hand on his back and when Dick looked down, he could see the handle of a pistol sticking out.

"Leave it go, King," said Dick in a hushed voice. "It ain't worth no trouble, not for no roughnecks."

King kept his hand on his back but began crossing the street diagonally, away from the trouble, and the others followed.

"Now there's a good little monkey," said the first roughneck.

"I wouldn't mind having me a tumble with that pretty Negress, though," said one of his pals, stepping toward the group. "How much darling?" he asked. Then, turning to Henry, "Or should I be askin' you? I can never tell husbands from pimps with your kind."

Henry withdrew his pistol, holding it close to his chest but pointed upward.

"They off the clock right now," said Henry, "but you gentlemen enjoy the rest of your evening, okay?"

The man laughed hysterically. Doubled over, he finally managed to compose himself enough to speak.

"Is... is a nigger pointing a gun at me?" he asked another man next to him

"It sure looks like it," said the third roughneck

"Nah, I ain't pointing it at no one but the stars," said Henry. "Now, we gonna keep headed where we was going. You fellas do the same, and there won't be no trouble for no one."

Caught off guard, the roughnecks were silent for a moment, assessing the situation. Then the first man put his arm around the second.

"Come on, there's plenty of nigger whores on this street," he told him with a laugh. "I'm sure we can find an even *pertier* one for you to have a go with, big fella."

The man he said it to paused for a moment and seemed to contemplate violence, before eventually laughing.

"Shit, you're right," he said. "It's payday. I think I'm gonna splurge and get me some white pussy tonight anyway. Come on, let's go get us another drink."

King Henry and the others continued down the street, where only moments later an Italian immigrant, also oil field dirty and clearly very drunk, stumbled toward them.

"Dove sono le ragazze? Miei amici, dove posso trovare una bella donna?" he asked, falling into Dick, who gently pushed him aside.

"English, man, English," said Dick, laughing. "You in America now."

"Girls, my friend," said the Italian. "I want girl for mine own."

The man held up a wad of bills in each hand.

"That way, man," said Dick, "right through that door up there."

Dick pointed toward a brothel about a block away, on the next corner, in the direction the man had been headed. The Italian patted his shoulder.

"Grazie, my compagno, my friend. Grazie."

Dick shook his head as he watched the man stumble up the street toward the brothel.

"Man, you should'a hit that fool over the head and took that fold, Dick!" said Freddy. "He must'a had more than ten dollars wadded up in those grimy hands."

"Nah, man," said Dick. "I ain't no hustler like that. He just had too much choc, and he want a little lady company."

He turned and smiled at his prostitute.

"Can't blame a man for that."

"Man fuck those filthy crackers," said Freddy, "always coming down here and startin' shit up."

"Is that right?" asked Henry, his arm back around the other girl. "Well, I didn't see you puffing out your chest like a bird when those four big Texans were testin' us? Besides, you think there'd even be a 1st Street if it weren't for all those roughnecks blowin' they wages up and down it? You think we'd be moving as much choc and brown as we do? It's all part of the same machine, Freddy. Half the dollars you spent tonight been through they greasy hands first."

"I mean you got a point, King, but... (laughs) fuck 'em anyhow!"

Henry shrugged, let out a sigh, and then laughed himself as they continued to shuffle down the street casually.

****

Lawton, Red, Willie, and Horse were watching from the alley as the Italian walked toward the brothel, which was located on the corner just past where they were standing. The man was singing in his native tongue and still had his money wadded up in both hands as he approached.

"Look at this fucking guido," said Lawton, "three sheets to the wind and looking for whores on payday."

"Wanna roll him, Lawton?" asked Willie, nervously.

"Shut up, Willie," he said, slowly sauntering out toward the street with both hands in his pocket.

"Hey... hey, *paesano*, what are you looking for, pal?" asked Lawton when he got about three feet from the man.

"Ciao, ciao. I come for the girls," said the Italian. "The Black men say this door for the beautiful girls."

116

"Oh, you're looking for some dark meat tonight?" Lawton asked. "You like that nigger pussy, do ya?"

Unfazed, the man smiled and held out his arms.

"Any kind of girls, I like. Beautiful girls! Bella!"

"Yeah, yeah this is the place all right," said Lawton, "but don't use that door, not if you want the girls. You gotta go in the back, and you gotta know the password."

"Oh! Grazie, grazie, friend. Can you tell me the password?"

"Sure, sure, come here," said Lawton, "I gotta whisper it though, so no one else hears it."

Lawton put his arm around the Italian man's shoulder and led him toward a very narrow alley that ran directly behind the brothel, as the other men followed a few steps behind. When they got to a metal door on the back of the building, Lawton leaned into the Italian's ear.

"When they answer the door, you gotta say, nigger lover."

"Yes?" asked the Italian, a bit confused.

"Yeah, I mean that's what you are, aren't you, ya fucking greasy, no good guinea."

Lawton, with his left hand still on the man's neck, punched him hard in the stomach with his right, immediately doubling him over. The drunk man could only vomit, then gasp in pain.

"Did you puke on my shoes, you filthy fucking wop?" asked Lawton, looking down.

Squared up with the man at this point, Lawton punched him in the ear with his right hand, and then sent a left hook crashing into the other side of his head, causing the man to fall to the ground hard, where Red and Willie began kicking him in the ribs and head. Lawton then pulled out a thin, lead pipe from the pocket of his overalls.

"Look out," said Lawton, and began hitting the motionless man with the pipe, screaming at him while the blows rained down.

"You think you can come to our town, take our jobs, then come down here and act like a filthy fucking animal with our money."

Lawton picked up the bills, which had fallen on the ground around the man's motionless body.

"Looks like there's gonna be an opening in one of the fields on Monday, boys," said Lawton. "Horse, put this piece of shit in the trash where he belongs."

Horse picked the man right up over his head, as Willie opened a dumpster that was against the building, opposite the brothel, in the alley. From a good two feet away, Horse body slammed the still man's dead weight into the half-full dumpster, where he crashed onto his back. Lawton walked up to the dumpster opening and saw a rat crawling across the man's chest. He sneered and put his hand on the lid.

"Sweet dreams, asshole," he said, slamming it shut.

Chapter 3

John Williams pulled up to the curb of his wife's confectionery shop in his fancy Chalmers convertible. He'd barely come to a complete stop when Bill, his 16 year-old son, exited the passenger side holding up several dead quail by the neck, a shotgun in his other hand.

"Mama, look!" shouted Bill.

Loula Williams, a very attractive and well-dressed Black woman in her late thirties, had her hands on her hips, shaking her head—her default reaction whenever her two boys were being boys in a manner that she only moderately disapproved of.

"John Williams, that boy is going to be late for school again, and he don't need to be gettin' in no trouble this close to graduation," Loula shouted to her husband who dropped his head on the steering wheel and grinned. "And you don't need to be late for work," she added with a wag of the finger in his direction.

John turned his head toward her and flashed a flirtatious smile from the driver's seat.

"I got special permission from the boss," he told her.

"Baby, you are lookin' into the eyes of the boss," she said, "and she don't recall issuing no such privileges."

Bill turned to look back at his father.

"Someone's in the doghouse now."

John shook his head and laughed. His wife finally cracked a small smile and winked at her husband.

"Go on, boy, mind your Mama. I'd best get to the garage before the boss's kettle goes hot."

Bill turned and headed toward his mother. His father drove off, honking the horn, waving and issuing pleasantries to people in the crowded street as he moved down it slowly, taking pride in the way they admired his vehicle. John Williams had been the very first man in all of Greenwood to own a motor car, a privilege he earned by becoming the first man in all of Tulsa to learn how to take one apart and put it back together.

A tinkerer by nature, he'd yet to come across a machine he couldn't come to understand with enough expertise to fix whichever part wasn't behaving in the manner it had been engineered to. A child of the industrial revolution, he'd come of age at just the right time for those skills to be of particular benefit and had ridden them from the railroads to the dairies and then to motor cars. Such was his superiority as a mechanic that even in Tulsa he had yet to come across a white man with any qualms about allowing him to put his Black hands upon even their most prized automobiles—or bicker over the premium prices he was smart enough to know such superiority could command.

He and Loula had come to Tulsa from Mississippi, where she'd been a school teacher and he'd worked for the rail line repairing steam engines. But Mississippi—where lynchings had become as regular as summer rain—was no place for a young Black couple starting a family. After two of her students discovered a Black man's body strung up from the branch of a large oak tree while playing in the woods near the school before class one morning, Loula had seen enough.

"How many dead bodies hangin' from trees do I gotta see, John?" she asked her husband as they ate dinner that evening, their son, who was only three at the time, seated next to them in his highchair. "How many does your son gotta see? How long before it's one of our faces looking down from that noose?"

"Where we gonna run to, Loula?" John asked, exasperation in his voice. "Tell me. Where's the Black man free from all that? We saw bodies in Memphis. We saw bodies in Chicago. Where's the place they don't lynch Negroes? Tell me and we'll go."

"I told you Sissy's people are down in Tulsa for more than a year now," she said, referring to a childhood friend she'd grown up with in Memphis. "More and more of her kin are making their way down there too. She and Arch are going themselves as soon as her momma gets well enough to travel."

"Again with Tulsa?" asked John. "That's your promised land? Where they got Negro cops and Negro nannies and Negro store owners? What, they ain't got no hate in Tulsa?"

"I'm not sayin' that, John," she said, feeding a spoonful of mashed potatoes to their son.

"I have good work here, Loula. The railroad's done right by us. It's brought us to Mississippi, and it will take us somewhere else when the Lord sees fit."

She shot her husband a sharp look.

"If the devil or the undertaker don't see fit to take us first."

John reached across the table and took his wife's hand.

"You can't keep out in front of hate, baby," he told her. "You can't outrun it, 'cause it's everywhere. Hate's been finding colored folks ever since they brought us to this place."

Loula rubbed his hand and turned her gaze back to their son, who was playing with the food on his plate, then back to John.

"I'd rather run ahead of it than stand still and wait for it in a place where it seems so eager to find us, John."

He took her other hand as she dropped her head, and she looked back at her husband, eyes wet but forcing a smile.

"Well, if you wanna run, you know you can always count on me to give chase," he told her with a smile.

Not long after, the young family had taken everything they owned and headed for Greenwood. And they hadn't known it then, but they could not have picked a better time to get in on the ground floor. It was one year after Oklahoma had achieved statehood, and John initially found steady work and handsome pay repairing the steam engines used by a large dairy in Tulsa, which he found to be simple compared to those used on the trains. When the motor car craze hit town, he initially figured it would be good side work and took in the occasional repair job, which he would do under the shade of a giant beech tree near their first apartment. It wasn't long at all, however, until he was faced with turning down work for lack of time.

Soon he decided it was in his best interest to quit his job at the dairy and work on cars full time. The couple took some of the cash they'd socked away and put a down payment on a three-story brick building in Greenwood, where they intended to put the garage, but, because of zoning restrictions, had ended up as Loula's confectionery instead, itself a rather prosperous concern.

After finding a suitable building for his service station, the couple later purchased another large brick building in the business district where they opened the Dreamland, a magnificent 750-seat venue that hosted live musical and theatrical revues, as well as silent movies with the accompaniment of a piano player. It was, without question, the hottest spot in Greenwood and took in a full till of cash six nights a week.

Not trusting white-owned banks enough to allow too much of their money to accumulate in one, John and Loula focused on real estate, adding several rental properties to their portfolio over the years. By 1921—just 13 years after they'd arrived in Greenwood—it was quite possible that they trailed only Stradford and Gurley in terms of wealth.

Beyond the Chalmers, however, you'd never know it from the way John Williams carried himself. Deep down, he was a simple man who liked simple things. Unless the occasion demanded formality, he dressed in plain clothing and spent most of his free time quail hunting, another skill at which he had proven so proficient that it was often said he was the very best shot in all of town, the vast number of Army veterans notwithstanding.

Loula on the other hand, had developed a taste for the finer things and didn't mind showing off their prosperity occasionally by way of a dress imported from France or a handbag that came from Italy. She had exquisite taste and, much to the chagrin of those women in Tulsa's elite white circle, was almost always the most regal looking woman in the room on the few occasions when their paths would cross.

John Williams was under the chassis of a small roadster later that morning when Horace Frank entered his shop, pausing when he realized that John had been engaged with a white customer. Horace watched as John turned the wrench a final time and then emerged, wiping grease from his hands with a towel as he stood. He then reached in with his leg and put a foot on the clutch as he turned the key. The car fired right up, as the customer stood there smiling and shaking his head in disbelief, before clapping his hands slowly.

"Hot damn, John," the well-dressed man said. "You are one hell of a whiz with these things, I do mean it. I didn't think this breezer was ever gonna turn over again."

"Oh she got loads of life left in her yet," said John. "The clutch plate just needed tightening. She shouldn't give you no problems for a little while, but I'd say you only got about another thousand miles or so until that clutch burns."

The man stroked his chin in consideration, then pulled out a shiny gold pocket watch to check the time. It occurred to Horace that the man's watch was probably worth more than all of the money he'd ever seen in his entire life.

"I'll tell you what, let's say I drop it off in 500 and we change it out, preemptive like?" asked the man, as he tucked the watch away in his vest pocket.

"Yes, sir," said John. "We can do that. Big job, though, take me a day or two depending on how much I got backed up when you come in."

"Ah hell, that's no trouble. I only get her out once in a while on the weekends anyway. I've got a car and driver through the week."

The man reached into the passenger seat, grabbed his sport coat, and took out a thick wad of cash from the inside breast pocket, peeling off several crisp bills.

"That seem fair, John?" he asked with a knowing smile.

"More than fair, sir," John told him with a wink. "Thank you, kindly. You bring her back in 500, and I'll fix that clutch real good, get the hoses and belts tightened too. Have her runnin' like the wind."

"I don't doubt it," the man said as he climbed into the car, struggling to work the clutch, and lurching forward a few times as he exited the garage bay.

"Was that a Stutz Bearcat, sir?" asked Horace, who'd slowly walked forward toward John, cap in his hands, as the man pulled out.

"It sure was," said John. "1914 model. You know your cars, I can see."

Horace blushed and looked down at his feet, still clutching his cap nervously.

"I only seen one a those in pictures. I never thought I'd ever see one right up close like that."

John offered his hand and the two men shook.

"John Williams."

"Pleased to meet you, Mr. Williams, sir," said Horace, again looking down.

"Look a man in the eyes when you talking to him, son," said John. "Let him know you're to be taken seriously. You get what I mean?"

Horace straightened himself, tightened his grip a bit, and looked John in his eyes as he answered, a bit more sand in his voice this time.

"Yes, sir. I'm Horace Frank."

John smiled.

"Good to know you, Horace. Now, what can I do for you today?" John asked.

Horace took out the calling card and presented it.

"Mr. Kelly over at the hamburger counter told me I should come see you. I done worked on some cars and motorbikes back in Fayetville, Arkansas, where we come from. He said you might have a need for me."

John looked at the card, then back to Horace and nodded.

"Son, if you can change oil, spark plugs, pump some gas and want to learn to rebuild engines, I can give you all the work you can stand. I got cars coming in here faster than I can look at them, let alone get 'em back out."

"Yes, sir, I'll learn anything you care to teach me, and I'll work as long as you put work in front of me. No problem with that, sir. Work wasn't easy for colored folks to come by back in Fayetville, truth be told."

John nodded, and set back about cleaning his hands with the rag.

"I know what you mean. Bounced damn near halfway around the country before we landed on our feet here in Greenwood. You got any of your people with you?"

Horace nodded.

"My sister, Bessie. She come down too. She 18, just finished up high school last year. She's back in the rooming house waitin' on me. I was gonna take her to look for work in Tulsa tomorrow, didn't want her going in on the streetcar alone, it being her first time in a city and all."

"That's a good brother," said John. "But I'll tell you what. You decide you don't want her working as a servant for rich white folks, you take her over and see my wife, Loula. We got the Williams Confectionery on Greenwood Street and the Dreamland Theater. Loula will put her to work taking tickets or making candies, pay her a fair wage and you need not worry about her living in some oil tycoon's servant quarters. If she's a pretty young lady, that's not always the best place to be, if you get me?"

"I do, sir," said Horace, "and I'd be happy if she could work around here in Greenwood instead."

"Alright then, you get her on over to see Loula right quick. She be at the confectionery this time a day, most likely. Tell her I sent you. She'll get her set up, and you can start here in the morning. Be here at 8 a.m. sharp, and we'll get to it."

Horace's smile lit up.

129

"Yes, sir. I won't be late, neither—ever!"

John smiled as he tossed the towel over his shoulder, shaking his head as he watched Horace run out of the garage in excitement.

****

When Ernie Wash approached the work site, a number of Black workers in hardhats were busy on the large wooden frame of a new project while Wilfred Dickinson was pointing things out on a blueprint to a white architect. As the architect nodded and rolled up the blueprints, Ernie raised his hand to get Wilfred's attention.

"Mr. Dickinson, sir."

Wilfred looked up.

"Hello, mate, what can I do for you?" he replied.

"Mr. Kelly sent me," said Ernie. "He say you were looking for workers on this here site."

"Got carpentry experience, have you?"

Ernie was a powerfully built man who stood just under six feet tall, but he was of a particularly shy disposition, and felt even more nervous and out of place than usual when he heard the man's accent.

"Yes, sir," said Ernie, trying to sound more assured than he felt. "I'm good at framin' too."

"Well, we've got this one good and framed already you can see, but if you're willing to lay plank, I can use you starting tomorrow."

Ernie felt slightly embarrassed about the framing comment but was instantly buoyed by such a genial offer of work.

"Yes, sir," he said eagerly. "I'll do whatever you need. That's no problem at all."

"Aren't you gonna ask what it pays?" said Wilfred.

"No, sir," said Ernie. "I hear you a real fair man. Mr. Kelly said so, and I believe him. I'll take whatever you're paying, sir, and be happy for the work."

As Ernie trotted off, Wilfred shook his head.

"Bloody hell," he mumbled to himself. "They never ask what we pay."

****

The confines of the Tulsa Star were not nearly as grand as the concrete fortress across the Frisco tracks that was the Tribune building. That said, they were far from shabby. A publication intensely focused on Greenwood and the issues that were of particular importance to the African-American community, the building was analogous to the paper itself in that it was neat and orderly, not an inch worth of space wasted on frivolity.

Its publisher, Andrew J. Smitherman, 38, was born in Alabama but moved to the Oklahoma Territory with his family back in the 1890s. They had been looking for a better home and found it. A.J., as he was often called, had been a precocious child and from a very early age demonstrated tremendous academic gifts, as well as a vehement distaste for social injustice. He learned early that education was the only method through which a Black male might attempt to level the playing field either for himself as an individual or his race as a whole and set about getting as much of it as he could manage, which was to say a considerable amount. He had become an honors graduate of both Kansas and Northwestern Universities with an additional degree in law from LaSalle University's extension school.

When he finished his education, Smitherman started writing for newspapers in Muskogee, Oklahoma, 50 miles southeast of Tulsa. In 1911, he started his own newspaper there while still in his twenties. He called it The Muskogee Star. Two years later, however, he heard Tulsa calling and convinced his wife, Ollie, to pick up stakes and move their young family. They settled in Greenwood where they more or less relocated the newspaper, rechristening it The Daily Tulsa Star, Greenwood's first newspaper of record and Tulsa's first Black-owned daily. His ad revenue coming exclusively from Greenwood's prosperous Black business community,

Smitherman proved bold, writing freely about African American rights, no matter whom he might offend.

Both Otto Gurley and JB Stradford were generous patrons of the Star's advertising space, where they would each promote their various business concerns. But while Stradford was the type to egg on Smitherman's most revolutionary inclinations, Gurley spent most of his time trying to convince him to dial them back. It could easily be said that Stradford was the more successful of the two men in this regard, but whatever restraint Gurley was occasionally able to inspire probably went a long way toward Smitherman's general well being.

In truth, Gurley liked Smitherman quite a bit, though he had for some time conceded him as a casualty of his ongoing proxy war with Stradford and his radical brand of politics. Nonetheless, he knew that Smitherman respected his opinion and considered his advice, so on the morning after the meeting at Mt. Zion, he'd shown up at the Star building to try and temper Smitherman's position on the march, the editor having given the promised support to the Black veterans via an editorial in that day's edition.

"What purpose can this sort of inflammatory rhetoric possibly serve other than to incite, Andrew, tell me?" said Gurley, waving a copy of that morning's Star, as he paced Smitherman's office.

Gurley opened the paper and began reading from it.

"To tell men such as Mann, who fought so bravely on the front lines in Germany, that their service is not worthy of recognition is only the beginning of an effort to deny its very existence, whitewashing and then rewriting history so that the contribution of our people in the Great War may be permanently erased."

Gurley stared at him as if to frame his reading as a question. To this, Smitherman leaped to his feet.

"It serves the purpose of informing the public's opinion, Otto!" said Smitherman at close to a scream. "Must I remind you, that's what the editorial page is for?"

Gurley tried to diffuse the intensity a bit with a softer tone.

"With all due respect, Andrew, we both know there's no one south of the Frisco tracks who isn't sleeping in servant quarters that reads your editorials. And our community is well aware of the reality of this situation and its injustice. But when you go on to implore their participation in this protest on Monday, you are stirring the pot in hopes of rousing the mob. What good can possibly come of that?"

Smitherman shook his head and glared at him before answering.

"You sound like the white businessmen who told the abolitionists that they were only making trouble, that slavery wasn't going anywhere, so why rock the boat."

The statement put some bass back in Gurley's voice.

"How dare you compare me as such!" he yelled.

"And how dare you make me out to be no better than the mouthpiece of a lynch mob," said Smitherman, calmer now that he'd roused the other man. "I am a journalist, sir, and I take my platform as a voice to and for this community with great seriousness. I'll not be muzzled just because being on the side of justice and equality might create discomfort for some of the most privileged."

"Stop making it as though I have only my own interests at heart, dammit," said Gurley. "Look what happened in Atlanta two years ago. Look what happened in Chicago. Yes, the more you had the more you lost, but you tell me, is it harder to lose most of a great deal or all of next to nothing? If that business happens here, it'll be the very people you think you're championing who'll have it the worst in the aftermath, and the one place in this country where a poor, uneducated, hard-working Negro can build a life of dignity and self-sufficiency will be gone forever—and you could be good and goddamned sure they'll see that there's never another."

Smitherman paused and the last trace of anger fell from his face.

"Look, Otto, if you think that you or I, or anyone else is going to stop Obie Mann and those boys from doing what they're intent to do, you're crazier than I am."

"I'm not talking about stopping the vets from trying to march, Andrew," said Gurley. "I'm talking about not doing your damnedest to make sure there are a hundred or so other Black folks from Greenwood standing behind them when they're told to go home. A show of numbers will only make people nervous, and when they crack heads it won't only be of those who are wearing a uniform."

Smitherman exhaled with an exasperated look that suggested he would give some ground.

"Obie is a man of his word, and he assured us they will go peacefully," said Smitherman. "This isn't about a fight, it's about looking injustice in the eye and forcing those around you to look as well."

"Wars are never about the fights, Andrew," said Gurley. "They're always about the principles. But the books are written about the fights for a reason."

Gurley pointed to a bookcase on Smitherman's wall.

"You said it yourself," he continued, "they lynched a *white man* in Tulsa just because they got stirred up over some cabbie they didn't give a hoot about. A white man! How little is it gonna take for this tension to explode? You want a peaceful revolution, but you won't even get a violent one. What you'll get is a damned massacre."

****

The nightly dinner table at the Williams house always held a bountiful feast. The family's array of operations kept both John and Loula quite busy, but every day began with the three of them at the breakfast table and every evening brought them back together for a late supper, both of which were prepared by their housemaid.

"It's just that it's Friday night and-" said Bill to his mother, who cut him off immediately.

"And what, young man?" asked Loula. "You gotta work, just like your father and I've done all week?"

John Williams shook his head.

"Boy when I think of how you have it, compared to how I had it, your mother had it?"

"I'm just saying-"

Again, his mother cut him off.

"And I don't want to hear what you're saying. You've got prom Wednesday, and that's costing us a small fortune. You were out running around last night, and I'm sure you'll be out tomorrow. And don't pretend like that little girlfriend of yours isn't going to be at the picture tonight anyway."

His father smiled.

"Oh, you done did it now."

"And another thing," Loula continued, "I've done told you about letting her and her girlfriend in with no ticket. You want a pass for someone, you come and ask me for one. Have I ever told you no?"

"No ma'am," said Bill, lowering his head.

"Everyone who goes through that door has a ticket," said Loula. "Period. Mr. Cotton tells me about anyone else getting let by, you'll work extra, young man. It don't do to have hardworking folks paying fifteen cent to get inside and then having to watch someone pass through for free."

"Yes ma'am," said Bill, finally raising his head. "It won't happen again."

"Pass me those potatoes, sweetie pie?" asked John.

To this, Loula smiled, coyly.

"Don't you sweetie pie me."

"Come on, not even just a little," asked John, with a wink and smile of his own.

****

O.W. Gurley and his wife Emma were dressed in fancy evening clothes, having tea in the ornately decorated library of their large home, while she knitted the beginnings of a blanket.

"You worry too much, baby," said Emma. "That bunch has always been a bit spirited, but I think it's mostly bluster."

138

"It don't have to be no more than bluster, Emma," said Gurley. "That's what they don't understand. It just has to be enough to act as the kindling. You get enough of it built up, and all it takes is one spark for the flames to rage."

"These young ones are of a different mind, I'll say that," Emma conceded, while continuing to knit.

"And that's what makes the bluster of someone like Stradford so much more dangerous these days," said Gurley. "I used to think he'd outlived his wild streak, that at 60, he'd finally be content to grow old with full pockets and a good life for him and his family."

Emma nodded.

"He does have both of those."

"Even Smitherman never really worried me, because it was just more of that intellectual, NAACP noise that never goes no further than dinner parties and social clubs," said Gurley. "But it's these young bucks like that Obie Mann that truly scare me. They got real fight in them. A man comes back from where they've been with a taste for blood, and then you force him to suffer not only injustice but humiliation?"

"And he's the type of Black man that scares them most," said Emma. "Big, powerful, outspoken."

"And without fear," added Gurley. "There's no deference in that man, not one drop, and they can see it every time they look at him, that he doesn't feel inferior to them. Heh, quite the opposite."

"Is that so wrong?" asked Emma.

"Not if there were a few million more of him, and they held offices, and ran police forces, and commanded armies," said Gurley. "But there's simply no leverage here, Emma. Obie Mann might not be afraid of any white man, but he's so greatly outnumbered that all the anger and ferocity in the world won't keep him above ground. And when he falls, they will unleash hell and all of its fury on Greenwood. Every bit of what we built will be gone."

As Gurley trailed off, he stared off to emptiness. Emma put down her knitting and laid her head on his chest.

"All we can do is the best we can, Otto. The Lord will take care of the rest as he sees fit."

"I'm not leaving it in the Lord's hands, baby. Not this."

****

From the street, the grand facade of the Dreamland Theatre seemed to light up the entire night. A marquee advertised, "Friday: Charlie Chaplin in The Kid. Saturday: Vaudeville Variety Show & Jazz Revue." The sidewalk was lined with people waiting to get to the ticket window as cars tried to negotiate the crowded road. A palpable energy rose through the streets as the hum of people and motorcars mixed with the neon buzz emanating from the building.

Inside, the lobby was brimming with well-dressed Black families, couples and teens. Andrew Smitherman, accompanied by his wife Ollie, raised his hand to get JB Stradford's attention when he saw he and his wife, Augusta, pass through the front door with Buck Franklin.

"Well hello there, Augusta," said Smitherman. "Don't you look lovely."

"Thank you, Andrew," said Augusta, "but I feel like window dressing next to your beautiful bride."

"Nonsense," said Ollie. "You look the belle of the ball, as always."

"And I see you lured Mr. Franklin out for an evening of good clean fun," said Smitherman.

Buck extended his hand and they shook.

"Mr. Smitherman, it's a pleasure to see you again."

"Please, call me Andy, or A.J." said Smitherman. "This is my wife, Ollie."

"Pleased to make your acquaintance, ma'am," said Buck, bowing, as he took her hand.

"Buck's family won't be coming up for a few more weeks, as things get settled on both ends," Stradford told the others. "So I thought it might do him good to get out for an evening. Get his mind off the loneliness and experience some of the cosmopolitan virtues of our fair community."

"Do you have children, Buck?" asked Ollie.

"Yes, my wife Mollie is a teacher, and we have a daughter, Mozella, who's a freshman at Lane College. My sons are with Mollie back in Rentiesville for the time being. Buck Jr., he's 14, and John is 6."

"Lovely," said Ollie. "I look forward to meeting them."

"Me too," said Augusta. "Meanwhile, I hear it's a delightful film—and funny. I find laughter to be a good distraction when you're missing loved ones."

"Indeed," said Smitherman.

"I hope you and Ollie will join us for dessert back at the hotel afterward, A.J.," said Stradford. "I've got a Cuban cigar with your name on it?"

"You had me at dessert," interjected Ollie.

Across the lobby, Bessie Frank and her brother Horace approached Bill Williams, who was taking tickets at the door to the theater. His girlfriend Hattie and her friend Estelle were standing next to him.

"Horace, how's it going, man?" said Bill with excitement when he spotted them. "I didn't know you guys were coming. Hey, Bessie."

"Hey, Bill," said Horace with a smile. "Yeah, we haven't been to the pictures in a long while. Thought we'd celebrate our first week in Greenwood. You know, payday and all."

Horace held up a bag of popcorn.

"This is Horace and his sister Bessie," Bill told the girls. "They just moved to Greenwood from Fayetville. This is Hattie, my uh ..."

"You'd best say *girlfriend*," said Estelle, sternly.

"Girlfriend," said Bill with a smile that Hattie returned.

"And her big-mouthed friend, Estelle," added Bill with a chuckle.

Estelle punched him on the shoulder, playfully.

"Pleased to meet you both," said Horace. "Well, we'd best not hold up the line."

"We'd better get in while there are good seats left, too," said Hattie. "Come on, you two can sit with us."

Hattie handed Bill their tickets and smiled. The four of them walked inside, as the next couple handed Bill their tickets.

****

The lunch counter was empty except for the sheriff, who was drinking his coffee, while Annie Shepton pretended to wipe the counter space that surrounded him.

"You gonna keep nursing that thing until we have to kick you out in order to close?" asked Annie, playfully.

"Savoring is more like it. It's particularly good this evening," said the sheriff with a wink and a grin.

"Always the charmer, this one."

The sheriff chuckled.

"I guess I been trying to work up my nerve."

"Yeah? How's that going?" asked Annie.

"Not so good, it seems."

"Well, you already ran out of daylight, sheriff. You'd best spit it out."

"Fair enough," he said, taking one final sip before clearing his throat and rising to his feet. "So, I was thinking that maybe if you weren't working on Sunday, perhaps you and me could actually eat a meal *together*, not here I mean, not that there's anything wrong with here or anything, it's just you know, I figured you'd maybe like a change of scenery."

"William McCullough, are you finally asking me on a proper date?"

The sheriff felt his cheeks warm and lowered his gaze.

"I suppose I am, at that."

"Well, I do normally work the breakfast shift on Sundays," said Annie, "but with Monday being my normal day off and it being Memorial Day, they got switched on account of the parade traffic."

"How do you think he knew to ask about Sunday?" said Evie from across the room, where she'd been wiping tables. "I figured if I didn't offer a hand, you two would be senile before you figured it out on your own."

The sheriff and Annie smiled at each other.

"I'll tell you what," said Annie, "I think the proper thing to do would be for you to take me to the 11 o'clock mass on Sunday morning and let folks see us together like that first. If you behave yourself, I'm sure you could talk me into going for some fried chicken at Millie's afterward."

The sheriff smiled.

"Then it's a date?"

Annie beamed.

"It's a date."

The sheriff tipped his hat and began to walk off.

"Don't you need my address?" asked Annie.

"I'm sure with my investigative instincts and all, I can sort it out," he said.

Evie, wiping tables and without looking up, said, "I already gave it to him."

Annie huffed.

"How'd you know I'd say yes?"

"The same way I knew the sun was gonna come up this morning," said Evie. "I just knew."

The sheriff gave Annie another smiled as he turned for the door. She was still blushing as she watched it close behind him.

"You gonna stand there like a smitten kitten or help me close up?" asked Evie, now beside her at the counter.

Annie playfully snapped her towel at her and then bit her fist, still looking at the door.

****

The Dreamland staff was cleaning up the lobby after the show. Horace, Bessie, Hattie and Estelle waited near the main doors, while Bill used a large vacuum to clean the carpet of the lobby. He switched the loud machine off as a slight man who looked like an accountant passed by to leave. It was Henry Sowders, the Dreamland's projectionist, as well as its lone white employee.

"You need a ride home, Bill?" asked Henry, dangling the keys to his motorcar.

"No, thanks, Mr. Sowders," said Bill with a friendly smile. "My friends are waiting."

Bill nodded toward Horace and the others. Henry smiled.

"Have fun, but stay out of trouble. Your mother is not a woman to be trifled with."

146

"Don't I know it," said Bill, shaking his head.

Outside the theater, Henry walked up to his shiny Studebaker, which was parked near the curb. The motorcar was his pride and joy. On his approach, Henry noticed a small smudge on the paint, took out a handkerchief and buffed it, taking a step back to admire the machine once he had.

Back inside the theater, Horace nodded toward the exit Henry had just passed through.

"Was that the manager?" he asked the group.

"Nah, Mr. Cotton's the boss," said Hattie, pointing to a well-dressed, middle-aged Black man, who was shuffling papers near the cash register of the snack bar. "Henry's the projectionist."

"You sayin' the white guy's boss is that Black man?" asked Horace in disbelief.

"Sure, why not?" said Hattie. "Miss Loula owns the theater, so she's all their bosses. She's Black."

"And she's a woman," Estelle added.

"I just never seen such a sight," said Horace.

"Me neither," added Bessie in similar disbelief.

"Welcome to Black Wall Street, y'all," said Estelle with a laugh.

Andrew Smitherman, Ollie Smitherman, John Stradford, Augusta Stradford and Buck Franklin were seated in an ornate sitting area in the lobby of the Stradford, to which they'd adjourned after the movie. The men smoked cigars, while the women ate finger cakes and drank tea.

"You see, it's also created a problem though," said Smitherman. "The lure of high-paying jobs across town has our high school dropout rate sky-high, particularly among males."

"By the time they're 15," said Stradford, "they can make more money as a waiter, a porter, or a shine boy than anything they're going to need that diploma for."

"If their momma's widowed or someone in the house is sickly, it's especially tempting," added Smitherman.

Buck shook his head.

"I hadn't considered that."

"Don't get me wrong," said Stradford, "it's that money from across town that built Greenwood and what makes it so different from the other Black towns in this state."

"But as we continue to grow," said Smitherman, "we need more doctors, lawyers, and accountants, people who will start their own Black enterprises so that we can continue to grow more self-sufficient and employ more of our own over on this side of the tracks."

"Understand," said Stradford, "even though there are some jobs where our people can do quite well over there, the majority are still toiling away for very low wages. Too many have got big families crammed into shacks made from corrugated tin on the north side. No indoor plumbing, lucky if they got gas or electric. They get old, they get sick, they best hope someone in the family can pick up the slack."

"And it's not just enterprise," said Ollie, joining the conversation. "We also need a better-educated community so that they are more likely to get involved in the political process and help make real change."

"People who understand the issues and see the big picture, especially now that we got our own voting district," said Augusta.

"Courtesy of Andrew, I might add," said Stradford, proudly pointing to his friend with a smile. "He led that fight."

"Of course there are those on our side who feel as though our success shouldn't embolden us," said Smitherman, "that we've got a good thing going here and shouldn't rock the boat."

Buck nodded knowingly.

"Of course."

"I'm sure you're a man who makes up his own mind," said Stradford. "We just want you to see where we're coming from, Buck. Where we stand on the issue of the Black man's place, not only in Tulsa, but throughout the nation."

Buck straightened himself and leaned forward subtly.

"And where exactly do you stand on that issue, if I might ask, Mr. Stradford?"

Stradford smiled and took a big puff from his cigar.

"You're direct, Buck," he said. "I appreciate that in a man. You see, I believe in the good book, and I especially believe that part about God having created all men equal. Personally, I'll not be satisfied until our people can enjoy a life that is actually protected by our rights, the same as every other citizen. And as good as we got it compared to some who've got it real bad, I'd risk it all to advance the larger cause."

"That's very noble," said Buck.

"What do you think of these cigars, Buck?" asked Smitherman.

Buck took another puff before answering.

"They are quite a bit better than I'm used to, I'll certainly admit that. Those folks down in Cuba have earned their reputation."

"They have indeed," said Stradford. "Let's have a toast, shall we?"

Stradford raised his glass. The others followed, men with whiskey, women with their teacups.

"To a long and prosperous life, and to Buck's success in Greenwood," said Stradford, winking at Buck with a sly smile.

"This really is an amazing hotel, JB," said Buck. "It's quite unlike anything I've ever seen."

"Thank you, Buck. I may have overdone it a bit, truth be told. But I just couldn't see a reason why there shouldn't be at least one place in this country where a Black man of certain means and refined taste could go to experience luxury on par with the world's great cities. Where he wouldn't have to use the back door or separate restrooms, where he could take his wife and they could indulge a bit, maybe feel... whole."

Augusta leaned in toward Buck.

"You'd be surprised, but we do a fair amount of business with folks right here in Greenwood," she said. "Anniversaries and such, you know, a night away from the house and kids. A holiday without having to get on a train."

"And where would they go if they did get on a train?" added Ollie. "Certainly nowhere like this."

"Not to mention that they'd have to travel there in the colored car," added Augusta.

Buck swiveled his head, taking the whole thing in.

"You've all built something quite special here, not just the hotel. This whole place is, well, surreal."

"We're hosting the prom for Washington High right here in the ballroom this Wednesday," said Augusta. "I'm so excited for those children."

"What a night it will be for them," said Ollie.

151

"Indeed," said Buck, looking around some more. "I'm not sure there's a negro class in the entire country that would consider themselves more fortunate."

Stradford leaned in and put his big hand on Buck's shoulder.

"Tell you what, when that wife of yours gets up here, and you get all settled, I'm gonna set you up with a suite—on the house. Any night you're free. We'll even sit for your boys. Consider it a welcoming present to the both of you."

"That's very kind of you, JB," said Buck. "I'm sure she'd be happy to take you up on it, as well."

"Just don't tell Gurley," said Stradford with a laugh. "I'm sure he already fears I'm corrupting you with my radical ideas."

Buck smiled, but in a way that suggested his discomfort.

"Oh, don't get me wrong," said Stradford, "Otto is a good man, and he often makes a lot of sense. Smart as a whip, to tell you the truth. We don't always see eye to eye on everything, but Greenwood wouldn't be what it is today if it weren't for him, that I'll be the first to tell you. The whole business district started with his building on Greenwood and Archer. It was his vision."

"He did pay me a visit earlier today," said Smitherman.

"Your editorial?" asked Stradford

152

"Mmm hmm."

Ollie smiled and squeezed her husband's hand.

"Always kicking the hornet's nest, my Andrew is."

"The role and interests of a free press and commercial enterprise are not always aligned, my dear," said Smitherman, bringing her hand to his mouth, where he kissed it.

"He leave happy?" asked Stradford.

"Our goodbyes were cordial, and so far he hasn't canceled any of his ad buys," Smitherman said with a laugh.

"That's because he would never give me the satisfaction of making them up to you," said Stradford with a laugh of his own.

Chapter 4

Kelly Ann O'Dell and Kathleen Brown, both in their senior year at Tulsa Central High, had been cutting through the school's parking lot on their walk home when two boys in a shiny roadster slowly rolled up next to them.

"Get in, ladies," said Johnny Gordon, who was driving. "We'll give you a ride in my chariot."

"No, thanks," said Kelly Ann, "we're enjoying the weather."

Elmer Porter, who spent as much time in detention as he did in classrooms, leaned toward them from the passenger seat.

"And what better way to enjoy it than from the back of a breezer. Come on, get in."

Kathleen grabbed Kelly Ann's arm and whispered in her ear.

"What are you doing? He likes you. Let's go."

Kelly smiled.

"Why not?" she said with a shrug.

The two boys got out, and the girls climbed into the backseat. When Johnny pulled off, Elmer slung his arm over his seat-back and turned toward them.

"Hey, how do you babysit a nigger baby?" he asked with a smile.

Kelly looked at Kathleen. Both girls wore looks of discomfort.

"You wet its lips and stick it to a wall," said Elmer, letting out a big laugh that was echoed by Johnny. Neither boy noticed that the girls weren't laughing.

"Johnny," said Kathleen, eager to change the subject, "I saw Kelly's dress for the prom last weekend."

She looked to Kelly Ann with a smile.

"You may wind up having the prom queen on your arm."

Johnny looked back at Kelly through the rearview mirror and smiled.

"I wouldn't be surprised in the least," he said, watching as she returned his smile before blushing and breaking eye contact.

"Hey, Kathleen," said Elmer, "I heard your date's gonna be your brother."

"And I heard you're taking Johnny's dog," she replied.

"Ouch!" said Johnny.

Elmer shrugged off the insult, unfazed.

"The house or the store?" Johnny asked Kelly Ann, again meeting her eyes in the rearview.

"The store," said Kelly Ann. "I've got to help my dad for a bit."

"Hey, I thought you were gonna recommend me to your dad for a stock boy job?" said Elmer, looking back at Kelly Ann.

"You did?" she asked with arched brows. "I recall laughing until I nearly cried when you asked."

"Hey! What's the matter with me?" he asked with a smile.

"You mean aside from that ugly face?" teased Johnny.

Elmer reached across and punched Johnny's arm.

"You smoke cigarettes, drink gin, you're shiftless and you're lazy," said Kathleen.

"Yeah, but believe it or not I've got some bad qualities too," laughed Elmer.

Kathleen rolled her eyes and Kelly Ann chuckled, shaking her head a bit as the car pulled up to the market. Once he stopped the car, Johnny got out and pulled up his seat to let the girls jump out. Kelly Ann's father, Gene O'Dell, a thickly-built man in his early forties, watched from the sidewalk where he had been receiving a produce delivery. Johnny waved to him.

"Hello, Mr. O'Dell," he said. "Good afternoon, sir."

Gene, expressionless, waved back but immediately turned his gaze to his daughter as she trotted over to where he was standing. Once she met him, Kelly Ann threw her arms around her dad in a hug.

"Go take over the register so Georgie can stock cans," said Gene.

"Sure, daddy," said Kelly Ann, waving goodbye to Kathleen who'd already begun walking down the street toward her house.

"Your mother's making some kind of new pot roast for supper tonight," said Gene. "She's in a mood, so make like you love it, no matter how it tastes."

Kelly Ann looked back and smiled lovingly at her father as she opened the door of their shop. He returned her smile, then lost it as he looked back toward the direction of the car once she had turned away.

****

"Right like that, child," said Loula Williams, as she dropped globs of milk chocolate into the molds. "Each one just to the top of the mold so that they's even sized. Now you try," she said, handing the ladle to Bessie, who repeated the process.

"Like that, Miss Loula?"

"That's it, baby. You're a natural."

Just then, Julia Jackson, an attractive woman in her early thirties, walked through the front door of the confectionery causing the bell to ring.

"Well hello, dear," said Loula with a big smile. "Don't you look the prettiest today?"

"Hey, girl," said Julia. "Am I the first one here?"

Loula shook her head.

"You know those two fools are always late."

Both women laughed.

"Julia, this is Bessie Frank," said Loula. "She just started this week. She and her brother moved down from Fayetville."

Julia turned to Bessie, smiled, and extended her hand.

"Well, hello," she said warmly as they shook.

"Pleased to meet you, ma'am," said Bessie in a shy voice.

"Bessie, Miss Julia here is a teacher over at the high school," said Loula. "Bill's favorite, truth be told, though I suspect that has as much to do with her pretty smile as anything else."

Julia smiled and slapped her on the arm.

"And her husband's the best surgeon out there," Loula added. "Famous all across the country."

"Don't tell him that," she laughed. "He'll get a big head and start thinking he could do better."

"Jack Johnson couldn't do better," said Loula with a laugh.

"Well, I'll settle for being Bill's favorite teacher," said Julia. "He's a good boy."

Loula smiled.

"That he is. Gets on my last nerve from time to time, but I got no right to complain."

The bell rang once again as two more women entered through the front door of the confectionery.

"We're here, sugar," said the first.

"Here *for* some sugar is more like it," said the second, laughing as she slapped the other woman's arm.

"It's about dang time," said Julia.

"You know who had to get her hair set," said the second woman.

"It does look correct," said Julia.

Loula introduced the women to Bessie as Pearl and Grace, explaining that they all served on the high school's prom committee together.

"This here is Bessie," said Loula. "She came in with her brother from Fayetville. He's working at the garage."

Bessie shrank a bit but gave the women a shy smile.

"Well, you'd better watch yourself in here, girl," said the one named Pearl."You can gain weight just looking at Loula's goodies."

Everyone laughed, even Bessie.

159

"I swear, my behind swells just passing through for these meetings," said Grace.

"Then maybe I should get rid of that tray of chocolate truffles I set up in the back?" teased Loula.

"You'd better bite your tongue," said Grace. "It's my time of the month, and I been dreaming about your chocolate all morning. I don't care if you gotta Crisco my hips to get me back out the front door."

The women laughed as they made their way to the back room for their weekly meeting. Once they were settled, Julia poured coffee, while the women put candies on small dessert plates.

"I hereby call this final meeting of the Booker T. Washington High School class of 1921 senior promenade volunteer committee to order," said Loula with facetious sincerity. "Decorations chair?"

"All set," said Grace. "We got the last of the streamers finished after church on Sunday, and Al's got us set up with the helium tank to do the balloons at the hotel Wednesday morning."

"And John will run the cakes over there in the afternoon," said Loula, shaking her head and letting out a sigh. "I just can't believe our babies are gonna have their prom. It seems like yesterday they were scared little freshmen nervous about startin' high school."

"Child, maybe to you!" said Grace. "My Duane done tried my nerves so many times, I'd swear that was eight years ago, not four."

The women laughed.

"Every mother says that," said Julia, shaking her head. "Then they all cry like babies when their babies are gone."

"Not me, child," said Loula. "Bill can come visit anytime he likes, but John and I are looking forward to acting like teenagers again our damn selves. No innocent eyes to worry about, we might not leave the house for the first few days."

"We see a closed sign on the door and hear a line of cars beeping their horns down at the garage, we'll know what's up," said Pearl.

The four women laughed.

****

Richard Lloyd Jones was behind his desk with his feet up. Chip and Tucker were seated across from him, looking slightly less relaxed.

"I am telling you that every bit of my journalistic instinct from the crown of my skull to the very tips of my toes is telling me Thaddeus is dirty on this, and no newspaper of mine will ever abide political corruption—not *ever!* Now what pray tell do we have thus far?"

"Well, there is one thing I got that involves the mayor to some degree," said Chip, "but the source was off the record."

Richard sat up, putting his elbows on the desk and leaning in toward Chip.

"Go on."

"Well," said Chip, "I go to see the contractor that won the project, and I'm amazed with how open he was with me, even though he'd stipulated that nothing he said could go on the record, obviously."

"Sure," said Richard, "he ain't gonna bite the hand that feeds him. What'd he say?"

"So, I ask him if it's all been business as usual, and he says, 'yeah, if you mean business as usual by this town's standards.' Then he starts going on about how after he'd been awarded the contract, he received a visit from someone who never bothered to identify himself, except to tell him that he belonged to a certain organization that was very unhappy to learn that 19 of the 38 engineers who were working on the project were Catholic. He says, so what? The guy tells him to can them or else he might find himself without the work."

"What's he say to that?" asked Tucker.

"He tells him to scram," said Chip, "but he figures he'll call the mayor just to make sure everything is copacetic. He says the mayor didn't exactly *tell* him to fire the workers, but he made it clear that it would definitely be in the best interest of everyone involved if he made the man who came to see him happy."

"And?" said Tucker.

"And he had to take them off the project or lose it standing on principle or, most likely, watch the poor Catholics get tarred and feathered, if not worse," replied Chip.

Richard, who'd been poker-faced thus far, shook his head.

"Mmmm mmmm mmmm," said Richard. "Those boys are a committed bunch, and they don't bend for anyone—least of all, Thaddeus. I don't agree with them on some things, of course, but you've got to admire their exactitude."

Chip looked at Richard slack-jawed with disbelief.

"Well, keep at it, kid," said Richard. "I'm sure we'll find something if we look in all the right places. Now, if you'll excuse me, I've got a telephone call scheduled. Send Miss Comstock in on your way out."

"Copacetic?" asked Tucker teasingly, once the door was closed. "That a Yale word?"

"He wasn't the least bit interested," said Chip, still beaming with disbelief. "What, does he hate Catholics too?"

"I don't think so," said Tucker. "Look, I told you, dollars to donuts it was the old exalted cyclops himself that paid that visit to the contractor. You saw how cozy the boss was with that evil bastard last time he was in here. He crosses the TBA and, next thing you know, half our advertisers fall out. We're already in hawk to the bank as it is."

"So, what do I do?" asked Chip

"Write it up dry for now," said Tucker, "nuts and bolts and, uh, like he said, keep at it."

Chip, clearly discouraged, frowned as Tucker walked off.

"Uh, Amy, the boss would like to see you," said Chip as Ms. Comstock approached, giving him the faintest smile as she headed toward Richard's office door. Chip sneaked a peek at her attractive figure once she'd passed.

****

At Wilfred Dickinson's construction site, a crew of mostly Black workers was nailing planks of wood to the floorboards of a framed house. A white construction worker in his early thirties was sitting nearby eating a bologna sandwich. The man looked flushed and clammy, like he had been nursing a hangover all morning and had given up on trying to make himself look busy.

"Hey, go on and get that section next," he said to a Black man working nearby. The man looked over at him, then back at the section he was referring to, then back to him. At this, the white man, clearly annoyed, stood, adopting an aggressive posture.

"What's a matter, stovepipe, you deaf or just stupid?" he asked. "I told you to start doing the same thing you been doing, just right there."

Charlie Mason, a stout and sturdy Black man in his mid-thirties who had been with Wilfred for several years and been promoted to foreman, walked over to address the ruckus.

"Lunch break been over for 15 minutes now," said Charlie. "Each man pull his own work on this site."

"Oh is that right, boy?" asked the white man. "Now I got a nigger telling me what to do? It must be upside-down day."

"I'm the job foreman," said Charlie, "and I say if you wanna work on this site, you'll mind your business and do the job that's assigned to you like every other man on the crew. Mr. Dickinson ain't paying you to eat bologna sandwiches and flap your gums."

The white man was visibly angered. He hopped to his feet, but in assessing the situation, saw that not only was he outsized by Charlie, but he was considerably outnumbered as well.

"Well then, that fuckin' limey cocksucker will have to tell me his own self that I'm supposed to be taking orders from the goddamned niggers!"

Having heard the commotion, Wilfred entered the site from behind the white construction worker.

"He won't have to," said Wilfred, "I've heard just about enough."

The man turned around. Wilfred extended his hand, offering a wad of bills.

"What's this?" asked the white man.

"Three days' wages," said Wilfred. "You've worked two and a half, but I'll round up so that there are no hard feelings. But I got no room for that business around here, mate."

The man looked confused as he counted the money, surprised to see it was in fact what he'd been told. He folded the bills and put them in his shirt pocket while contemplating Wilfred for a moment.

"Hell, you can keep this fucking job, anyway," the man said. "It's nigger work for nigger pay. Besides, no decent white man should have to smell nigger sweat all day long while he's working to feed his family."

"Haven't seen you doing much work, to be honest, sir," said Wilfred. "But if that was the problem, we've got it sorted. You'd best be moving along now, I think."

The man took two aggressive steps toward Wilfred and poked him in the chest.

"Look, friend," he said through gritted teeth, "you obviously don't know how things work over here yet, but you might find this here ain't a friendly town if you go siding with the darkies just 'cause they work on the cheap."

Charlie stepped aggressively toward the white man, but Wilfred put his arm in front of Charlie's chest, which had puffed up like a bird's.

"That won't be necessary, Charlie. Our friend here's about to be on his way, aren't you, mate?"

Wilfred continued to look at the man with a serious expression until he started away from the site. Once he was a safe distance away, the man looked back.

"Fuckin' nigger lover!"

****

Gene O'Dell was enjoying a splendid dinner with his wife, Megan O'Dell, and his daughter Kelly Ann in the dining room of their upscale home, though his face suggested that he was not at ease.

"I told you, Daddy, they just gave us a ride straight home," said Kelly Ann. "It's not like we were out racing along the country roads."

"I don't care," her father said. "Cars are dangerous."

The girl looked to her mother.

"Mom?"

"Listen to your father, dear," said Megan.

"Besides," said Gene, "anyone dumb enough to hang around with that other knucklehead, that Porter kid, isn't exactly showing sound judgment."

"Elmer's a moron," Kelly Ann conceded, "but he's harmless, Dad. He just doesn't know better."

Gene pounded the table, and Megan put her hand atop his fist.

"You see, that's what I'm talking about," said Gene. "Both them kids come from wealthy families! I mean, a 17-year-old with a motor car? They got all the advantages, yet they still don't *know any better*? That worries me. Says something about how they been raised, the values they got."

"Johnny's different, Daddy," said Kelly Ann. "He's smart, and he doesn't drink or get in trouble. He doesn't even smoke."

"Yeah? Well, I know the crowd his father runs with," said Gene, a little louder now. "Member of the TBA, that one. Lord knows what else."

Kelly Ann shrugged.

"So?"

Her father's nostrils flared.

"So? So, it's a front group for the Klan!"

"He's a banker, Daddy. Every banker in town is in every civic group and social club. You know that."

Her father stood up and pointed.

"Civic group my ass."

Megan grabbed his arm.

"Gene! Not at the kitchen table."

Gene looked at his wife.

"What? You think the old man's never worn a hood and sheet?"

"Daddy! Johnny's not like that," his daughter shouted.

"Really?" asked Gene. "Let me ask you this, does he know you're a Catholic? Do his parents know he's taking a Catholic—an *Irish Catholic* at that—to prom?"

His daughter looked confused.

"I don't know, it's not like he asked me what church I go to."

Gene sighed and relaxed his tone.

"Look, you've led a pretty sheltered life, young lady. You've been lucky that way. I've had to bust my hump to get something for us in this town, and there are a lot of people who don't like a family like ours having three grocery stores, a motor car, or a house in this neighborhood. They think we might be doing a little *too* well, and when I see you running around with the kids of the people who'd rather we not, it concerns me."

Miss Annie, the O'Dell's Black, live-in servant, entered from the kitchen with a pot of coffee.

"Y'all like some cake now that you through, Mrs. O'Dell?" Annie asked.

Megan smiled warmly.

"Yes, but just a small sliver for me, Annie," she said.

Miss Annie filled Gene and Megan's cups before making her way toward the kitchen, as Gene resumed.

"You think Miss Annie would let any of her kids run around with anyone whose family had ties to the Klan?" he asked the two women.

His wife gasped.

"Gene!"

"What?"

"That's different," said Megan in a hushed but firm voice.

"Only because it'd be more obvious," said Gene. "You don't have to wear the thing they hate about you on the outside. It don't mean they're gonna hate you any less for it when they find out."

Just then, Miss Annie returned with a tray of cake, serving out the three slices.

170

"Your father is right to be worried, young lady," said Miss Annie. "There's a hate in this town that would chill the devil himself. And I done seen sweet little boys grow up to be monsters as men for no better reason than they was raised by monsters themselves. I don't know this boy, nor his daddy, but you'd be wise to mind yourself if your father is so concerned."

"Thank you, Annie," Megan said with a warm smile and a voice that conveyed her embarrassment.

"I'm sorry if it wasn't my place to say so, Mrs. O'Dell," said Annie, looking to the floor.

"Don't be silly," said Megan, again with a warm smile.

Miss Annie nodded and left the room. Megan's gaze was fixed upon her husband who shrugged in genuine confusion.

"What?"

Megan shook her head.

"Really, Gene, to compare our plight to hers?"

"If you don't think-"

Megan interrupted her husband, which was something she rarely did.

"I know the Klan hates Catholics, but if you don't think that woman's lot in life is decidedly worse than ours," she said, motioning with her hands at the finery around them.

Gene waved her off with his own hand.

"That's not what I was saying."

"But that's the way it sounds, dear. I can only imagine what it must be like for her, and then to hear us of all people complain as though we share her suffering?"

Gene shrugged again, turning his palms upward.

"She's got it better than most," he told her. "I mean we treat her good, pay her well. She's practically family."

"Is she now?" asked Megan, her dander having risen. "Living in our servant quarters six days a week and seeing her three kids for one? And *we* have it better than most, too. Let me remind you of that, Gene O'Dell."

Gene was back to looking confused.

"What are you getting all sore at me for?" he asked. "I'm talking about our daughter here. And what am I supposed to do? We agreed we'd get some help when the last store opened. She asked us for the job—was thrilled to get it, too."

"That's my point," said Megan, a bit calmer now. "She's thrilled to be over here because it's the only way a woman in her position can take care of her family. Yes, it might be a blessing for her, and it might be uncommon that we treat her with basic human kindness like we would any other of God's children, but she can probably do without hearing us tell her that we share her struggle."

Gene, genuinely perplexed by his wife's anger, shrugged again. Kelly Ann smiled at her mother.

"Don't smile at me like the cat who just swallowed the canary, young lady," she told her daughter. "You listen to your father. As clumsily as it may have been made, he has a point. If you get even a faint whiff of anything that makes you uncomfortable, you extricate yourself from the situation immediately. You understand me? And so help me, God, if there's any gin on prom night, drank by you or anyone else in your party, you'll be locked in your room all summer."

Gene smirked at Kelly Ann.

"Yeah, what she said."

Gene smiled and winked at his wife, who held her stare for a moment before finally giving him a bit of a smile in return.

****

Maddie Dickinson, a small, attractive woman in her late twenties, was serving tea to her husband Wilfred in their well-appointed living room, which was adorned with many reminders of their native England.

"Well, it sounds like you did the right thing, then," she told him as she poured. "You'll do well not to have a bloke like that on your crew."

Maddie stirred a spoonful of sugar into the tea and handed him his cup.

"No, I certainly don't," said Wilfred, "it's just that for the first time I've got an entirely Black crew on the job is all."

"Careful, it's hot," she said as he took his first sip. "That worries you?" she asked.

Her husband shrugged his shoulders and winced a bit.

"Only so much as I know it can create hard feelings."

"You think you'll have a harder time bidding on jobs?" asked Maddie.

Wilfred put another spoonful of sugar in his cup as he weighed an answer.

"Always stingy with it, aren't we?" he said with a smile.

"I'm looking after you, love," she said. "You have got too sweet of a tooth."

"I might not have found you had that not been the case," he said to her with a wink.

Maddie giggled.

"Listen to Mr. Sweet-talker changing the subject."

Wilfred took another sip and sighed.

"This place scares me a bit, Maddie," he told her. "People look at the Negroes like they're dogs. They don't mind them doing the dirty jobs, and they don't mind getting cheap bids from people who'll hire them, but there's a delicate balance, and you can't always be sure what it is until someone decides it's out of whack."

"But you pay everyone the same?" said Maddie.

"And I pay a little less," he told her.

"But that's how you win the bids, and because you get more jobs, you can give them all more work."

"I do," said Wilfred, "and I can hire the best Black workers for that wage, but I only get the shiftless whites. They're not much use to me, to tell you the truth. Between their slow work and the trouble they start with the Blacks, it never seems worth it."

"Then what's the trouble in not having any whites?" asked Maddie.

Wilfred shrugged.

"None, I should hope. But, as I noted, this town is peculiar that way. There are unwritten rules you can't always know or understand, and it seems like there's always a wild bunch who are on the verge of violence. I worry for us sometimes, Maddie, and I worry for Margaret, not just her safety but what she'll see and learn from it."

Maddie took her husband's hand and leaned in toward him.

"What she'll see is her father, a good man doing the right thing, and what she'll learn is that even when the world is a complicated place, *that's* the thing to do."

"I hope so, Maddie. I do."

Just then, Margaret burst into the room.

"I'm done all my work, mum," the girl said. "Can I have a biscuit now?"

"Not until you've come over here and given your father a hug you can't," said Wilfred.

The girl blushed.

"That depends," she said.

Wilfred feigned indignation.

"On what, young lady?"

The girl smiled.

"On whether you've cleaned up from work or you still stink."

Margaret laughed as her father grabbed her and pulled her tight, tickling her a bit once he'd drawn her in.

"Well, am I smelly or not?" he said.

"No, but your whiskers scratch," Margaret shrieked through a laugh. "Let me go."

Maddie, who found her husband's deep and unabashed love for their daughter to be an irresistible quality, smiled as she watched the two of them.

****

Kelly Ann O'Dell, Kathleen Brown, Elmer Porter, and Johnny Gordon were hanging out in a soda shop that was crowded with white teenagers when Kelly Ann tugged Johnny on by his arm.

"So, my mother said I can miss my cousin's graduation and go to the movie on Tuesday night, but that they have to drop me off and pick me up," she told him. "My dad's not very keen on the idea of me riding in cars with boys."

Johnny leaned in and smirked.

"You make it sound like it's a regular thing?"

Kelly Ann bristled.

"No! The two times you've given me a ride are the only times I've ever even been in a car aside from his!"

Johnny gave her a big smile.

"Where's your cousin graduating from?" he asked.

Kelly paused and felt anxiety as she recalled what her father had said.

"Holy Family? It's a middle school."

Johnny seemed to consider the answer for a moment, then nodded.

"Oh yeah, over on Boulder. Swell, I'll just wait in the theater lobby and we can meet up."

Kelly, relieved at his ease, still winced at the answer.

"Uh, no," she said. "You'll get there early and wait out front so that they can see you. You'll get my door when the car pulls up, and you'll say, 'hello, sir, hello, ma'am,' shake hands and all that. Got it?"

Having overheard, Elmer slapped Johnny on the back.

"Yeah, dummy. You gotta make her old man think that you're not a louse before you can get her alone and be one."

Kathleen punched Elmer on the arm.

"I swear, Elmer, can you not be a creep for like one minute!"

Elmer giggled as he rubbed the spot where her fist had landed.

"You're just mad because it's not a double date, doll face," he told her.

"As if!" huffed Kathleen.

"Tell you what, sugar cakes," said Elmer, "if you buy my ticket and maybe a pop too, I'll go with you, so long as we can sit at least two rows apart."

"I wouldn't go with you if you were the last man alive, you bought the tickets, and we were 10 rows apart," said Kathleen.

Johnny slapped Elmer on the back.

"You're making progress, pal."

"Yeah? How's that?" asked Elmer.

"Well, she referred to you as a man instead of a creep for once," said Johnny. "I mean there was an *if* in there, but still."

Elmer wadded up a napkin and threw it at Johnny, as they all had a good laugh.

Chapter 5

Memorial Day

Dick Rowland was sitting at the kitchen table with two other Black men who'd been staying on as boarders. Aunt Damie set plates of toast and glasses of apple juice on the table, as the men ate their grits.

"What'chu doing today, Dick?" asked one of the boarders, a short thin man in his mid-twenties. "Gonna watch the end of the parade from 1st Street?"

"No, sir, I be a working man today," said Dick.

"You ain't got off?" the man asked. "I surprised how many places shut down. We don't go back 'til tomorrow."

"Nah," said Dick, "holidays be the busiest time. That's when you make the good coin, too. People more generous on they day off for some reason."

"I'd work half a day then," said the other boarder, "make full pay."

"It ain't like that," said Dick, as he sopped up some grits with a piece of toast. "You don't work your box regular, Mr. Virgil give it to someone else who will."

"But you're Diamond Dick Rowland, man," the first boarder said. "Everybody want that diamond shine."

Dick laughed and sipped his juice.

"To Mr. Kerwin, I just be plain old Dick, and the only thing he wants is his half of that cabbage."

Aunt Damie put her coffee cup on the table and pointed her finger at each boarder as she addressed them.

"Now listen, I told y'all I don't want to hear that fool nickname in this house. And it's good you'll be working today," she said to Dick. "That'll keep you from getting in trouble down on 1st Street, and if you boys have any sense, you'll stay clear of that devil's den too. Nothin' but trouble down there normally—twice as much today, I expect."

"Yes, Miss Damie," said both boarders, nearly in unison as they lowered their heads and fiddled with their grits. Dick stood up with his empty plate, looked at the men, then to Damie, shook his head, and smiled. She gave him the eye before returning the smile and playfully snapped her dishtowel at him as he put the plate into the sink.

"You mind yourself today, Dick Rowland," she said. "Same for you two fools."

****

Inside the Williams Confectionery the next morning, Bessie Frank was helping Loula make candies on a large marble slab table, while two other women of middle age worked behind them at a different table.

"This one here is ready, Miss Loula," said Bessie.

"We best do two more batches still," Loula told her. "Believe me when I tell you, child, it will get crazy in here today. Half the town's got the day off, other half will hit the streets as soon as the work whistle blows. The fountain sodas and lemonade will be the main thing, but we'll sell plenty of chocolates, too. And it's better to mark it down later in the week than to turn people away today."

Bessie nodded.

"If you say so, Miss Loula."

"Think about it," said Loula, "if something cost you a nickel to make, you sell it for 15 cent. You gotta mark it to a dime later, you still make a nickel on each. But if you turn people away when it's busy, you're losing a dime every time."

"I guess you're right," said Bessie.

"You better believe I'm right, child, but I only know it from having been wrong," said Loula with a laugh.

"Pay attention, too. I didn't give you this job so you could learn how to make candy."

Loula lowered her voice as to not be heard by the others.

"Any fool can do that. I want you to learn how a business runs."

"What for?" asked Bessie.

"Well, you want more than this for yourself someday, don't you?"

Bessie shrugged.

"I haven't really thought about it, ma'am. In Fayetteville, it was hard just to find any kind of work. When you gave me this here job, I didn't think there was anything better in the whole world."

Loula smiled.

"Well, there is. Lots of things. And in a town like this, the possibilities are endless."

"You mean my own store, like this one here?" asked Bessie.

"Sure, but it doesn't have to be a confectionery," said Loula. "It could be anything. Business is business. It don't matter if it's a beauty parlor, or a sundry, or the cleaners. In fact, ain't much difference between this place and the theater, or even the garage for that matter."

"Really?"

"Mmm hmm," said Loula with a nod. "It's still just seeing where there's a need for something, finding what people will pay for it, figuring out how you can make it for less than that, and then making sure everyone does their job."

"You sure do make it sound easy, Miss Loula," said Bessie, "but truth be told, you about the smartest person I ever met. I don't know if anybody else could do all the things you do."

Loula laughed and slapped her knee.

"I don't know about that, child. Before we came here, I was just a teacher in a tiny little town in Mississippi, and John was working on the rails."

"For real?" asked Bessie, genuinely surprised.

"I swear it," said Loula, holding up her hand. "He got a job at the dairy cross town when we got here because they needed someone who knew about steam engines. Then when motor cars became the craze, he started tinkering with them— I tell you, that man can figure out how any kind of machine works."

"Horace say he a genius," said Bessie.

"Well I don't know about that, sugar," said Loula, "but it did turn out he was the only person in town really knew how to fix them things, and soon he couldn't keep both jobs up. Fixing cars paid better, so he opened his own place. It was gonna be right where we're standing now at first."

"What happened?"

Loula nodded.

"Well, we bought this building, but we were so green we didn't know there was a rule against having a garage underneath where people live. So we found another place, but we were already living upstairs and had the third floor rented out, so I figured we just needed another business down here, and that's when I started this here confectionery."

"How'd you wind up with Dreamland?" asked Bessie.

"That was another fluke. John read in the newspaper about a theater that was going out of business in a town nearby. There was no place Black folk could go see a picture show in Tulsa at that time, so we went up on the train, bought all the equipment, brought it down here, seats and all. I said, okay, let's figure out how a movie house runs."

Loula laughed at the recollection.

"Don't get me wrong, we made plenty of mistakes in all of those ventures, but we learned from them and figured it out together. Having someone you love with all your heart, someone you know done got your back? It sure do make it easier, child, I will say that."

Just then, John and Bill Williams entered the confectionery with Bessie's brother Horace at their side. John was holding a large dead turkey by the neck in one hand, his shotgun in the other. The boys were holding two dead pheasants each.

"Lookie, lookie, we set to have a Memorial Day feast," said John to his wife. "Your boys brought home the goods today, baby."

Loula put her hands up and dropped her jaw, as the men put the game on one of the empty slabs.

"Oh hell, no," said Loula. "Outside with them birds. Nah uh, John Williams, not unless you gonna pluck, clean, and cook it all your damn self."

The boys quickly exited. John was taken aback and sat his gun in the corner, turning to hand the turkey to Bill as he reentered. Then he turned back toward his wife.

"Baby..." he said, as he walked toward her.

"Uh uh, do not *baby* me," said Loula. "How many times I told you I got a full plate today. Half the theater staff is off. I'm covering for Earnest at the matinee, and we ain't even ready to open here. And I gotta go to Mabel's and get my hair set in half an hour. *Nuh-uh!*"

"What you talking about, get your hair set?" asked John with a smile. "My baby look like a queen."

"Don't sweet talk me, John. I done told you we don't need all this game, we can't use all the meat and-"

John reached his wife, put his hands on her shoulders, and gave her a flirtatious smile.

"Now how many times you heard it told that I'm the best shot in Greenwood?" he asked playfully. "That I can hit a dime from a football field away?"

He dropped his hands to her waist and drew her closer.

"I'm just a true provider, baby girl. I can't help it. I told you back when we first met, I do the huntin', you do the gathering, and we be good."

John started to dance with his wife, but she resisted.

"You'd best gather up that game and get it off my sidewalk," Loula said, though her posture softened some.

"Miss Loula, Bessie and me know how to prep birds real good," said Horace, who'd just reentered the room. "We can clean 'em up quick if you want."

Loula contemplated the idea for a moment.

"Tell you what," she said, "you take Bill in the back with you, teach him how to do it while you're at it, and his father will wash his filthy hands and help me finish in here."

"Yes Ma'am," said Horace.

"And when you're done, take all that bird down to the rooming house," said Loula. "Tell 'em happy holiday. I done already made chicken salad for lunch and somebody promised me we were going to the Little Cafe when I finally get done tonight," she said turning toward her husband. "I told you I got a hankering for that smothered steak."

Horace, Bill, and Bessie went out front to gather the birds.

John smiled and giggled at his wife as he drew her back toward him by her hips. "I do remember making that vow now that you mention it."

Loula remained bristled.

"Hmm hmm. If you think just cause you make 'em in a time of need, I'm gonna forget about them, you ain't been paying attention."

John kissed her on the mouth and drew her in tight.

"Speaking of needs..."

"Nuh-uh, John Williams, ain't no time for that business right now. Go clean your hands."

****

In the downtown Tulsa business district, street crews were putting up red, white, and blue bunting and streamers, and tying balloons to light polls. Proprietors and their employees were decorating storefronts with similar fanfare. Between two light poles, city employees were stringing up a large banner that read "1921 Tulsa Memorial Day Parade, Sponsored by Tulsa Chamber of Commerce, Tulsa Benevolence Association."

Outside of a small apartment building, just blocks away, muffled voices could be heard fighting inside, not a particularly uncommon occurrence for either the unit in question or the neighborhood in general, where many low-wage boarders resided.

Inside the small, dingy efficiency apartment, one of several housed on the back of a commercial building, Sarah

Page, a 19-year-old divorcee who worked as an elevator operator argued with her married boyfriend, Ed Kline, a Tulsa police officer, as the two finished putting their clothes back on.

"Cripes, Sarah, it's not like I can come over here and have sleepovers with you," said Ed as he buttoned the navy shirt of his uniform. "I'm married for Christ's sake, you know that. I've got kids. It's hard enough getting here before my shift."

"Oh, can it already, Ed, will you?" said Sarah. "I know you're married, and I know all that noise about leaving her was just talk back when you were first trying to get me in the sack. I may be ditzy, but I'm not stupid."

Ed sighed.

"It's not that simple."

"It's exactly that simple!" shouted Sarah.

"What, you think I can divorce her, just like that?" screamed Ed, snapping his fingers. "Take up with a 17-year-old girl? You don't think people would put it together?"

Dressed by this point, Sarah began brushing out the knots in her hair in hard angry strokes, while Ed buttoned the cuffs of his shirtsleeves.

"What, you afraid your friends in the Klan won't approve of the moral implications?" asked Sarah, arching her brows.

"What are you talking about?" asked Ed. "I'm on the force, there's just things you can't do."

"I know what you *can* and *can't* do, Ed," said Sarah. "You *can* come over here for some young tail before work, or when you finish at the bar with your buddies. What you *can't* do is treat me like a decent human being, like I'm more than a hole to stick that dirty thing of yours in."

Ed shook his head, unmoved by the familiar bating.

"Oh, like you got it so bad?" he asked her. "Are you in that boarding house anymore? Didn't I get you set up in a place of your own, just like I said I would?"

"You couldn't bang me at the boarding house, Ed," said Sarah with a mocking laugh. "You rented this shithole so you didn't get caught at no motel."

"What shithole?" said Ed, his voice rising as his patience waned. "How's it any worse than the last place you laid your head?"

"There were bed bugs when I moved in!" screamed Sarah.

"And didn't I get a new mattress?"

"Whatever," said Sarah.

"Oh, what's a matter, doll face?" asked Ed, affixing his tie. "Not up to her highness's standards? Maybe you shouldn't have left that husband of yours back in Kansas City if you were so used to living high on the hog."

Sarah turned quickly toward him from the mirror and pointed the brush at his face.

"You shut your mouth," she warned. "You don't know a goddamned thing about me or where I come from."

Ed cocked his head and sneered.

"I know you act like you're a damn sight better than the dumb cunt that's standin' before me."

Infuriated, Sarah threw the brush across the room at his face. While Ed was able to get his arm up and partially block it, the heavy wooden instrument still managed to hit his head. Enraged, he charged her. Sarah tried to hit him with her right hand, but he caught it with his left, and grabbed her by the throat with his right, pushing the much smaller woman to the counter of the kitchenette where her head slammed against a cupboard. Ed tightened his grip to the point that he was choking the life out of her when she was finally able to grab a metal ladle that was on the counter and hit him over the head with it, stunning the man for a moment. He screamed and put both hands on the top of his head where he was struck. As he did, Sarah spun quickly toward a drawer, opened it, and pulled out a long kitchen knife, pointing it at Ed, quivering as she spoke.

"You get the hell out of here right now, you son of a bitch," she told him, her eyes burning holes in his. "You get the hell out and never come back or I swear I'll open your throat where you stand."

191

Ed was seething. But after regarding the knife and studying the woman's face, he quickly rethought any notion of going at her. After a brief staredown, he forced a laugh.

"All right, Sarah," said Ed. "Have it your way."

He walked over to the door, grabbed his hat and the belt with his holster and revolver, looked back at Sarah, who was still trembling against the counter, and shook his head as he exited. Sarah, breathing heavy as she slumped to the floor, closed her eyes and began to sob heavily.

****

Annie and Evie were dealing with a very full breakfast crowd from behind the lunch counter as other waitresses worked the tables at a frantic pace. It seemed like half the city had planned to get their breakfast at the small diner en route to the parade.

"Well?" asked Evie, as she wiped the part of the counter next to where Annie was busing the dishes of someone who'd just eaten.

"Well, what?" asked Annie with a coy smile.

Frustrated, Evie stopped working and put her clenched fists on her hips.

"Are you gonna make me ask, or are you gonna tell me how it went?"

Annie finished topping off a coffee, then stopped cold, set the pot down, and sighed through a smile as she turned toward her.

"It was just lovely. He was a perfect gentleman and so shy and nervous. It was adorable."

"You make plans to see him again?" asked Evie.

"Nothing specific, but he did say he'd like to do it again soon, and I told him I'd like that very much."

Evie shook her head and chuckled.

"Good lord, are you gonna make me push you two reluctant fools toward each other again?"

"You think it'd be too forward to invite him over for Sunday dinner next week?" asked Annie.

"Forward?" yelled Evie. "You flirted near every day for four months straight just to get to the first date. You're practically in reverse the way it is. You can use a bit of forward, darlin'."

"It's just... you know," said Annie, looking side to side to make sure no one was eavesdropping.

"I don't have any damned idea," barked Evie, much less careful not to be heard.

"People look at war widows a certain way," said Annie, just above a whisper, "and, it's just..."

"Oh, don't give me that nonsense, Annie, not today of all days," said Evie. "Some gave all, isn't that what they say?

You lost a husband, and not that I'd ever speak ill of the dead, but we both know he was a no-good son of a gun."

Evie looked at a man seated at the counter who had been listening.

"What? It's true," she barked. "Mind your own damned business if you don't think so."

She turned back to Annie.

"What are you supposed to do, turn into an old maid in honor of the memory of his sorry ass?"

Annie gasped, but with a trace of a smile.

"Evie!"

"Don't Evie me? You know me long enough to know not to ask a question lest you want a truthful answer."

Evie looked back to the male customer, picking up the coffee pot.

"Let me top that off, Wally."

At a nearby table, Bill Rodgers was having breakfast with Chief Gustafson.

"You don't say," said Rodgers, mocking surprise, "a concussion?"

"Yep, and that was the least of his problems," said Chief Gustafson. "Nurse said he was up pissing blood half the

194

night. Bruised kidney, three busted ribs, fractured orbital, lost three teeth, and they had to wire his jaw shut."

Rodgers started to laugh.

"I miss somethin'?" asked the chief.

"I'm just trying to picture the poor son of bitch eating his spaghetti," laughed Rodgers, miming someone sucking in a single strand of spaghetti through pursed lips, in a hyper-animated fashion.

The chief shook his head and chuckled.

"I know, I know, it's a shame," said Rodgers. "Though I will say my sympathy is limited, considering the trouble those filthy roughnecks cause, especially the ones that aren't even decent whites."

Chief Gustafson gave him a knowing smirk.

"I'm sure they are rather limited," said the chief. "I don't suppose you know anything about who was involved?"

"Oh, I only hear whispers, John," said Rodgers.

"Whispers?"

Rodgers shrugged.

"I wouldn't go looking too hard is all," he said. "Besides, I'm sure some good will come of it. He'll go back to wherever he came from, and one of our boys will get on out in the fields. Hell, we have a few more dozen of his kind slip and fall while drunk in an alley like that, we'd probably have all our out-of-work vets set up."

"I see," said the chief.

"Shame when a good Christian white boy comes home from serving his country and has to do nigger work while looking around him to see outsiders prosper," said Rodgers, arching a brow. "It has a way of building a dangerous sort of resentment, John. But I wouldn't worry too much. These things have a way of sorting themselves out."

Chief Gustafson nodded and went back to work on his food.

"That they do."

****

Outside of Mount Zion Church, Obie Mann stood in front of a group of 15 Black WWI veterans, in uniform, as two kids unrolled a cloth banner off to the side. Meanwhile, a congregation including JB Stradford, McKinley Mann, Andrew Smitherman, and Reverend Whitaker watched from the church steps.

"Let me say it again, we are not going over there looking for trouble," Mann told the men. "Same as last year. They already denied our permit application. We show up to march. They tell us to go home. Every white face still gotta look and see the Black ones that fought to defend them while they was back here safe and warm."

Obie turned toward the kids, who now had the banner completely unfurled, each one holding a side. There was a stenciled picture of a buffalo head with the words: 92nd Infantry Division, 366th Infantry Regiment 93rd Infantry Division, "Buffalo Soldiers" 369th Infantry Regiment "Harlem Hellfighters", 370th Infantry Regiment, 371st Infantry Regiment, 372nd Infantry Regiment, stenciled below.

The men on the steps admired the banner.

"That is a beautiful site, gentlemen," said Stradford, as the others nodded and smiled.

"We gonna thank Reverend Whitaker over there and the Mt. Zion ladies auxiliary for this beautiful banner that will precede our formation," said Obie, looking toward the steps, where the reverend gave a nod and wave.

Obie then produced a piece of paper from his pocket, unfolded it and began to read aloud.

"We must not eat with them, must not shake hands with them, seek to talk to them or to meet with them outside the requirements of military service. We must not commend too highly these troops, especially in front of white Americans."

Obie looked up at the men.

"That was General John J. Pershing in a secret letter to the French military in 1918 before many of us were sent to serve with them," he said, before looking back at the letter

197

and resuming. "But I cannot commend the spirit shown among the colored combat troops enough. They exhibit a fine capacity for quick training and eagerness for the most dangerous work."

Obie folded the paper back up and returned it to his pocket.

"You see, this white man knew what he was talking about. They used to call him *Nigger Jack* 'cause he fought with the first Buffalo Soldiers in the 10th Cav. He knew we were needed this last time and allowed us to be the first American soldiers to ever serve under a foreign power. His words embody the same mentality we'll face today, but it is one of deceitful denial. Whether they wanna know it or not, five thousand Negroes fought in the revolution that created this nation. Three thousand more fought in the War of 1812. Some 200,000 Negroes enlisted in the Civil War that ended slavery for good, emancipating 400,000 of our people. Another ten thousand fought in the Spanish-American War, and by the time we beat the Jerries, 350,000 of us had served on the Western Front. We have paid for our freedom in both blood and toil, and it will not be erased. It will not be forgotten. We go in peace, but they will look us in the eye and know that *we* fought, *we* bled, and *we* died so they can be free today, and they'll have to have that somewhere in their minds when they tell us that our people shouldn't really be free back home."

The soldiers, enthralled by Obie's charisma, began to hoot and holler. On the porch of the church, Smitherman was equally entranced, writing furiously on a notepad.

"Boy, my little brother's got a head full of steam today," said McKinley.

"Gentlemen, if Oklahoma were ever to elect a Black Congressman, Senator even," mused Stradford.

"Senator?" quipped Smitherman. "He's what, 22? He could be our first Black president someday!"

"Someday?" asked the reverend. "I'll be happy if he doesn't get himself killed on *this* day. You keep an eye on him, McKinley. I mean it. I'm gonna go inside and tend to a few things. I suppose a few prayers wouldn't hurt neither."

With that, Reverend Whitaker marched up the steps. Meanwhile, the soldiers began to assemble into formation behind the kids carrying the banner.

****

Kelly Ann O'Dell was helping her mother decorate the front of the store with red, white, and blue bunting when Wilfred Dickinson and his daughter Margaret approached.

"Well hello, Megan," said Wilfred. "Good to see you. You look lovely, and let me guess, this is your sister who's in town visiting for the holiday?"

Kelly Ann blushed and lowered her head.

"Good morning, Wilfred," said Megan, turning her attention to his daughter. "Why hello, Margaret, don't you look pretty today?"

Margaret beamed.

"Thank you, Mrs. O'Dell," said the child. "Good morning, Kelly Ann. My dad knows who you are. He's always joshing like that."

"You're the one we should be teasing about growing up so fast," said Kelly Ann. "Look at you!"

"My, she has shot up like a weed now, hasn't she?" said Megan.

Wilfred laughed.

"It's this American food, I tell you. She can't get enough of it. Is that husband of yours inside?"

"He sure is," said Megan. "Give him the business a bit while you're in there, eh Wilfred? It keeps him on his toes."

Wilfred winked and tipped his flat cap.

"Of course."

Inside, Wilfred and Margaret found Gene in an aisle, sorting cans of vegetables on one of the shelves. Wilfred motioned to his daughter to be silent, and they sneaked up close from behind.

"Where might I find the marmite, my good man?" Wilfred nearly shouted. "You seem to be out."

Gene looked over his shoulder and smiled.

"I'd tell you where to look if there weren't young ears around," he said with a chuckle.

"Are you always this saucy or is it just when the limey comes by?" laughed Wilfred.

"I did get some more of those fancy crackers in for you," Gene said. Then he knelt before Margaret. "And for you, young lady, pick out any piece of candy at the register, and it's on Uncle Gene. Special holiday treat."

The young girl's eyes widened.

"Can I have a lollipop?"

"You bet."

****

Chip Bennett and Gary Kale were walking downtown toward the staging area as businesses continued to make preparations for the parade. Gary was shooting pictures, while Chip took notes. They turned a corner to see that the entire cross-street was filled with Klansmen, preparing to assemble.

"Holy shit!" marveled Chip.

Gary glanced at the spectacle, then back to Chip.

"What, they don't march in the parades back in St. Louis?" he asked facetiously.

"There must be 500 of them," said Chip in disbelief.

"I'd say 300," said Gary, indifferently, as he looked at his watch. "But I'm sure there are more coming."

As Chip surveyed the crowd he noticed a mother fussing with the outfit of a young boy of perhaps six, who was sporting his own Klan robe. The boy was clearly excited. When she managed to get the shoulders straight, she affixed his hood, stood back, and beamed with pride.

Chip shook his head.

"Kids?"

"They start 'em young around here," said Gary. "I swear, damn near half of the Halloween costumes that have come to my porch past couple of years have been the hood and robe."

Chip stood by slack-jawed and limp figured as Gary took shots of the Klan members. As he closed in, the Klansmen next to the little boy put his arm around the child and the woman, who appeared to be his son and wife. The three mugged proudly for the camera.

****

Dick Rowland and was shining shoes next to Bump, while men in casual clothing and fedoras read the paper on their seats. Parades were good business, as shine boys could make nearly a day's wages in just a few hours, as the swells passed by on their way to the parade. Rather than having to kill the down time between the morning rush and lunch, they could count on a wave of steady work leading up to the parade, while still finishing early in the day.

"What, no jokes today, Dick?" asked the man whose shoes Dick was working on. "Don't worry, Marty here's no prude," he added, elbowing the man in Bump's seat. "This kid's a riot."

"Let me think," said Dick, continuing to buff the man's shoes. "Okay, I got one. A woman posts an ad in the newspaper that says, looking for a man who won't beat me up, or run away from me, and is great in the sack. She gets a bunch of guys showing up, but none of them is right. Until one day, someone rings her door. She say, who is it? He say, I'm your perfect guy. I got no arms, so I can't beat you, and I got no legs, so I can't run away. She asks, but what makes you think you're great in bed. He say, hey, I rang the doorbell didn't I?"

The whole group roared in laughter. Virgil, a white man in his forties who owned the shine stand, looked annoyed as he peered over his newspaper from the nearby booth to see what the commotion was. Dick finished his shine with a snap of his towel and leaped back to admire his work.

"Yes, sir, that's that diamond shine," he said. "I can see my smile in them wingtips. Now, you try not to go blinding nobody today when they catch the sun."

203

The man rose, looking down at his feet approvingly as he shook his head in disbelief.

"I tell ya, I was about to toss this pair. Never thought they'd come back to life like that. Thanks, Dick. Enjoy the day."

As he stood, the man greased Dick's palm with a bill and tipped his fedora. As Dick walked off toward the curb, marching band instruments could be heard getting in tune from the distance.

"Diamond shine," yelled Dick. "Can't go to the parade without that diamond shine. Still get'cha in before they step off."

Sarah Page was walking in the oncoming direction when Dick took notice. She was in her uniform but looked disheveled and wore a foul look on her face, having just left the apartment and her fight with Ed Kline. Dick smiled, as usual, but when she didn't even look as she passed the curb from three feet away, his hope deflated.

"Diamond Shine... get it," he continued to bark with considerably less enthusiasm.

Bump walked up beside him.

"See, I told you to stick with the sisters," said Bump. "Ours got that mean look all the time. Leaves less to uncertainty."

Both men chuckled, but Dick's heart wasn't in it.

****

On the portion of Main Street that was along the parade route, the streets were already full on both sides, even though it was still an hour before the parade would step off. In the staging area, Horton McGuire stood with a chart in his hand, accompanied by Tate Brady and Wash Hudson. McGuire stood before a white marching band, checking off the chart as they moved down the line. The next group was the KKK. The three men were very chummy with the Klansmen, shaking hands as they passed. In the center, Bill Rodgers stood tall, wearing a red robe. As he was just about to put his hood on, he smiled and waved to the three men, who waved back enthusiastically. Suddenly, a young man named Billy ran up to Horton, breathlessly heaving from his efforts.

"Mr. McGuire, Mr. McGuire!" screamed the boy.

"Jesus, Billy, slow the heck down, you're too young for a heart attack," said McGuire, smiling.

"You're gonna wanna get down to the staging area right quick, sir," said Billy.

Obie and the vets marched toward the staging area from a side street, where a small crowd of Blacks watched on

205

nervously. Just then, McGuire, Hudson, and Brady turned the corner.

"Ah, hell no," said Hudson. "What in the fuck do they think they're doin'?"

His face turned crimson, and he picked up his pace and walked ahead of the others toward the soldiers.

"Ah, boy. I guess you ought to go round up some police officers, Tate," said McGuire.

Brady shook his head and sighed, before starting off in the opposite direction.

"You'd best just turn back around and head in the other direction, fellas," said Hudson. "This is my parade, and I already made it clear you ain't marching."

"There was an open call for veterans, sir," said Obie, firmly. "Read it in the Tribune."

"Look, boy, if you can read," said Hudson, "and you been reading the Trib, then you know good and goddamned well you ain't marching in no parade today, not unless they're having one over in Little Africa, which y'all best be headin' back to before there's trouble."

By this time, a sizable crowd had assembled from around the corner. Tate was returning in a jog with police officers when he pulled up next to McGuire and Hudson.

"I ain't no boy, mister," said Obie with intensity burning in his eyes. "And I can read anything you put in front of me."

"Now you look here you big, Black son of a bitch," said Hudson, "if you think I'm gonna be intimidated by some cocksure halfbreed..."

Obie's nostrils flared and his eyes filled with rage as he struggled to keep his composure. From a nearby crowd, Smitherman, McKinley Mann, and Stradford ran over to his side. At the opposite corner, white vets approached, along with Mayor Evans and a small entourage. In a matter of moments, all parties converged and the tension rose dramatically, as the white and Black vets stood face to face with Lawton Mercer out at the front of the white soldiers.

"Ain't gonna be no spades marching with us today, fellas," said Lawton with a sneer. "Best go back to Niggertown or, better yet, over to *Gay Paree* if you wanna celebrate."

The whites laughed.

"Well, there you have it, boys," said Hudson. "The vets aren't allowing it, so there's no point in making a scene."

"What do you mean *the vets*?" asked Stradford, looking to the Black soldiers. "They are vets, served same as your boys."

"The hell you say," snapped Lawton. "We didn't let no niggers in our regiments, old man."

Stradford clenched his fists and ground his teeth, as Smitherman moved quickly to put a hand in front of his chest.

"No, no, JB," said Smitherman. "Come on now, we're here to keep the peace, not spoil it."

Two blocks away, Gary was photographing a family who was set up on the street to watch the parade. Chip ran up and grabbed his sleeve, ruining the shot and startling him.

"Follow me, quick. Some Black soldiers are trying to march and something's about to go down."

Chip turned and ran back in the other direction with Gary following. The crowd all looked, with some following behind.

A man who did not give chase turned to his wife.

"Can you believe this?" he asked. "Them fucking darkies, they gotta go and ruin stuff like this all the time. Can't stay over in Niggertown and be left alone. Always looking for trouble."

A man next to him chimed in.

"Those monkeys don't know any better. They get their freedom, but they don't even know how to use it. They'll wind up locked up or worse."

"Should end up swingin' from a tree," said the first man.

Chip and Gary arrived at the standoff just behind the mayor, who'd shown up with a small entourage of additional police officers.

"All right, all right," said Mayor Evans, "you've made your point, boys, but let's end this little standoff before there's real trouble. Nobody wants that."

"Then do the right thing, Mayor Evans," said Smitherman. "These brave men fought for you and every other citizen of Tulsa. Black men bled and Black men died, same as the whites. This city owes them the same debt of gratitude."

The mayor shook his head and smiled condescendingly.

"Mr. Smitherman, you're not helping matters," said the mayor. "One might even think you're stirring up the pot."

At that, the largest police officer who'd arrived with the mayor wrapped his nightstick against his palm menacingly.

"Hey, Mayor," said Lawton, "why don't you let 'em march in the back, clean up the trash like they did in the Army."

Sensing that the worst was about the come, JB Stradford turned to face Obie and the soldiers.

"All right, men," said Stradford. "You did what you came to do. Look how many people are watching. The rest will hear about it. Let's head back."

Obie turned to the soldiers and yelled in a commanding voice, "Platoon, *atten-hut.*"

The men snapped to attention.

"About face," said Obie, prompting them to turn around in unison.

"Forward march."

The soldiers began marching in the opposite direction.

"Every fuckin' time," said Tate Brady. "When will they learn?"

"They can't learn, Tate," said Wash Hudson. "That's half the problem."

"All right, enough of this already," said Horton McGuire. "We got a parade to run."

"I gotta get back to my motor car," said the mayor as he hustled off.

The white vets were laughing and smiling as they watched the Blacks march into the distance.

Gary was taking pictures of them, as Chip approached Lawton.

"Excuse me, sir, can I have a word?" Chip asked.

Lawton stuck his middle finger in Chip's face in reply, then looked to Gary.

"Listen, Nancy," said Lawton, "you take one fucking picture of this here face, and I'll shove that camera up your ass sideways, get me?"

Gary lowered the camera, and both men cautiously backed away from the vets.

****

Dick and Bump were still at their shine boxes with two other bootblacks, but there was no business to be had, now that everyone had gone on to the parade. Virgil emerged from his nearby booth.

"Won't be no one coming by now that the parade's stepped off," announced Virgil. "Go on and get out of here, but you know the rules, be back in the morning bright and early or someone else works the box."

"Wanna go catch the streetcar?" asked Bump.

Dick paused in consideration.

"Nah, I'm gonna head over to the Drexel and take a leak," he finally said.

Bump gave him a knowing look.

"Hmm hmm."

Dick shrugged.

"Where else can a Negro piss around here?"

Dick left him with a smirk. Bump shook his head and frowned toward the sidewalk after he watched the young man run off toward the big building.

Dick walked down an empty downtown street. He could hear the parade revelry in the background and see crowds of people watching it as he passed the corners of intersecting side streets. After a few blocks, he ducked into a brown brick building. The lobby was mostly empty. The department store on the ground floor was dark and its gate closed. He kept his hands in his pocket and his head down as he made his way toward the elevator on the other side of the lobby, where he saw Sarah looking at him with a smirk.

"Lemme guess," she says, "4th floor?"

"Only choice we got," said Dick, as friendly as he dared be.

Once inside, Sarah closed the door and turned to Dick before starting the elevator.

"What'd you say your name was?"

Surprised by being asked, Dick spoke nervous and fast.

"They call me die... Diamond Dick."

Sarah frowned and looked at him like he had two heads.

"What in the hell is a *diamond dick*?" she asked, glancing toward his crotch.

"No, not diamond-dick — *Diamond Dick*," he tried to explain, pointing to his finger and repeating, "diamond," then to his chest, "Dick."

Sarah seemed to have lost interest.

"Whatever."

She pushed up the lever and they jerked forward. Dick startled a bit.

"Don't worry," said Sarah, "it's just been doin' that lately."

"You seem angry or something," said Dick. "You okay?"

"Fuck do you care?" asked Sarah, seeming to go frosty all at once.

"I care," said Dick, stammering a bit. "I mean, I just do is all."

Sarah sighed.

"Well don't, it's none of your business, okay?"

"Okay," muttered Dick, shoving his hands into his pockets and leaning over against the opposite wall to put more distance between them and perhaps make the young woman less uncomfortable.

"You just seem like a nice lady is all," Dick said after a few moments, "and usually you seem, well, happier."

Sarah sighed deeper this time.

"Well, I ain't, okay."

"Which one," asked Dick, "nice or happy?"

Sarah relaxed a bit, exhaled, and rolled her eyes, but with much less hostility in her mannerisms this time.

"Neither is prolly the most honest answer if you wanna know the truth."

She gave him the faintest smile, and he returned it with a broad one of his own. Sarah's hand was on the lever, and when she pushed it up a moment later, the elevator jerked again, only this time, much harder. Dick's hands were still in his pockets, causing his to fall forward as he struggled to get them out in order to steady himself. The momentum threw him straight toward Sarah, and it was all Dick could do to get his hands out of his pockets before his head crashed into hers. He instinctively put his hands in front of him to brace the impact, and one landed on her shoulder, while the other fell to her chest, pushing her back against the elevator wall as the door opened. Sarah was half startled, half angry when she pushed Dick off of her.

When the car arrived, a clerk who'd been waiting for the elevator stood there, his eyes wide and his mouth gaping.

"Get off that woman!" screamed the clerk.

Dick had his hands up defensively and was backing away from Sarah, who was by now slapping at his shoulders and arms, which he'd raised to cover his face.

"Don't you ever put your dirty, fucking hands on me!" Sarah screamed.

Instinctively, Dick grabbed her wrists as she continued to swat at him, while the clerk rushed to step between them.

"Unhand her, you animal," the man yelled.

Sarah stopped hitting Dick, as the clerk got in front of her. Dick slunk into the corner of the elevator, looking to the man in fear.

"I didn't do nothin', sir," he pleaded. "I slipped. The car jerked."

The man shook his head in disgust as he screamed toward the hallway.

"Call the police! There's been an assault."

Dick's eyes widened and his jaw dropped.

"What? No, I didn't assault nobody. I didn't do anything, I swear it."

The clerk was now half in front of Sarah, facing Dick with his left arm guarding her while his right was up in the air as if to possibly swing.

"Call the police!" he screamed once more.

Dick looked to the hallway, where he saw an open office door, then to Sarah, then to the clerk. He turned quickly out the door and hung a hard right, sprinting toward a door marked "Stairs," which he slammed open and ran through. Dick sprinted down the steps of the unlit and musty stairwell two at a time, sweat immediately beginning to flow from every pore. With his hands on the rail, he swung around the landing and bounded down another flight. When he got to the last landing, he jumped off of it to the ground floor, where he burst through another door marked "Exit."

As he stumbled into the street, Dick paused for a moment. There were a couple of people on foot who looked over toward the door, so he didn't want to draw attention to himself by sprinting. Instead, he fought his instincts and walked off as normally as he could manage until he was sure no one was looking. His stomach burned and sweat continued to pour from his body. Once he was certain it was clear, he opened up into a full sprint, running down a side street and toward a large field.

****

At the Tulsa Police Station, Herman Bowers, the clerk from the store who'd thought he'd seen Dick Rowland attack Sarah Page, sat at a desk across from Chief Gustafson, while three uniformed officers flanked him.

"So, you seen him attack the girl?" asked the chief.

"Yes!" said Bowers. "The door opened and he was on top of her, groping her breasts and... and..."

"And what?" asked the chief.

"Well, he clearly had intentions to have his way with her," said Bowers in an indignant tone.

Chief Gustafson leaned back in his chair, unimpressed.

"So you witnessed him trying to rape the girl?"

"Yes," said Bowers. "That's what I'm telling you. Isn't it obvious?"

The chief leaned back in, putting his elbows on the table.

"Listen, pal, nothing's obvious. None of us were there. You were, so we gotta be thorough. Get me?"

The man dropped his head and cowered some.

"I'm sorry, I'm very sorry, officer, I..."

"Chief," said Gustafson.

"Yes?" asked Bowers.

Gustafson shook his head and sighed.

"*I'm* the chief of police, *you* call *me* chief. These guys are officers."

He pointed with his thumb over his shoulder at the men surrounding him.

"Of course, apologies, sir," said Bowers. "I mean chief. It's just, I'm a bit, it was something of an ordeal, as you can imagine. I suppose I'm a bit taken back."

"Someone get him a glass of water," said the chief, looking to the officers around him, one of whom volunteered.

"So you step between them," continued the chief, "what happens next? He go after you?"

The man paused briefly before answering.

"No... he was, well, clearly surprised to be seen by someone. He sort of backed away against the wall. I yelled for someone to call the police, I mean I couldn't go back to the office and call myself. I had to stay with the girl."

"Of course," said Gustafson. "There were other people up there?"

"Yes," said the man. "The store was closed today of course, but there were a few of us in the upstairs offices working on the books."

The officer returned with a glass of water he handed to the clerk, who quickly drank half of it down.

"You guys canvas the building?" asked the chief, looking to one of his officers.

"Yeah, the lobby was empty with Renberg's being closed, and no one on the third or fourth floor saw anything," said the cop.

Chief Gustafson looked back at Bowers.

"So what happens next?"

"Well, he starts yelling that he didn't do anything," said the man, "like I didn't already know what happened, hadn't seen it with my own eyes. I yell again to call the police and he ran off faster than anything I'd ever seen move."

"Those monkeys sure can run," said the other officer. "I once chased a nigger for ten blocks, lost half a block with each one we ran."

The chief looked back over his shoulder, glaring at the young patrolman.

"Sorry, chief," said the officer.

"So, you take chase?" the chief asked Bowers.

"I beg your pardon?"

"When he ran, you chase after him?" asked the chief.

Bowers seemed a bit shaken by the question.

"Well, no, I mean, like I said, he was gone before I had even realized he'd taken off. I was glancing back and forth between him and the girl. She was pretty shaken up. I mean she had bruises on her neck and everything. I just stayed with her until someone came over from the office, John Halsey, our account manager, and I had him call you guys."

The chief chewed his gum as he studied the store clerk.

"All right," he finally said, "that's good for now. You can go home, and we'll get in touch if we need you."

"That's it?" asked Bowers. "You don't need to ask me anything else?"

The chief shook his head slowly.

"You said you didn't know what his name was. You know where he lives? Where he works?"

"Uh, no," said Bowers.

"Then what else do I need to ask you?"

"Right," said Bowers.

The man rose to his feet a bit sheepishly and then walked off with much greater purpose. After watching him for a moment, the chief looked to one of the officers.

"See if he needs a ride."

Then he looked to the patrolman at his other side.

"Send in the girl."

****

Aunt Damie was busy doing dishes in the kitchen when Dick burst in the back door of the boarding house. She was startled by the sound and panicked when she saw that he was totally out of breath and sweating profusely.

"What in the lord's name is wrong, child?" asked Damie. "Look at you."

Dick was doubled over, panting as he struggled to catch his breath. Aunt Damie grabbed a glass and filled it with tap water from the sink. She handed it to Dick, who could barely rise well enough to take it. He sipped it eagerly but began coughing and spitting some out. He continued to gasp as he tried to recover.

"Dick Rowland, what's this all about?" she screamed. "You're scaring me."

"Somethin' bad happened, Aunt Damie," said Dick, still short of breath as he struggled to force out the words.

He up-righted himself and finally began to settle his breathing. Damie walked over to him and put her hand on his shoulder.

"What happened, baby?" she asked with a calmer voice. "Tell me right now."

"I didn't do nothin' wrong, I swear," said Dick, tears beginning to well in his eyes.

"Okay, well what's this about then?" she asked.

"There was this girl, the elevator girl at the Drexel," he began.

"Dick Rowland, what kinda trouble you get yourself in?" snapped Aunt Damie, grabbing hold of his arm.

Dick shrugged and tears began to roll down his cheek.

"I didn't do nothing, Aunt Damie, I swear it. I just tripped."

"Make some sense to me this instant, boy," Aunt Damie said firmly.

"Mr. Virgil let us go once the parade started and there was no trade around," explained Dick. "I had to use the bathroom before I came home, so I had to go over to the

Drexel like always. Mr. Virgil got it set up for us to use an old one on the 4th floor, rents it off them like."

Damie let go of the boy's arm and put her hands on her hips.

"And?"

"So, the elevator girl there, her name Sarah, she took me up. But the elevator was all herky-jerky. It jumped when we started, and when it stopped it jerked real hard. I fell toward her and we crashed into each other, just as the door opened. She was all excited and screamed, but there was a white man waiting for the car when the door opened. He start yelling to call the cops, some girl been attacked. I didn't attack no one, Aunt Damie. I just tripped 'cause the car jerked."

She took Dick into her arms and stroked his head.

"Alright, Child, I know, I know."

Damie withdrew, putting each hand on one of his shoulders.

"But that ain't gonna matter if they got it fixed in they heads that you did. Now you tell me, Dick, what happened next."

"I ran," he said. "I ran as fast I could, down the stairs, across town, all the way here. I didn't stop or look back once."

"Were they chasing you, baby? Did anyone yell after you?" she asked.

"No, I don't think so. I didn't hear or see nobody but that man."

Damie turned away toward the sink, pacing the kitchen with her palm on her forehead.

"Oh lord, I hope they got it straightened out before they called the police," she said.

"Sarah, she know me, Aunt Damie," said Dick. "I have to go up that elevator two, three times every day. She know I wouldn't hurt her. She was just in a bad mood today is all, and she was startled real good. She'd a told 'em it was an accident once she settled down and sorted it out."

"Good lord, I hope you're right, child," said Damie. "How many times have I done told you not to even go lookin' at them white women, huh?"

"But I didn't do nothin' wrong, Aunt Damie. I gotta use that bathroom, it's the only one for coloreds in the whole downtown. She the elevator girl at the building. You not supposed to take the steps unless there's a fire or something. It say emergency only."

Damie shook her head and pulled Dick in for a hug, patting his back.

"I know, baby, I know," she told him in a more gentle tone. "You didn't do nothing wrong and that should be all there is to it, but it ain't. It just ain't, and it's no good, but it's the way this world is."

223

****

In the lobby of the police station, Officer Ed Kline was standing with another patrolman behind a tall desk. He glanced over to where Sarah was seated nearby, fidgeting nervously as she took quick and frequent puffs from a cigarette.

"I gotta go take a leak," said the other officer.

"Sure," said Ed, watching him walk off before hurrying over to Sarah once he was out of sight.

"Hey, I heard what happened," he said to her. "You okay?"

Sarah gave him a cold look.

"What do you care?"

"What do you mean? Of course, I care," he told her.

Sarah took another short drag.

"Yeah, right."

"Hey, you're the one that threw a fucking hairbrush at me," he said before lowering his voice. "Hit me with a ladle, threatened to cut my throat. And I still ain't sore at'cha."

Sarah frowned as she cocked her head and dropped her shoulders.

"Look, they're gonna ask you about your neck," he said. "It's still a little red."

She looked at him with violence in her eyes.

"All I'm sayin' is..."

"I know what you're sayin', Ed, and you can stop worrying. I ain't gonna tell 'em about us."

Ed put a hand on her shoulder.

"That's my girl."

Her expression didn't change.

"I gotta get back to the desk," he said delicately. "It wouldn't be good, you know, if they saw me talking to you."

Ed withdrew his hand just before another officer came in from the back.

"Miss Page, can you come back here, please."

Sarah rose, shooting Ed a quick look as she followed the police officer through the doorway, where Chief Gustafson was waiting on the other side with Detective Morris, who he'd assigned to the case after interviewing the clerk.

"So, how you holding up?" the chief asked Sarah.

"It's like I told the other officers, I'm fine," she said, putting out the stub of her cigarette as she sat down.

"Good, I'm glad to hear it," said the chief. "This is Chief Detective Morris, he's gonna be the lead investigator on this case. He'll need to ask you a few questions, then we'll get you home."

Sarah looked over at the portly, disheveled man wearing a crumpled fedora, his shirt sleeves rolled, his collar opened with his necktie loosened.

"Have a seat, Sarah," said Detective Morris.

Once Sarah was seated, Gustafson walked off.

Sarah took a cigarette from her purse and held it up toward the detective.

"You mind?" she asked.

Detective Morris pulled out a Zippo, reached over, and lit for her before pushing an ashtray over to her side of the desk.

"I've been trying to quit myself, but..." he said, pulling a pack from his shirt pocket and lighting one for himself. After a quick puff, he put his elbows on the desk, leaning toward her a bit.

"Can you tell me exactly what happened, Sarah?" asked the detective.

"I already told them everything I remember," she said sharply.

"Yeah, I know you did, but you see they're not detectives, and most of them are dumber than bricks, I'm afraid," he said with a chuckle. "So I'm gonna need to hear it directly from you myself if that's alright."

Sarah ashed the cigarette as she slowly exhaled.

"We was coming up the elevator and when we got to the top, the car jerked. He went tumbling into me-"

"The nigger boy does?" asked the detective.

Sarah looked perplexed.

"Yeah."

"And it's just the two of you in the elevator?"

"Yeah," said Sarah, "Renberg's was closed for the holiday. The place was practically empty."

Detective Morris scribbled on a legal pad.

"Okay, go on."

Sarah took another drag, rolling her eyes as she exhaled.

"So he comes flying into me, and he grabs onto my jacket," she said. "I screamed, started hitting him. The door opened. He grabbed my wrists to keep me from swatting at him, and that man from Renberg's came in and started yelling for the police."

"So, you saying it was an accident, or that when he bumped you, he grabbed a hold and attacked?"

"I dunno," she shrugged. "He might a just tripped. It all happened so fast. I was scared."

"Of course," said the detective, "who wouldn't be? Little thing like you, big buck nigger grabs a hold of you by the chest."

227

Sarah rolled her eyes again.

"It wasn't like that."

"What do you mean?" asked the detective.

"He sort of fell like, and then he grabbed on," she told him.

"You said the chest, but you got marks on your neck?"

"I don't know," she said nervously, "it all happened so fast."

"It's okay, darling, I just need to get this all straight. Did the nigger choke you around the neck, or not?"

Sarah's demeanor shifted rapidly. She seemed suddenly unnerved by the question.

"I don't know," she told him. "No, I don't think so."

"Well those marks couldn't have put themselves there, now, could they have?" he asked her.

She looked down

"No, I don't suppose so."

Detective Morris made another note on his pad.

"So, we'll just presume that he grabbed you around the neck and not the chest, or that he did both."

"I don't think he meant to hurt me," she told him.

Detective Morris glared at her for several moments.

"You know this boy?" he asked. "He familiar to you?"

228

Sarah fidgeted in her seat.

"What d'ya mean, *familiar*?"

"You ever have occasion to take him up to the 4th floor prior?" he asked.

"I don't know, prolly. It's the only bathroom down that ways they can use. I take half dozen of 'em up and back a day."

Detective Morris shook his head and sighed.

"Yeah, they do tend to look alike, don't they? They're like monkeys that way. Hard to tell 'em apart. That must be awful, though. I mean the smell alone of all those filthy niggers riding in the car all day, but then again I don't suppose we can have 'em pissing in the streets either."

Sarah puffed on her cigarette in quick short bursts.

"Is that it?" she asked.

"No."

"Well?" she asked, even more impatiently this time.

Detective Morris paused, staring at her intently.

"You friendly with any of those nigger boys you take up and down the elevator?"

Sarah jumped to her feet.

"No!"

"You got a boyfriend, Miss Page?"

"What's that got to do with it?" she asked.

The detective shrugged.

"Nothing maybe. Maybe something."

"I ain't got no boyfriend," she snapped. "I'm divorced. Came here from Kansas City afterward to start over."

The detective was unfazed. He stared at Sarah until she sat back down.

"Parents back there?"

"Ain't got none," she told him. "Grew up in an orphanage. Married the first guy who asked me just to get out of that rotten place."

"But it didn't work out?" he asked.

She rolled her eyes again.

"Obviously not."

"How come?" he asked.

"Because when I met the son of a bitch, I thought there was no place in the world I could ever want to be less than that godforsaken orphanage."

"And?" he asked with a shrug.

"And I was wrong, goddammit. I'd gone and found the one life more awful than the one I left."

"Is that so?" he asked indifferently.

"I just said so, didn't I?"

Sarah stubbed out her cigarette in the ashtray. Detective Morris reached back into his shirt pocket, took out his pack, and gave her another, leaning toward her to light it once she'd put it in her mouth.

"It's just a dangerous situation, is all," he told her. "Your job, that is. I mean these niggers, especially the young bucks, they're like wild animals when they rut. They catch a whiff of a pretty little white woman, and it sets 'em off, can't help themselves. I'm surprised something like this didn't happen to you earlier, truth be told. Whoever thought it'd be safe to put a young white girl—how old?"

"Seventeen."

"Seventeen?" he asked, shaking his head. "Lord have mercy."

"It's a job, and I ain't never felt unsafe," she told him. "There's usually lots a people around. They're usually too shy to even look up."

"That's 'cause they're yella," he said. "But, the first time this one comes in and Renberg's is closed, and there's nobody around, he figures he can have him a taste, I suppose?"

"What are you sayin'?" she asked.

"I think you know exactly what I'm saying."

"No, I don't, so you got a question, spit it out," she yelled.

"You see, some girls enjoy getting the niggers all wound up," he told her with a sneer. "It's like a game to them.

They like to see 'em get all flushed and excited when they smile or bat their eyes. Gives 'em a sense of control, like they got something the beasts want, but that they know they can't have, which I suppose makes 'em want it even more. But you push 'em too far and, well, like I said, wild animals."

"It ain't like that," she said in a softer tone.

"Good," he said, nodding his head. "I'm glad to hear it. I didn't figure you for a nigger lover."

Sarah glared at him, but the detective had already gotten the better of the exchange and met her eyes with a devilish smile.

"Anything else?" she asked.

"You know this boy's name?"

"No," she told him

"Where he works?"

She shrugged.

"He looked like a shine boy. The way he was dressed and all."

"All right then," said the detective. "Good enough. Let's get you home."

****

At the Tulsa Hotel, in their usual room, Richard Lloyd Jones was in bed, on top of Amy Comstock, pumping vigorously when the phone rang, breaking his concentration. Richard reached toward the desk while his secretary/mistress covered herself with a sheet.

"What the hell do those fools want now?" he wondered aloud as he reached for the receiver. "Hello?"

"Mr. Jones?" asked the hotel operator.

"Yes, what is it?"

"There's a call for you," the voice said. "They wouldn't say who it was. Should I put it through?"

"Man or a woman?"

"It was a man, sir."

"Put it through," said Richard. "Hello, who's this?" he asked after hearing the click.

"It's Morris," said the new voice on the other end of the line. "I might have a tip for you, and it's a doozie if I do."

"How'd you know I was here?" asked Richard.

"I'm a detective," said Morris. "Called the paper, they told me you work from the Tulsa sometimes for a few hours after lunch."

"What'cha got for me?" asked Richard.

"Might be that a nigger attacked a white girl in an elevator at the Drexel this afternoon," said Detective Morris. "Not sure yet."

233

"Is that so?" asked Richard, excitedly. "You got the boy?"

"Nah, haven't identified him yet. Ran off when a clerk saw him. It shouldn't be too hard though."

"Let me know the second there's an arrest?" asked Richard hopefully.

"Usual fee?"

"Listen to me, you boys make an arrest, and I get it in time for the afternoon edition, I'll pay you twice our usual arrangement."

"Sounds good," said the detective. "I'll be in touch."

"What was that about?" asked Amy, as she buttoned her blouse.

"Not sure yet," said Richard, "but it could be the biggest story we've had all year."

Richard grabbed a hold of her and kissed her cheek, then turned away, sporting a fiendish grin.

****

Once Smitherman had been tipped off about the incident, he immediately called on Stradford, who summoned Buck Franklin and Isaiah Spears from their office. Fearing the worst, the four men quickly made their way to the boarding house to assess the situation.

"Thank you, ma'am," said Stradford, as Aunt Damie topped off his coffee

Damie, looking at once anxious and tired, nodded and took the last seat at the table.

"Thank you all for coming over so quickly," she said, fighting back tears. "I sure do appreciate it. I hope I'm not wasting your time, neither. I was just so scared they might have called the police."

"You did the right thing," Stradford assured her.

"You think it's gonna be alright?" she asked the men.

Stradford put his hand over hers and leaned in, looking the old woman in the eyes.

"We are going to make sure it's alright," he told her. "If everything happened the way Dick says, and I believe it did, there's not gonna be nothing to worry about, Miss Damie. You got four men with law degrees sitting in your kitchen, and if they try and come after him for something he didn't do, I'll direct every resource at my disposal toward fighting it. I promise you that."

"That's kind of you, Mr. Stradford, but I ain't worried so much about courtroom justice," she said. "It's the other kind that scares me. I done seen plenty of it in my time."

"We won't let that happen either, Miss Damie," said Smitherman. "I'll call on my contacts in Oklahoma City, and we got the NAACP on our side too. There won't be no lynching of our boys. I promise you that."

"And no one has been by the house, not even Barney?" asked Isaiah.

"No, sir," Dick told him.

"Then my guess is they haven't reported anything to the police," said Isaiah. "It wouldn't be too hard for them to figure out where Dick lived, especially if the girl knew where he worked."

"You think we should move him outside the house, just in case?" asked Buck.

"Sure, I can put him up in one of our rooms, or at my house even," said Stradford.

Dick looked to Damie, then to Stradford.

"If y'all don't mind none," he said, "I prefer to stay here. I appreciate it, but I don't wanna leave my auntie alone, and she got the business to run."

The men exchanged looks.

"Okay," said Stradford. "Isaiah's probably right. If they were coming today, they'd likely be here by now. If they figured it out and just want to ask you some questions, they'll more likely stop by the shine stand tomorrow."

Stradford began writing on the back of a calling card.

"You might want to lay low for another day or two, but the next time you do go to work, as soon as you get there, I want you to give this card to whoever you trust the most. You tell them that if you should get picked up, they're to get in touch with Andy or me at one of these places immediately, you understand?"

Stradford handed Dick the card.

"Yes, sir, thank you," said Dick, as he put the card in his pocket.

Once they were outside, Stradford and Buck waited near two motor cars, as Smitherman walked around to get in the driver's seat of one, Isaiah the other.

"You think he's in the clear?" Buck asked Stradford.

"*Sheeyit*, son, this is Tulsa. Ain't no Black man ever in the clear. He might be alright though, with just a store clerk seeing it. Had it been four or five white men, each afraid of what the other would think if they didn't call for blood? Then we'd have a real problem on our hands."

"Thank heaven for small blessings," said Buck.

"Girl was probably shaken up good, but once he got her calmed down, she probably told him it was an accident. Dick said she told him the elevator had been jerking like that, so she would have put it together once she got settled."

"I hope you're right," said Buck.

"Me too," said Stradford as he entered the passenger side of Smitherman's car. "Me too."

****

Detective Morris was sitting across from Sheriff McCullough at the sheriff's desk with Deputy Barney Cleaver standing behind them.

"Tall, thin kid, about 18 or so," said Detective Morris. "She figures him for a bootblack."

"Dozens of shine boys in Greenwood," said Deputy Cleaver. "*If* he was a shine boy, that is, detective."

"Right," said the detective.

"I served divorce papers on that Page girl a few months back," said the sheriff. "Came in from Kansas City. If even half the stuff that was in that file were true, she'd be... less than reputable. Besides, it don't sound like she's saying it even was an assault."

Detective Morris sat there rolling his pencil between his fingers, as he regarded the sheriff.

"Poor girl was shaking like a leaf, and who could blame her?" said the detective. "There was a lot of gibberish coming out to be sure, but it's the clerk's account I'm concerned with."

"Can't have a crime with just a witness, detective," said the sheriff. "Need a victim too, it seems."

"Right," he answered. "Like I said, I'd be remiss if I didn't follow up on what was reported by the clerk. Can't have these niggers just putting their paws on a white woman

238

anytime the urge strikes. Something like this, well it might embolden the others, and I don't need to tell you there are organizations set up to prevent that from happening, should we fail to do so, sheriff."

The sheriff rose.

"Well, like I said, we'll look into it," he told the detective. "Let you know what we find."

Detective Morris stood and shook the sheriff's hand.

"Please do, sheriff."

Once Morris had left the room, the sheriff turned to Barney.

"I imagine you were keeping your cards tight to your vest?"

"Yes, sir," said the deputy.

"Good idea, Morris is high up in the Klan, as I understand it. He gets a lead on the kid, he's liable to turn him right over to them rather than run him in."

"Don't I know it," said the deputy.

"You know who the kid is?" asked the sheriff.

"No, but I got some ideas. I'll figure it out by morning when they all head to work."

"Good, now listen," said the sheriff. "Don't scare the kid, but bring him in once you do, and not to the police station. Bring him here. I'll call Gustafson, and if they're gonna charge him, there'll be no reason for him to leave the jailhouse or even the cell for that matter. We'll be able to keep him safe until this blows over. He'll go to court, or he'll go home, but he will not be handed over to a mob."

"You mind I head over to Greenwood now, see what I can find out?" asked Barney.

"Yeah, go on and do that."

"Sheriff?" said Barney.

"Yeah?"

"Thanks."

The sheriff tipped his hat as Barney set off with purpose.

****

That evening, the pool hall on the north end of Greenwood Avenue was jumping like a juke joint. A jazz band played lively tunes, as men and women spilled into the street only to be replaced by more revelers seeking entry.

Inside, a buffalo soldier still in uniform, sent a cue ball crashing into the racked balls on the pool table with a thunderous crack that could be heard above the music. Obie and McKinley Mann stood against the near wall, observing the competition. McKinley offered Obie a belt from his pint of bourbon, which he accepted, pulling a generous snort.

"Well, you didn't get your big Black ass shot today," said McKinley with a grin. "I suppose that's something. You satisfied?"

Obie regarded his older brother with a smirk.

"For today," he eventually told him.

"And tomorrow?" asked McKinley.

"We'll see come tomorrow, I guess," said Obie, a bit more serious this time.

"What more you want, Obie?" asked McKinley.

"All of it, brother," said Obie with a dark look in his eyes. "I don't ever want to have to bow down to no man, not never. I want those guys today to look at me and not figure I gotta do what they say because it's their world, and when I have kids of my own someday, I don't just want them to be *born* free, I want them to actually be able to *live* free."

McKinley shook his head and turned back toward the game.

"You picked a hell of a town to make that stand, little brother."

"This is where we were born," said Obie. "No choice in that."

McKinley turned back toward his much larger sibling.

"I'm proud of you, little brother," he told him. "You stood tall. Not that you can help it."

Obie smiled and palmed the top of his brother's head, mussing his hair. McKinley leaned away, but Obie easily pulled him in for a hug, kissing the crown of his head in a very rare exchange of physical affection between the two men. As they released, the band struck a final note and Obie took the pint bottle and held it high, looking out to the crowd.

"To the Buffalo soldiers!"

The rest of the room whooped, raising beers and pints in a toast. Every face in the room was filled with pride and the contentment that the morning's moral victory had brought, even if it was only symbolic and would soon fade with the next day's reminders that nothing had in fact changed. That night, however, the men drank with the revelry of soldiers who had just won a battle, content just to fight on another day.

****

At the hospital, Dr. A.C. Jackson walked into the lobby from the hallway, where a lone nurse manned the main desk.

"What in the world are you still doing here, Dr. Jackson?" the nurse asked. "It's nearly 10 p.m. and on a holiday, no less."

"Mrs. Watts still isn't out of the woods yet with that infection," said Dr. Jackson. "It's been as stubborn as any I've seen in quite some time."

"Well, you get home," she told him. "I'll check on her and ring you at the house if she takes a turn."

Dr. Jackson, clearly exhausted, nodded.

"Please do. And if Julia Calls, tell her I'm on my way, but I was stopping at my father's real quick first. I won't be long."

"Sure thing, Dr. Jackson," said the nurse. "See you in the morning?"

"I've got to stop by the Smith's, check on Sissy's scarlet fever, and then make a couple of house calls out on the north end," he told her. "Probably more like lunchtime, I imagine."

"Okay, Goodnight, Dr. Jackson," said the nurse.

"Goodnight," he said, tapping the desk with his hand as he left.

****

Captain Jackson was sitting on his porch, rocking in his chair and petting a large basset hound, while whistling an old battle tune. His son heard the sound before turning the corner and smiled. When his father saw him approach, the son held a paper bag in the air.

"Hey, old soldier," he said, "I brought you some boiled peanuts."

"At this hour?" asked his father with a smile.

"I had to attend to a patient," Dr. Jackson said. "I'm on my way home."

He sat down on a second rocking chair that was next to his father's. It was the one his mother used to sit in and, as such, it always caused him to feel a bit out of place, though the captain had told him more than once how happy it made him whenever one of her children took up the post. A.C. snapped his fingers toward the dog, who lazily ambled toward him for some attention as the two men spoke.

"Don't keep that wife of yours waiting too long," said the captain, "not in that big lonely house of yours, anyway."

"I told you, if you'd move in with us, like we asked, you'd both have more company," said A.C.

"Oh, I'm not much company these days," said the old man, as he shelled a peanut. "Can barely keep a conversation in my own head. Besides, I like being close to the shop. No one's here, I'm home. Someone shows up, I'm at work."

"Well, consider it a standing offer," said the son. "I know Julia would love to have you around."

"That's a good woman you got, son," said the captain. "Reminds me of your mother more and more all the time. You always made the right choices and marrying her was no exception. I'm proud of you as any father got a right to be."

Dr. Jackson put his arm on his father's shoulder.

"I believe you looked happier today than I've seen you any day since she's passed," he told him.

His father smiled and broke off eye contact to look straight ahead.

"That was a pretty sight, wasn't it?"

"It sure was," said A.C. as he continued to pet the hound. "Make you miss your old wild ways a little?"

His father laughed.

"Maybe just a touch. Those boys done good today, though. Heard they marched all the way up to the staging grounds cross town, gave them peckerwoods some hell."

His son smiled, happy to see the flicker of life in the old man's eyes.

"You should've gone with 'em," he teased.

His father laughed.

"Heh, heh. Nah, my wild days are done. I had me more than my share of giving white men hell, that's for sure. Never did me no good, neither. That's why I brought you up different. Taught you to prove it with this," he said, tapping his temple with his index finger, "instead of this," he added, shaking his opposite fist.

A.C. smiled.

"You did good, pops. Real good, not just as a dad. I'm proud of all you've done."

The old man waved off his son's comment.

"All I done?" he said with a good-natured chuckle as he shook his head slowly.

"I ever tell you about what finally drove me from Memphis?" he asked.

"The Irish?"

"Nah, they drove us from the police force, that's true. We was only on it because we stayed when the yellow fever broke out, and there were no white officers left. The Irish had been told they was beneath niggers for years, but I guess after being kicked around for so long, they finally lost their accents and, well, they can blend in a bit better than us."

The old man seemed to stare off far beyond anything in their line of sight, pausing for a moment before continuing.

"So, they gave them the police forces, and they were happy to take them. Kick the Black man around because there was finally someone to look down on. Ain't it funny how that happens?"

"What's that?" asked his son.

Captain Jackson looked him in the eyes.

"One group's at the bottom with nothing. They get treated like dogs by those at the top who got everything. Then they climb up, just a little bit, and who do they hate the most? Is it the ones at the top who'd kept them down? Nope. It's the other poor fools they just passed."

A.C. shook his head and returned to petting the dog.

"I never thought of it that way," he said.

His father let out a sigh.

"When you get old, everything slows down, I suppose. You see some things you missed when they was moving faster. I used to hate those Irish sons of bitches with every bone in my body. Not no more. They just wanted something for their own like we did. Being hated brings out the worst in people, so far as I've seen."

A.C. loved these rare moments when his otherwise quiet-mannered father opened up a bit, and he always tried to keep the conversation going when it occurred.

"That's when you and mom came to Guthrie, right?" he asked.

"Nope, I stuck around for a while. Thought I'd show 'em that they could take my badge, but they couldn't *win*. One day, I don't know what came over me, but I had a head full of steam and I just walked myself into a white store on Beale Street, picked up a cigar, and put it on the counter."

A.C.'s eyes widened.

"You didn't!"

The captain laughed.

"God as my witness, I surely did. That clerk knew who I was. He's standing there dumbstruck, so I just throw a coin on the counter, say, keep the change, I pick up a pack of matches and light it."

"No way," said A.C.

His father raised his right hand.

"Hand to god," he said with a laugh.

A.C. slapped his father's leg.

"There was three or four white men in the shop with they mouths hanging down 'bout to the floor," the captain continued, "and I just walk out onto Beale and smoke my cigar, walking right down the middle of the street."

"What happened?" asked A.C.

"Damned near got myself lynched is what happened," his father replied. "Got word that a mob was forming to come and hang me from a tree."

His son's expression became more serious.

"Were you scared?"

His father shook his head.

"I felt one thing, son, you know what that was?" he asked.

"What?"

"Shame. Not fear, not anger, not even resentment. Just plain old shame."

"What for?" asked A.C., puzzled.

His father put his giant hand on his son's arm.

"That I'd put the woman I loved in danger and done it for something so foolish."

"What'd you do?" asked A.C.

"I gathered your mother and as much stuff as we could carry and got us on the first train out. That is how I ended up a jailer in Guthrie."

A.C. shook his head.

"How have I never heard that story?"

"Like I said, it had been nothing but shame in my mind. Tried not to think of it. Wasn't 'til your momma passed on that I could laugh at my foolishness a little."

A.C. shook his head and smiled, and both men broke into a laugh before the old man again grew serious.

"But I've stood by a promise I made to myself way back then to never endanger the ones I love that way and to raise my children to know better," he said. "And they do."

His father smiled, and A.C. stood, leaned down and embraced the old man.

"Well, I better get home to Julia," he said as he stood back up. "You gonna head inside?"

His father stroked the hound, who'd nuzzled up against his leg as soon as A.C. had risen.

"I think I'll stay out here for a little while yet," he answered, opening the bag of peanuts. "I enjoy it out here at night. So does Rufus. This part of town is so quiet, and when the weather is as perfect as it is right now, it just makes me think about how good we got it here, what a special place you all made in this town."

Dr. Jackson put his hand on his father's shoulder.

"I love you, pop."

The old man smiled.

"I love you too, son."

"Don't let him fall asleep on that chair, Rufus," A.C. said to the dog.

His father laughed.

"He's no help there. Many a night I've dozed off and didn't wake until I heard roosters crowin'. It don't do me no harm. The fresh air's good for my health."

"Goodnight then," his son said, patting his shoulder.

"Goodnight, son. And kiss that pretty wife of yours for me."

Dr. Jackson turned back and gave him a thumbs-up as he descended the stairs of the porch. As he walked out of view, he could hear his father begin to whistle once more, the same tune as earlier, and it warmed him with a comfort that made him feel as though life had never been better than that particular moment.

As he continued down the street, Dr. A.C. Jackson took a moment to survey the neighborhood and consider all of the other old, tired, Black men like his father who were warm and safe inside of those homes and how little of such peace those men had surely known throughout there lives. Without thinking about it, he soon found himself whistling that very same tune, and it made his heart warmer still.

Chapter 6

The sky was still mostly dark and the roosters had just begun to crow when Aunt Damie poured coffee into two mugs at the breakfast table. It would be at least an hour before any of the boarders came down.

"You get any sleep last night?" she asked Dick, taking a seat beside him as she spooned some sugar into her cup.

"Some," said Dick. "You?"

Damie shook her head and sighed.

"Not a wink, child. Not a wink."

"If nothing happened through the night, it's all good, Aunt Damie," Dick told her, trying to sound more confident than had been the case.

"I still don't want you leaving this house today," she said with a wag of her index finger.

Dick shrugged and let out a groan.

"I'll lose my box if I don't go in!"

"You listen to me, Dick Rowland, Mr. Virgil is a businessman," said Damie, matching his volume and intensity. "He make a lot of money off your work, and he ain't about to say goodbye to it tomorrow because you stay home today. Now you just tell him you was sick."

"It ain't like that, Aunt Damie," said Dick. "He busy all the time. I get better tips than the other boys, but he still be shining shoes steady, if I'm there or not. Either way, he get his cut and that man like nothin' less than someone upsetting the order of things."

"And I'd like nothing more than keeping your skinny Black behind among the living!" said Damie.

Dick shook his head and thought for a moment.

"Look, I'll be a little late, so I can see if the police be waiting on me," he told her. "If Bump say no one been around, then there's nothing to worry about. If they was after me, they wouldn't be takin' they sweet time."

Damie regarded him sternly, shook her head, and took another sip of coffee.

"You make sure you got that calling card, the one Mr. Stradford gave you."

"Yes ma'am," said Dick, relieved.

****

Elliot and Hooker's Clothing Emporium was an upscale store where Greenwood's socialites shopped for their Sunday best. Its proprietor, Samuel Hooker, had started small but quickly realized that the wealth being created in Greenwood would create the same demand for fine clothing imported from exotic places that existed across the Frisco tracks.

Hooker was the sort of Black man who could easily navigate commerce with ambitious white wholesalers. He was genial and slightly deferential. They could tell he was neither a fool nor a sucker, yet he knew the limits of his leverage in any negotiations and played along nicely enough. The white men he dealt with might have described him among their own as a "good negro who was bright enough to know his place," never imagining how much pain and discipline had been invested in maintaining the facade that he was any less incensed by such social realities.

That morning, Sam was on the sidewalk giving direction to a worker who was painting the sign above his shop when Mickey Kemp, a salesman he bought much of his inventory from, pulled up in his motorcar and walked over to greet him. Like Sam, Mickey was a businessman above all else and remained pragmatic when it came to matters of commerce. The two men enjoyed a mutually beneficial relationship that was framed by polite conversation and forthright dealings with each other.

Sam felt as though he genuinely liked Mickey Kemp and, more importantly, that the feeling was reciprocated. Mickey always asked about his family and would often take a minute or two to play with Sam's kids when they were around. If he had to guess, he wouldn't have figured Mickey for a bigot. His work put him in front of a lot of people, both Black and white, and Sam had always felt as though whenever that was the case, all else being equal, the person would come away having learned that people have far more in common than they ever would have suspected. In fact, Sam often felt that because the most racist people seemed to have the least actual experience with those they supposedly hated, this sort of interracial commerce went a long way toward healing the historic riffs that still remained, a little more than half a century since slavery had been abolished.

"Mr. Kemp, how are we on this beautiful morn?" asked Sam, as he extended his hand for a shake.

"Samuel, if I were any better, there'd have to be two of me," said Mickey with a jovial laugh.

Sam smiled and wagged his finger at him.

"Wait right here," he said. "I want to show you something you're not going to believe."

Sam walked into the store and grabbed a blue dress that was hanging near the door. When he got back outside, he held the hanger with one hand and supported the garment from behind with the other, showing it off with a giant smile. Mickey's jaw dropped.

"Get out of town!" he said. "That's what you wanted the length of blue satin for?"

Sam smiled, beaming with pride.

"The misses plain insisted on making our oldest daughter's dress for prom tomorrow evening herself," he said.

"That's gorgeous, Samuel!" said Mickey, clearly floored by the craftsmanship. "She'll be the belle of the ball for sure."

"I just can't believe I've got one graduating high school already," sighed Sam. "They do grow up fast."

"Don't I know it?" Mickey sighed. "One more year and all three of mine will have struck out on their own."

Samuel's six-year-old daughter Olivia and his eight-year-old son Sammy Jr. emerged from the Hooker's house, which was attached to the store. They were carrying their school sacks. Olivia ran to her father and hugged him.

"As you can see, I've still got a while before that will be the case," Sam laughed.

"Hey, who are you, and what'd you do with little Sammy Jr.?" Mickey said to the boy, putting up his hands to play box with him.

The boy smiled from ear to ear as he punched Mickey's palms, which were held out as targets.

"And you?" said Mickey, turning to Olivia. "You must be the prettiest little girl in all of Greenwood. Come here and give your Uncle Mickey a hug."

Olivia hugged Mickey as he reached into his pants pocket and pulled out some candies wrapped in foil.

"How'd you two like a piece of candy for the walk to school—if your pops says it's alright, of course?"

He looked to Samuel, who smiled and nodded.

"Just don't tell your mother," Sam told his children with a smile, as they ran off toward the school. The two men smiled as they watched the children run down the street, then Mickey waved Samuel toward the back of his truck.

"Wait to you see what I got in the truck," he told him, pulling out a box from the back.

"Men's silk shirts, straight from the Orient," he said, pulling a white one from the box. "They shine like they got lights on 'em! Pricier than cotton, but..."

Sam stroked his chin.

"How much pricier?"

Mickey held up three fingers and Samuel cringed. Mickey put up his palm defensively.

"But the swells pay top dollar for 'em, so your margins are higher. Plus, they're a lower volume seller, so you only have to inventory a few of each in the popular sizes. And I got a good deal on some stiff white neck collars I can go half on to make it less painful."

Holding the shirt in one arm, Samuel inspected the collar Mickey produced in his other hand.

"Sure, bring them inside and we'll put a small section together in the front," he told him.

Mickey smiled.

"I love you, Samuel Hooker!"

****

Olivia and Sammy Jr. were unwrapping their candies as they walked to school.

"Uncle Mickey always gives us candy," said Olivia.

"I know," said Sammy. "I like him."

"Myra at school says that all white people hate Black people," his sister told him somewhat indifferently, "that they used to own us like dogs and beat us for not even doing anything wrong."

Sammy scoffed.

"Nuh-uh."

Olivia shrugged.

"That's what she says."

"She's stupid," said Sammy. "Every white man that comes and sees Daddy is nice. They shake hands and smile and give us stuff."

"I know," she said. "I told her, and she didn't believe it."

Sammy shook his head.

"She's a dummy."

****

Back at the shop, Samuel was counting out money to Mickey at the back of his truck.

"I've got a shipment of dresses coming in from London, should be here next week," said Mickey. "I'll come by and let you look at them when I do, check on how the shirts are selling."

"Sounds good, Mickey," said Sam.

"You take her easy, Samuel," said Mickey.

"You too, Mickey. Don't work too hard."

Mickey waved him off.

"Ah you know me, I'm like a shark. Keep moving or else I die."

"I hear you," said Sam, "but I try and remind myself to stop and smell the roses every now and then."

Mickey climbed into the cab of the truck and leaned out the window as he started off.

"I'll try and remember to do that," he told him with another smile. "Hey, give my best to the wife, and I hope your little girl has a great time at her prom. So long now, Samuel."

"So long," said Sam, watching him drive off before turning toward his store and admiring the fresh coat of paint on its sign.

****

The sun had risen high enough to light the room as John Williams and his son Bill ate breakfast at the kitchen table. When Loula entered, dressed to the nines, John's head snapped.

"Good Lord have mercy, woman!" he said, springing to his feet to fondle her. "Surely, I can't allow you to leave the house looking so good."

Their son rolled his eyes.

"Stop it, you," said Loula, smiling as she pushed him off. "You're gonna mess my outfit."

"I can't help it," said John, giving chase and smacking her bottom as she scurried away from him. "My baby is the prettiest! I might need her to go back into that room and put a potato sack on though. Can't be having other men drooling over my girl, now."

"Why you dressed so fancy, momma?" Bill asked.

"I gotta get to the bank this morning," Loula said. "They were closed yesterday for the holiday, and we did a lot of business at the theater and the candy shop, plus the normal Monday deposit."

"She going across the tracks, so she wanna turn it up a notch, show those uppity white women what a real queen looks like," said John with a chuckle.

260

Bill laughed as Loula shook her head, walking to the table to give her husband a kiss on the cheek. He quickly pulled her in and peppered her with kisses.

"John!" yelled Loula, trying not to laugh as she pulled away.

"Sorry, baby," he told her with a big smile. "You know I need a little sugar with my coffee."

Loula smiled and shook her head before turning her attention to Bill.

"You make sure you get over to the Stradford right after lunch period ends and help Miss Julia with the table decorations."

"She got it set up for us to all walk over together after third period," said Bill. "Mr. Stradford's gonna give us lunch when we get there."

Loula pointed her finger at Bill.

"And you make sure to thank him profusely for that *and* for lending out his hotel for prom. He and Augusta are really doing a nice thing for you all, and you best make sure none of your knucklehead classmates do anything to disrespect that man's property, or I will kick their behinds myself."

"Yes ma'am," said Bill.

John laughed.

"Your mother won't have to," he said. "JB will do it his own self. Sixty-years old or not, that is not a man to trifle with."

Bill shook his head and sighed.

"I know it. Mr. Stradford's nice and all, but he's scary too. I sure wouldn't wanna be on his bad side."

"No you wouldn't," agreed Loula. "Bye," she said, kissing her son on top of the head as she walked off.

****

Dick Rowland looked more than a little bit nervous as he walked down the street toward the tracks. His head was pointed down toward his feet, his flat cap pulled low, and his hands were in his pockets. He was hunched, almost shrinking himself in an effort to be less visible.

Deputy Barney Cleaver was sitting outside a cafe having coffee when he spotted the young man from a block away. He quickly ducked into the cafe and waited in the doorway, watching Dick get closer. When the boy was only a couple of feet away, Barney stepped out.

At first, Dick froze like a deer in headlights. For a moment, it looked like he would run. Barney put his hands out, palms down as he tried to appear as non-threatening as possible.

"Easy now," said the deputy. "Don't run off, son. I can tell you're thinking about it. I don't mean you no harm. We just need to talk."

Dick's face contorted as he tried to weigh his instincts against his better judgment. For a moment, it looked like he might break into tears over the mental juxtaposition, but Dick ultimately let his posture fall, throwing up his arms in an exaggerated shrug.

"I didn't do nothing wrong, Uncle Barney," he screamed. "I swear."

The kids who mostly managed to stay out of trouble always called him Uncle Barney. That's what he'd been teaching them to do since they were youngsters in the streets. Deputy Cleaver was something of a rare bird to his people in Greenwood. Most understood that it behooved the Blacks in town to have one of their own among the ranks at the sheriff's department, but it didn't stop others from calling him things like an "Uncle Tom," or a "house nigger." He was, after all, the man they usually sent to run in Blacks who had warrants, if only because he knew who everyone was and where to find them. In that sense, it could be accomplished with much less fanfare and potential for things to go sideways than if a cadre of white deputies were to roll into Greenwood looking for someone based on a description or a nickname. Still, some of his people looked at it no differently than as if he'd taken up as a soldier on the side of an occupying force. Those with young kids, however, usually appreciated that there was someone like Uncle Barney out there mediating these kinds of events, and Dick had been raised by Damie to respect and listen to Deputy Cleaver.

"And I believe you, Dick," said Barney.

Dick's eyes began to fill.

"You gonna run me in?" he asked, his voice cracking.

"I just need to talk to you for a minute," said Barney, both men still tense and in wide stances that suggested they weren't sure what was coming next. "You know what about?"

A tear fell down Dick's cheek and he relaxed his stance.

"The girl from the Drexel?" he asked.

"That's right," said Barney, palms pushing toward the ground, as his own posture softened.

"I didn't do nothin'," pleaded Dick. "I just slipped. I swear it."

"Okay," said Barney, "that's what I thought. But listen, there's a detective from the Tulsa PD looking for you, and I think it'd be way better if you come down to the sheriff's office, and we have him meet us there. Otherwise, he's gonna run you into the Tulsa station, and I can't make any promises as to how they might handle the situation. Get me?"

Dick, scared and confused, put his hands on his face and rolled his neck, as he contemplated what Barney had said.

"It's okay, Dick," Barney told him. "We just gonna talk to him. Sheriff McCullough's a good man, and he gave me his word he won't let nothing bad happen to you."

Dick nodded, his eyes closed tightly to stop the tears from falling.

"Okay," he finally said. "I'll go."

"Good," said Barney, taking some steps toward him and putting his hand on Dick's shoulder when he got close. "That's good, Dick."

****

Hattie Carter was trying on her white prom gown in front of a tall mirror, while her mother sat by, pinning it in place. The girl beamed as she turned to both sides, looking at the back of the gown.

Her mom swelled with pride. Marveling at her daughter's transition from girl to mother, she couldn't help but think that soon it would be a wedding gown gracing her form.

"Now I still gotta take just a little in right here," said Mrs. Carter, tugging at the sides of the gown that rose up under her daughter's arms. "But I can do that today, while you're at school. I just wanted to make sure I'd gotten the length right."

"Oh, momma it's beautiful," beamed Hattie, continuing to admire the way she looked in the dress. "Bill is gonna love it too. Thank you so much!"

"I just can't believe my baby's all grown," said Mrs. Carter, looking warmly at her daughter, as she cupped her cheeks, before taking her hands. Just then, Hattie's father walked into the room. Stopping dead in his tracks upon seeing his daughter, he smiled ear to ear.

"Well, lookie here," Mr. Carter said. "That just can't be the same little, fuzzy-headed girl that used to bounce on my knee."

As he closed the distance between them, Hattie gave him a hug.

"You look beautiful, darling," he told her.

"Thank you, Daddy," she said, still radiating.

"Now you better go on up and put your school clothes on," her mother interjected. "You late, they liable to not let you go."

"Yes, Momma," said Hattie, taking one more look at herself in the mirror before running up the stairs.

"I guess the next one'll be a wedding dress?" said Mrs. Carter, once they'd finished watching her ascend the steps. Hattie's father leaned in and kissed his wife on the cheek.

"Bite your tongue," he laughed. "Let me get used to her dating before you go talking about weddings."

****

Otto Gurley was reading the Tulsa Star in the lobby of his hotel, while Cecil busied himself behind the desk.

"Front-page news, Cecil," Gurley told him, holding up the paper. "Crisis avoided and a happy ending, to boot. Of course, Smitherman had to go on and on grandstanding about the daring adventure across the tracks, but all is well that ends well, I suppose."

"Dat's what they say, Mr. Gurley," said Cecil in his usual agreeable tone.

"They do indeed," said Gurley. "Let's hope those rabble-rousers got most of that spunk out of their system, anyway. I keep thinking old JB will eventually start acting his age, but one can only hope, I suppose."

Just then, Buck Franklin walked down the stairs and into the lobby.

"Good morning, Mr. Gurley," said Buck. "Heck of a parade you through yesterday. That was really a sight to see and quite a surprise."

"Oh, I try to put a little bit of sugar on top whenever the opportunity arises," said Gurley with a smile. "How are things going over at the firm? Keeping you busy?"

"Oh yes, sir," said Buck. "Mr. Spears and Mr. Chappelle got steady work, caseload bigger than I've ever seen—wills, trusts, real estate contracts. Plenty to keep me busy for some time."

"Glad to hear it," said Gurley. "They say idle hands are the devil's playthings."

"Indeed," said Buck. "I best be off. Good day to you as well, Cecil."

"So long, Mr. Franklin," said Cecil. "I'll see you later."

Buck tipped his hat as he exited.

"I'm not sure of what to make of that one yet, Cecil," said Gurley. "He presents himself as a reasonable man in every way, but I still feel as though I might be underestimating his radical side. Sure does seem to get on well with Stradford and Smitherman."

"I think he alright, Mr. Gurley," said Cecil. "He seem like he just one them type o' men get along good with everybody."

"Perhaps you're right, my boy," said Gurley, twirling his mustache. "Let's hope so, anyway. We have a delicate balance right now, and a man like that just might tip the scales."

****

Like most mornings, Kelly Ann O'Dell and Kathleen Brown were talking next to their lockers before the bell rang to start class.

"I can't believe she's letting me miss the ceremony, but thank god, they're so long and so boring," said Kelly Ann.

"You're so lucky," said Kathleen. "Johnny is the cutest! What are you going to see?"

"The Four Horsemen of the Apocalypse at the Majestic."

Kathleen's eyes bulged.

"Your parents are letting you see that?"

"Well, with all of the warnings about going with a boy, I don't think they thought to ask what the picture was."

"Won't they see it on the marquee when they drop you off?"

Kelly Ann shrugged.

"By then it'll be too late."

Kathleen laughed.

"You're the worst!"

Kelly Ann smirked.

"Besides, I hear there's this actor in it, Rudolph Valentino, who is the bee's knees!"

"I wish someone was taking me to a picture show," said Kathleen.

"There's always Elmer Porter," Kelly Ann said with a sarcastic smile.

Kathleen rolled her eyes.

"Oh, please, that hoodlum? He makes me want to upchuck."

Both girls giggled as the bell sounded.

****

At the sheriff's office, Dick was sitting across the desk from Sheriff McCullough, who was flanked by Deputy Cleaver and Deputy Evers.

"And that's it, sheriff," Dick said, repeating his account of the events from the day before. "I kept running until I got to my Auntie's house. I swear, that's how it all happened."

The sheriff nodded.

"Alright, I got no reason to suspect otherwise. The girl's story was sketchy, and it sounds like the clerk could have made a reasonable assumption, even if it turned out to be untrue."

"I won't get in no trouble?" asked Dick.

"I can't say for certain," the sheriff admitted with a shrug. "This isn't my jurisdiction. It's Tulsa PD's, and their detective is still gonna need to talk to you, son. You just tell him what you told me, though, and I think it'll all work out."

The fact that Dick was beyond panicked was written all over his face.

"You think?" he asked the sheriff.

"I got no reason not to," said McCullough, more confident this time. "Listen, you got someone you wanna call, let 'em know you're here?"

"Yes, sir. Please."

The sheriff stood.

"Deputy Evers, take Dick up to the front and let him make a call to his people. After he gets a hold of them, give it ten minutes and call over to Detective Morris. Let him know we brought someone in."

"Will do, sheriff," said the deputy. "This way."

"You believe him, sheriff?" Barney asked once Dick and Deputy Evers were out of the room.

"Yes, I believe I do, Barney," said the sheriff with a nod. "You?"

"I surely do, sheriff," said the deputy. "Known that boy for a long while, his auntie too. He just ain't got it in him. Besides, he's too scared right now not to blurt it out and beg for mercy if he had."

The sheriff nodded again.

"Yep, let's hope our friends in blue are equally convinced, though."

****

In the lobby of the Exchange National Bank, Loula Williams was glancing impatiently between the "Colored Line" and the clock on the wall. She noticed two white women in the other line ogling her, as they whispered comments to each other and snickered. Loula, dressed regally in a fine hat, a conservative dress, a boa-style scarf, and plenty of jewelry, took a deep breath, stood up straighter, and looked forward, smiling as she struggled to project the illusion that they hadn't made her uncomfortable.

"I swear," the pale blonde woman said loud enough to ensure Loula would hear, "have you ever seen a tackier outfit?"

"Where would someone even get such a thing?" sneered the other, a middle-aged redhead.

Loula looked over at the two women and smiled.

"Elliot & Hooker's Clothing Emporium in deep Greenwood, ma'am," she told them politely. "Mr. Elliot gets much of his wares from New York and Paris, so I imagine the styles might be unfamiliar to *some*, even if they're all the rage in the big cities of the world."

The women kept talking as if Loula hadn't spoken.

"They should just drop the Elliot," laughed the redhead. "It certainly would be more clear as to who their clothes are for."

The women giggled, and Loula turned back toward the front, clenching her teeth tightly.

"Can you even imagine ever leaving your house looking like that?" said the blonde woman.

"Gives a whole new meaning to *Coco* Chanel," laughed the red head.

The last woman in front of Loula, a Black woman in a maid's uniform, finished her transaction. As she turned to leave, she gave Loula a sympathetic look, touching her arm as she passed.

"You look beautiful, ma'am," said the housemaid.

Loula gave the woman a closed-mouth smile, tugged her sleeve to stop her, and leaned in so she could whisper.

"Watch this."

Loula put her purse on the teller's counter and looked over at the two women who were now at the front of their line. The blonde was opening her pocketbook.

"You should go sometime," Loula said loudly, looking over toward her as she took thick stacks of cash out of her purse, pausing as she set each one down on the counter. "You see over in Greenwood, we don't discriminate," she added, as another stack fell from her hand. "Anyone who can afford to shop at Mr. Elliot's is welcome," she said, slowly dropping yet another stack of bills. "Word to the wise, though?" she added, dropping a final stack. "Their prices are rather dear."

Loula smiled at the housemaid whose mouth was wide open, joy in her eyes. She looked back to the two white women while the teller was giving her a deposit receipt, then sauntered passed them with her nose high in the air. Tilting her head toward the ceiling, she sniffed around, then looked back to the women with a displeased squint, her nose scrunched.

"He sells a wide array of perfumes as well, in case you're interested."

Every eye in the place was fixed on Loula as she slowly walked out, proud as a peacock. As she got into her sedan and closed the door, however, she immediately put her head to the steering wheel and began to cry. After just a few moments, she squeezed the wheel tight with both hands, threw up her head, and screamed in a futile attempt to expel the all-too familiar humiliation she felt deep down inside of her being.

****

JB Stradford was on the telephone in the lobby of his hotel. It was clear that the person on the other end of the line was excited, his voice ringing out loudly enough for others to hear.

"Now calm down, son," said JB. "I told you, we're not going to let anything happen. You just sit tight and don't talk to no one else until we get there, okay?"

"But they're bringing some detective from the city police over," said Dick on the other end of the line.

"I understand," JB said, "but you don't have to say another word without an attorney present, no matter what they say. That's the law. Now let me hang up, so I can get over there right quick."

Stradford hung up the phone, slamming the desk with his hand, before starting off quickly toward the door.

****

The sheriff was sitting at his desk, again flanked by Deputy Evers and Deputy Cleaver. This time it was Detective Morris and Chief Gustafson sitting across from them.

"So, where's he at?" asked Detective Morris.

"One of the deputies has him in the back," said the sheriff. "His lawyers are on their way over. He asked to have them present."

"He asked for an attorney?" shrugged Morris, rolling his eyes as he glanced to the chief.

"Like I said, they're on their way," said the sheriff.

"They? Oh it's a team of legal geniuses, is it?" quipped Morris.

"He asks for his attorneys to be present during questioning, he gets it," said the sheriff. "That's the law."

"Cripes, Bill," said Gustafson, "why didn't you just bring him to the station in the first place?"

The sheriff stiffened his posture.

"Because I didn't know we had the right guy until we talked to him. Besides, he'd have told you the same thing he told us, that is unless you've got different... *methods* when it comes to interrogation?"

Gustafson sighed and rolled his eyes. Detective Morris looked to Barney.

"And what do you know about this kid, deputy?"

"Good kid, detective," said Barney. "Used to be a football player at Booker T, halfback, pretty good too. Quit school a few years back to go to work as a shine boy, though. He lives with an elderly aunt who has a little boarding house and sundry over on the north side. Walks her everywhere she goes, takes real good care of her."

"He ever get in any trouble?" asked Morris.

"Not one bit, detective," said Barney. "He keeps his nose clean. Might mess around down on 1st Street once and awhile, but just normal kid's stuff."

Morris nodded, "Kid's stuff, eh?"

Deputy Shoemaker poked his head in.

"Sorry to interrupt, sheriff, but the Rowland kid's people are here."

"Excuse me," said the sheriff, as he stood and left the room.

Aunt Damie was standing in the lobby with tears in her eyes—Stradford, Buck Franklin, Andrew Smitherman, and Isaiah Spears behind her—when the sheriff walked in with Deputy Shoemaker.

"Alright, folks, I'm Sheriff William McCullough. Now I talked to Dick earlier, and I think maybe this is just a misunderstanding, but it's not my jurisdiction. It's Tulsa PD's, and they wanna question him. One of you a lawyer?"

JB chuckled.

"Everyone of us is, sheriff," he told him. "Well, accepting Miss Damie here, of course," he said, patting her on the shoulder. "She's Dick's auntie. Raised him as her own."

The sheriff was clearly surprised. He tipped his hat to Damie.

"Well, how about one of you go back as his lawyer of record then?" he said.

Stradford looked around.

"What d'ya say you let me get this one, fellas?"

Smitherman and Buck grinned. Isaiah nodded. JB may have had the least overall experience of any of the men when it came to actual barrister work, but his knowledge of the law was almost as mythical as his ability to debate men of high intellect. They knew he was better equipped for this sort of encounter than anyone else in the room, especially when you factored in his still intimidating physical presence.

In the holding room, Dick sat at a desk across from Detective Morris. Stradford took a seat next to him, while Gustafson and the sheriff stood against the back wall behind Morris.

"Your name is Dick Rowland?" asked the detective, holding a pencil above a yellow legal pad.

"Yes, sir," said Dick, trying desperately not to appear as nervous as he felt.

"That short for Richard?" asked Morris.

"No, sir," Dick told him. "Just Dick Rowland."

"Your friends down at the shine stand gave your name as Diamond Dick," said Morris. "What in the hell is a diamond dick?" he asked, looking toward Dick's waist.

Stradford rolled his eyes.

"No," said Dick. "Diamond Dick. Like *diamond*," he said, pointing to his finger, "and *Dick*," he added, pointing back at his own chest.

In the lobby, Detective Cleaver was standing with Buck and Smitherman, while Isaiah comforted Miss Damie on nearby chairs.

"The sheriff may well be all that," said Smitherman, "and he's certainly an improvement over the last bozo that held this office. But with all due respect, Barney, the city police have the numbers and the jurisdiction, and I know for a fact they got Klansmen on that force, and not just a few bad apples, either."

"Andrew, I can appreciate your concern," said Barney, "but this thing is gonna happen right. I promise."

"What do you know about this Morris character?" Buck asked Barney.

"Worst kind of white man, best I can tell," said the deputy. "Gustafson is no better. But like I said, Sheriff McCullough ain't gonna let there be no vigilante justice. You can take that to the bank."

Seated nearby, Isaiah offered Aunt Damie his handkerchief to dab the tears, which continued to well in her eyes and fall down her cheeks.

"I'm not really his aunt, you know?" Damie told him. "Not by blood."

"No?" said Isaiah.

Damie shook her head, still looking down.

"More like a mother than anything. I used to live up in Vinita, had a little sundry wasn't no bigger than this here lobby. My husband killed hisself sharecropping bad land that didn't wanna give up no food. I got by canning fruit and vegetables, sellin' 'em during the winter months—*barely*, but I got by."

She looked up at Isaiah and smiled before continuing.

"One day, this scrawny little boy, maybe four years old, wanders up onto my porch looking like he about to fall over. Gaunt, belly sticking out, eyes looking but not really seeing. He just say, *I hungry*. Now I tell you, I ain't never seen nothin' so sad in all my life. Took that boy inside, fed him up, and after a bit, he came to life. Told me about how he'd been living in the streets with his sister, but didn't know where she was. That boy been with me ever since. Name was Jimmy Jones, he said. But told me after a bit that he wanted my name, wanted to be a Rowland. So I says, okay, you can be Jimmy Rowland, and he said no, Dick, Dick Rowland. Don't know where he got the idea, truth be told."

Isaiah put his hand on top of the old woman's. It was small, shriveled, cold, and veiny.

"He's lucky to have you, Miss Damie."

Damie looked back up to him and smiled warmly.

"Him? Other way around, I tell you. I never had no children of my own, Mr. Spears. My husband and I prayed on it, but the Lord didn't see it fit, I suppose. That made me sad for a long time, all the way until that little hungry, homeless boy showed up on my porch, and I finally realized why God had never given me a baby. The lord sent Dick to me 'cause he knew that boy needed a whole lot a caring for, and he knew I had all my momma love stored up," she said, breaking into sobs as the tears rolled back down her face, this time with much greater volume.

Isaiah embraced Aunt Damie in a hug and patted her back. She put her face in the handkerchief he'd given her and began to let go of a hard, muffled cry.

"And that's all that happened?" Detective Morris asked when Dick again finished telling what had transpired at the Drexel building.

"I swear it," said Dick, right hand raised.

"Just one thing that don't figure," said Morris. "If you didn't do anything wrong, why'd you run?"

To this, Stradford slammed his giant palms on the table and then put both of his hands in the air.

"As I live and breath, detective, did you seriously just ask my client, a Black man, why—in Tulsa, Oklahoma of all places—he feared that a simple misunderstanding of that nature could prove less than *simple*, and perhaps even fatal?"

Detective Morris remained unfazed.

"I'm just saying that nine out of ten times, a suspect runs?"

"A Black suspect?" asked JB.

"Any suspect," said Morris, speaking much more sternly now.

JB gave him a wry smile.

"That would presume there's no difference?"

Morris shrugged.

"If he's innocent then-"

"Are you trying to assert that an innocent Black man has nothing to fear in this town, or that his situation under such circumstances doesn't drastically differ from a white man's?" JB asked in a voice that neared a scream. "A *white man*—of the professional class, no less—accuses him of assaulting a *white* woman, he attempts to explain that the man simply mistook what he saw for something that it wasn't, and that man's response is to call him a liar and yell for someone to call the police? He's supposed to assume in that moment of duress that the prudent thing to do is stand his ground and explain himself further to other such white men?"

Morris sneered.

"Look, pal-"

Stradford shot to his feet.

"Pal? I'm not your pal, detective. My name is JB Stradford, and I'd appreciate it if you would address me with

282

the same courtesy I've shown you, sir. Now anything you have on my client is circumstantial at best and outweighed by the lack of corroboration from the very person the crime was supposed to have been perpetrated upon. So what exactly are we doing here?"

Morris sat silently, waiting for Stradford to come to his senses and sit back down. When that didn't happen, he continued calmly, as to ensure him he hadn't been rattled by the theatrics.

"Your client is accused of attempted rape, Mr. Stradford. We got an eyewitness to the incident who says he saw him clearly mauling her in a sexual manner, a witness who will testify that he tried to stop him and that your client ran. Her dress was torn, had red marks on her neck. I'm not sure a jury would be so sympathetic."

JB took his seat but leaned in toward the detective, elbows on the table, before answering.

"Only the girl hasn't accused him of anything. In fact, it sounded to me like her story came far closer to corroborating *my* client's statement than the witness's."

"The girl was shaken up," said Morris, a bit of grit in his voice now. "We don't feel as though we've gotten a complete statement from her yet, so, as it stands, we've got the witness and the flight."

"Then you have nothing, detective," said JB.

The sheriff took a step forward, putting his hands up in a defensive manner before speaking.

"Alright, gentlemen, let's calm down," said McCullough. "Detective, you might well have just barely enough to charge him, but you ain't got any kind of real case without the girl. Everyone in this room knows that. Way I see it, we either hold him under those charges until she gives a full and complete statement, which by this point she should be more than capable of doing, or you cut him loose. We know where to find him if things change."

The detective shook his head as he tapped his notepad with the back of his pencil.

"We cut him loose, and he's on a train," said Morris. "We're booking him. Take him over to the station."

Dick put his head in his hands. Stradford waved off the suggestion and sighed toward the sheriff's direction.

"No," said McCullough, looking toward Chief Gustafson. "He stays."

Stradford looked at the sheriff, as surprised as the chief and his detective looked to be.

"What the hell you talking about?" asked Morris. "It's a Tulsa PD arrest. He gets processed down the street."

The sheriff, arms folded, shook his head.

"This is too sensitive of an issue to take the threat to the prisoner's safety that lightly. I'm in charge of prisoners in this county, detective, *all* prisoners, and you can process him here, and we will hold him here until if and when there's a trial. Take it or leave it."

Morris looked back to his boss.

"You gonna let him do this?"

"He doesn't have a choice in the matter," McCullough said sternly, again looking to Gustafson, who glared at him for a moment before answering.

"He's right," the chief finally said, looking to Morris. "But fuck it, that makes it his problem instead of ours."

The chief started toward the door but looked back to the sheriff before he left the room.

"And you'll have your hands full on this one, Bill. You had better believe that."

****

Loula fumed, as she sat in the office of John's shop, where he was sitting on his desk wiping dry his hands, while she paced, still infuriated from what had transpired at the bank that morning. John, however, was laughing, though a bit nervously, after he heard her recount the events.

"Loula Williams you did what?" he asked with a big smile, as he shook his head, far from surprised by his wife's exploits.

"Oh, I couldn't help it, John. It was all I could do to not slap those two peckerwood women right across they chubby pink faces!"

"Now no good is gonna come of that, baby girl," he said, more seriously this time.

Loula just threw her hands up in the air and continued pacing.

"I know, I know, I know," she sighed. "I was just so mad! John, if you could have seen these bitches' faces, just filled with resentment, looking down on me like I made as much sense as a gorilla stuffed into a tuxedo."

Her husband stood, put himself in front of her, and placed his hands on his wife's shoulders.

"Baby, you got it all wrong. They wasn't looking down. They was looking *up* at you, and that's what they hated. If you were white, they'd have just admired you and thought about how nice it'd be if they could look like that."

"But because I'm not, because I'm Black, they gotta make me feel like I'm... I'm *sub-human*?"

John drew her in, holding her in his arms as he rubbed her back.

"Baby, they just don't know better. You said they was dressed kind of plain, right?"

"Yeah, so?" she asked.

"So, they prolly wasn't as well off as us," he told her. "They got poor people on the other side of them tracks too, plenty of 'em. Them other guys I worked at the dairy with wasn't rolling in jack. Some of them didn't have a pot to piss in or a window to throw it out of."

John laughed, which finally elicited a smile from his wife.

"So that gives them the right to-"

He put up his hands, waving off the thought.

"Nah, it don't give them no right. I'm just saying they got problems too, and when they down, they tell themselves, well at least I'm not no nigger, 'cause that's all they got, and it's all they ever been told. So, when they see a beautiful Black queen of a woman come in looking all cosmopolitan in her fine clothes, they're not gonna think, *oh look, she's better than we thought, after all, let's be nice to her.* They gonna try and tear her down."

John reached down and lifted Loula's chin with his finger and thumb.

"But they can't touch my baby," he said, "because she's on a higher plane, way up above all that noise."

He gave her two soft kisses on her forehead. Loula pouted.

"I just wanted to scream, baby."

John gave her a devilish grin.

287

"Then maybe my baby needs to let out those screams?"

Loula gave her husband a coy smile.

"Where's Horace at?"

"Lunch," said John, softly.

Loula sauntered toward the door, her heels clacking on the vinyl tiles of his office flooring. Taking the doorknob in her hand, she looked back at John.

"Those hands clean?" she asked, a lustful look in her eyes.

"Yes ma'am."

Loula slammed the door shut and began to disrobe.

****

Detective Morris was at a payphone on a city street, looking around to make sure no one was listening as he spoke.

"Yeah, it's me," he said into the receiver. "We just booked him."

In his office at the Tulsa Tribune, Richard Lloyd Jones tightened his grip on the receiver, a giant grin spreading over his face.

****

Sarah Page was sitting across from Ed Kline at the small table in her efficiency, smoking a cigarette. Her posture was unmistakably hostile.

"Look, darling," said Ed, "I'm just trying to look out for you is all."

Sarah snickered and puffed her cigarette.

"Put a cork in it, Ed. You're looking out for yourself, no one else."

"I'm not talking about that," said Ed. "I know you didn't tell 'em about us, but Detective Morris wants this guy. He sort of hinted that he thought you may have been, you know, *familiar* with him. If you just tell him that the shine boy grabbed you, he'll leave you alone."

"And if I don't?" she asked, stubbing out the butt in an old cracked ashtray that sat on the table.

"What gives?" asked Ed. "You weren't... you know?"

"Jesus Christ, Ed," she sighed, "what the hell is it with all you guys and that? For the love of Christ, no, I wasn't screwing the colored boy."

Ed shrugged.

"I'm not-"

"Look, I was in a pissy mood because of you know who," she said, leering at him. "That kid tripped when the elevator jerked, fell into me, and I socked him. I didn't even

289

realize what had happened, but the boy was scared as hell, and that clerk didn't help none. I told all of them the same thing. That detective can go screw himself, so far as I'm concerned."

Ed sat silently for a moment, tapping the table while Sarah took a big drag from her cigarette.

"I just don't see why you don't tell him what he wants to hear is all," he finally said. "It's just some darkie that's probably up to no good half the time anyway. A stint in the can might do him good, straighten him out before he does get bold enough to attack some white girl."

"I already told everybody the same thing," Sarah yelled. "I ain't gonna change my story now and wind up getting my own self in trouble on that asshole detective's account."

Ed sighed and shrugged his arms.

"Well, I'm sure he's gonna wanna talk to you again, Sarah. Tell him whatever you want, but a word to the wise, Morris isn't a guy you want looking to give you a hard time."

Sarah leaned across the table toward him, an icy look in her eyes.

"He ain't gonna though, is he, Ed?" she asked coldly. "You're gonna see to that. I keep my mouth shut, you get him to scram and leave me the hell alone."

Ed stood up to leave.

"I'll do everything I can, Sarah, you know that. But he's chief detective. I'm just a patrolman."

Sarah lit another cigarette and spoke calmly.

"Then I suppose you better pucker up and kiss his ass real good then, Eddie boy."

****

Over at the Tulsa Tribune, the newsroom was humming with activity, when Richard came bursting through the door from his office.

"Hold the press," he screamed. "Hold the press!"

The entire newsroom stopped what they were doing, turning to their boss.

"I have always wanted to utter those sweet words," Richard said, "and I finally have good cause. We're not leading with that beauty pageant story, gentlemen. We got a real bombshell. Tucker, get that dummy sheet into my office. Miss Comstock get us some coffee, please. We got work to do and not much time to do it.

****

With Morris and Gustafson having left, the sheriff remained in the front lobby of his office with Smitherman, Stradford, Buck, Aunt Damie and Isaiah.

"Another thing you all might want to consider?" he said.

"What's that?" asked Smitherman.

"I'd think about getting him a lawyer from over this side of town."

Smitherman arched an eyebrow.

"A *white* lawyer, you mean?"

"Yep," said McCullough flatly. "No offense or anything, but you're gonna want someone who knows the judges and the folks in the DA's office."

"Because they'll have our boy's best interest at heart, sheriff?" asked Smitherman.

"Because there's not much of a case here, and the right attorney will likely be able to get it tossed before it ever goes to trial," said the sheriff. "You start making it a Blacks versus whites thing? Well, it could take on a different gravity, so to speak."

"I hardly think one can say we'd be the ones making it a case of Blacks versus whites, sheriff," said Isaiah.

Aunt Damie looked around at the group.

"I don't know," she said. "I feel much more comfortable with you all."

Stradford put a hand on her shoulder and shook his head.

"No," said JB, "he's right."

Smitherman looked at him, somewhat surprised.

"We won't let them go and railroad Dick or nothing like that," JB said. "You have my word, Miss Damie. But the sheriff has a valid point. You should've seen the look on that detective's face when I gave him an earful. Didn't matter that I was in the right. It became about every colored man he never liked, rather than about Dick, and we don't want that. It goes to trial, we can think it over again, but we'd be better off with someone who knew the right way, politically speaking, to navigate this part here. And don't worry none about cost. I'll cover everything."

"I sure do appreciate all your help," Damie said, "the rest of y'all too."

Stradford looked to the sheriff as he answered her.

"We just looking out for our people is all," he said. "That's how we do, sheriff."

The sheriff tipped his hat.

Chapter 7

At the Tulsa Tribune, Chip Bennett was sitting at Tucker Johnson's desk while his boss stood over other reporters who were working to reassemble the dummy sheet.

"I didn't know what else to write," said Chip. "We don't even have a police report, let alone first-hand witnesses. He's getting everything from an unnamed source? It's basically, *a Black kid was reported to have been arrested by an unnamed source who claimed other people had seen him attack someone, possibly a female elevator operator.* He didn't even want me to call the station."

Tucker nodded.

"That means he got it *from* the station. He pays good money for tip-offs, probably got it from the arresting officers."

Chip stared blankly for a moment, then spoke.

"Well, we never would have run it with so little-"

Richard barged out of his nearby office.

"Get ready to move those sheets, Tucker," he said, sporting a devilish grin.

With every eye in the room cast upon the boss, Richard put on his reading glasses. He looked up to ensure he had the room's full attention, then held forth a sheet of paper, cleared his throat, and began to read.

"Police Nab Negro for Attacking Girl in Elevator," he said, reading the title and then looking around the room for affirmation. "A negro delivery boy who gave his name to the public as Diamond Dick, but who has been identified as Dick Rowland, was arrested on South Greenwood Avenue this morning and charged with attempting to assault the 17-year-old white elevator girl in the Drexel building early yesterday. The girl said she noticed the negro a few minutes before the attempted assault. He had been looking up and down the hallway on the third floor of the Drexel building as if to see if there was anyone in sight, but she thought nothing of it at the time. A few minutes later he entered the elevator, she told police, and attacked her, scratching her hands and face and tearing her clothes. Her screams brought a clerk from Renberg's department store to her assistance and the negro fled. He was captured and identified this morning both by the girl and the clerk, police say. Tenants of the Drexel building said the girl is an orphan who works as an elevator operator to pay her way through business college."

Chip's jaw was nearly dragging on the floor when Richard smiled and nodded toward him proudly, before hustling over to the dummy sheet to show Tucker where its placement should be.

"Now, if y'all will excuse me," said Richard, "I'll obviously have to prepare an editorial as well. Leave that block right below it open, Tucker."

Richard headed back toward his office.

"That does not even remotely resemble what I wrote," Chip screamed at Tucker once Richard's door had closed. "I don't want my name on the byline."

Tucker shrugged with a look that seemed designed to garner sympathy for his own predicament, though none was to be had.

"There's no byline on it," he finally answered. "I'll leave it like that."

Chip shook his head and exhaled forcefully in disgust.

****

Dick was playing gin rummy with Deputy Evers at a small table that the deputy had pushed up against the cell, allowing Dick to play through the bars.

"Get outta here," said Evers. "No way Jack Johnson could'a beat Dempsey. Look what Dempsey did to Willard, and Big Jess creamed Johnson."

Dick waved him off.

"Man, everybody know Johnson threw that fight 'cause he was in trouble with the law. Besides, Willard was a old man when Dempsey walloped him. I saw it on the newsreel at the Dreamland. All big and slow."

Dick stood up, comically pantomiming the lumbering heavyweight.

"You're crazy," said Deputy Evers. "You should'a seen it when he knocked out Billy Miske. Brutal."

Dick waved him off once more.

"Man, who Billy Miske? He won't fight no Harry Wills. You ever see Harry Wills? Now that cat can scrap."

"Uh uh," said Evers with a shake of his head.

"See, they ain't be puttin' no Harry Wills on the newsreels at the Majestic, I expect," said Dick. "Negro Heavyweight Champ of the World, right there. Dempsey be ducking him like a wild left hook. Instead, he gonna fight that little Frenchman, Carpenter or whatever his name is."

Deputy Evers knocked on the table.

"That's gonna do it."

"Man, I hate rummy," said Dick. "What else you know? You play blackjack?"

"Sure," said the deputy. "I'll deal."

****

Chip, Tucker, and Gary Kale stood over the dummy sheet at Tucker's desk, each looking at the editorial their boss had sent to Tucker, via Miss Comstock.

"Is this a frigging joke?" asked Gary.

297

"Mob to Lynch Negro Tonight?" read Chip. "That's not a headline *or* an opinion, Tucker. That's a goddamn directive."

"An uppity negro, and Little Africa has plenty, is a dangerous example for other Black men?" read Gary.

"It gets better," said Chip. "The worst of the worst are the lowest scum of this Earth."

Tucker, finally having had enough, walked off with purpose toward Richard's office, dummy sheet in hand. A moment or two after he knocked on the publisher's door, it opened, Amy Comstock exiting. By the time he entered the room, Tucker already looked less assured. When he entered the office, Richard didn't even look up from his desk.

"What is it, Tucker? I'm busy."

"Richard, I implore you to rethink this," Tucker said, holding up the new front page.

Richard looked up at him confused.

"Rethink what?"

"This editorial. The lead story is bad enough, but we run this," Tucker said, pointing toward the editorial's headline, "and we're practically asking people to lynch that boy."

Richard waved him off.

"Who's asking anything? The mob's gonna lynch that nigger. You know it. I know it. I'm just explaining to our readers as to *why* they're going to do it."

Tucker sighed in exasperation.

"It doesn't exactly read that way, Richard."

"We are five minutes from press, son. You want me to pull the edition and go late to the streets because you're worried about... what? Impacting the already sealed fate of some nigger rapist?"

Tucker shrugged.

"See, that's what I mean. We have no evidence at all that this Rowland boy is a rapist, or that he even assaulted this girl, yet we sound as though we're reporting both."

At this, Richard chuckled and finally looked his editor in the eye.

"Tucker, Tucker, Tucker, my dear boy. My contacts at the Tulsa PD are high up and they are plentiful. I have it on good authority that he was arrested and will be arraigned. I know they got the clerk who saw the filthy beast mauling that young girl. I know that she showed up to be interviewed with bruises on her neck and chest."

"But you didn't talk to her?" asked Tucker. "So her account is second hand? And did anyone go down to the Drexel? Who's the source on her being an orphan paying her way through business college? Shouldn't we wait until that boy goes before a judge to condemn him to death?"

Richard, clearly irritated by this point, put his palms on the desk and looked at Tucker with cold eyes.

"Gimme that sheet," he told him in a stern tone. "I'm taking it and the others downstairs personally, and we're going to press right this moment. You got any problems with that, then you go right over to your typewriter and compose a resignation, you hear?"

Ashamed at having been so easily defeated, Tucker dropped his head and handed the sheet to his boss, wishing he could find the will to be a stronger man while knowing he was ultimately powerless to stop him even if he could muster enough courage to try.

****

At 3:00 p.m. that afternoon, a young, white newspaper boy was standing on the corner of a busy intersection with a large stack of papers at his feet.

"Fresh off the press," he screamed, "police nab negro for assaulting white girl, mob to lynch negro tonight. Get your copy, fresh off the press."

A gaggle of white men in suits immediately began to converge. There was a loud murmur among the crowd, and they quickly began to purchase copies. Over the next half hour, similar scenes played out at at least a dozen more spots in Tulsa. By the time people were leaving work, nearly half the city had heard the story, and by the time families were sitting down to dinner that evening, the other half had gotten up to speed.

The mayor was standing in his office when an aide handed him a copy of the Tribune just before he left for the day, causing him to sigh when he read the headline.

"Good Lord have mercy," said Thaddeus to his chief of staff. "I need this like I need an extra hole in my head. Get me Bill Rodgers on the phone and send for Chief Gustafson."

****

At the luncheonette, the sheriff was at the counter having coffee and pie while talking to Annie when Deputy Shoemaker ran in with a copy of the newspaper.

"Sheriff, you'd better look at this," he said, holding it up.

"Ah hell," said McCullough, "that trouble-making son of a bitch."

Deputy Shoemaker nodded.

"There's already people starting to gather, sheriff."

Annie could sense it was serious.

"What's the matter?" she asked the sheriff, who held up the paper, dropping a dollar on the table before he hurried out with the deputy.

McCullough and Deputy Shoemaker moved with purpose toward the courthouse steps. As they approached the crowd of around a dozen people, the sheriff began speaking without slowing down his pace.

"Nothing to see here, folks. Go on back about your business."

"You got that nigger up there, McCullough?" asked one of the men. "The one that raped the orphan girl?"

"We got no one charged with rape of anyone," said the sheriff. "We're still sorting through an alleged assault at this time."

"That's not what it says in the paper," said another one of the men.

"Tell you what," said the sheriff, "you stop reading that rag, and you'll feel yourself getting smarter right away."

The sheriff and his deputy continued past the crowd and through the doors to the courthouse building. Two deputies were up in the front lobby when they entered the sheriff's department.

"Don't let no one past," he told them.

****

At the Gurley Hotel, Otto was on the phone at the front desk with Cecil next to him.

"I see, yes, I certainly share your concern... Well, I'll do everything within my power to see that it does not, you can be sure, but this could get volatile... Alright, yes I will. Thank you for alerting me."

Gurley hung up the phone and looked to Cecil.

"Cecil, get the car and meet me out front. Come on, be quick about it.

Cecil snapped to it.

"Yes, Mr. Gurley, sir."

****

At the jail, Dick and Deputy Evers were still upstairs. Dick sat in his cell as the deputy remained standing outside of it.

"What about Pop Lloyd?" asked Dick.

"Who's that?" asked Deputy Evers.

"Man, you ain't never heard of Pop Lloyd or Oscar Charleston?" asked Dick. "They the two best ballplayers in the world!"

"Babe Ruth hit 54 homers last year," said the deputy. "I mean, 54! Shattered the record—*his own record!* He's already got 13 and it's not even June. Hell, he might hit 60 this season."

Dick smiled and shook his head.

"Dat's 'cause he ain't gotta face Bullet Rogan."

"Who?" asked the deputy.

"That new pitcher for the Kansas City Monarchs. Man, I'm telling you, if Babe Ruth had to play in the Negro League, he'd be lucky to hit 20 home runs."

Just then, a voice cried out from the square, its words ringing through the room's large, open windows.

"We know you're up there nigger, and we read what you did to that little, white orphan girl. You'll get yours you son of a bitch."

Deputy Evers walked over to the window.

"Don't pay them any attention," he told Dick.

"How many out there now?" the young man asked.

"More than before," said Evers. "Maybe three dozen or so."

Dick hung his head. Sheriff McCullough and Deputy Shoemaker entered the room.

"Hey, sheriff," said Deputy Evers.

The sheriff nodded, then looked to Dick.

"How you holding up, young man?" he asked.

"I be better once I get back to my side of town, sir, truth be told."

"Well, don't let that crowd out there get to you," said the sheriff. "They're all talk. Making sport of other people's problems helps 'em forget about their own, I suppose."

Dick nodded.

"Hey, Rowland," said another voice. "You're gonna hang, you Black son of a bitch. If the court don't see to it, we will."

The sheriff walked over to the window.

"You all go home now," he shouted down to the crowd. "There's nothing for you here but trouble."

The crowd dispersed a bit, breaking eye contact with the window, but without fully dissipating.

The sheriff looked to his deputies.

"I want you two to grab shotguns from the weapons room. Deputy Evers, you're to guard the stairwell on the north side, Deputy Shoemaker, you've got the one on the south end. As soon as you get back, we're gonna disable that elevator so that those are the only two ways up or down. Anyone comes up, you order them down. They don't obey, you shoot. Am I clear?"

Both men nodded.

"Yes, sheriff," they said in unison before hurrying off. The sheriff just kept staring off at the window. He could nearly hear the buzz of mounting tension. "Dear God, let this pass over," he mumbled mostly to himself.

****

"I was fit to be tied for sure," said Loula Williams, recounting her exploits at the bank to Bessie as they turned slabs of pecan brittle on the marble table. Just then, Bill ran into the confectionery with an urgency that immediately got his mother's attention.

"Momma," shouted Bill as he opened the door.

"What'chu all running like that for, child?" said Loula.

Panting from his run to the store, Bill took a deep breath before answering in quick words.

"Mrs. Jackson sent us home. Something's happening. They got some boy from Greenwood at the jail, and they think there's gonna be trouble."

"What are you talking about?" she said. "What kind of trouble?"

Her son shrugged.

"I don't know. They closed the school and everything."

"Stay here and help Bessie," Loula told him. "I'm going down to get your father. Do not leave this building, you hear?"

"Yes, ma'am," said Bill.

****

Obie Mann was doing inventory with his brother when a young boy of around seven entered their grocery.

"Obie, Mr. Brown wanted me to give you this," the boy said somewhat nervously, as he handed the giant man a copy of the Tribune. Obie snatched the newspaper and looked at the front page.

"Awe, hell no they ain't," he said after reading the headline.

"What's up?" asked McKinley.

Obie held the paper up to his brother. Upon seeing the headline, McKinley put his head down and rubbed the bridge of his nose.

"Go get the shotguns, the pistols, and all the ammo you can get your hands on," Obie told him. "Wrap it all in a blanket. Put it in the truck. Wait for me here."

McKinley sighed.

"Obie, we don't even know-"

"Do it," his brother said with a look McKinley knew to mean there was no room for debate on the subject. McKinley nodded and Obie ran toward the door.

****

John Williams stood with Horace and four other men in front of his garage, looking at the paper with disbelief when Loula sped into the lot in their sedan. She parked the car haphazardly and ran to her husband.

"Baby, what's happening?" she asked as she hugged him.

"There might be some trouble," John said. "They got Damie Rowland's boy over at the courthouse. They're saying he attacked some girl, and there's talk of a lynch mob."

"What?" said Loula. "That's crazy. Damie's boy's a sweetheart. He was a few years ahead of Bill in school. I see him all the time walking Damie around town."

"I know it," said John, "but they got him down there, and there's no telling what'll happen if a mob gets it in their mind that he did it."

John handed his wife the paper. Her face went pale as she began to read the lead story.

"What do we do?" she asked John.

"You go back to the house," he told her. "Tell Bessie she's staying with us tonight. Make sure you keep Bill there too. Tell him he don't go nowhere at all. We're gonna head over to Greenwood and Archer, see what we can find out."

Loula hugged him tight and kissed him on the cheek. Then she turned to Horace.

"You don't go nowhere without John, you hear me," she said sternly.

"Yes, ma'am," said Horace, trying to mask the fear in his voice.

****

The scene at the county jail had begun to take a turn for the worse. Throngs of people were attempting to push into the lobby from outside. Four deputies tried desperately to maintain order, steering them back toward the steps. As the noise grew, Sheriff McCullough came out from his office.

"Everybody outside," the sheriff screamed. "Let's go."

The crowd let up just enough that the deputies were able to successfully steer them away from the doors. The sheriff followed behind them to the front steps of the large building, from which he addressed the crowd, which looked to number around 70.

"Listen up," he said, in a loud, commanding voice. "I don't care what you read in no newspaper today, there ain't gonna be no lynching tonight, or any other night for that matter. Anyone gets arrested in this county, they go to trial, just like the law says. We don't do vigilante justice."

"A nigger rapes a white girl in Tulsa, he hangs, sheriff, and we ain't gonna count on some jury to see to it," yelled one man from the crowd.

"Look, friend," said the sheriff. "I told you how it's gonna be. Now I suggest you all disperse and go home to your families. Anyone who tries to take my jail *will* be shot. Make no mistake about that."

The crowd booed and hollered as the sheriff walked back inside the fortress of a building. As he left, a couple of people threw paper cups and other pieces of rubbish toward the steps, but he didn't turn around. Bill McCullough had been in these situations before, and he knew how volatile they could be. At the moment, this was still nothing more than a curious crowd filled with the nervous energy of any newly formed congregation. He knew, however, that the mob mentality was fickle and that the larger the group of people assembled, the easier it was to provoke agitation and for otherwise cowardly men to momentarily grow both brave and dangerous. It was a powder keg, and he'd have to do everything possible to ensure that the fuse didn't get lit.

****

Back at the offices of the Tulsa Star, Smitherman, Stradford, Buck, Isaiah, Gurley, Samuel Hooker, Philip

Spears, Pastor Whitaker and Deputy Cleaver were all engaged in a heated debate.

"Listen to Barney, will you?" said Gurley. "I was just at the courthouse. The sheriff gave me his word that he would lay down his life before turning Dick over to the mob."

"Ah, come on, Otto," said Stradford. "Look, Barney, I think the sheriff's a good man. I really do. He did right by us when we were down there this morning. But he ain't gonna be able to fend off a few hundred Klansmen if they come looking to lynch our boy."

"Mr. Stradford, I understand your concern, sir," said Barney. "I really do. But you gotta understand that anything you do is only gonna make the chances of that happening better. You go down there to protect him, and they gonna see it as you went down to spring him. Then they'll use that as an excuse to come after the whole lot of you. And them boys in the blue uniforms ain't likely to see it different, neither."

"So what then, we sit on our hands and wait for them to do him like they done Roy Belton?" asked Smitherman, referring to the white man who'd recently been taken from the courthouse and hanged by a mob.

"Andrew, please," said Gurley. "McCullough wasn't in office when Belton was lynched."

"Is that right?" said Smitherman. "Well, who was it that just invoked Belton on Friday to remind me that they lynched a white man, a white man who was being held at the

311

same courthouse? Sheriff McCullough might have honorable intentions, but they'll only get him so far. At the end of the day, *we* need to protect Dick Rowland. He's one of our own."

****

In an alleyway behind one of the choc houses he ran, King Henry was with Freddy, confronting a teenager named Harold. The boy looked scared, backed up against the brick wall in a very defensive position. Henry was inches away from him, face in his face, pointing with his right hand, while his left carried a wad of cash.

"Now I done been doin' business with the chink for 'bout long as you been on this Earth, Harold," he told him. "And he ain't never done me wrong."

"Maybe he made a mistake, King?" said the boy.

"He ain't never made no mistakes, neither," said Henry. "Now, you know why that is, Harold?"

Harold shook his head.

"'Cause them Chinese cats don't be fucking up when it comes to numbers. Been using abacuses and shit since back before Jesus walked the Earth. Now, if you gave the man the right count on the choc, I know he gave you the right count on the green. So, reach into your motherfucking trousers and make sure it didn't stick to the lining of your pocket or some such shit, before I run out of patience with your narrow ass."

Harold slowly reached into the front pocket of his jeans and began to pull out a bill, his eyes growing wide.

"Yeah, yeah, that's it, King," the boy said nervously. "You smart as a motherfucker. That's exactly-"

As Harold carefully finished pulling the bill out, Henry reached into his own back pocket, from which he pulled out a blackjack and, lightning-quick, brought it down on the top back of the young man's head, immediately dropping him to the ground. Freddy leaped forward, looking down at the boy, who was still conscious, though clearly loopy from the forceful blow.

"Damn, son," Freddy said, "you fell like a sack of potatoes. Serves you right too, stealing from the King. Fuck's wrong wit'chu?"

Harold just moaned and began to move a bit. Freddy reached for the $10 bill on the ground, but Henry put an arm in front of his chest.

"Nah, let this here motherfucker give it to me."

Harold reached for the bill, then held it up.

"You want I should bend down and get it, motherfucker?" Henry asked him, reaching out his leg and stomping the wrist that held the bill into the ground. "I look like someone who bends down to pick up a measly $10 bill?"

Henry began grinding the young man's hand into the street with the heel of his boot as if outing a cigarette butt. Harold screamed in pain. When Henry let up, Harold sprung to his feet and handed the bill toward Henry.

"Now you can take it, Freddy," Henry said.

He looked back to Harold as Freddy collected the bill from him. Harold's other hand rubbed the bruise on his head, where a knot had already risen. When he brought his hand forward he saw that there was a thick coat of blood on his fingers.

"I guess you'd best check your pockets better, Harold," said Henry, "because the next time you come up short on my money, you be gettin' a bullet through the same spot."

The alley door just to the left of Harold crashed open, startling all three men. It was Mooch, who was excited and out of breath as he tried to speak.

"Yo, they got Dick!" he blurted out.

"Damn, Mooch, you scared me half to death," said Freddy.

"They got Dick!"

"Man, who got dick, your moms?" asked Freddy.

"They got Diamond Dick," said Mooch, frustrated. "They gonna string him up."

"What'chu talkin' about, fool?" asked Henry.

"They picked him up this morning," said Mooch. "Talking some noise about him raping a white girl cross the tracks yesterday."

"Man they can't be meaning Dick Rowland," said Freddy. "They confused or some shit, prolly."

"No, man, listen to me," said Mooch. "It's in the newspaper, they got his full name and everything."

Mooch hurriedly pulled out a rolled up copy of just the front page from his back pocket. Henry grabbed it from his hand and began to read with Freddy leaning over his shoulder.

"See," said Mooch, "they used his whole name, even said that they call him Diamond Dick."

"Where they got him at?" asked Henry.

"The courthouse, I heard. All the big men in town are down on Greenwood and Archer talking about what to do."

King pushed past him and through the door. The other two men followed while Harold caught his breath, silently grateful for the interruption.

****

Courthouse: May 31, 7:00 p.m.

There was now a crowd of around 100 people assembled outside the courthouse, and they had grown even more bold and rowdy. Many were on the steps. More were yelling up to the window where Dick was being held. There were a few city police officers strewn about, but they were relaxed and talking to the members of the crowd in a way that suggested they weren't very concerned about what the mob might do.

Inside the building, Sheriff McCullough was in his office, meeting with Chief Gustafson. Deputy Cleaver stood next to where the sheriff sat and SGT Butch Carlson stood next to the chief's seat.

"Bill, what do you want from me?" said the chief. "You wanted to hold him here. He's here. I warned you it wouldn't be no stroll through the park. You wouldn't listen."

McCullough was a very deliberate man. He never spoke too quickly because he always chose his words very carefully and delivered them in a way that adequately expressed his sentiment. After a considerable pause, he leaned forward, resting his elbows on the desk as his face got closer to Gustafson's.

"What I want," he said, in a firm and measured tone, "is for you to do your goddamned job and police this mob out front."

The chief smiled but was clearly offended.

"Whoa," he said, "easy now, don't forget who you're talking to, sheriff."

"I'm talking to the man responsible for keeping the peace out there," the sheriff said, not giving an inch or softening his tone.

The chief shrugged.

"I just posted four officers out front. They can't force the people to leave a public square—right to peacefully assemble and all that. They'll stay and make sure they remain... *peaceful*. Things get outta hand, just call the station, and I'll send over more guys. But I can't bring the whole force over here right now. I got an entire city to police."

The sheriff stared intensely at the chief. After a few seconds, Gustafson shrugged again.

"Come on, Butch," he said. "Let's let these men get back to work. Looks like they got a long night in front of them."

As they left, Gustafson smiled at the sheriff.

****

As the chief exited the courthouse, he wore the look of a man without a care in the world. He smiled and waved to people he knew in the crowd out front and walked casually among them.

Back inside, the sheriff was standing over his desk, palms on it, head down. Barney stood across from him.

"They're not gonna be no help at all, are they?" asked the deputy.

"Nope," said the sheriff without looking up. "When we didn't turn him over this morning, I'm sure we took any chance of cooperation off the table."

"No good choices, huh sheriff?"

"There rarely are, in my experience, Barney. There rarely are."

The sheriff stood upright and walked toward a small window in his office, from which he could look out at the crowd in the square.

"How'd it look over in Greenwood?" he asked Barney.

"Not good, if you wanna know the truth."

The sheriff chuckled.

"I wasn't expecting good, Barney," he said, turning from the window to his deputy. "I just want to know *how* bad is more like it."

"They concerned, sheriff. Soon as copies of the Tribune got over that way, they started congregating. Truth is, they believe you'll do right by the kid, but they don't think we got the manpower to stop the mob if things get outta hand, especially if the Klan gets involved."

McCullough shook his head and exhaled deeply.

"I got half a mind to go over to the Trib building and grab that Jones character by the neck, drag him down here and horsewhip him on the front steps while they watch."

Barney laughed.

"I'd give a week's pay to see that, sheriff. I surely would. Two if you'd let me get a few licks in."

The sheriff again gave his unique chuckle, restrained and with a closed mouth. It was as close as the serious man ever got to a full on laugh.

"That was over the line—even for a slippery bastard like him," the sheriff said. "Yet he's home counting all the money he made today while we're dealing with the fallout."

"You think it'd do any good to call on the mayor, him being a Republican and all?" asked Barney.

The sheriff rolled his eyes.

"Thaddeus? That plum simple son of a bitch doesn't know shit from shinola. Besides, he's thick as thieves with that TBA crowd ever since he got elected. If you think he'd stick his neck out for a colored boy, even an innocent one that was about to be lynched, think again."

Both men turned as a deputy ran in from the lobby.

"Sheriff, there are some men here asking to see you."

The sheriff gave him a cross look.

"I told you, deputy, we ain't lettin' no one in."

"I know, sheriff," said the deputy, nervously, "and I'm sorry, but I don't think they're from around here. I think they might be from the state police or even the feds."

The sheriff grabbed a shotgun that was next to his desk and moved toward the door with great purpose. Barney and the other deputy followed at his flanks. In the lobby, there were two well-dressed men in suits and fedoras waiting. They seemed calm and professional, and most people would have assumed they were law enforcement of some kind, but Sheriff McCullough knew better. They were Klan organizers and their eyes bulged a bit when they saw him coming, shotgun in tow.

"Can I help you gentlemen?" asked McCullough.

"Sheriff McCullough, thanks for making the time," the first man said, extending a hand that the sheriff did not shake.

"I ain't got none to spare," he told them. "So say your peace quick like."

"Well, I can appreciate that, given the gravity of what you're facing," the man said. "Suffice it to say that we're here to make things go easier for everyone."

"Is that right?" asked the sheriff, arching an eyebrow cynically.

"Sure," said the other man, "just release the boy to us, and we'll get this thing handled in a... *tasteful fashion*, far away from the courthouse of course, and it can be resolved as having been achieved by... unidentified out-of-towners?"

The sheriff's eyes narrowed and he cocked the shotgun, pointing it toward the ceiling.

"Now you two listen good because I'm only gonna say this once," he told the men. "The prisoner under my charge isn't leaving this building until he's been tried in it, and any man who attempts to do otherwise is gonna go on to his glorious reward much sooner than expected. We clear?"

The men's faces registered shock and fear. They clearly weren't expecting a sheriff in these parts to react that way. Both men extended their hands in front of them in a defensive posture.

"Steady now, sheriff," said the first man. "We were just trying to offer you an easy way to sort this thing out. We don't want no trouble."

"Then I suggest you get the hell back to wherever you came from, and do it as fast as you can manage."

The sheriff looked at them with determination, eyes narrow, jaw clenched. They kept their hands out and slowly backed toward the door before turning quickly and exiting.

Chapter 8

Johnny Gordon was waiting out front of the Majestic when the O'Dell's car pulled up to the curb. Inside, Gene O'Dell put the car in park. Turning his head to address his daughter, who was seated in the back, he caught a nervous look from his wife in the passenger seat.

"You remember what I said," he told Kelly Ann.

"Yes, Daddy," she answered eagerly.

"And what *I* said, too," her mother added.

She nodded her head quickly.

"Yes, mother."

Johnny approached the passenger window, which was down. He looked past Mrs. O'Dell to Gene.

"Hello, sir," he said, reaching across to shake his hand. Gene leaned over and they shook.

"Hey, kid."

Johnny nodded at Megan.

"Mrs. O'Dell."

They shook hands. Then he turned to Kelly Ann and smiled. She returned the smile, nodding toward her door. Johnny jumped, remembering he was to open it. Once it was ajar, Kelly excitedly jumped out, nearly tripping on the curb.

"I'll pick you up at the soda shop next door like we talked about," Gene said out his wife's window.

"Yes, Daddy," Kelly Ann replied.

Gene looked to Johnny.

"And just the movie and the soda shop, nowhere else."

Johnny nodded.

"Yes, sir, of course."

"Have fun, dear," Megan told her daughter. "Nice to meet you, Johnny."

"You as well, ma'am," he said, then nodded to Gene. "Sir."

Gene held his stare for a moment, then turned, put the car in gear, and pulled off.

****

It was dusk at the corner of Greenwood and Archer, and a large, all-Black crowd of mostly men had assembled in the street. They had grabbed whatever armament they could find and while most carried shotguns and pistols, others had bats, shovels, and even rakes.

JB Stradford and Andrew Smitherman stood in front of a car, at the center of it all, facing the crowd. They were surrounded by Buck Franklin, Pastor Whitaker, Samuel Hooker, O.W. Gurley, John Williams, and Horace Frank. Obie Mann and a group of vets faced him. King Henry,

Mooch, and Freddy approached from the side, nodded to the others, and posted up.

"We got word from the courthouse that the crowd is over 100 right now and getting rowdier by the minute," Stradford said. "Now I'm here to tell you that they got intentions to lynch that boy. The sheriff done gave us his word he wouldn't let that happen, but when push comes to shove?"

The crowd jeered.

"They ain't gonna save that boy," said Obie.

"Well, that's why we're fittin' to go over there and offer our assistance," Stradford said. "We're taking three cars. Obie, if you wanna fill this one here, John's got a crew, and the four of us will ride in mine."

There was conversation among the crowd. Obie started pointing out the people he would be taking with him. It was clear from his body language that Gurley was not pleased by the plan, but he remained silent, nonetheless. Buck turned to Isaiah.

"What do you think?" he asked him.

"I really don't know," Isaiah said. "Carloads of Black men showing up at the courthouse? Armed no less? It's liable to set this thing off."

Buck nodded.

"I know it. At the same time, it doesn't sound like things are very far from going sideways over there as it is. It'd be hard for the community to sit on its hands and wait for that boy to be hanged."

Isaiah nodded.

"A rock and a hard place."

****

Sitting in his cell, the noise from outside the courthouse had grown much louder and was making Dick Rowland nervous, when Deputy Evers returned with a tray of food.

"Hey, you gotta be starving," said the deputy. "They just sent this up. It's from the luncheonette on the corner."

He handed Dick a tray with fried chicken, mashed potatoes, green beans, and a bottle of orange soda.

"Thanks," said Dick. "I'm hungry, but at the same time, my stomach's in knots. Not sure it'll stay down, know what I mean?"

The deputy nodded.

"Look, I know it sounds bad down there, but we got two deputies with shotguns at the top of the stairs, and the elevator is disabled. Anyone tries to overtake the jail, we got orders to shoot to kill."

Dick nodded toward the window and forced a chuckle.

"Sounds like a big crowd out there," he said. "You sure you got enough bullets?"

The deputy smiled.

"Trust me, people like that are only brave when they feel safety in numbers. They try and storm a stairwell and see the business end of a shotgun at the top looking down? They go yellow quick."

Dick shook his head.

"I do hope you're right, deputy, I surely do."

Dick looked down at the food and took a bite of mashed potatoes, washing it down with some soda.

"Mike," said the deputy.

"Hmmm?"

"My name, it's Mike," said the deputy.

Dick extended his hand and the two men shook.

"Pleased to meet you, Mike," said Dick.

The deputy smiled.

"We're gonna get through this, Dick. I promise."

****

Courthouse: May 31: 8:00 p.m.

When the three cars from Greenwood pulled up at the courthouse, the noise stopped and the crowd immediately focused its attention on the men getting out of their vehicles. Stradford, Smitherman, John Williams, Obie, and McKinley Mann were out front. Horace, the vets, and several others followed behind them as they moved nearly single file with either pistols in their hands or shotguns on their shoulders.

The crowd, unarmed, grew nervous and were mostly still as they passed. The sheriff was in his office with Barney when another deputy ran in.

"Sheriff, you're gonna wanna see this," said the deputy.

Without saying a word, the sheriff walked toward the lobby with Barney following. The Greenwood crowd was assembled there when he arrived.

"What in the Sam Hill is this?" the sheriff fumed.

Stradford answered.

"Sheriff McCullough, we're offering ourselves as protection against the lynch mob. You can deputize us and allow us to stand guard out front and make sure no one tries to storm the jail."

"Have you lost your damn mind?" McCullough said to him. "Do you know what the sight of a dozen armed Black men on the courthouse steps will do to that crowd? You know how many more it'll draw? I'll have a damned bloodbath on my hands!"

Smitherman stepped forward.

"Well, it's looking more and more like we're gonna have the lynching of an innocent man on ours."

The sheriff clenched his teeth and exhaled through his nose, as he looked at each of the men.

"I already told you that ain't gonna happen," he finally said. "But you all being here like this ain't making my job any easier."

Sensing the sheriff's growing impatience, Barney stepped forward with his hands up and addressed JB.

"Look, Mr. Stradford, I told you, I can appreciate your concern, I really can. I know things look rough right now, but you all are going about this the wrong way."

Before Stradford could answer, Obie Mann cut him off.

"How you expect we go about it then? There are a hundred men out there, and I don't see but half a dozen 'round here."

Barney remained composed.

"Dick is secure," he told the group. "He's in a cell on the fourth floor. The elevator's disconnected. Only way up is a narrow stairwell, and the two men at the top of it got orders to shoot if anyone tries to rush them."

"As many people out front as there are, they wanna overrun it, they can," said John Williams.

Barney nodded.

"If they were that determined and willing to die for it, sure, but that ain't the way things work."

At this, the deputy looked to Obie and the vets.

"You all know how it goes. You think one man gets a load of buckshot blown through the back end of his belly, and the rest of those men out there are gonna keep chargin' up the steps, no guns of their own?"

Barney shrugged. The vets looked at each other, mostly nodding in agreement.

"You got a bunch of cowards out there," he continued. "If we turned Dick over to them, sure, they'd muster the courage to do him harm, but we ain't gonna do that, no how, no way. You have my word."

At this, the sheriff stepped forward and retook control.

"Go on back home," he told them, "and I promise, if things start looking worse and I can use the backup, I'll send word over to Greenwood for you to come back over. I mean it."

Stradford and the others looked at each other, talking low among themselves for a moment.

"Alright, we'll leave," said Stradford. "It's in your hands, sheriff, and we're taking you at your word. But we will not abide any harm coming to that boy. And I mean that."

The sheriff nodded and the men left. Outside, the building, Lawton Mercer had just shown up with Red, Willie, and Horse, along with a group of around a dozen more younger men. Lawton walked up to a man in a short-sleeved shirt and tie who was looking on with the others.

"What gives?" Lawton asked the man.

"A big group of niggers just went in the courthouse," the man said. "They're armed to the teeth, too. I think they're trying to spring the Rowland boy."

Lawton looked around at the other men. They all had confused expressions, as the Greenwood men descended the stairs and headed toward their cars.

"Well I'll be dipped in dog shit," said Lawton, "I never thought I'd see the day."

"That's that big son of a bitch that brought his monkey soldiers to the parade yesterday," said Horse, nodding toward Obie.

Red pointed to Stradford.

"And the old man who was their mouthpiece."

The Greenwood crew piled into their cars and pulled off without incident. Lawton moved quickly toward the steps, the others following behind him. The crowd watched and when he reached the top, he already had the mob's attention.

"What in god's name are you people doing standing around like this is the county fair?" he screamed. "I just saw a nigger army walk through here. They got one of their own right up there," he said pointing to the window of Dick's cell. "Raped an innocent orphan girl—on Memorial Day, no less. Now, if you're any kind of real man, and the sanctity of our women means anything to you, you'll go home and get your hunting rifle or your pistol and all the ammo you can muster. If they come back, we'll be ready for them."

The mob, having been given a collective voice, began whooping and hollering in approval.

"Go on now, men, get out of here and arm yourselves to the teeth!" screamed Lawton.

The crowd dispersed eagerly.

"I got two shotguns at the house," said Red. "You wanna run over and get them, Lawton?"

Lawton gave him a sinister smile.

"No, I got a better plan for that."

****

Inside the Majestic Theater, a Black and white silent film rolled with live piano accompaniment. In the back row, Kelly Ann sat close to Johnny.

"You want some?" he asked, offering a bag of popcorn in her direction.

"Thanks," Kelly Ann said nervously, as she took a small handful.

"I asked them for extra butter," Johnny told her with a wink.

"It's good," she said.

When she finished eating it, Kelly Ann put her hand on the armrest. Johnny put his hand on top of hers and looked over to see her smiling.

****

At the Gurley house, Otto and his wife Emma were in the library. She was seated on the couch while her husband paced the floor.

"Do you think they'll try and lynch the boy?" Emma asked.

Her husband threw up his hands.

"I don't know, dear, I really don't. What I do know, however, is that if they try and a couple dozen Black men with hunting rifles attempt to stop them, they will succeed only in setting off a war that we are destined to lose."

Just then, a housemaid entered the room.

"Mr. Gurley, sir, there's a telephone call for you. It's the hotel."

****

The sheriff was sitting at his desk, rubbing his face, while Barney and another deputy stood by.

"Deputy, call over to County Commissioner Short's house," the sheriff said. "See if you can get him on the phone for me."

"Yes, sheriff," said the deputy, leaving quickly.

"You think he can help?" asked Barney.

"I don't know," said the sheriff. "Ira Short's the only honest politician I know of in this town, though, so if anyone can, it'd be him. Hates the Klan, knows Gustafson and the mayor aren't worth spit. I believe he'll try and do what's right."

"Can't ask for more than that," said Barney.

"Sure you can," said the sheriff. "You just won't get it. Not around here, anyway."

Barney laughed. The two men looked out the narrow window to a crowd that had grown smaller, though some had shotguns and more seemed to be arriving on foot.

"You think that'll be the end of it, sheriff?" asked Barney.

The sheriff stroked his chin.

"Depends."

"On?" asked Barney.

The sheriff sighed.

"How many left because they've had enough, and how many went home to arm themselves, then how many of those see their families and come to their senses before heading back."

"You want me to go back to Greenwood, see what it looks like, maybe try and cool some heads?" Barney asked.

The sheriff paused before answering.

"No," he finally said. "We're gonna need every hand on deck if things get worse here. You've reasoned with them already. If they decide to come back, there won't be any talking them out of it, I'm afraid."

"You're right about that," said Barney. "I wish you weren't, but I know better."

****

Otto Gurley was on the phone in the kitchen with his wife Emma standing nearby.

"Good job, Cecil," he said into the receiver. "Thank you and do continue to keep me apprised of the situation."

He hung up the phone and looked to Emma.

"Cecil said the men have returned from the courthouse."

"Crisis averted?" his wife asked hopefully.

"Looks like it," Gurley said with a shrug. "For now, anyway."

"If we can just get through the night," she said, "maybe the whites will lose interest some by morning."

"My thoughts exactly," her husband responded. "It's a good thing it's a Tuesday. Folks have to be up for work and aren't as likely to be getting liquored up. If this were a weekend..."

Emma walked toward him and hugged his shoulders.

"We'll get through it, darling," she said softly into his ear. "We always do."

****

A full congregation was assembled inside of Holy Family Catholic Church that eventing as Father Herring addressed them from the lectern.

"And now that the mass has ended, I hope you will not only go in peace but join us next door for the graduation ceremony, followed by a reception in the church basement," he told them.

Moments later in the back of the church, Gene and Megan O'Dell were greeted by Megan's sister, Mary, and her husband. The couple's 13-year-old daughter Ann Marie was at their side.

"Hey, Willard," said Gene. "Good to see you. Mary."

"Gene, thanks so much for coming out," said Willard, as both smiled.

"Wouldn't miss it," he said, turning to Ann Marie. "Congratulations, kiddo."

"And where pray tell is my beautiful niece this evening?" asked Mary.

"I'd say under the weather, but I can't tell a lie in church," said Megan hesitantly. "She's out on a date."

Mary gave her a look of disapproval, to which Megan put up a hand defensively.

"I've already gotten an earful from this one," she said, pointing to her husband. "It's the boy who's taking her to the prom, and it was the last night prior that they could get together, and she really wanted to get to know him a bit first, which I thought was a good idea too. I'm sorry it meant her missing Ann Marie's graduation."

Willard waved her off.

"Oh, come one, Mary, she'd be bored to death anyway," he said to his wife. "She had to sit through her own already, not to mention, what, half a dozen at least for all the other kids?"

Mary shrugged.

"I suppose," she said, glaring at Megan. "Come on, we'd better get next door."

****

Obie Mann was standing on the corner of Greenwood and Archer, surrounded by other vets. There were three cars in front of him when a fourth pulled up filled with young Black men. Obie walked over to the car.

"What's it look like?" asked Obie.

"Less people," the man said, "but some got guns now. Seem like maybe they went home to muscle up after we left."

Obie looked down the street for a moment before turning back.

"Alright," he told the man. "Give it 10 minutes and then make another roll through."

The young man nodded, then looked to the driver, and the car pulled off.

****

On a dark street in downtown Tulsa, Lawton, Red, Willie and Horse led a group of 10 men as they approached a sporting goods store that had already closed for the evening. Lawton carried a large rock in his hand. He took off the button-downed flannel that he had been wearing over his t-shirt and wrapped the rock with it as he walked up to the front door. With one swing, he easily broke the glass. He reached his hand in, careful to avoid the remaining shards, and opened the door from the inside.

"Watch your step," he said to the others behind him as he pulled it open and walked inside, turning on the lights as he entered.

The men quickly found the hunting rifles in a locked wooden case with two large glass doors. Lawton used the same rock to smash them open and then began handing out rifles to the men. There was no question who was in charge.

"Red, go over there and issue ammo to each man," he commanded. Red moved swiftly toward the boxes of bullets behind the cashier counter.

****

Henry Sowders was in the projection booth looking out to a near-empty theater when the manager, Earnest Cotton, walked in.

"It's getting pretty bad out there, Henry," Earnest said to the white man. "You might wanna be thinking about getting back across those tracks while you still can. Miss Loula asked me to stay open, figuring that giving people a place to go and escape the craziness might prevent them from doing something stupid, but she agreed you should probably scram."

"Who'll work the projector?" asked Henry, somewhat aloof to his boss's concerns.

"I'll take care of it myself," said Earnest, shaking his head. "Don't you worry none about it. Now, go on while you can still get home safely."

Henry paused, looked forward at the screen, then nodded and left the booth.

On the street outside the theater, he walked toward his car only to find it with the top down, four Black men sitting in its seats, the two in the back holding shotguns.

"Hey, that's my motor car!" he screamed at them indignantly. "Get out of it at once."

The four men laughed to each other.

"I mean it," he said. "Let's go."

The men stared at him blankly.

"It's been commandeered, man," the one in the driver's seat finally said. "Your people across the way trying to lynch one of ours. They got the cops, so we gotta fend for ourselves. You'll get it back when it's all over."

Henry's jaw was clenched and he tightened his fists.

"What?" said the man in the passenger seat. "You heard the man. Beat it."

The man raised a pistol into the air. Henry tried to speak but could only stutter. He jumped when he felt a giant hand on his neck and turned around to find Obie Mann.

"Come on, Mr. Sowders," Obie said. "We gonna get you home."

Obie walked him over to a different car that had two men in it.

"Get in," said Obie.

Henry looked back toward his treasured vehicle.

"But... but my automobile."

"Do another drive-by," Obie told the men inside. "Drop Mr. Sowders once you cross the tracks. Don't let no harm come to him."

The men nodded and Henry reluctantly got into the sedan, staring back at his shiny Studebaker as they pulled off into the night.

****

At the courthouse, the crowd had continued to grow to around 80 people, many of whom were now armed. The sheriff, having grown nervous at the crowd's rejuvenation, came through the main doors to the veranda at the top of the steps.

"Alright, now listen," he shouted. "The folks from Greenwood have gone on back home peacefully. They are not trying to break the Rowland boy out of the jail. They only want to see that justice is done through the courts. There's no reason for these guns, and they're only gonna lead to someone getting hurt. I'm telling you again, go on home to your families. Mind your business, and let justice take its course."

"To hell with that," one of them shouted back. "They got an army of niggers with guns. If they're looking for a fight, we'll give it to them."

Near the back of the crowd, Lawton and his crew approached the scene. Lawton smirked with pleasure when he saw how many people had returned armed. His head spun, however, when three motor cars sped by the street running behind them filled with Black men holding shotguns. Horse drew his rifle, but Lawton reached out quickly and lowered its muzzle.

"No, not here," he told him.

The sheriff walked through the doors back into the courthouse where four armed deputies waited on alert. He continued straight back to his office, where Barney was waiting inside.

"They gonna have to run out of steam on their own, it seems, sheriff," said the deputy.

The sheriff shook his head.

"That it does, Barney. That it does."

Just then, County Commissioner Ira Short walked in. A small, neatly-kept man in his fifties, he looked more like an accountant than a politician.

"Ira, thanks for coming down," the sheriff said.

"Of course, Bill. It's not looking very good out there, though, is it?"

The sheriff looked back at the window and shook his head.

"No, not by a long shot."

"Tell me what I can do to help," said Ira.

The sheriff shrugged.

"Anything that you think might."

Ira nodded.

"It seems rather touchy at the moment. It's hard to say what could help and what could further escalate the situation."

"Don't I know it," said the sheriff.

"At least the coloreds have gone back across the tracks," said Ira. "Maybe they'll tire of this soon if there's nothing to rile them. It is getting late."

"From your lips to God's ears, commissioner."

"I take it the city police have been no help?" Ira asked.

Barney sighed.

"None too much," said the sheriff.

"Have you spoken to Thaddeus?" asked Ira.

"He called about an hour ago," the sheriff said. "Never heard a man that needs so many words to say so little."

Ira snorted.

"Yes, I suppose there's not much to be hoped for there. Have your men eaten?"

The sheriff shook his head.

"Probably not."

"Tell you what," Ira said, "I'm gonna run down to the diner real quick and get them to put some sandwiches and cokes together. It's likely to be a long night and they'll need their strength."

The sheriff nodded.

"That would be much appreciated, Ira."

The sheriff began writing on a legal pad.

"Listen," said the sheriff. "There's a waitress named Annie who'll be at the counter, most likely. Do me a favor and give this to her? If you can't find her, give it to Evie."

Ira took the paper and looked him in the eye.

"You bet."

****

Two older Black men walked up to the door of King Henry's choc house and knocked on it. Mooch carefully opened it just enough to stick his head out.

"Yo, man, we closed for the night," said Mooch. "Go home, come back tomorrow."

Inside, King Henry was counting out bullets at a card table where several pistols were laid out. Next to him, Freddy inspected a shotgun. The two tables next to the one they were seated at had four more men sitting at them, each of whom were also counting ammo.

"Yo, man find a piece of paper or something and make up a sign saying we closed until tomorrow," Henry told Mooch. "We don't need people knocking every five minutes."

"Alright. I'll find something," said Mooch.

Mooch pulled a thin piece of wood from a crate. He took out some bootblack from a nearby desk and began writing on it with a rag.

344

"We got 50 shells for this here double barrel, King," said Freddy. "That's 25 rounds."

Henry smiled.

"Look at you, must have some Chinaman way back in your line."

Freddy blushed.

"Nah, my grand-mamma used to say we got some Cherokee in us though."

"Negro, please," said Henry, pointing to the choc beer. "You might have drunk enough of that stuff to have some Choctaw in your blood by now, but that's the only Indian shit you know about."

Mooch held up the sign, which read, "Close to tomorrow."

Freddy roared in laughter.

"Now this motherfucker definitely ain't got no Chinese in him," howled Henry.

"What I do?" asked Mooch, confused.

"Close to tomorrow?" asked Henry. "No kidding, motherfucker. It'll be tomorrow in just a few more hours."

Mooch frowned, while Freddy took the sign.

"Man, give me the damn thing. Close and close, they spelled the same. You gotta put a "d" on the end to make it closed, like it been done already. Otherwise, you're telling the fool to close something."

Henry shook his head, chuckling with the others.

****

At the luncheonette, Evie was handing Ira two large bags of food at the counter while he counted out his money.

"No charge, commissioner," she told him. "Seems the least we can do."

Ira smiled and handed some bills.

"No chance, young lady."

Evie didn't accept but Ira, still smiling only now tilting his head, laid the bills on the counter.

"Well, either you get it or whoever wipes the counter does."

Evie shook her head and collected the money.

"Is that girl over there Annie, by chance?" he asked.

"Sure is, why do you ask?"

He pulled the note from the inside pocket of his sports coat.

"Sheriff McCullough asked me to give this to her."

He handed it to Evie.

"Thanks again, ma'am."

They both nodded solemnly and Ira made for the door. Evie walked down to Annie, who was just finishing taking an order and handed her the folded paper.

"It's from your sweetie pie," she said with a smile.

Annie hurriedly unfolded the sheet and looked at it for a second before reading aloud.

"Annie, tell Evie to close up the diner. Things are getting ugly over here, not sure how long it'll be safe. Get home, lock your door, and don't answer for anyone. Bill."

She looked up to Evie with horror in her eyes.

"That's good enough for me," Evie said, turning toward the dining area.

"Alright, y'all, listen up. We're closing up early. Everybody finish up and pay your tabs. No more orders. Sheriff says everyone should go home and stay in their houses."

****

Back at Greenwood and Archer, Obie was leaning on a garbage can, surrounded by a throng of vets, when three cars pulled up. He quickly rose and walked out to meet them. A man was yelling from the passenger seat of the lead car.

"Yo, they on the attack."

"Say what?" shouted Obie.

"There are men coming from the courthouse with guns and shit," said another one of the men. "I think they might have got him already, man."

Obie whistled and gave the signal with his finger to circle the wagons. The men immediately jumped into four other cars parked at the curb. All were carrying weapons. As they pulled off, Obie slapped the outside of the door from the passenger seat of his vehicle, yelling out to others on the street.

"Come on, round up, and move out. It's on. Let's go, over to the court house. Move!"

John Williams was standing next to his car talking with Horace, Bill Williams, and two other men outside of the confectionery when he heard Obie's directive. They all jumped into John's car, but when Bill moved to enter his father put up his hand.

"No, you stay here."

"But I wanna go with you," Bill protested.

"I need you here watching over your mother, Bessie, and the shop," John said firmly. "Get inside, son."

Bill hung his head.

"Yes, sir."

The car sped off behind the others and Bill could feel his stomach hit the floor as he watched the taillights fade into the darkness.

Once across the tracks, the cars all turned off their headlights.

"Park right over there in that open area," said Obie, pointing to an empty patch. "We don't want them to know where we parked. Might try and disable the vehicles."

Once the eight cars were parked, around three dozen men got out of them. They grabbed their weapons and assembled into a loose formation. Obie faced the men.

"Alright, listen," he told them in a hushed but firm tone. "We head over in a double column, that way if they fire on us, they don't have a broad target. You hear shots, you fall back to the side, get cover behind a car or something before you return fire. Understood?"

The men all nodded.

The crowd at the courthouse was back to around 100 strong when it came into sight. There were lots of guns, and a menacing tension seemed to fill the air. Men from the mob continued to heckle Dick. One of them spotted Obie and his men on the approach and stopped mid-sentence.

"Hey, look," he shouted. "Over there. The niggers are back."

As they got closer to the square, some of the whites raised their weapons a bit.

Inside, Ira, the sheriff, and Barney were eating ham sandwiches in the sheriff's office when they heard the commotion. Barney hurried to the window.

"Ah shit," he said. "They're back, sheriff. It's Obie Mann and his boys this time. All of them got guns."

Sheriff McCullough rushed to the window then turned and hurried toward the door. Ira and Barney followed. As they passed through the courthouse lobby, the other deputies put their sandwiches down and quickly fell in behind them as he burst out onto the steps. Obie and his crew had reached the bottom of the steps by that point and the sheriff met him and a few others halfway.

"What in the hell is this about, young man?" the sheriff said to Obie, standing two steps above him and still looking up to meet his eyes. "I thought we had an understanding?"

John Williams stepped forward.

"We got word across town that the mob had made a run at the jail."

Sheriff McCullough clenched his jaw and shook his head.

"Well you heard it wrong then," he told them firmly. "Now every time you all come over here, you make the situation more volatile. I appreciate your intentions, but if you'd just stay over in Greenwood, it'd be a lot easier for me to do my job."

Obie looked around and could see that they'd been misinformed.

"Obie," Barney plead, "I assure you, Dick is fine and he's gonna stay that way. Y'all need to get back over to Greenwood and stay put before it goes bad."

"Wish y'all would work half as hard gettin' this crowd to disperse as you do us," Obie said.

"Noted," said Barney, "but we're just trying to keep the peace and get through the night. And this is the best we can do, right now. Now y'all are making things harder still."

Obie looked around at his men.

"Alright, boys, back out the same way we came in," he told them. "Be on guard."

When they walked off, there was some jeering from the crowd. Looks were exchanged and the scene got tense, but the group was ultimately able to leave without incident.

****

Bill Williams was sitting in the confectionery with Bessie and a handful of customers when Loula came in from the back.

"What's wrong?" Loula said when she realized he'd returned. "Where's your daddy at?"

"They went back over to the courthouse," he said. "Horace too. He wouldn't let me go."

Loula's jaw dropped.

"Back to the courthouse? What for?"

Bill shrugged.

"Obie said they got word they were trying to lynch Dick."

Loula took a deep breath.

Bessie, who hadn't said a word in what seemed like hours, finally spoke up.

"Miss Loula, I'm scared."

Loula went to the young girl and took her in her arms.

"Now you don't worry none, child," she said tenderly. "John won't let no harm come to your brother. It's good he's there. He's a level-headed man, might keep them others from doing something foolish."

"How come Horace gets to go but not me?" said Bill.

Loula turned to her son.

"Because your daddy knows I'll snap his neck if he takes you over there. You're 16 years old, Bill Williams. Horace is 21. He's a grown man, and he can do as he pleases, but you are under my roof and my care, and I ain't having you in a situation like that at your age."

Bill lowered his head.

"Yes ma'am."

Loula drew both of them in, one arm around each.

"Now you listen to me," she told them. "We gonna get through this night, and we gonna get through it together."

****

Back at the Stradford, JB, Buck and Smitherman were seated in the lobby with Ollie and Augusta having joined them.

"You think we're out of the weeds on this?" Stradford asked Smitherman.

"We won't know until it's over," Smitherman said, "but I'd say we're through the most dangerous part. They showed up, but they didn't get him."

Stradford cocked his head in consideration.

"Mobs tend to grow braver as time goes by and more show up," he said.

"But it's after 10 p.m.," Augusta said to her husband. "People have to work in the morning. I think if they were going to do something, they would have done it hours ago."

"I think Augusta is right," said Ollie. "If it were a Friday night, I'd be more worried, but a Tuesday on a holiday week is probably working in our favor."

"I hope you're right, darling," said Smitherman.

"Then we've got to focus on getting him released before the weekend," said Buck. "The attorney that was recommended said we should be able to get a reasonable bail set when he's arraigned tomorrow."

"Don't count on it," said Smitherman. "They're going to argue he's a flight risk and that he be held without bail."

"They'll need a corroborating statement from the girl for that to be entertained," said Buck.

"And don't count on them not getting one, either," said Smitherman. "Seventeen-year-old girl in that situation will scare easily."

Buck nodded in agreement.

"Well, if you all will excuse me, I'm going to get back to the office," he told the group. "Isaiah is going to meet me there, and we're going to settle in for a long night of pulling relevant case law, see if there's anything we can pass along that might help."

"Is there anything I can do, Buck?" asked Stradford.

"No," he told him, "but I'll send word if that changes."

"I'm happy to help any way that I can too," said Smitherman. "Tomorrow's edition will include an article laying out the baseless nature of the charge. Hopefully, it'll put a little pressure on the judge to land on the right side of this thing, particularly given its volatility."

"Only the right side morally and the right side politically aren't always the same," said Ollie.

"Amen to that," added Augusta.

"True," said Smitherman, "which is why it's important to remind the powers that be how bad something like this looks from the outside. Tulsa is a city trying to sell itself to the more refined places of the world and all their deep-pocketed investors. Nonsense like this doesn't play well in places like New York and Philadelphia."

"You make a good point, Andrew," said Buck, rising to leave.

Stradford and Smitherman stood to shake Buck's hand as he bowed his head to the ladies.

****

Aunt Damie was kneeling in prayer at the end space of a pew in a mostly empty Mt. Zion Church when Pastor Whitaker walked up to her and placed a hand on her shoulder. He smiled when she looked up at him.

"Mind if I pitch in some prayer, Miss Damie?," asked the reverend.

Damie looked up at the man with glossy eyes.

"That would be right kind of you, Pastor Whitaker," she said.

As he knelt beside her, the old woman turned toward him.

"Do you think God delivers justice in this world, pastor, or does he wait until judgment day?" she asked.

"Honestly?" he said to her. "I'm not sure. The gospels tell us much about justice. It is said that when justice is done, it brings joy to the righteous and terror to the evildoers. But I believe that speaks to man acting justly toward his fellow man. There certainly are enough instances in which the wicked seem to prevail and justice fails to deliver. Often, there's scant evidence that the pious and devout are protected from the wickedness of the wretched—at least here on Earth. But I like to think that God gives us great latitude in both making and fixing our place on his Earth. If he doesn't intervene as often as we'd like, or as early as we'd like, I don't believe it's because he's indifferent. I believe it's just that he's giving us every opportunity to right the ship ourselves before he casts eternal judgment. But we are promised that God shall judge both the righteous and the wicked and that the meek shall inherit the Earth."

"My Dick is a good boy, pastor," she said, tears beginning to stream down her cracked cheeks.

"I know it," he told her, taking the woman's hand and squeezing gently. "And I promise you that the good Lord will see to it that he gets his reward, and whether it's here on Earth or at his side in Heaven doesn't matter none. And whether those who would do him harm are punished through their fate on this Earth or in spending an eternity in the flames of Hell while the righteous bathe in the glory of his light is of no concern to his true servants, for we submit that vengeance is his and that the Lord will repay."

Damie smiled at the man and the two of them turned forward to pray, hand in hand.

****

The men from Greenwood walked from the courthouse toward the area where they had stashed their cars without incident. When they arrived, they began to get load into the vehicles. The first two cars, led by John Williams, pulled off. As the others were still loading in, however, several armed whites from the courthouse crowd called out to them.

"Hey, what are you niggers doing with them guns?" yelled an old white man who looked to be in his eighties.

Obie looked around and saw that it appeared to be mostly a crowd of old men who looked to be unarmed.

"Don't you worry about it, old man," he told him. "I suggest you be on your way."

However, a few others had by this point turned the corner, including Red, Lawton, Willie, and Horse.

"You'd best mind your manners, boy," said Red, shotgun on his shoulder. "That's no way to speak to a white man, especially one that's your senior."

At this, several of the Black vets drew their weapons and there was an audible sound of guns cocking on both sides.

"Well, looks like we got a bold bunch of blackies here, don't we?" said Lawton with a sneer, as he emerged from the shadows.

Emboldened by the backing, the old man walked up and tried to grab the barrel of Obie's shotgun. Obie, as much annoyed as anything else, pulled it away, but as the old man released the barrel, the gun went off. Shots were fired from both sides, immediately. It became clear that the old man had been hit, though whether by the initial shot or crossfire was impossible to tell. One of the Greenwood vets screamed out in pain as he fell to the ground, blood soaking the leg of his pants. Red drew his rifle on Obie and stepped toward him in the street. Obie quickly turned his rifle and shot him point-blank in the chest, killing him instantly.

John Williams heard the shots ringing out and slammed on his brakes.

"What was that?" screamed Horace.

"Gunfire, son," said John, whipping the car around to head back toward the fracas. After a block, he could see two men from their group moving toward the car. It was the vet who'd been shot in the leg. He had his arm slung over the other man's shoulder.

"What happened?" asked John.

"They shot him," the man said. "They shootin' it out in the alley now. Came up on us right after y'all took off."

John stopped the car, and all four men got out to help.

"Here, put him in the back," said one of the other men. "John, you get him back to the hospital, we'll stay and help."

Horace and John put the man across the back seat, while the other three men headed back toward the fighting.

Obie and the other vets had taken cover behind the cars. Lawton and the whites had done the same, and the groups continued to fire back and forth with bodies from both sides lying dead in the street that separated them.

At the courthouse, Sheriff McCullough, having heard the shots, ran out onto the veranda. He looked around but didn't see anything. The crowd also seemed to be confused, heads quickly swinging in every direction. The sheriff ran back into the lobby where Barney and Ira were waiting with a couple of deputies on guard.

"Everyone upstairs, now!" the sheriff screamed.

He locked the double doors, then turned a flagpole standing in the corner of the room sideways, wedging it between the bars of the two doors, further reinforcing it.

Upstairs, Deputy Evers was still watching over Dick, as shots continued to ring out.

"You think that's them tryin' to come for me?" Dick asked nervously.

"Nah, I don't think so," said the deputy, who'd carefully backed up against the wall to the side of the window so that he could get a look outside without presenting a target to any would-be shooters. "It sounded like it came from too far away."

The sheriff and the others, plus Deputy Shoemaker who'd been guarding a stairwell, ran into the room. The sheriff swung a large metal door with a small, barred window closed, sealing off the area outside of the three individual cells from the hallway. He pulled a key ring from his belt and locked it.

"What's going on?" asked Deputy Evers.

"No idea," said Deputy Shoemaker.

"There's gunfire outside," said the sheriff, "not sure from who, but if they're gonna try and take the jail, they'll likely do it now. We hunker down in here and there's no way for that to happen."

Ira, Barney, and the deputies jockeyed to see through the small window from its corners but there was only confusion on the ground.

As the men from John's car returned to the alley, their shooting forced the whites to take deeper cover, giving Obie and his men a brief opening.

"Fall back toward the tracks," Obie screamed to his men. "Go!"

The men abandoned the cars and moved on foot, using them for cover as the whites fired in futility in the dark from a good distance away.

Once they were out of sight, Lawton, Horse, and Willie kneeled over Red's body in the street.

"Those sons of bitches," said Lawton. "They're gonna pay in blood."

Willie, attempting to pull back his tears, couldn't help but let out a sob.

"You sure he's dead, Lawton?" the boy asked.

Lawton stood abruptly and grabbed him by the collar of his shirt.

"Of course he's fucking dead, look at him! You wanna cry over it, go home to your mom. You wanna do something about it, buck up, get your shit together, and let's go."

Horse put his hand on Lawton's shoulder.

"Easy," he told him. "It's not him you're mad at. He's just shaken up. Come on, let's move."

Lawton spat on the ground and signaled for the men to follow him down an alley that ran in the opposite direction.

****

Gene and Megan O'Dell were eating ice cream with the others in the basement of the church after the graduation ceremony when Father Herring burst in.

"Excuse me, everyone, I need your attention," he shouted. "Listen closely. You all need to go home immediately. Get inside your house, turn off the lights and pull down the blinds. There's trouble outside, the worst kind. Go now, please."

Everyone began to panic. Megan looked to Gene in horror.

"Kelly Ann!" she screamed.

"Come on, let's go," he said, grabbing her hand. "Get them home right away and stay there," he told Willard. "We gotta find our daughter."

At the soda shop, Kelly Ann and Johnny were enjoying their cola floats when they heard a loud ruckus outside. Before they could even process the sounds, people began pouring inside the shop from the streets.

"What's going on?" a kid next to them yelled.

"There's a gunfight at the courthouse," one of the men yelled. "The niggers are shooting at the whites. There's gonna be a war."

Kelly Ann looked to Johnny, panic-stricken. He squeezed her hand.

"Come on," he said, "I'll get you home right away."

She hesitated.

"But I'm supposed to meet my dad here."

He tugged her arm.

"It might not be safe by then," he told her. "Come on, we have to go."

****

The main area lobby of the Tulsa Police Department was packed with people—both civilians and police. There was confusion and shouting. Officer Ed Kline walked swiftly toward Chief Gustafson's desk. He was followed by an old man. When they arrived, the chief was holding court before a group of detectives, civilians, and patrol officers. He didn't stop to acknowledge them, so Ed gently tapped his shoulder.

"Chief, this guy's saying he was there for the shooting," said Ed.

"Is that true?" asked the chief, looking suspiciously at the man across from him.

"Sure is," the old man said, holding his right hand in the air. "They shot my buddy."

"Who did?" asked the chief, his hands now on his hips.

"Them damned niggers," the man howled, "who you think?"

"Calm down," the chief told him. "Now tell me exactly what happened."

"They came back to the courthouse," the man said, "must've been fifty of them, all carrying guns. My buddy Skinny Lewis, he tried to disarm one of them, and they shot him dead right in the street. Then they opened fire. We shot back. There's bodies lying all over the street."

The chief slammed his hands on the desk.

"Goddammit," he screamed. "Officer Kline grab another patrolman and go down there with this man now and check it out."

The chief looked toward another officer.

"Get me the mayor on the phone."

****

Lawton, Horse and Willie were walking up an alley, when they came across an old, Black waiter walking slowly on his own. Lawton raised his rifle.

"Easy there, partner," he told the old man. "Where you think you're going?"

The man, clearly confused, raised his hands.

"I'm just walkin' home, sir," he said. "Just done finished work for the night down at Carter's. I wait tables there, have for near 11 years."

"I'm afraid you're on the wrong side of town, old man," Lawton told him.

The man cocked his head, now even more confused by the statement.

"But this the side of town the restaurant's on," he said genially. "Mr. Carter's place over on Detroit, been working there 11 years come this September. I just got done. I gotta walk back to Greenwood since the last bus already came by that way."

Lawton shook his head and spat on the ground, as he walked closer, lowering his rifle.

"You sound like a broken fucking record," he said, delivering a blow from the butt of his rifle into the man's stomach. The old man immediately doubled over, vomited, and fell to the ground in a heap. Lawton turned to Willie and handed him the shotgun.

"What's this for, Lawton?" asked Willie, equally confused.

"For Red," Lawton told him.

"But Red's not here," Willie said innocently.

"I know that, you simple son of a bitch," screamed Lawton. "It's for you to get revenge for what they done to him. An eye for an eye. Now shoot this old, raggedy nigger."

The man tried to climb up from the ground, getting only to his knees before he doubled over again. Willie still looked to be confused. He turned toward Lawton, then back to the old man, then Lawton again.

"But he didn't shoot Red, Lawton. He wasn't even there."

Lawton sighed and shook his head.

"The niggers shot Red," he finally screamed. "He's a nigger. An eye for an eye, just like the bible says. They killed our friend, we kill their... I don't know, uncle or some shit. They all seem to be related."

Horse let out a laugh, but Willie was still uncertain as to what was happening. The old man finally lifted his head.

"I mean you men no harm," he said. "I swear it. I just wanna go home to my family."

"Get a load of him," said Horse, "he means us no harm. Ain't that a fuckin' relief?"

Horse and Lawton laughed. Lawton looked to Willie who was trying to form words, though he couldn't quite manage. Willie looked at the shotgun, began to lift it, then lowered it again and inspected the weapon as if it was the first time he'd seen one. Lawton, frustrated, pulled a pistol from the back of his waistband.

"Oh Christ on a goddamned cross, you're as useless as tits on a bull," he screamed, shaking his head.

Lawton turned the pistol toward the old man and shot him point-blank in the chest, dropping him onto his back. Blood began to pool around him.

"See how easy it is, Willie," he said with indifference. "You just squeeze the trigger."

Willie looked down at the man's empty face as blood pooled in his mouth and began to spill over his cheeks. He looked to Lawton with shock, but his friend only sneered and spat down onto the old man's lifeless body.

****

John Williams and Horace pulled up to the Greenwood Hospital with the wounded man still alive in the back of their car, though he'd passed out from blood loss by that point.

John slammed the car in park right in from of the main doors and the two men carefully picked him up from the backseat and carried him toward the hospital steps.

They began yelling for help from the moment they opened the door, and the desk nurse ran to hold it open.

"Dr. Jackson, come quick," the nurse screamed.

Seconds later, Dr. Jackson came running into the lobby from the hall, just as they'd succeeded in getting the man through the doors.

"He's been shot," said John Williams. "One in the leg and another under his arm. The second one is bleeding pretty bad."

"Dr. Adams, bring a gurney, quick," yelled Dr. Jackson.

Moments later, Dr. Adams, a tall Black man in his thirties, came around the corner with a gurney. John and Horace laid the man onto it, and Dr. Jackson further ripped his shirt where it had been torn to put pressure on the wound, as Dr. Adams removed his belt and began tying off the entrance wound on the man's leg.

****

Obie and the 19 men who were still with him continued to move down the dark street in a column, weaving when there were cars they could take cover behind. They'd successfully made it several blocks and were only a couple of more from the Frisco tracks when they began taking fire.

At first, they couldn't tell where the shots were coming from. On Obie's command, they continued to move forward, popping up from behind the cars that lined the street to return fire in the general direction of the sound, whenever possible.

Back at the courthouse, many of the armed whites had left, though they had been replaced by even more unarmed and curious onlookers, including some women. As two green, three-quarter-ton Army trucks rolled by, the crowd cheered.

Inside, Barney, the sheriff, and the deputies were at the window looking out when the trucks passed.

Barney looked to the sheriff.

"You think the governor sent the guard in?"

The sheriff shook his head.

"Those boys are from the armory, and I doubt they'll be any more help than the police."

"Good news is, seems like most of the troublemakers out front been drawn away by the fighting," said Barney. "Expect maybe they given up on gettin' their hands on Dick?"

The sheriff shrugged.

"For now, maybe."

****

At the Tulsa Police Station, Henry Sowders looked lost as he staggered around the lobby, confused by the crowd and their excitement. He finally made it to the front desk.

"Excuse me, officer... officer, excuse me," he said, trying to get the attention of the desk sergeant.

"What?" the officer finally answered in a perturbed tone.

"I need to report a robbery," Henry Sowders told him. "My car, it's been stolen. I work-"

The sergeant cut him off mid-sentence.

"Look, we ain't got time for that, you'll have to come back. You wanna be deputized?"

Henry was confused.

"How's that?" he asked.

The desk officer held up a tin badge that read "special deputy."

"Deputized?" asked Henry, still confused.

"Deputized," the officer repeated, loudly. "If you're gonna shoot niggers tonight, you gotta be sworn in and meet out front. Otherwise, you're on your own."

Rendered speechless by the suggestion, Henry shook his head and backed away, bumping into another man as he turned to run toward the door. In the parking lot, he looked up to see a national guard commander standing on the back of a flatbed.

"All right, listen up," the soldier said. "If you're a minor, you need to go home. If you're a military veteran, go over to that area," he said as he pointed to his left where several guard soldiers were. "If you're a civilian, you need to see Sergeant Carlson to be deputized and issued ammunition. All prisoners are to be taken to the convention hall."

"Prisoners?" one man in the crowd laughed. "Grab a gun, shoot a nigger. Ain't gonna be no prisoners tonight, boys."

Nearby, Sergeant Carlson was handing out tin badges and hurriedly swearing people in as temporary deputies. A civilian next to him inspected their weapons and then gave them the proper ammo.

"I hereby deputize you," said Sergeant Carlson as he pinned one man. "I hereby deputize you," he repeated, pinning the next. "Ah shit," he said, looking around. He bent down and felt his hands around another box behind him.

"Alright, we're out of badges," he finally said. "I'm gonna give the rest of you a ribbon to keep with you."

Henry was still spellbound, walking sideways and bumping into people nervously as he looked around, trying to exit the scene. As he passed a city patrolman, he overheard the officer talking to two civilians.

"Most of the action is on Second Avenue right now, from how I hear it," the officer said. "They got a bunch of niggers pinned down. More fighting' going' on a few blocks north near the Frisco tracks, too."

Henry got a few blocks down the street when he came upon a crowd of men standing outside of a hardware store. He watched with them as one man threw a rock through the glass door. The crowd, some of which were wearing tin badges, immediately entered, and, in a matter of minutes, people began emerging with rifles, loading guns from boxes of ammunition.

****

Gene sped down the city streets, both he and Megan looking nervously in all directions. Suddenly, a group of people ran in front of the car and Gene slammed on the brakes, barely avoiding hitting them as the car screeched to a halt. He lurched forward in his seat and could see the lights from the theater a half-block ahead. Gunshots rang out and he looked to his wife, grabbing her hand.

"Listen to me," he told her. "Stay right here."

"Gene! No-"

"Listen to me," he screamed. "When I get out, lock the doors. I'm gonna leave the engine running. I'll grab her, and we'll go. That's the safest way."

His wife went pale as her jaw dropped. Gene broke away from her hand and jumped out of the car, running toward the theater. Though it felt like an eternity to his wife, he emerged just moments later, ran a couple of doors down to the soda shop but quickly exited without Kelly Ann, sprinting back toward the car. Megan fumbled with his door, and he jumped back into the driver's seat once it had been opened.

"Where is she?" Megan cried.

"The soda jerk is pretty sure she left about 10 minutes ago," he told her as he turned the key. "It's crazy in there."

"Oh my god-" she cried.

"Stay calm, Meg, listen. I'm taking you to the house. You wait there in case she comes home. I'll head back out to look."

"I'm not-"

"Meg, listen to me. She'll go to the house. We don't want her there alone. We don't even know what it's like over our way."

****

Obie and his men were dug in on 2nd Street, shooting it out with a much larger force this time, some of which were firing at them from rooftops.

"They get more men firing from high ground, we in trouble," one of the vets said to Obie, as more shots rang out in the distance.

"Gunfire's comin' from both directions down that way," Obie said. "That's good news, at least."

"Sounds like maybe the tracks, down around Detroit?" asked McKinley.

"Greenwood Avenue, most likely," Obie replied.

"That's only six blocks once we hit the tracks," his brother said, "but we gotta get past 1st Street, which might be lit up."

"Be harder farther east we go," said Obie. "We cut back a block, cross, and then double back, less of a chance we lose men."

"How we get outta this nest?" asked the other vet.

"You gonna go down the line and tell each man that when he see the one to his right break, count to five and break behind him," Obie instructed. "Run like the devil chasin' him, but keep they heads low. We'll lay down fire while they move. These peckerwoods ain't gonna follow. Frisco tracks at Greenwood Ave is the rally point. You be first out the gate so they follow."

374

The man squatted down low and began doing as he was instructed. Obie turned to his brother.

"Hey, McKinley?"

"Yeah?"

"We get outta this, I'm gonna let you buy those refrigeration units."

McKinley laughed, and both men took aim from a prone position and began shooting as the first men moved out.

****

A mob of armed whites roamed a crowded street in downtown Tulsa, as nervous onlookers stared, unaware of what was happening. Four men from the mob broke off, storming into a crowded restaurant. Guests screamed as the armed men entered. The man in front pointed a gun toward the maître d' and tugged his badge with his other hand. The maître d', petrified, raised his hands into the air.

"We're sworn deputies ordered to round up all niggers," the man shouted. "Go get all your nigger help from the back and bring 'em up here now."

Frightened half to death, the maître d' was unable to manage words. He just nodded his head and ran toward the back.

Gene stopped the car in front of the O'Dell house and looked to Megan.

"Get inside the house," he told her. "If she's in there, you blink the porch light one time and I'll come in. If not, you blink it twice. Don't come out. Lock all the windows and doors, and pull down the shades just like Father said. She gets home before I come back, you put the porch light on, so I'll know."

Tears running down her cheeks, Megan nodded, opening the door. Before she closed it, she looked back at her husband, who'd seemed to age several years since they left the church.

"Bring back our baby, Gene."

He reached out and squeezed her hand.

"I will," he said. "I promise."

Megan hurried into the house. Gene fidgeted, looked at his watch and then up to the porch where Megan was closing the door. A moment passed and the light blinked twice. He sighed and lowered his head to the wheel. After another moment had passed, he snapped to and pulled off into the night.

Outside of the restaurant, four men had three Black dishwashers up against the outside of the building, legs spread, palms against the glass panes, while patrons look out with wide eyes—some horrified, some only curious. The leader checked the pockets of the first man, taking out a wallet. He emptied its money and tossed it into the street, putting the cash in his pocket. The dishwasher at the far end looked over at him.

"What's this about, sir?" he asked. "You can't rob us in the street like this. That ain't the law."

The man walked down to the dishwasher, who lowered his head in fear, causing the man to smile. He gave a tug to the tin badge on his shirt.

"Listen, nigger, you see this here badge? That means I *am* the law. I can do whatever I want. We have orders to round y'all up, and since we ain't getting paid to collect niggers tonight, I think it's only fair that we impart a little darkie tax this evening."

While he was speaking, the man he'd just tossed took off in a sprint down the street. The second mobster quickly drew his rifle and shot him in the middle of the back, causing the man's corpse to collapse forward in a pool of its own blood.

"Looks like we only gotta walk two of them down to the convention hall now," a third man said with a laugh that was reciprocated by the others.

The first mobster went back about his work, kicking open the feet of the man who'd just questioned him and going in his pocket as well. This time, the man offered no words.

****

At one of the many boarding houses on 1st Street, a white man in dirty clothes was banging on a pot with a large spoon in the hallway to wake the boarders.

"Wake up," he screamed. "It's nigger day. Wake up."

In one of the dark rooms, a man stirred on a cot. Once awake, he hit the light and then opened his door to the hallway, squinting as he looked out, still half asleep. Other doors opened.

"What in Sam Hill is goin' on out here?" one of the men asked.

"It's nigger day," said the man beating the pot. "They're warring in the streets, and tonight you're allowed to shoot as many niggers as you want. Can't get in trouble or nothin'."

****

Obie and his men were high-crawling along the gulch between the Frisco tracks. A train, slowing as it approached the depot, lit the area around them. When its whistle blew, Obie stood and whistled through his teeth, waving the men to the other side of the track, while running down to the back of the formation. As the train moved by slowly, he waited until an open freight car passed and jumped in, pulling up the next man. The rest followed.

At a stretch of tracks closest to Greenwood and Archer, around a dozen Black men fought from positions on the Greenwood side. A shot rang out from one of the windows, then another. It was the Williams Building and inside John Williams was positioned in an upper floor window, aiding the battle as a sniper. He fired off a shot and handed the gun to Bill, picking up a different rifle. Horace was against the wall with a pistol breathing heavily.

"Reload that," John told his son. "Loula," he screamed toward the stairwell.

Loula ran to the door of the room.

"Baby, it's time to get Bessie and drive straight out to Henrietta's house," John said. "That's a good mile out in the country, won't be no trouble out there tonight."

Loula tilted her head in shock.

"I am *not* leaving our house, John Williams. I'm not leaving our-"

John turned around sharply. He was generally deferential to his wife, whose intelligence and independence he admired greatly. But this was no time for questioning the plan.

"Baby, you listen now, and do as I say," he told her. "We got this here. You get Bessie and you get in the Chalmers, and you drive north until you get to Henrietta and Del's. I'll come get you tomorrow, but it ain't fit for women here right now."

Loula looked at him and began to speak but nothing came out.

"Go on now, baby," he said. "Do as I say."

Loula kissed the top of Bill's head and ran out of the room. John turned and fired out the window. Horace nervously turned and shot the pistol without aiming. Bill handed John the other gun.

****

Samuel and Olivia Hooker's mother had made them hide under the kitchen table when the white mobsters began pounding at the door. Neither could understand what was happening when the men entered and angry voices started

380

questioning their father's whereabouts and asking about weapons that were kept in the house.

Were the men police? They thought it all may have been a joke or a misunderstanding until the hatchets began destroying their belongings. Their mother shrieked as a man crashed his ax into the family's piano where their older sister would entertain guests. She begged them to stop, as they shattered her precious record collection after looting the family's Victrola record player.

Chapter 9

At the convention hall, there were already nearly 100 Blacks sitting on the floor. A police officer sitting at a card table with two civilians was writing down names when a white man walked in with four Black women in tow.

"More?" asked the officer, annoyed. "What's with all the women? They don't fight. Stick with the men. The place will be full in an hour if you bring me every mammy in Tulsa."

A few blocks away, a Black man was sprinting down an alley, five white men closing in on him from behind. The man unexpectedly cut hard to his left, slamming into a door in the alley, which opened. He ran inside.

It was the Rialto Theater, where a handful of people watched a movie, obtuse to what was happening in the streets outside. The small crowd gasped when they saw him and, as he ran up the center aisle, a shot rang out from the door. The man fell dead, blood pooling from the bullet hole in his lower back.

****

Miss Annie and Megan sat quietly in the sitting room just beyond the foyer of the O'Dell house, fidgeting nervously, looking at the door. There was a noise at the steps that caused both women to jump to their feet. Before either could get to the door, it opened and Kelly Ann fell forward, Johnny behind her. Megan hugged her daughter tight as she began to sob loudly.

"Oh my God in Heaven, I was so worried," Megan shouted.

"Mother, it was awful," said her daughter, still crying. "They're killing people in the streets. They dragged a Black man down Boulder Avenue! He was tied to the bumper of a motor car!"

Miss Annie covered her mouth in horror. Megan pulled her daughter to her. Then she stepped toward Johnny, one arm still over Kelly Ann, and took his hand.

"Thank you for getting her back here safely," she told him.

"Yes ma'am," he said.

"Do you need to call your parents and tell them you're alright?" Megan asked.

"No ma'am," he assured her. "I think I'd best just hurry back quickly."

"Are you sure it's safe?" Megan asked. "You are welcome to stay here."

"Yes ma'am. It's... I'm... not in any danger," he said, looking somewhat apologetically toward Miss Annie, who was still crying. He reached out and touched Kelly Ann's arm on his way to the door.

"See you at school?"

Kelly Ann looked up and nodded, her eyes red and puffy from their tears.

****

As the train continued down the Frisco tracks toward Greenwood, the shooting momentarily stopped if only because it was obscuring much of the field of vision. As it pulled by, however, the vets jumped off and the other Blacks cheered their arrival. Almost simultaneously, three cars pulled in from Greenwood Avenue. King Henry, Mooch and Freddy got out of the lead vehicle. Seven others fell in behind them, all armed. Henry looked toward Obie.

"Hey, big man," said Henry.

Obie looked over to him.

"We wit'cha if you need us," Henry said.

Obie nodded.

"Fall in," he told them, and the men hurried into positions as the last cars began to roll down the tracks. Obie signaled for everyone's attention, while the cover still existed.

"When that last car passes," he said, "unleash hell on these pecker woods."

On the other side of the train, many of the whites had moved down closer to their position, using the train as cover, hoping to charge from behind the last car. However, when it passed, shots rang out furiously and they were caught off guard by the new men. Several of the whites fell and more retreated.

From the window above the street, John Williams emptied his gun as they ran back to their position. Now he had both Cecil and Bill switching them out for him. With a new gun, he dropped two of the white men before drawing the rifle back up to aim. He fired and another man fell.

"You weren't expecting that, now was you?" he screamed. "Whoooh! Ain't nobody taking Greenwood on this night, boys. We defending the promised land."

Bill and Horace tried to put on brave faces, though they were clearly petrified by fear.

****

Lawton and his crew had made their way to the fringes of Greenwood, where others had already been looting the homes. Lawton, Horse, and Willie were moving down a dark street when shots rang out at a distance, frightening Willie.

"Why we moving so far west, Lawton," he asked nervously.

"Rest of them are going about it wrong," said Lawton. "What they teach us in the Army? Attack from the flank, right? The niggers are gonna defend Greenwood and Archer the hardest, so we're gonna come in from Boston Ave and work inward."

"That's smart, Lawton."

Lawton looked at Willie and shook his head.

Shots rang from closer to where they were positioned and the men ducked down to move forward. Turning a corner, they saw three white men behind a wagon, shooting it out with a Black man in a second-story window.

At the base of the building, another white man poured gasoline. Once it was good and doused, he lit a match and the building began to go up in flames. Moments later, the Black man ran out the front door and was immediately shot dead by one of the others. Back at the wagon, one of the men removed the cover, revealing that it was filled with jerrycans of gasoline.

"Worked even better than I thought," he said to Lawton, Horse and Willie. "Gentlemen?" he asked looking toward the gasoline.

Lawton smiled.

****

In the O'Dell house, the three women remained in the sitting room waiting for Gene. Megan was holding Kelly Ann, while Miss Annie continued to rock in her chair nervously when a loud knock shook the door. All three women were startled.

"Who's there?" Megan yelled.

"Police," screamed the voice, "open the door."

Megan motioned for the others to be silent, walked to the door and looked in the peephole where she saw two men in plainclothes who did not look like police officers. She quickly walked to the window and looked down, where she could see three Black women and two Black men sitting in the middle of the street. Three white men had rifles trained on them.

"Open up now," the voice screamed, "before I kick it in."

Megan ran back to the door.

"You don't look like police," she said, her mouth nearly pressed up against it as she looked into the hole. "What do you want?"

The man tugged his tin badge toward the peephole. Megan saw it and cautiously unlocked the door, leaving the chain lock in place.

"What's this about?" she asked.

"Ma'am, unlock that chain, or I kick it in, so help me god," the man said.

Not knowing what else to do, Megan complied, looking at Annie, who was now being hugged by Kelly Ann from the side, with tears in both of their eyes.

"The nigger's coming with us," the man said. "We got orders to round 'em all up."

"What orders?" shouted Megan. "From who? That's preposterous."

Miss Annie rose.

"Miss Megan, it's okay," she said walking toward the man. "I'll go. I don't want no trouble for y'all."

Megan put her arm out in front of Annie's chest and turned back to the man.

"Over my dead body, you will," she said.

The man cocked his shotgun. Kelly Ann shrieked.

"Look, lady," said the mobster, "you turn her over, or I shoot her where she stands. We already killed us two niggers tonight. Three won't make no difference, but you should know they bleed like a river. It'll ruin that fancy rug for sure."

As the man drew the rifle, Kelly Ann whaled, falling to the floor crying. Megan put her hands on her face and Annie hurried over to the man, who grabbed her by the arm.

"That's a good girl," the man said. "See? Easy as pie."

Kelly Ann looked at her mother, horrified.

"It's okay, now, don't worry," Miss Annie said to her. "I'll be okay."

The man shoved Annie out the door and walked her down the steps. Another man yelled for the other Blacks to rise, kicking one in the bottom when he stood. The white men laughed uproariously and continued toward the next house on the block.

****

On Boston Avenue, near Archer Street, a white man ran out of a house with a phonograph player as smoke began to billow from the upstairs windows. He threw it onto a flatbed truck full of housewares they'd pilfered. Next door, Horse led a Black man out his front door at gunpoint. When they got to the curb, he kicked the man in the back, causing him to fall to the ground. As he laid there muttering, Horse held up a jerrycan and began dousing the floor inside the house from the doorway. As he started to light the match, the man cried out in horror.

"No, no, my wife and children are in the attic."

Horse struck the match and dropped in on the carpet and the doorway went up in flames.

"And you swore you were all alone in there," Horse said to the man, shaking his head. "I guess you'd better go up and get them then."

The man ran to the door and looked at the flames. He began to move in but jumped back when he felt the flames burn his skin. He looked back at Horse, who was laughing as he watched the scene unfold with amusement. The man blocked his face with his forearms and tried to run in again, getting a little further before running out, choking on the smoke that filled his lungs.

Inside a nearby house, Lawton was filling two pillowcases with silver, jewelry and other valuables when Willie walked into the room.

"They won't leave," Willie said sheepishly.

"What do you mean they won't leave?" asked Lawton. "You've got a fucking gun in your hand, don't you? *Make* them leave."

A tear rolled down Willie's face.

"They still won't listen, Lawton."

Lawton gave Willie a cross look and dropped the bags so that he could pick up his shotgun. He walked off quickly and climbed a flight of stairs where he found an elderly Black couple who were on their knees, bedside, praying in loud whispers. Lawton shook his head and raised his rifle.

"I'm afraid prayers won't help tonight, folks," he said.

Downstairs, Willie winced as two shots rang out.

Lawton and Willie emerged from the house moments later with two pillowcases each. Horse was waiting with the jerrycan.

"Torch it," Lawton said, looking back toward the house they'd just left.

Horse entered the living room, doused the walls and floor, then dropped a match. When he stepped back outside, the man from the previous house was tumbling out the door with his wife and two daughters, covered in blankets. Lawton raised his rifle at them.

"Nah, let that one go," laughed Horse. "He's got some real grit."

Lawton lowered his rifle and spat on the ground. As the family trotted away sheepishly, he raised his gun in the air and let go of a round. Without looking back, the family took off, hand in hand, sprinting. Horse and Lawton doubled over with laughter at the sight of their fear. Meanwhile, Willie felt happy to see them get away and thought about slipping off while his two friends were laughing but couldn't muster the courage.

****

Ira, the sheriff, and deputies Cleaver, Evers, and Shoemaker were still hunkered down in the holding cell room, unaware of how bad the fighting had gotten. Only Ira, the sheriff, and Barney remained awake, with Dick asleep in his cell, and the other two deputies catching some sleep on the sheriff's orders.

"This is likely the only chance to get him out, Bill," said Ira. "They've lost interest for now, but if this thing gets worse—and it still might—they'll be back, and there'll be a lot more of them."

The sheriff drew a deep breath, rubbed his face, and began to pace the room.

"Might have worked up the courage by then, too," he conceded. "He won't be safe anywhere in this state, Ira, you know that."

Ira nodded.

"You got any ideas on where to stash him?"

The sheriff paused in contemplation.

"I know a sheriff up in Kansas City that I trust," he finally said. "If I can get in touch with him and he agrees to help, you think we can get the kid up there tonight?"

Ira folded his arms and looked out the window.

"The depot will be too risky, and that's a hell of a drive, especially on no sleep," he said.

The sheriff nodded toward Evers and Shoemaker.

"They should be rested enough to drive in shifts."

"Sheriff," said Barney, "I can go. I'm wide awake with adrenaline. No way I could sleep if I wanted to."

The sheriff nodded but began shaking his head as he spoke.

"No, I want you to get back over to Greenwood, look in on your family, get some rest, be ready for whatever comes at us tomorrow."

"Are you sure?" he asked.

"Yeah, might be safer for them to be running him around tonight anyway."

Barney nodded and the sheriff walked over to the door, unlocking it.

"Wake up those two Sleeping Beauties," he told Barney, nodding toward Evers and Shoemaker.

****

In the second-story offices of Chappelle, Spears & Franklin, Isaiah and Buck were peeking through the blinds into what seemed to be empty streets.

"It looks like they may have given it a rest for a while, at least over this way," Isaiah said.

"I hope you're right," said Buck. "The shots seem to be much less frequent now, and they all seem to be coming from down by the train depot."

"I can't figure whether it'll be better by morning or worse," said Isaiah.

"You mean will they wake up with shame for what they've done, or with a taste for some more?" asked Buck.

"Exactly."

Buck sighed.

"You know, when I was at the courthouse today to drop that petition off, I overheard something that I didn't put together until far too late."

"What was that?" asked Isaiah.

Buck paused for a moment, biting his lip before responding.

"There were a bunch of white attorneys standing in the lobby when I left, and they were excited about something. I heard one say, 'No way, I've known that kid for years. Doesn't have it in him,' and another answered, 'Me too, been going to his stand forever, nicest kid you'd ever want to meet.' Finally, a third one says, 'None of that will do him any good now.' Then, on my way home, I heard a newsie saying something about a negro attacking a white girl. It wasn't until JB sounded the alarm much later that I put it together."

"Surely, you're not thinking you could have prevented this, Buck?" said Isaiah.

"I don't know," he said, shaking his head with a sigh. "Probably not. I just thought that maybe if I'd known who those two attorneys were, I could have... I don't know."

Isaiah turned toward him and put a hand on Buck's shoulder.

"Hell, half the men involved know Dick didn't do it," he told him. "This has nothing to do with the kid. He was just an excuse."

Buck nodded as he yawned.

"You're probably right."

"Hey," said Isaiah, "why don't you get a little sleep on that couch. I'll watch the window, and we'll sleep in shifts until daybreak."

"That's not a bad idea," Buck conceded. "I could surely use the rest. Wake me in an hour and we'll switch?"

Isaiah nodded and Buck laid down, falling asleep within moments.

****

Gene O'Dell was in his car, stuck behind of large line of vehicles that were honking their horns. He got out and walked quickly alongside of them to see what was holding up traffic. At the front, he finally saw a young Black man lying in the street, writhing in a pool of blood. Three white men were standing over him. Two held pistols, one had a shotgun, while an unarmed man in a suit argued with them.

"You can't leave him there in the street blocking traffic all night," the man in the suit said.

"You wanna drag him over to the curb, be my guest," said the man with the shotgun.

The man in the suit looked down at the hemorrhaging Black man, shook his head in frustration, and got back inside the first car in line. Gene stared at the scene, mouth agape.

Moments later, a siren rang out and an ambulance arrived from the opposite direction. Two white medics dismounted, but the man with the shotgun aimed it at them. The medics raised their hands.

"Get the hell out of here," the man said. "Touch that nigger and I'll shoot you myself. We got shot up white people all over town, and you're gonna treat a nigger? What's the matter with you?"

The medics looked at each other.

"Sir... we..." the first attempted.

But another shot rang out and when everyone turned back, one of the men with pistols was standing over the body.

"There," he said, "ain't nothing to talk about no more. Now get back in your wagon and go find some whites to help. Ain't got no time for nigger lovers tonight."

Gene was both shocked and horrified, but unarmed and outnumbered found himself unable to do anything buy get back into his car, instantly shamed by his own inaction.

When Gene finally made it back to the house, his heavy heart was lifted by the sight of the porch light burning brightly. He exhaled deeply in relief, dropped his head to the wheel for a moment, and then quickly parked the car and ran to the front door.

"Meg," he yelled before even getting to the door, and his wife jumped up, unlocked the latch and threw herself into his arms as he entered.

"Oh thank God you're alright, angel, I was so worried," he said to Kelly Ann as she came into view from behind Megan and hugged the two of them.

"They took Annie," Kelly Ann sobbed.

"What?" said Gene. "Who took Annie?"

"Men who said they were deputies," said Megan, crying. "They had these stupid little tin badges on and were rounding them up from all the houses."

Both women were crying. Gene pulled them both in and rubbed their backs as they sobbed.

"They're doing a whole lot worse downtown," he said, shaking his head. "Meg, I ain't never seen nothin' like it."

"Is it the Klan?" she asked.

"It's hard to say," Gene told her. "No one needs a hood tonight, they're killing people right out in the open."

Megan's face grew even more serious.

"Are we in danger, Gene?"

He shrugged helplessly.

"I dunno, honey. I really don't."

Gene walked over to the wall and took down a crucifixion cross hanging from it, then a picture of the Christ that hung nearby.

"What are you doing, daddy?" Kelly Ann asked.

"It's only the Blacks now, but who knows what they'll do next," said her father.

Megan cocked her head.

"You don't think-"

"Meg!" he screamed. "You didn't see them out there. They look like wolves who've smelled blood. They come in here and see we're Catholic?"

Gene put the cross and picture frame on the floor and ran to the closet from which he grabbed his shotgun. He put it down momentarily and removed the medal of St. Martin from his neck.

"Take those crosses off your necks," he told his wife and daughter. "Put all this stuff in a closet upstairs someplace. The last one somebody would look in."

****

Back at the Stradford, JB, Augusta, Smitherman and Ollie were in a third-floor hotel room. Stradford was talking with his wife and Ollie, while Smitherman kept a lookout from the front window with a rifle at his side.

"Look, I'm not saying put them out in the street," Stradford told the women, "but you've got to let every person here know just how dangerous of a place the hotel is right now."

"I did," his wife pleaded. "Some of them still won't leave. It's the best-built building in town, John. Some of these people live in shacks."

"And where do you think they're gonna wanna burn, Augusta, the shacks, or the mighty Stradford Hotel?" her husband asked.

"He's right, Augusta," reasoned Ollie. "This place will be the crown jewel of their conquest, and if you and John don't leave they're liable to put his head on a spit and parade it through town."

Augusta picked up a crystal tumbler and threw it at the wall. It smashed into hundreds of pieces. Her husband picked one up and did the same.

"Go on," he told her, "throw them all. Ain't gonna be here in the morning no how."

He threw two more and she grabbed him to make him stop and he hugged her tight to his body.

"I'm sorry, baby," he said, "this is just the way it is. Lord, you know I'd change it if I could."

"There's a pretty big crowd headed this way, JB," Smitherman said.

Stradford looked at his wife.

"We either go down fighting, right here, right now, or we leave, and live to fight another day?"

"But everything we have is here," she said, tears welling in her eyes.

"Well, you wanna die and be buried under its rubble, we can do that," he told her. "But we're not going to save it, not this time."

Smitherman picked up his rifle and ran over to them.

"Augusta, he's right," he said. "We have no choice. We have to leave, and we have to go now. We don't have the firepower to hold off a mob that size."

She nodded silently.

"Get the bags and go down the back way to the car,"
Stradford told her. "I'll meet you there."

Outside the building, a band of around 30 white men
and about a dozen women approached the hotel, many
carrying burning torches. Inside, Stradford opened a safe and
began shoving stacks of cash into his breast pocket, then his
pants pockets, and finally inside his shirt. He grabbed bearer
bonds, the rest of the cash, some jewelry and shoved it into a
pillowcase, grabbed his pistol, and left the safe open.

Back outside, a man picked up a brick and fired it at
the front of the hotel, smashing a large pane of glass.
Smitherman, Ollie, and Augusta descended a set of external
fire stairs and loaded their things into a fancy black sedan at
the bottom of it, then got inside. JB emerged from a bottom
floor exit and ran to the car. As soon as he was inside, the car
sped off.

Back at the hotel, the mob had gotten inside. Men with
shotguns rounded up Black men, while white women with
pillowcases began filling them with candlesticks, lamps, and
other fixtures in the lobby.

****

Four men in suits sat in a dimly-lit office. One was on the phone, while the others sat quietly.

"Okay, thank you, mayor. I will. Goodnight," he said, hanging up the phone.

"Well?" asked one of the other men.

"He's calling the governor," said the man who'd been on the phone, "asking him to send in the guard."

"That'll take until morning at the earliest," said the third man. "They'll have to send in a train from Oklahoma City, most likely."

"Time to make the other arrangements then?" asked the first man.

"Yes, call the airfield," said the fourth man, speaking for the first time.

The man who'd been on the phone picked it back up. The other two looked at the fourth man.

"Go on and start getting everyone organized," he said to them. "We go in at dawn, but make sure some fighting keeps up through the night. Wear them down. Keep rounding up the men and the guns."

"Yes, sir," one said.

The man got up and left. The other man hung up the phone and looked at the remaining two.

"These opportunities don't tend to present themselves often," he said to them. "Got to make the most of them, I suppose."

****

Sheriff McCullough, Deputy Evers, Deputy Shoemaker, Ira, and Dick were in an alley behind the courthouse, where a patrol car was waiting. The sheriff opened the trunk and looked at Dick.

"Trust me," he said to him, "much safer than the back seat on a night like this."

Dick, already nervously scanning the alley, looked at the open trunk with skepticism.

"Will I be able to breathe?"

"Sure," said the sheriff. "It might be stuffy, but you'll be in no danger. My deputies will pull over and let you into the backseat just as soon as they get to the edge of town and there's no chance of anyone seeing you back there."

Dick nodded and looked back to McCullough.

"What'll happen to me, sheriff?"

"Sheriff Dunnigan in Kansas City is gonna hold you until he gets word from me," the sheriff explained. "He's a good man. Just listen to him, and you'll be alright. I won't bring you back here until we have your legal status sorted out, and I know it's safe."

Dick looked at the trunk then back to the sheriff.

"Will you tell my Aunt Damie I'm okay?"

The sheriff nodded.

"I sure will."

"Sheriff?" Dick asked.

"Yes?"

"Thank you," he said and then turned to the others. "Thank all of you."

"We're just doing our job, kid," the sheriff told him. "Mind yourself up there and this will all work out, alright?"

Dick nodded.

"Yes, sir. I sure will."

Cautiously, Dick climbed into the trunk. When he'd finished contorting his long body into the small box, Ira carefully closed the deck lid. The sheriff walked Deputy Evers up to the driver's door and leaned down after he climbed in.

"Remember, you don't stop for anything, and I mean anything," the sheriff said. "Anyone tries to interfere with you, you're under orders to shoot the sons of bitches, you understand?"

"Yes, sheriff," the deputy told him.

The sheriff banged the side of the driver's door, and they pulled off, leaving just he and Ira.

"You think they'll make it up there alright?" asked Ira.

"Yeah," the sheriff said. "Evers is a good kid, sharp too. Shoemaker's a little slow on the uptake sometimes, but his heart's in the right place."

Ira laughed and the two men watched until the taillights faded in the distance.

****

Lawton, Horse, and Willie were among a crowd of men waiting outside the police station to be issued ammo. Seeing two local guardsmen standing next to a large-caliber machine gun that sat on the back of a flatbed, Lawton left the line to engage them.

"Browning M1919, nice," he said, admiring the weapon.

"You familiar with it?" one of the soldiers asked.

"I was a gunner over in Germany," he told him, then pointed to Horse. "That big bastard over there was on my team. He was the one that humped it."

The soldier nodded as he sized up Horse, clearly impressed by the man's gargantuan stature.

"What the hell's it doing gathering dust over here though, while people are getting shot?" Lawton asked. "We could end this whole mess in an hour with that thing spitting out 30 cal shells at those monkeys."

"We're gonna see if this thing dies off through the night," the other soldier said. "If not, we'll set up it and another we got on the tracks in the morning. Push them back."

"Why set 'em both up on the tracks, corporal?" asked Lawton. "We should get this one up on Standpipe Hill. If we wake up in the morning and there's still fighting going on, we'll rain down on them from above."

The guardsmen looked at each other, then around to see who might be listening or looking.

"Couldn't hurt to get in position?" the first one said.

"Fuck it, why not?" said the other. "It'd end it quickly if it's still going by then."

Lawton smiled.

"See, it's practically the humane thing to do."

He let out a muted whistle to get the attention of Horse and Willie, then signaled them over, looking back at the guardsmen with a smile.

****

Gurley and his wife carefully peeked out from behind the curtains of a room on the third floor of their hotel. They could still hear gunshots and could see fires burning on the horizon.

"Look at it, Emma," he said to her. "Look at it burn. There will be nothing left when they're through. All that we've built, all that we've worked for."

Gurley clenched his jaw and pounded his fist on the sill as tears welled in his eyes. His wife put a hand on his shoulder and rubbed it.

"You did everything you could, Otto. You did everything possible to stop this."

He clenched his fist and held it up.

"I told them they'd burn us to the ground," he said angrily. "I told them we had no chance. And for what? The kid's probably hanging from a tree right now anyway."

Gurley dropped his head and began to weep. His wife kissed him on the back of his head as she continued to rub his shoulder. Soon, tears began rolling down her cheeks as well.

****

The convention hall was nearly at capacity. Annie was being checked in at a desk set up near the main entrance.

"Name?" the police officer asked her.

"Brown, sir," she said, her voice cracking. "Annie Brown."

"Age?"

"32, sir."

"Go ahead and take a seat on the floor wherever you can find one," the officer said indifferently. "You're free to lie down and sleep if you want. Next."

"Can you tell me if any of my people are here, sir? I have three children, one is-"

The officer looked up at her with anger in his eyes.

"What the fuck does this look like to you, lady, central information? Take a look around, we got thousands of your kind in here. You're probably related to half of these animals given the way you people mate."

He shook his head.

"Next."

Miss Annie put her head down and began to walk away, trembling when something deep inside of her welled up to the surface with a force that wouldn't allow her to take another step. She clenched her fists and looked up to the sky, mumbling in prayer for a moment before turning back to the officer.

"I got three children, officer," she said, her chin held high. "They daddy—*my husband*—was a good man who died in Germany, fighting for this here country. I live and work in servant's quarters on this side of town, get to see them but once a week, but I'm blessed that my momma can look after them when I'm gone. I didn't do nothing to nobody, and yet these men dragged me from they house and put me in this pen like I'm some kind of stray dog. I-"

Before the next word could pass her lips, the deputized mobster who'd brought her in delivered the butt of his rifle to her gut, doubling Miss Annie over on the ground where she writhed in pain. He grabbed her by the hand and dragged her along the floor, away from the table.

"Alright, that's enough from you, loudmouth," he told her. "What I tell you about all that noise?"

He finally let go of her arm and she remained on the ground, prone on her stomach, weeping loudly. With her fist, she pounded the ground with an open palm and cried harder.

****

As Stradford drove his Rolls Royce out of town, he looked over to Augusta, whose head was resting against the passenger window. Ollie was nestled into Smitherman's chest in the back seat. They all kept looking toward the passenger side where there was a complete view of the city in the night, small sections of smoke billowing up against the skyline.

Augusta, whose head pressed against the glass of the passenger seat, couldn't bear to look back at her husband as tears rolled down her face. Stradford looked back to the road, and then back to her window as they all watched Greenwood burn.

****

Sheriff McCullough pulled up to the front of a small bungalow on an empty, quiet street, looking at it for a moment before he noticed that one of the lights were on. He closed his eyes and tapped the wheel for a moment, then got out of the car. He paused again on the porch before finally rapping on the glass of the front door very softly with the back of his knuckles. He fidgeted nervously and had turned to leave when he heard the door unlock. He turned and Annie opened it, wearing a nightgown with a robe over top.

"Bill!" she said, somewhat surprised. "What are you doing here?"

"I... I don't know," he stammered. "I'm so sorry, this was stupid. It's late. I just was on my way home and I saw the light was on-"

"There were gunshots," she said. "I couldn't sleep."

"I just wanted to make sure you were safe is all," he said, "I'm sorry, I shouldn't have-"

Another gunshot rang out in the distance and Annie abruptly pulled him forward by the collar. He inhaled the scent of her hair, and she raised her head. Pressing her mouth to his forcefully, she began kissing him with a passion neither had known in many years. The sheriff was surprised for a moment but then eagerly began to return the kiss, pushing her across the threshold and into the house where she pulled him against the wall and kissed him with even greater intensity, unbuttoning his shirt as he pushed closed the front door and opened her robe.

****

At the same moment, inside the Tribune building, Richard Lloyd Jones crashed his torso into Amy Comstock, who was looking back at him, while bent over his large desk as he roughly took her from behind. The phone rang loudly as he finished with a final thrust. He moved quickly to answer it, causing his paramour to frown.

"Hello?" said Richard into the receiver. "Georgia, dear, what are you still doing up? Oh nonsense, you wouldn't be any safer at Fort Knox… Well I'm just finishing up some stuff for tomorrow's edition. As you can imagine, things are crazy around here... I was gonna just catch a few winks on the couch to tell you the truth."

Amy, clearly annoyed, began to quickly dress herself. Richard grabbed her arm and gave her a consoling look while shaking his head.

"No, I won't," he continued into the receiver. "Okay, dear. I love you too. Tell the children I'll see them when I get home tomorrow night."

Richard hung up the phone and put his arms around Amy's hips.

"Now don't you go all glum, sugar plum. You know you're the only girl for me."

"I feel like she's right there in the room with us every time that happens," she told him, still pouting.

He tried to nuzzle her cheek, but she turned toward the window from which some of Greenwood could be seen burning in the nearby distance.

Richard slid up to her again from behind, put his arms around her waist, and looked over her shoulder.

"I assure you it's just you and I, darling," he told her, admiring the view that he knew he'd helped bring to fruition. "It's nearly three, what do you say we go over to the Tulsa and get a little rest before things get going again here?"

"I don't know. I should probably go to my place," she said.

Richard began swaying his hips, pulling her closer.

"Come on, sugar plum. I'll make it worth your while. Breakfast in bed, dessert to follow."

Amy rolled her eyes, but then smiled, relaxing her body and allowing him free range of it.

"Can I order whatever I want?" she asked.

He smiled.

"You can order the entire menu if you like. Steak and eggs, biscuits and gravy, hash, whatever your heart desires, baby doll."

She pursed her lips.

"I want blueberry hotcakes."

"Then you shall have them, my dear."

"What if they have no blueberries?" she asked.

"Then I'll go out and pick wild huckleberries my own self."

The young woman smiled as he began kissing her neck.

****

Operating on only adrenaline by this point, an exhausted Dr. Jackson furiously worked to remove a bullet from the abdomen of a middle-aged Black man bleeding profusely on the gurney. The nurse who was assisting him had two fingers on the man's neck.

"I'm losing the pulse," she screamed. "He's bleeding out!"

"I can't stop the bleeding," he barked.

"He's gone, doctor," she said to him, as he continued to work.

"Doctor! He's gone."

The doctor threw his head back in exasperation and removed his surgical gloves. Then he picked up a nearby pan and looked at the three bloody slugs that were in it. He turned to his left and pitched it against the wall with all his might.

Moments later, as Dr. Jackson sat against a wall in the hallway with his head in his hands, Dr. Bridgewater, a tall man in his forties, approached.

"There was nothing you could do, A.C.," he told him.

Dr. Jackson snorted.

"That's when it's most frustrating, though, isn't it?"

"Get some sleep," his colleague told him. "It's slowed down. I can handle it until you come back in the morning."

Dr. Jackson nodded.

In the lobby, there was a desk nurse who'd been jockeying between handling the influx of victims and assisting with procedures. She looked even more exhausted than the others on staff and broke off a yawn halfway as Dr. Jackson came into view.

"Dr. Jackson," she called out. "Julia called. She said your brother managed to get your father out there a few hours ago. She wants you to call her at your sister's when you're free."

He nodded.

"Finally some good news."

"Room three is open if you want to catch some sleep," she told him.

"No," he said. "I'm going to head over to the house. We have a nice old man renting our basement apartment. I'd like to check in on him."

She gave him a nervous look.

"Is it safe to be out there?"

"I called Professor Hughes a little while ago," he told her, "and he said it's been quiet over that way all night."

He shook his head.

"Too close to the whites on the hill, I suppose," he said, feeling guilty about the fact.

"Please be careful, Dr. Jackson," she said.

"I will. Make sure Dr. Bridgewater gets some rest though, will you?"

The nurse nodded.

Walking to his truck, Dr. Jackson could hear gunshots ringing out in the distance. As he drove off from the lot in his truck, smoke billowed on the horizon. He didn't need to get too close to where the fighting was happening and the short ride to his house was non-eventful. When he pulled onto his street, it was still dark and desolate with no evidence of the horror that had occurred. When he climbed out of his truck, however, he realized that he could still hear the faint sound of gunfire off in the distance. He walked to the basement door and noticed a candle burning inside. A few seconds after he lightly rapped on the windowpane of the door, an old man who looked to be in his seventies opened it.

"Oliver, are you alright?"

"Oh yeah, Doc," the man said, genially. "No one bothering me, but there's something going on out there for sure. Been gunshots and noise all night."

Dr. Jackson nodded.

"Yes, there have been some terrible events, I'm afraid. We had more than a dozen gunshot victims brought to the hospital tonight, only two of them survived."

Oliver gave a toothless gasp.

"Oh, Lord have mercy."

Dr. Jackson leaned his head inside the cracked door.

"Do you mind if I stay down here with you tonight, Oliver?" he asked. "I think we'll be safer. If anyone comes to the house, they're likely not to look down here."

Oliver quickly opened the door.

"Of course, of course, come on in, Doc. Where's that wife of yours? She safe I hope?"

Dr. Jackson nodded.

"Yes, fortunately, I was able to get her out to my sister's this afternoon after they closed down the school. My father and brother are out there as well."

A gunshot, louder than the others, rang out, causing Oliver to jump.

"Oh, lawdy lawdy, come on in," the old man said. "Let's get this door closed."

Oliver bolted the door and walked toward a small table where two folding chairs were set up and a candle burned.

"Here, sit down. Sit down, Doc."

Dr. Jackson took a seat.

"What's this business all about?" Oliver asked. "Have you heard?"

"A young Black man was accused of attacking a white woman across the tracks yesterday," Dr. Jackson told him. "They're holding him at the county jail, and apparently a mob showed up to lynch him. Some folks from Greenwood went over to try and stop it, and some fighting broke out. Next thing we knew, there was shooting all over deep Greenwood, men coming in all shot up with bullet holes."

A horrified expression washed over the old man's cracked face.

"Smells like smoke, too?" he asked.

"Yes, I think they might have set fire to some of the buildings over on Archer."

"Oh no," the old man said. "Do you think they'll leave us be way up here, Doc?"

He shrugged.

"I hope so," he finally said. "There are a lot of prominent white folks who live on the hill over yonder. I don't think they'll allow it to burn, but you never know what a mob might do."

Oliver nodded.

"Ain't that the truth? I done seen some terrible things in my life, Doc. I mean it when I say that nothing does surprise me no more when it comes to the evil that men do."

Dr. Jackson looked at the old man, imagining for a second how many horrid memories he must have had to draw from.

"I don't imagine it would, Oliver. I guess we'd just better hope that mankind's better angels persevere tonight and that by morning the worst of it is through."

****

As the sound of violence grew louder, Gene O'Dell decided not to take any chances and moved his family down into the damp, unfinished basement of their home. Tulsa wasn't an easy city in which to be a Catholic, even if it wasn't nearly as difficult as it was to be Black. Gene worried that if the mob couldn't quench its bloodthirst on that side of town, it wouldn't be a big leap for them to turn their angst toward families like his, along with Jews and other groups that the Klan regularly vilified.

Megan and Kelly Ann were huddled up against him on the floor, slumped against a wall. Worried that mobsters could break into the house, they sat with only a single candle lit. He'd already removed the light bulb at the top of the stairway. If they heard noise coming from above, they would extinguish the flame and hope the mobsters would either forgo checking the basement or at least give up when they couldn't find any light. There was a crowbar at his feet to pry open the metal access doors that led to the street should someone set fire to the house.

It burned his heart to feel his daughter sob into his chest.

"Why is this happening?" she finally managed to ask.

Gene stroked her hair.

"I don't know what to tell you, angel. I wish I understood it myself."

She sobbed.

"Why do people hate each other so much? What could make someone want to..."

"Look," her father told her, "there are a lot of hard feelings that go back a long ways, I guess. My father, Grandpa Ed? He hated coloreds like it was a part-time job. Grammy wasn't no better. I never did understand it, to tell you the truth."

"But they don't do anything to us," his daughter said. "Best I can tell, they just want to be left alone."

Gene shrugged.

"I think there's a lot of fear that because they were, you know, kept as slaves for so long, that... if the whites don't keep them in... "

His wife shot him an icy look.

"In their place?"

Gene sighed.

"I didn't say that. I just mean, you know, that they might harbor a lot of... anger... and if, I don't know, given the chance..."

"Pay back the white man?" his wife asked in the same tone.

Gene was flummoxed.

"Cripes, Meg, what are you coming at me for? You know I ain't prejudiced. Neither our families were even over here yet when they were emancipated."

"Well at least tell her the truth," his wife told him with unmistakable coldness in her voice.

Gene was genuinely clueless as to her meaning.

"Which is?"

"That it's all about fear of anything different," said his wife with a sharp tone Gene wasn't used to hearing. "That and sex."

Gene's eyes bulged in shock.

"Meg!"

"Oh, come on, you know it's true."

Gene gasped.

"No, I don't and anyways, she don't need to hear-"

"Are you serious?" his wife asked. "We're hiding like rats in our basement right now, hoping that they don't bust the door down just because we pray to the same god and the same book but in a different church! If we're gonna meet our end, she at least deserves the truth."

"Look, I just think we should focus on gettin-"

Megan cut him off and began speaking to their daughter.

"You know all those mulattoes you see, the *half-breeds* as they call them? You ever wonder why you don't see Blacks and whites together but so many Blacks have light skin? That's not the way they came over here."

Kelly Ann was confused.

"Then how-"

"The white slave masters took them at will, that's how," her mother said, as her father sat by speechlessly. "They raped them indiscriminately. Sometimes they impregnated them on purpose just because the offspring would make more sightly house slaves."

"Sure, that might be part of it," said Gene, "but it's a lot more complicated. I mean-"

"What's so complicated about it?" Megan screamed. "What set this off? What's the easiest way to rile up the rednecks? Tell them a colored boy eyed one of their women, or worse yet, touched her. They're so afraid that the Black man is just waiting to take their revenge, or maybe that white women will like it."

Gene stood, candle in hand.

"Megan! Enough!" he roared.

His wife put her hands on her face and began to sob.

"I'm just so tired of it, Gene. I'm exhausted by all of the petty, shallow hate, all of the stupid rules and taboos. We all go to Christian churches every Sunday. The people in Greenwood, the people in the Klan, the people on this street. We all read from the same book that says the same things, yet we turn around and act like the devil's own. What kind of world is this, and what good are we doing by sheltering her from a truth she's only gonna learn the hard way? You tell me."

Gene pulled his wife close and she began sobbing more loudly. He looked to his daughter, whose face seemed blanketed with both fear and confusion. He drew her in with his other arm and shushed.

"It's gonna be okay," he told them. "We just gotta get through this night, that's all. Let's just relax and get through this night."

Chapter 10

June 1, 1921

At exactly 5 a.m., a loud, shrill work whistle began to blow. In a shot-up warehouse just off Greenwood Avenue, Obie, McKinley, and around a dozen other vets began to stir from their sleep. Nearby, on the top floor of the Williams building, John awoke, looking around in confusion as Bill and Horace came to.

While lying on Bill McCullough's chest in her bed, Annie Shepton also heard the sound and began shaking him to wake up. In an abandoned rail car near the Frisco tracks, throngs of white fighters who'd fallen asleep jumped to attention, making their way from the car to the street as the piercing noise continued to ring out into the still-dark sky.

As the whistle finally died out, a mob organizer facing a still groggy cadre of armed white men one block north of 1st avenue held his rifle in the air and screamed, "charge." The men began trotting toward the tracks, rifles aimed forward. Within moments, shots were ringing out.

"Let's go, let's go," Obie screamed out. "They on the attack."

His men quickly exited through a small back door that led to an alleyway, ensuring that no one was waiting to ambush them before setting out into the dark.

Nearby, King Henry, Mooch, and Freddy were just coming to when bullets began piercing the side of the covered bed of a delivery truck they had taken cover in for the night.

"Open the door," screamed Henry. "Go!"

Mooch swung open the back door and climbed down to the street. As shots continued to ring out, his body immediately began to flail as large-caliber bullets tore through his flesh. Two white men ran toward the back door. Henry, who was holding a large single-shot pistol in each hand, fired each of them simultaneously, dropping each man.

As a third man came into view, Freddy unloaded a shotgun in his center mass, blowing him back five feet before he hit the ground. The two men reloaded as they exited the truck. Freddy paused for a moment when he saw Mooch's body lying lifeless, chest up in the street, a river of blood flowing out from beneath him. Henry pushed him forward violently.

"Go," he screamed, "ain't nothing you can do for him now."

A tear rolled down the young man's face. He clenched his jaw and raised his shotgun, running sideways right in front of Henry as they looked for cover along the street.

By this time, John Williams was perched in his window with a long-barrel shotgun pointed toward the tracks. When a white man carrying a Molotov cocktail came into view, he fired, hitting the man in the chest and killing him

425

instantly. He quickly tossed the gun to Horace, then turned to take another one from Bill. In one motion, he swung back toward the window, took aim, and dropped another armed white man who was headed their way while Horace reloaded the first shotgun. John turned and handed the spent weapon to Bill, grabbed the other gun from Horace and swung back to the window, quickly killing a third white man as he emerged from behind a smoked out car just below their position. It was an efficient process, considering the armament and ammo that remained, as well as the fact that neither Bill nor Horace were nearly as reliable of a shot. It also allowed him to keep the two young men as far from harm's way as possible. Still, he knew that he would not be able to keep a large number of men at bay all by himself.

At Greenwood and Archer, Obie led his squad as they moved in a low crouch toward the fighting at the tracks. A white man popped out from behind a car and fired a pistol, dropping one of the vets. Obie spun around and fired, killing him with a blast from his shotgun.

The reality of the situation had sunken in. The night had done nothing but forestall the inevitable. They were at war, being hunted by a larger and much better-armed force that seemed to have at least the tacit support of the local government. The only advantage he and his men held was a superior knowledge of the battlefield on which they were fighting.

****

Standpipe Hill was a piece of high ground to the west of Greenwood, on which the city of Tulsa had constructed its first water tower some fifteen years prior. It was built in the shape of a stovepipe, which was how it got its name. From a tactical perspective, it was the essential high ground in the battle and had the combat unfolded in a more traditional manner, rather than an unthinkable invasion, the people of Greenwood would have certainly sought to hold it.

As it were, Lawton, Horse, Willie, and the two guardsmen from the night before had staked it out and were setting up the machine gun at the top of the hill just as the morning fighting broke out. Once they had it positioned, one of the guardsmen began feeding bullets into the machine. Lawton took position behind it, Horse at his side, just like their Army days. A nervous Willie stood nearby.

"What'cha waiting for, Lawton?" he finally asked.

Lawton didn't turn from his position.

"People, dummy, what do you think?"

Embarrassed, Willie sought to redeem himself.

"Won't it pierce those houses?"

Annoyed, Lawton turned his head toward him this time.

"What are you, fucking Superman all a sudden? Got X-ray vision and all that shit? What good is it firing up a bunch of houses, getting the bitch all heated up or jammed just so we can put them on notice we got a machine gun? They hear the other guns firing and they'll start congregating. That's when we mow them down."

"Smart, Lawton," said Willie. "Real smart. Get a few of them for Red while you're at it."

Lawton swung his head back into position and closed one eye to aim.

"I sure as shit will."

****

Annie stood next to the sheriff in her robe, drinking coffee, while he hurriedly dressed.

"I know you gotta go and all," she said, "but I wish you could stay. I just wanted you to know that."

Sheriff McCullough stopped for a moment, turned and took her cheek into his callused hand.

"Me too," he told her with a wink. "I mean that."

She smiled and he set back about putting on his clothes.

"Listen," he told her as he buttoned his cuffs, "you stay in here all day. No reason for the diner to open. Call Evie, tell her I said to stay home."

She nodded.

"You'll come back later if you get a chance?"

The sheriff leaned down and kissed the crown of her head.

"You bet."

****

By dawn, Greenwood and Archer looked like a full-on war zone. Bodies were lifeless in the street, most of the cars were burned out, and smoke billowed from several buildings, darkening the sky and creating an ashy dust that covered the air. The fighting had died down and there were only scattered gunshots ringing out every minute or so when the buzzing sound of the JN-4 biplanes started humming toward Greenwood.

The fighting stopped as everyone in the streets looked up to see the small planes coming in low on the horizon. No one knew what to make of the sight until the biplanes, which had been used for flight training at a nearby base, passed and the balls of fire began to drop from airplanes onto the tops of buildings, a few landing haphazardly on the street.

Immediately after the planes passed, a machine gun roared out and more white combatants stormed across the tracks.

From a nearby alley, Obie and the vets began firing up at the first airplane to no avail. Buck and Isaiah watched from the window as the buzz of the planes continued, eventually making a second pass during which they dropped even more of the fiery, turpentine-dipped tarballs onto the rooftops of buildings, quickly sending them up in flames.

The armed whites took advantage of the confusion caused by the air raid and began taking and holding more ground as more and more Black fighters fell. Obie and his band of vets continued to fire but were forced to do so defensively, moving backward with each shot. When he saw that he was down to just eight soldiers still standing on his side, he finally gave the order to retreat.

"Fall back to the church," he shouted. "Fall back!"

Conceding Greenwood and Archer meant that it would burn, but Obie could see that such would be the case, regardless, and knew that if they were to have a fighting chance with such decimated ranks, his men would have to secure a well-fortified base. Having just been constructed, and built of the most solid materials, the Mount Zion Church was their best option.

Almost immediately, the whites sensed opportunity and began dousing the nearby buildings with gasoline from their bases to the bottom of their first story windows before lighting a match. Once the fire caught, someone from the street would throw a Molotov cocktail into a window and the flames would quickly intensify. From there, it was just a matter of time before the building was consumed.

John Williams stopped firing and looked down to the street at the large crowd that was continuing to advance toward their position. Blacks were coming out of neighboring buildings with their hands up. Rather than shooting them on-site, however, this time the whites were rounding them up. He turned to Bill and Horace.

"Down the back stairs," he barked. "Go!"

All three dashed down the stairwell. At the bottom, John opened the door just a crack, peeked out, then swung it open fully. Seeing no one, he turned back inside and made the hardest decision of his life.

"Listen to me closely," he told Bill and Horace. "We get outside, you lay down your gun and you empty your pockets of any shells. We need to get out of here, and we need to split up."

"Daddy, no," Bill protested.

John grabbed the boy's shoulder.

"Son, now you listen up. We can't fight our way outta this, and if they see three Black men together, they're liable to shoot first and ask questions later. Now, they seem to be taking kids peacefully it looks like, so they see you, you don't run. You put your hands up and go with them. We'll figure it all out when this is through. We ain't got no time to fuss. Come on, move."

John opened the door with his shotgun drawn and saw that it was still clear. He placed the gun on the ground and motioned to Bill and Horace to come out. The boys laid down the other guns and emptied the shells from their pockets. John motioned in three different directions, and each of them took off. Bill looked back for just a moment, tears in his eyes, as he tried to catch a glimpse of his father's face, hoping he'd change his mind and take him.

John could sense his son looking at him and could feel his own tears welling up, but he bit down on his lip and opened his stride without looking back. Tears ran down his cheek as he tried to fully convince himself he'd done the right thing by playing the odds rather than allowing his emotions to rule. Every bit of him wanted to take the boy and the gun and use every last bullet to keep him safe or die trying. No part of him wanted to explain to Loula why he'd separated from her baby. But he knew, as counterintuitive as his choice seemed, that it gave his son the best chance of survival—as long as those odds might presently have seemed.

****

O.W. Gurley was standing outside of his hotel surveying the situation. The building right across the street was still on fire after burning through most of the night. It was far beyond saving. Two more smoked up the block. When he turned to see what the south end looked like, a group of six young men with guns and jerrycans turned the corner. Gurley immediately put up his hands.

"Please, don't shoot," he screamed. "I'm unarmed."

"You better get your Black ass back in there and tell all your customers to come out, old man," the boy in front said. "We're about to burn this place down."

Gurley, panic-stricken, nodded his head with his hands still raised, then ran back inside the hotel. Others from the group were banging on the doors of the surrounding buildings, hollering for occupants to come out.

In the room where they had slept, Emma Gurley was kneeling next to a couch praying furiously when the door burst open, nearly sending her into cardiac arrest.

"Emma, come on," her husband screamed. "We gotta get out of here, it's about to go up in flames."

"Oh, Otto, where will we go?"

"We need to get out of Greenwood quick," he told her. "If we can get over to the other side of the tracks, people there know who I am. We'll be safe."

"You want to go into town when they're the ones burning Greenwood?" she asked, clearly confused by his logic.

"Look, Emma, these hoodlums are gonna march right through here, burning everything they see. They won't know or care who we are. We just need to get to the bank or even City Hall. I can reason with those people."

She hesitated.

"I don't-"

He grabbed her arm.

"Come on now, there's no time."

****

At the bottom slope of Standpipe Hill, Blacks began emerging from houses, looking around confused.

"That's it," said Lawton from high above, "just a few more, come on now."

Once a few more joined and it didn't look like any others would follow, shots started ringing out from the machine gun. Bodies dropped hard and fast as the giant rounds tore through flesh like it was a wet napkin. Some people scattered, others froze like deer in headlights.

"That's it," cheered Horse, "mow 'em down, baby. Mow 'em down. Whooohooh!"

Lawton had a sneer on his face as he fired. In less than a minute, the entire crowd was dead in the street, save one or two who'd managed to scatter.

****

Kelly Ann had convinced her parents that she needed to go to school the next day, and though he insisted on both dropping her off and picking her up afterward, Gene reluctantly allowed it. She was sitting in second period when the assistant principal entered and gave the class an update on what was happening. While all females were to stay in school that day, he told them, boys in the junior and senior class would be permitted to leave if they wanted to "participate," and though their female teacher was mortified at the suggestion, she bowed her head in silence.

Elmer Porter was among a number of boys who began whooping and hollering at the announcement. He turned to Johnny.

"Come on, man. Let's go. We can load the backseat of the breezer with all the loot we can find."

Johnny paused for a moment and turned to Kelly Ann, who tilted her head and gave him a desperate look that was clearly imploring him not to.

"Come on, man," screamed Elmer. "We're gonna miss all the good stuff."

Johnny turned away from Kelly Ann and took off toward the door, Elmer patting him on the back as they hurried off.

Kelly Ann's eyes welled and a tear ran down the young woman's face, as her bottom lip began to quiver.

****

Back in deep Greenwood, Bill Williams walked down the street cautiously. As he turned a corner, he immediately saw a group of four white teenage boys with rifles. He ducked back, but someone had already seen him.

"Hey, get over here, nigger," the voice screamed.

Bill froze, took two steps back, and put up his hands. In seconds, the boys turned the corner with their rifles pointed at his face.

"Where's your gun?" the same boy asked, his muzzle inches from Bill's nose.

"I don't have one," said Bill in a sheepish voice.

"Bullshit, if you're lying to us, we'll shoot you dead."

Bill tried to be brave, though his knees were shaking so hard he thought he could hear them clack.

"I ain't lying," he said, feeling tears begin to form and fighting with all his might to keep them at bay.

"Maybe we should shoot him anyway," one of the others suggested.

"How old are you?" the first asked.

"Sixteen," Bill said.

"Nah, we ain't supposed to shoot minors unless they're armed. Take him over to where they're rounding them up."

"Looks like you're a lucky little nigger today, doesn't it?" the other kid asked.

As Bill started walking, the boy jabbed the muzzle of his rifle into the middle of Bill's back. The tears he'd managed to fight off began to fall.

The boys marched Bill over to a group of Blacks who'd been corralled on a corner. Minutes later, they were marching toward the tracks where flatbed trucks awaited to take them across town. As they passed the Williams building, Bill watched as a short man with a thick mustache emerged wearing his mother's leopard-printed jacket. The boy seethed in anger at the sight. Moments later, the Dreamland came into view and he watched flames continue to burn as more of the structure fell to the pile of cinders smoldering on the ground.

At one point, another teen who was marching a skinny, middle-aged Black man, his rifle poking his back, stopped the group.

"Hold up," the boy yelled. "I got another nigger for you to take."

"Did you check his pockets?" the boy leading the group asked.

"No," the other boy said.

"Get him over there against the wall," the boy told him.

The teen marched the Black man to the sidewall of a brick building, just feet from where the other Blacks were assembled. When his face was less than a foot from the wall, the boy jabbed the rifle tip into his back, and the man put his palms up against the brick.

The other boy began rifling through his pockets, but the man swung his hips.

"You got no right to rob me," he screamed.

The teen held up his pistol, just inches from the man's head, and he pulled the trigger. Blood spattered across the brick wall, as the crowd of Blacks gasped and whelped in horror.

The boy reached down and stuck his hands in each of the dead man's pockets, collecting a few dollars that he'd managed to tuck away.

****

Obie, McKinley, King Henry, Freddy, and four other men moved through a quiet alley, crouched, on the lookout. Obie gave the signal to halt as they approached a field that would offer no cover and turned back toward them.

"Listen, we don't want to get in no kind of exchange out here. We don't have enough ammo, and we're sure to be outnumbered. Too many of the buildings are on fire, there's too much smoke, and there's not much cover. I'm gonna sprint over to the field and hit the ground. I give the signal, you start to follow, each man waits until the one in front of him is across. We'll low crawl across the field and we'll just about be at the church once we've crossed."

When Obie took off, King Henry tugged on McKinley's shirt.

"What if it's an ambush?" he asked. "They see him go, wait a bit, see who follows, then light us up once we're all out in the open?"

"Nah, these pecker woods aren't thinking tactical," McKinley told him. "They see a big Black man with a rifle, they gonna open up."

Convinced, Henry nodded, and when Obie gave the signal, he jumped the line and volunteered to go first. One by one, the eight men made it into the field where they began the long, arduous task of crossing it on their bellies, pulled along only by their elbows and knees.

****

Buck and Isaiah continued to look out of the second-floor window, surveying the situation. Flatbed trucks were in the street and whites poured out of buildings, loading valuables onto them, as fires raged. The two men were amazed that their building had somehow been spared but sensed that their luck was running out.

"We need to get out of here before they torch it," Buck said.

"I know," said Isaiah, "but I am in no hurry to walk into those streets, Buck. They might shoot us on sight."

"They might," Buck admitted, "but it looks like they're taking those who surrender into custody. That'll give us a chance, at least. They set this place on fire, we might not be able to get out from up here."

Isaiah nodded.

Moments later, the two men were cautiously descending the stairway. When they got to the bottom, Buck turned to Isaiah.

"Best not to go out together," he told him. "Two men might make them nervous. I'll go out first, slowly, with my hands up. Once you see it's safe, you do the same."

Again, Isaiah nodded. Buck pulled out a white handkerchief from his pocket and opened the door. He walked out, hands up, gently waving the white cloth.

"I'm unarmed," he yelled to any of the men in the street who might hear him. "I want no trouble. I'm an attorney and I am surrendering myself."

Two white men with raised shotguns moved toward him.

"You better not be fooling us, nigger," one of them said. "Turns out you got a gun, I'll send you straight to hell."

Buck was careful not to move a muscle.

"I've never carried a gun in my life, sir. Now listen, my partner is in there. He's gonna walk out too, as soon as you say it's okay."

The men looked at each other with apprehension.

"He ain't got no gun?" the other man asked.

"No, sir."

"Well get on out here then," the first man hollered toward the door. "We'll turn you over to the deputies. We're about to burn this whole block."

Isaiah walked out, hands up, petrified.

****

Mickey Kemp hadn't participated in the murderous shooting the night before, and he tried to tell himself that he was taking *mostly* his own goods—goods he hadn't yet been paid for—as he ran out of Elliot and Hooker's Clothing Emporium, two arms filled with silk shirts and fine dresses.

Surely, Booker T. Washington High School's prom would be canceled and if he hadn't taken the blue satin dress, it would have either burned or been looted anyway. If he could sell it to another shop on the other side of the tracks, it would barely make up for the losses he was sure to incur now that one of his most profitable markets had been erased from his territory. Lots of people have done much worse, he rationalized as he tried unsuccessfully to keep his shame at bay.

****

Otto and Emma Gurley emerged from the hotel with guests behind them. Most of the block was already engulfed with flames. Gurley pulled Emma by the hand and they began running toward the tracks, opposite the other Blacks they saw, who walked toward the north.

"Hey, where you niggers running to?" a middle-aged white man with a pistol called out when he saw them. The mobster drew and fired. The others in his group turned and opened up as well. Gurley and his wife continued to run but Emma fell flat to the ground. Gurley turned back toward her in horror.

"Emma!"

"Run, Otto," she pleaded. "They'll kill you!"

Gurley looked at Emma, then to the mobsters who were running toward him as they reloaded. He took one more look at his beloved wife who nodded before he took off running, shame burning in his chest.

****

Five white men slowly drove down Detroit Avenue in a flatbed truck loaded with jerrycans of gasoline. Ten more followed on foot. Judge Oliphant, one of the most well-connected whites in town, who happened to live in a big house on that street, suddenly came running down the hill from his porch in a robe and pajamas.

"Hey, what the hell do you hooligans think you're doing?" the judge shouted at the men.

The truck stopped and the notorious Cowboy Long, a murderous outlaw known all over the state, jumped out of its passenger seat.

"Burning down Niggertown, old man, what's it look like we're doing?"

The judge's jaw dropped, as he looked at the houses that were burning further up the street in the truck's wake.

"Hey, I know who you are," the judge screamed. "You're that bootlegger fella. Now you listen here, I'm a judge, and I'm telling you not to light these houses. You see that row of homes up on the hill?" the judge asked, looking behind him. "Well, I live there, along with a lot of other white men who have a considerable amount of influence in this city."

Cowboy laughed as he spat tobacco juice on the road, inches from the judge's slippers.

"Well, your honor, maybe y'all shouldn't have built your big fancy homes so close to the niggers then, huh? Whatcha wanna be over here living with them filthy animals for anyhow? You a nigger lover or something?"

The judge was indignant.

"Now you listen to me, the people who live here are doctors, lawyers, professors. They've got no part in this and cause no trouble for no one. They pay a lot of property taxes in this city too, all of which will go away if you burn them out. You go on now. Off with you."

Cowboy put his hand on a holstered pistol.

"No, you listen, judge. I'm the one's gonna tell you how it's gonna be today. Now you'd best turn your wide ass around, and go stand outside that big home of yours so everyone knows it's not a nigger house, and then, just maybe, it'll be spared. Go on now, git."

Cowboy spat another stream of tobacco juice at the Judge's slippers, this time dousing them good. The other men laughed. Incensed, the judge stomped off toward his house.

Across the street, Dr. A.C. Jackson and Oliver were looking out the window, watching the scene unfold outside.

"I think we'd best go out there and turn ourselves in, Oliver," A.C. said.

Oliver shrugged.

"Whatever you say, Doc."

"I'll do the talking, and we'll just cooperate with whatever they say. I'm sure it'll all be fine."

Oliver nodded dutifully.

"Yes, sir, Doc. I won't make a peep."

As Cowboy and his crew laughed at Oliphant, Dr. Jackson and Oliver emerged from the side of his house with their hands up. One of the boys standing on the road noticed first and trained his rifle on them.

"Hey, whatchu niggers doing?" he said, drawing the attention of the others.

"I'm Dr. Jackson. This is Oliver. We wish to turn ourselves over. We want no trouble with you."

"Get him," one of Cowboy's other henchmen said, "*he* don't want no trouble."

The first gunmen moved toward them, his rifle still trained in their direction, swinging back and forth between the two men, who kept their hands high. Doctor Jackson crouched a bit and lowered his hands halfway. Oliver crouched to hide behind him.

"Easy now, son," the doctor said, "we mean you no harm."

"Who the fuck you calling son, nigger?" the boy yelled. "I ain't your son."

Sensing the young man's fearless hostility, the doctor began to grow more nervous by the moment.

"No," he said, "of course not, no, I'm just-"

A loud shot rang out and Dr. Jackson fell to the ground hard.

"No!" screamed Judge Oliphant from a distance.

Just then, a National Guard Jeep pulled up behind the truck and its two guardsmen dismounted. The judge was running back down the hill furiously. Dr. Jackson was lying on the ground. Oliver sat next to him, having put his head on his lap. He looked to the mobsters then to the doctor, who had a large bullet wound in the center of his chest that was bleeding profusely, though he was still breathing, eyes open.

"What the hell have you done?" the judge screamed. "That's A.C. Jackson, you fool! He's one of the most famous doctors in the whole damned country."

The men all looked at each other in confusion. The guardsman driving the Jeep was the first to finally speak.

"You serious?"

"Yes, I'm serious, you jackass! Why the hell do you think he lives in a big house on Detroit Avenue, you fools?"

"You better get him on that truck then, and get him over to the park," the guardsman said to Cowboy. "They got medical staff there. Go on, hurry."

Cowboy and his men unloaded the jerrycans from the back of the truck, and three men lifted Dr. Jackson onto it. Oliver seemed to still be in shock but managed to get up into the truck with him, where he resumed holding the doctor's head. Oliver began to weep when he saw the weak look on Dr. Jackson's face. Judge Oliphant took the doctor's hand as the truck began to take off, silently mouthing out the words, *I'm sorry.*

****

O.W. Gurley was running down a dirt alley when his legs simply gave out from underneath, causing him to fall flat on his chest. Exhausted, he nonetheless pulled himself from the ground. Breathing heavily and sweating profusely, he forced himself forward even though he could only manage a trot.

Out of nowhere, a young Black man ran right past him. Seconds later, a shot rang out and the boy was flung forward to the ground. Gurley looked back to see a white man staring at him as he fumbled in his pocket for a shell to reload his shotgun. The sight gave the old man just enough adrenaline to open back up into a sprint and he ran right past the boy's body, looking down to see a large, red circle of blood spilling out of his white t-shirt near the middle of his back.

Rather certain he was about to be shot in the back himself, Gurley nonetheless managed to turn the corner before hearing another shot. Losing steam, he headed down the cross street. After half a block, he saw a Black man in a second-story window with a rifle pointed out of it. He kept running as best he could, now barely a slow jog. Moments later, he heard two more shots, turned back, and saw the Black man falling from the window.

Again, the same white man was looking at him while trying to reload in time to shoot. Gurley turned right at the next corner. After a few more strides, he vomited all over himself. His body had completely given out. He looked to the middle school at his left and saw that there was a crawlspace beneath it. It was all he could do to fall to the floor and roll beneath the building. Seconds later, the white man turned the corner, his now loaded weapon drawn. Two other white men soon arrived behind him.

"Hey, what's up?" said one.

"I chased some nigger down here, saw him turn the corner, but now he's gone," the man said.

"Maybe he crawled underneath?" the man asked.

The third man walked over to the crawl space, pointed the rifle underneath, and fired. Gurley closed his eyes and held his breath, silently praying for his life.

"He prolly crawled out the other side," the second man said. "Come on, there's hundreds of them to shoot out here anyway."

****

Obie and three men were low crawling through another field that led toward the back of the church. McKinley, King Henry, and Freddy were no longer with him, however, having been separated when a firefight broke out in an alley between the two fields. On the other side of the church, in the near distance, was Standpipe Hill, where a crowd of whites remained, firing off an occasional shot.

"Stay low until we directly behind the church and 10 or 15 yards away," Obie told them. "I give a whistle, y'all sprint to that back door."

In addition to Lawton, Willie, Horse, and the two Guardsmen, there were now a dozen more cars and trucks, around two dozen men and a dozen women on the hill. They were standing around like spectators at an event, looking down on the burning town, while comparing their hauls from the houses. One of the women modeled a fur coat.

"Can you believe it?" she asked. "I think it's mink. I mean it's a shame it's been on a nigger and all, but it was just too beautiful to pass up. I had to darn near wrestle another lady for it."

"You can always get it cleaned," the other woman said. "Look, I got this ring, this necklace, about a half dozen broaches. There were some nice hats too, but no way I was gonna put those on my head on account of the way their hair is and all."

Another man showed off his stolen rifle.

"He just walked out with it above his head and sat it on the ground. Nicest rifle I've ever seen. Killed two of them bastards with it later in the morning. I'll use it as my main hunting gun from now on."

A man next to him laughed.

"I tell you, we should have us a Nigger Day every year. It's better than Christmas."

"You know, it just really creases me though, them having all this nice stuff, you know what I mean?" said the man with the rifle. "There's decent folk on our side of town who can't find work, and some of them are living like J.D Rockefeller over there. It just ain't right. I mean we was taking out new Victrolas, Kelvinators, fanciest fucking couches I've ever seen in one of them there hotels they got."

"*Had* is more like it," the other man said as they both broke into a laugh.

"Maybe now they'll start remembering their place again, at least," the other man said. "Won't be no uppity niggers left after today's over, I'll tell you that much."

Down at the church, Obie and the men had made it to the back door. He pounded on it with an open hand.

"Who's out there?" a voice yelled. "I got a gun. I'll use it."

"It's Obie Mann. We're here to help."

The door slowly began to creak open and an old Black caretaker cautiously poked his head out with the tip of his rifle pointed upward.

"Easy now, old-timer," said Obie. "We're on your side."

The man lowered the gun as if he'd forgotten he had it.

"Oh, don't mind me," the caretaker said, "I'm just supposed to keep watch on the door, case any of them pecker woods on the hill come down. Reverend Whitaker and a few others are down in the basement. Come on, I'll take you."

"We'll put a man on the door," Obie said, "give you a break."

Obie turned to a vet behind him as they walked in.

"Hang up here for a bit, and I'll rotate men up every hour. See if you can find some stuff to reinforce that door with, okay?"

The vet nodded. The caretaker led Obie and the rest of the men down a set of stairs to the basement of the church where Reverend Whitaker was pacifying a young Black man in his twenties who'd been shot in that morning's machine gun assault by Lawton and his boys up on the hill. The man was lying on the ground, clutching a bloody shoulder that had been badly wounded by just a glancing blow from the large bullet. His wife was at his side, holding his hand and sobbing. A small child sat next to her occupying himself with a toy of some kind.

"He been shot?" Obie asked the reverend.

"Yes, damn near took his shoulder off," said Reverend Whitaker. "They made it into the church and I cleaned it best I could, but I don't have no kind of proper medical supplies here."

Obie had seen more than his share of gunshot wounds in Germany. He knelt beside the man to inspect the wound.

"It's not too bad," Obie told him. "Seen a lot of men survive worse."

"Will he live?" the wife asked hopefully.

Obie turned to the woman and answered in a much softer tone.

"I ain't no doctor, ma'am, and I'm sure he's hurting real bad, but I expect he'll make it as long as we can get him help in the next day or so. It looks like the bleedin' is under control. Infection's prolly his biggest worry right now."

Obie turned to the reverend.

"You got any way to heat up water?"

"Yes, there's a stove upstairs," said Reverend Whitaker.

Obie turned toward the caretaker.

"Go on up and put a pot on. Pull it just before it gets to a boil."

He nodded to one of the vets.

"Give him a hand."

The vet followed the caretaker up the stairs. Obie moved to a narrow window near the ceiling that looked out to ground level.

"They been firing on the church?"

"We took some shots upstairs," said the reverend. "Couldn't tell if they was firing on us or just crossfire from the fighting in the streets. They got a machine gun up on that hill. Was a damned massacre when they first opened up. Dozens of folks shot to pieces, just dying in the streets."

Obie shook his head and looked out the window with disgust.

"You think they'll come for us?" the reverend asked.

Obie turned to him, stone cold.

"You can count on it."

The reverend seemed confused.

"In a house of god?"

"They just see a nigger church, reverend," said Obie with a snicker.

"What'll we do?" the reverend asked.

"Y'all stay down here, tend to him, and pray with all your might. We'll set up in high positions upstairs. When they come, we'll give 'em all we got."

The reverend nodded.

"God bless you, son."

Obie smiled.

"He already has."

With the Convention Hall having been filled far beyond its capacity by the middle of the night, McNulty Park, the largest fenced field in Tulsa, had been turned into a makeshift internment camp by morning. Thousands of Blacks were huddled together, while armed white men, police, and national guardsmen patrolled the park. From just beyond the gates, a flatbed truck pulled up, its bed filled with Black men. As it came to a stop, an armed man jumped out of the front seat and pointed his rifle at the men, Bill Williams among them.

"Alright," the man screamed. "Off with you. Get on over to the gate and sign in. No funny business or I'll fill your Black asses full of lead."

The men dismounted, tied to each other with a rope that passed through a couple of belt loops on each man. They dropped their heads and moved sheepishly toward the gate.

A table was set up at the entrance. Two white women were signing people in.

"Sign this card right here," she told Bill when he approached. "And make sure it's legible or we'll have no idea who you are if someone comes looking for you."

Inside the camp, people were clinging to the fence, looking out to see if they knew any of the incoming arrivals.

Wilfred Dickinson was among the crowd on the outside of the park. He was walking the fence's perimeter looking for any of his men. When he finally spotted one, he cupped his mouth to yell.

"Jack, Jack!"

A young Black man ran toward the fence.

"Mr. Dickinson!" he screamed.

Wilfred ran to the fence and clutched the metal, putting his face as close to it as he could.

"Are you alright, my boy?"

"Yeah," the young man said. "They burned us out, but we made it alive at least."

"Is Charlie here?" Wilfred asked.

"Yeah, I saw him 'bout half hour ago," the young man said, pointing to a corner of the park. "Over by those bleachers with some of the crew."

Wilfred nodded and smiled.

"Alright, listen, Jack. Go find him for me, okay?"

"Yes, sir, Mr. Dickinson," said Jack, before running off toward the bleachers.

Once he'd been in-processed, Bill Williams walked the grounds of the park in a daze. After a few minutes, a young boy from his school recognized him.

"Look, it's Bill Williams," the boy called out. "They even bringing the rich kids down here."

Two other boys laughed. Bill lowered his head.

The boy was tossing a football up into the air.

"I guess we've got plenty of time to practice," he said, holding the ball up.

"Don't feel much like it today," Bill said.

The boy shrugged and turned back to his friends as Bill walked off.

Back at the gate, a caravan of Ford panel trucks with the Red Cross symbol was pulling in. Alma Clarke, a young woman in her thirties, dismounted and immediately took charge, pointing to a guardsman at the gate.

"I need this gate open," she barked. "We can't well carry all of the supplies that far. Let's go."

The two guardsmen looked to her in confusion.

"I got orders to keep her locked, ma'am," one of them finally said.

Alma glared at the young man, nonplussed.

"And these are your new orders, mister. Let's go. Snap to it."

At this, both guardsmen seemed dumbstruck.

"Come on, young man," she quipped. "You heard me. Now, open this gate."

The other guardsman began to speak but Alma just pointed sternly at the gate. Not knowing what to do, he turned and opened it and the trucks passed through.

Inside the park, Chip Bennett was sitting notepad in hand next to a Black couple who looked to be in their seventies. He turned to watch the trucks come in, then back to the man.

"I'm sorry, go on," he told him.

"Wasn't much more to it," the man said with indifference. "They just came in and told us to get out, that they was burning the house down. Asked me if I had a gun. I said no. We went out into the street, barely turned around and it was in flames. Everything we ever owned, up in smoke."

"Wasn't much," the man's wife added, "but it was all we had."

"I'm so sorry," Chip told her. "I can't even imagine what that must have been like."

"Could have been worse, I suppose," the woman said. "Seen dozens of folks lying dead in the streets on the way over."

"Had 'em stacked up on a truck like cords of firewood," the man added.

Nearby, Alma was instructing other volunteers as they set up a tent when another guardsman approached, this one in his mid-thirties.

"Ma'am," he said, "Captain Miller, Oklahoma National Guard. I can't have you set up here. You're blocking the-"

"We need to be close to the gate," Alma bellowed without looking at him, "so we can get supplies in here efficiently. This is the only spot that will do. I'm sure you can manage, captain."

Captain Miller was confused.

"Ma'am-"

Alma finally looked him in the eye.

"Alma Clarke, American Red Cross."

"Well, Ms. Clarke, I just can't have you coming in and doing as you please. This is a-"

"This is a disaster, captain, a shameful, god-forsaken disaster, and while it is not of our creation, it seems that we are the only ones who've considered the logistical needs of interning thousands of American citizens in a prison camp."

"This isn't a prison camp, ma'am, we're just trying to protect-"

To this, the woman pointed a finger at the officer.

"Look around, captain, and tell me again what this *is* and *isn't*. Protect them from whom? Best I can tell, there was no effort to protect them at all when they needed it, which is why you and I are both presently standing where we are right now. So I suggest you get out of my way and let me help these people so that an already putrid situation doesn't quickly turn worse. You've got people starving here, wounded who have not been tended to, and it doesn't seem that your outfit has any answers as to how that's going to change, does it? Best I can tell, you've got a bunch of able-bodied men standing around this mess holding guns and telling people like me what they *can't* do."

"Ma'am-"

Alma tilted her chin and shot the officer a piercing glare. He hung his head.

"Yes ma'am."

Alma stomped off and began pointing out more directions to her staff.

"So, where will you stay?" Chip Bennett asked the old couple he was interviewing.

"Don't know," said the old man. "Look like everything burned down. I got people in Mississippi, but I expect what money we had at the house was either burnt or stolen. Don't even know how we could make a phone call."

Chip reached into his pocket and pulled out a couple of bills, handing them to the man.

"What's this?" he asked.

"I know it's not much," said Chip, "it's just what happened was... I'm not even from here. I only arrived-"

The old woman put her hand on his.

"Bless you, child," she told him. "We been around long enough to know that ain't all of you in league with the devil."

Chip dropped his head and felt shame burning deep inside of him.

On the other side of the fence, Wilfred was waiting for Jack to find his foreman and good friend Charlie Mason when he was spotted by Mayor Evans, who was on hand to give the ordeal at least the appearance of an orderly, government-sanctioned operation.

"Wilfred, old boy, I suppose you're down here looking for some of your workers," the mayor said, extending his hand.

"Yes," Wilfred told him as they shook. "I found one and it seems some others are being detained as well."

"Only for their own safety, of course," said the mayor. "I've seen a few that I recognized as yours. We're getting it set up so that the workers can be released if an employer will vouch for them. We can't have them starting up again."

"How's that?" asked Wilfred, clearly confused.

The mayor shrugged.

"Come on, now, they were bound to set off something like this sooner or later. All that talk of equality those uppity Negroes across the tracks have been spouting off so much about. It gets the dumber ones all riled up. Shame of it is, if it weren't for those troublemakers, most of them—your boys, for example—are happy to do honest work and live a clean life, gracious for benefactors like you."

Wilfred's blood boiled, but he held his tongue, wanting to help his men more than engage in a futile debate with a man whose mind was incapable of change.

"Right, well I'd appreciate anything you could do for them, mayor. Of course, I'd be happy to vouch for them all."

Thaddeus chuckled.

"I bet you would," he said. "Plenty of work to be done, I'm sure."

The mayor punctuated his sentence with a wink and tipped his flat brimmed hat as he walked off.

****

O.W. Gurley was still in the crawlspace under the school trying to look out into the street. From his vantage point, he could see that a crowd of feet had begun to assemble. As he scooted closer, he could see that one had a jerrycan. The man came closer to the crawlspace and began dousing the building. Another struck a match, and Gurley could instantly smell the building's wood beginning to burn as the air around him grew warmer. He crawled out, immediately putting his hands in the air.

"Don't shoot," he screamed. "Don't shoot."

Several men trained rifles on the ragged, dirty man, who was bleeding from multiple cuts and lacerations, but none of them fired.

****

The truck carrying Dr. Jackson and Oliver pulled toward the park entrance. The man in the passenger seat looked back at Oliver when they stopped.

"He still alive?"

He looked down at Dr. Jackson whose body was still.

"His eyes are closed," Oliver said, "but he still seem to be breathing. He don't look so good though."

"I don't expect he does, considering he got a belly full of lead and all," laughed the driver.

The other man climbed down from the passenger seat to take a look.

"He's still breathing," he said, then grabbed Oliver by the collar.

"Now you make sure they know he was alive when we brought him, you hear me?"

Oliver flinched and put up his hands defensively.

"Yes, sir."

"You make sure you tell that to anyone you talk to about this. We did all we could, and he never told us who he was before he got shot."

The driver leaned over toward them.

"We hear you been telling tales, old man, and we'll be back for you."

"Yes, sir," said Oliver.

****

At Lawton's direction, Horse had led a dozen men from the hill on a patrol of the church, hoping to clean up anyone who might run out from the building after he and the guardsmen spent what was left of the machine gun ammo on one final offensive. Obie Mann had posted up in the church's tower when they approached with pistols and Molotov cocktails, the latter of which they lobbed toward the church once they'd gotten close enough. Obie shot one man in the chest with his rifle, a five-round Springfield, and ducked back into the tower for cover as two return shots rang out. During the pause, he leaned back out and shot another one of the men center mass.

Below, another Black vet fired from a church window but missed, drawing return fire from nearby, but the bullets bounced off of the church's sturdy brick exterior. Horse, who was armed with a rifle, fired a shot in the air and then pumped his arm skyward three times. This was the signal for Lawton to open up with the machine gun.

In the basement, Reverend Whitaker and the wounded man's wife were still praying over his body while he writhed in pain when the machine gun rounds began ripping out. The building shook, and the couple's young boy began crying hysterically.

464

On the hill, Lawton and the guardsmen continued to fire. Willie, the second guardsmen, and a crowd of about a dozen other men aided, firing their rifles at the windows. Bricks began to shatter from the building as the machine gun rounds blasted its walls.

In the tower, Obie took a small-caliber bullet in the arm. He set down his rifle to clutch the wound. But as the machine gun fire got closer to his position, he picked up his rifle with his good arm and descended the stairs.

Black vets continued to fire from the windows of the church. One was hit in the chest and, as he fell, gasping for air, he saw two more men were already dead on the ground. Large holes where the brick had crumbled from the large-caliber machine gun rounds flooded the room with light. Seconds later, a Molotov cocktail sailed through one of the larger openings and flames engulfed the center pews.

Obie slumped against a wall, ripped a piece of his sleeve, and fashioned a tourniquet from it, tying off his arm above the wound. Once he'd finished, he took off for the basement where the reverend was still tending to the wounded man.

"How's he doing?" Obie asked.

"He's hanging in there?" Reverend Whitaker said.

"Can he move?"

The reverend shrugged.

"Do we have a choice?"

Obie looked toward the window.

"No, no we don't."

The reverend shook his head.

"It'll be two months Sunday since we celebrated our first service in this building. Took six years to build it and all of six hours to bring it down. Is nothing sacred?"

Obie shook his head.

"Not to some folks it ain't."

"Your brother, McKinley, he make it?" asked the reverend.

"Not sure," Obie said. "Our group got split in two during a firefight on North Elgin on the way over here."

"I'll pray for him-" the reverend began to say when a Molotov cocktail passed through the basement window.

Obie ran to the window and began firing out from it. A vet ran down the steps into the basement.

"Obie, we gotta move, now. The church is on fire and we're outgunned. We can't hold them off much longer."

Obie lifted the wounded man to his feet. He writhed in pain.

"Listen now, partner," Obie told him. "You got two good feet. Won't do nothing but slow us down if I gotta carry you."

The man nodded.

Obie ripped off another piece of his sleeve and wadded it up into a ball.

"Bite down on this as hard as you can," he told the man. "And run like your wife and baby's life depends on it. You understand?"

The man nodded again and bit down on the fabric, his face wincing and his eyes full of water.

The last two remaining vets upstairs continued to fire out the windows, but the flames were quickly becoming worse. As Obie climbed the stairs with the others from the basement, he called to them.

"Let's go, move out."

The vet from the basement kicked open the back door and immediately shot a white man moving toward it. He stepped outside cautiously and looked for others, then motioned for the reverend and the couple who followed with the woman clutching the baby against her chest and covering its head with her hand and forearm. Obie was behind them with the last two vets who fired toward the massive openings on the front end of the church as they backed out slowly.

Finally, they reached the back and turned toward the door, but two of the white men had entered through a now gaping hole in the brick at the front. One of them shot the Black vet who was pulling up the rear in the middle of his back. He fell forward, eyes open, blood pooling from his mouth. The vet who'd been in front of him turned and shot one of the men, and Obie shot the other. The vet kneeled down and tried to help his fallen comrade, but Obie grabbed his arm.

"Come on, man, you can't do nothing for him now."

The vet pulled the dog tags from the dead man's body, blessed himself in the sign of the cross, and followed Obie as they headed toward the door, which had swung closed since the others had left. The other man stepped forward and kicked it open, while Obie covered him from the side. When the door swung outward, however, Horse was standing a few feet in front of it and blew a shotgun hole in the man's chest. The buckshot burned Obie's neck and arms, sending him crashing into a nearby wall and causing him to drop his weapon. Less than ten feet away by that point, Horse started to reload but when he saw that Obie was reaching for his own rifle, he decide to charge, belting the equally-gargantuan man in the jaw with the butt of his rifle once he'd closed the distance.

Blood from Obie's mouth sprayed across the wall as his chin whipped sideways from the blow. His knees buckled and Horse pushed the rifle's stalk against his windpipe with all of his strength. When Obie's head met the back of the wall, the wooden stalk began choking off his airway. His face turned purple as the flames began to consume what was left of the building.

Sensing that only moments of consciousness remained, Obie stomped his right heel onto the toes of Horse's left foot, pulled him forward by the shirt and brought the his right knee into the man's groin with tremendous force. This caused Horse to double over, and Obie dropped low before sending a right uppercut crashing into his chin, followed by a wide left hook into his jaw. The punch hit the mark, and the white behemoth fell to ground, splayed out on his back and barely conscious. Obie picked up his rifle and sent the butt of the weapon crashing into Horse's face, which seemed to explode with blood.

Just then, a large wooden beam at the ceiling broke off and dropped within a foot of the men, flames rising up from it. Obie turned and sprinted to the door, choking on smoke as he made his way toward daylight. When his feet hit the grass, he sprinted toward the others who had ducked down halfway across the field behind the church waiting to see if any of the Black vets emerged. When Obie was halfway to their position, the stained glass windows on the side of the church blew out and flames shot from the opening as if a bomb had exploded. It was clear that no one who remained inside could have survived.

****

Deep in the woods beyond Greenwood, a preacher led a congregation of about thirty Black men, women and children through a wooded area and into a clearing. They were sweaty, covered in ash and grime, and looked to be utterly exhausted.

"Yea, though I walk through the valley of the shadow of death," the preacher said, "I will fear no evil, for thou art with me. Thy rod and thy staff they comfort me. Thou preparest a table before me in the presence of mine enemies. Thou anointest my head with oil; my cup runneth over. Surely goodness and mercy shall follow me all the days of my life."

The group arrived at a stream, where they began cupping water to their mouths and splashing it on their sweaty faces.

"Easy now," the preacher said, "I know you are parched with thirst, but go easy or your body will cramp. We must keep moving."

****

Dozens of Red Cross relief workers were serving soup, cheese sandwiches, water, and coffee outside of medical tents that were tending to the wounded at McNulty Park, which seemed more like a prison camp in some dystopian novel than a field in an American city. O.W. Gurley stumbled through the crowd in a daze. His clothes were torn to shreds and he was filthy. Blood trickled down his head from a wound above his hairline. Other Blacks pointed and whispered as the wealthy man walked past them.

"Otto! Otto!" a woman's voice cried out.

Confused, Gurley looked about, pawing at his head wound when he finally saw Emma running toward him.

"Otto, you made it," she yelled.

"Emma?" he asked, confused. "Emma? Is that you?"

When Emma reached her husband, she threw her arms around him in a big hug.

"Oh, darling," he said, "I thought you were gone."

He pulled away from her and looked at her body.

"You had been shot," he said, still confused by her presence. "In the street."

She shook her head.

"No, I think I just fainted when I heard the blast. They brought me over here. I didn't think I'd ever see you again, Otto. I thought for sure you were-"

Gurley grabbed Emma and pulled her tight to his chest.

****

Outside of town, a flatbed truck moved down a seldom-traveled dirt road. A handful of Blacks who'd survived the shooting in Greenwood had jumped into the tall grass next to it when they heard the engines. As the trucks passed, they peeked up where they could see the corpses of Blacks stacked three and four high on its bed like cords of wood.

****

At a phone booth in downtown Tulsa, a man in a tailored suit was looking around nervously as he spoke into a payphone.

"Morty's got the last hundred or so," the man said. "Already got the steam shovel out there. I told him two grand in cash if no one makes a peep. He's got his best men on it."

The man paused to listen to the voice on the other end.

"Hal put the rest of them on a barge," he finally said. "They're gonna weigh them down and dump them in the river."

The man paused again.

"I know, I told him we can't have any floaters washing up down shore. Right. You got it."

The man hung up the phone, looked in both directions, and walked off, trying to appear casual as he swiveled his head, attempting to see anyone who may have been watching.

****

A floating barge with the dead bodies of Blacks killed the night before stacked high floated out from a dock on the Arkansas River. Its pilot had a sickened look on his face.

****

In a large, country field, miles outside of town, two white men tossed the corpse of a dead Black man into a giant pit that been dug in the middle of the field. The pit was teeming with bodies, thrown one on top of the other. A steam shovel began to lower dirt on the hole. As they walked back toward the flatbed, one of the men looked to the other.

"Cripes, I thought they stank when they were alive."

The man who spoke laughed. The other one gave him a dirty look, as he shook his head.

****

John and Loula Williams were alone in a room of a friend's house on the northern outskirts of Greenwood. They were standing in the middle of the room facing each other, and it was clear that Loula was deeply upset.

"How can we just sit here, John? We have no idea where our son is, or if he's even alive."

John put his hands on his wife's arms.

"Loula, baby, please. I know how hard it is, but you have to trust me. There is nothing we can do that will help right now."

"We ain't heard no gunshots all day," she pleaded. "They never came this far north. What if he's..."

John put his hand on her chin.

"Listen-"

Loula threw up her arms and turned away from him.

"I'm tired of listening! I'm tired of waiting, I'm tired of not knowing, John. How can you just stand there and-"

John moved toward his wife, grabbed her shoulder and turned her toward him with as much physicality as he'd ever handled her.

"You think I don't want to know?" he screamed. "You think I don't want to find our son? You think I'm yellow? That I don't wanna grab one of Del's rifles and point it at every white man I see until one tells me where Bill is? But that ain't gonna do him, me or you no good, Loula!"

"Then what do I do?" his wife sobbed.

"You wait until Del tells us what's what. He can pass," he said of their mulatto friend, "but he's still taking a hell of a risk going into town like that. Let him find out whether they still holding people, whether it's safe to go across the tracks, whether they got a price on my head—or yours even. You think they ain't gonna look for a handful of coloreds to blame this on, say they started a riot and the whites were just defending themselves and they property? Everyone knows whose building I was firing from."

Meanwhile, Horace and Bessie Frank sat next to each other on a couch in the living room of the same house. They could hear the couples' argument.

"I feel guilty, Horace," said Bessie, whose face indicated she was still in shock. "Loula got me outta there, and you were able to follow John, but they own son's gone missing. They done nothing but be good to us since we got here, and there ain't nothing we can do for them."

Horace nodded.

"I know it, but put that outta your mind for now, sis. We didn't do nothing wrong. Bill's a smart kid. He would've gotten away. He probably just don't know we out here is all."

In the other room, Loula had calmed down some, though tears were still running down her face.

"He's my only child, John. I couldn't live if he's gone."

John took his wife into his arms.

"Hey, now, don't even talk like that. He's not gone. He's just separated from us temporarily, and I know that's the scariest thing in the world right now, but he's alright, I promise."

"You don't know that, John, you don't," she said, pulling away. "Don't make me promises you can't keep."

"There was so many bodies in the street, Horace," Bessie told her brother. "Little kids, old ladies, and you know there had to be a lot more who never made it out of those houses before they went up in smoke."

Horace turned toward his sister and put his hand on her back.

"Hey, listen to me," he said, "put that out of your head, you hear? Don't think about any of the things you seen right now. Not today. We safe now. That's all that matters."

The front door opened and Del, a very light-skinned Black man who looked almost completely white, walked in. John and Loula quickly entered through a door on the side of the living room.

"Did you find anything out about my baby?" Loula asked him.

"I'm afraid not, Loula. I'm sorry."

"What's it like out there, Del?" asked John.

"Not good, I'm afraid, though it seems like the fighting is finally over."

"What are they doing with the people they rounded up?" asked Loula.

"They got most of 'em held up at McNulty Park," said Del. "Looks like a giant outdoor prison over there. I mean thousands of people, Red Cross relief workers tending to them. They won't let anyone inside. I got up to the fence but couldn't find Bill or anyone who knew him."

"They still rounding people up?" asked John.

"I can't say, but it don't look like it. Got no more room for 'em probably. Some colored folks were wandering around the ashes in Greenwood. The whites who were picking through the rubble looked to be leaving them alone."

"How bad was it there?" asked John.

"Greenwood? It's gone, man. I'm sorry. Deep Greenwood burned all the way to the ground. The Dreamland, the confectionery, even the Stradford... gone. Garage looked like it was mostly okay, at least."

"I don't care about none of that," screamed Loula, as she looked upward and clasped her hands. "Lord, hear me now, you can take it all from me, every bit of it, just leave me my Bill. Please, God, spare my son. He's a good boy."

John took her in his arms and tried to calm her sobs before looking back to Del.

"Del, you think it's safe for us to go into Tulsa?" he asked.

477

"I'd wait until tomorrow, John, I really would. There wasn't no colored folks out in the open over there. I didn't even feel safe myself. I'd wait and see what the afternoon paper says. See if there's heat on you. If Bill's at the park, he'll be alright, and you wouldn't be able to get him out nohow. You all are welcome to stay here as long as you need to. Most of the stores were closed, but I was able to get some food at least, and there's a good bit of canned provisions in the pantry."

"Thank you, Del," he said, shaking his hand. "You've been a good friend. I can't tell you what it means to us."

"Least I can do," Del told him. "Y'all always been there for me."

John nodded as he continued to comfort Loula.

****

Obie and the two remaining vets from the church moved quietly through the woods outside of Greenwood. They had been able to place the reverend, the wounded man, and his family with a group of Blacks they had crossed paths with who were making their way out to the country by way of sneaking across farms.

The trio had then taken some fire at Sunset Hill and though Obie was able to kill one of the whites who'd

478

ambushed them, they had to flee when their ammo had dwindled to just a few bullets.

When he heard a rustling in the bush ahead, he motioned for the other men to stop and get low.

"Don't shoot, Obie, it's me," said the voice, which Obie didn't immediately recognize but could tell was familiar.

Freddy emerged from the bush.

"King and your brother are pinned down at a grocer's on the north end," said Freddy. "They down to a few men and not many bullets, so they sent me toward the church to see if I could find you."

They moved out at a fast jog and were able to use their last few bullets to lay down enough cover for the last two survivors—McKinley and a vet they called Gyp—to get out of the building and over to their position behind a delivery truck.

"Where's King?" Freddy asked McKinley.

McKinley just shook his head. A tear fell down Freddy's cheek.

The men pooled their ammo, but the writing was on the wall. Obie loaded his rifle and began to take position. His older brother pulled on his massive shoulder before he could rise.

"Obie, this ain't no hill to die on, brother. Hell, it ain't even our store."

Obie looked at his older brother, knowing he was right.

"Alright, move out from behind," he told the men. "I'll only fire if they shoot, so we don't waste ammo."

He turned to Freddy.

"Once you all have turned the corner to that alley, whistle."

Freddy stood up straight, puffed out his chest, and nodded, proud to have been given his first real assignment in the whole thing, aside from being sent away to fetch Obie. When they backed out from behind the truck, Obie got into position, but no one fired. He heard the whistle, waited, and when a man finally raised his gun from behind a car on the diagonal corner he shot him right in the head, then turned and ran to the alley. Obie, Freddy, McKinley, and Gyp silently made their way for the hills and that was it. The last of the resistance had ended. The fighting was over.

****

Chip Bennett entered the newsroom where he approached Gary Kale, who was seated at his desk.

"How creased is he gonna be that I'm passed deadline?" Chip asked.

Gary gave him an awkward look and tapped his pencil on the desk nervously.

"What?" Chip asked. "I've got great stuff, and it's copy ready."

Gary shrugged.

"Um, the good news is he's not gonna be mad at all, most likely."

In Richard's nearby office, he was dictating to Amy Comstock. Gary motioned for Chip to be quiet and then put his hand to his ear, indicating for him to listen. Chip could hear Richard Lloyd Jones' voice and moved closer to his open office door so that he could better hear what was being said.

"Tulsa residents witnessed a most unusual spectacle this morning when a motley procession of Negroes made its way over the city's most prominent streets and thoroughfares on their way to McNulty Park. The men walked with both hands held high above their heads, hats in one hand, a token of their submission to the white man's authority. They will return not to the homes they once occupied, but rather to heaps of ash, the angry white man's reprisal for the wrong inflicted on them by the inferior race."

Just beyond the open door, both Chip and Gary were now off to the side, eavesdropping.

"The Negro women, by nature more brave and brazen than their male counterparts, tried at first to put a bold front on the entire affair, but as they ruefully gazed on the unfriendly street throngs looking down on them, they seemed to sense it was a most serious epic in their lives, and the

481

bravado had fallen by the time they reached the encampment."

****

Tucker Johnson was standing over the editorial desk looking at a dummy sheet with a section editor when Chip stomped over to the desk, Gary behind him.

"Are you fucking kidding me?" said Chip.

Tucker looked up, shocked and confused. He finally shrugged.

"He's gonna run one of his long-winded, self-righteous, bigoted, racist rants today? Today?"

The section editor's face registered shock. He picked up some papers and walked off, while Tucker looked around nervously before speaking, leaning toward Chip so that he could keep his voice just above a whisper.

"He's the publisher, Chip. I don't know how it works in St. Louis, but around here, he tells us he wants to handle the lead piece, he handles the lead piece."

Chip threw up his hands.

"Un-fucking-believable! We caused the goddamned thing, Tucker, *this paper!* Is he gonna take credit for that? We incited a mob for Christ's sake. We set it all in motion and

482

now hundreds maybe thousands are dead, an entire community has been burned to the ground because of *us*."

Tucker's eyes bulged.

"There have been dozens of race riots across the whole damned country, Chip. Surely you don't-"

"Race riots?" Chip screamed. "Race riot? You've got to be joking. Have you even been out there? That was no riot, my friend. That was a goddamned extermination. It was a holocaust!"

Everyone's body language suddenly shifted. Chip shrugged and Tucker nodded toward the area behind him before looking to the ground, scratching his head. When Chip turned around, Richard was staring at him, arms folded across his chest.

"You got something you wanna say to me, *cubby*?"

Chip rolled his sleeves.

"I got a lot I want to say to you."

Chip began to move forward as he spoke, but Gary put himself in front of him, reaching out an arm across his chest. Richard sneered and rolled up his own shirt sleeves with Amy standing at his side, looking nervous.

"Let him come if he wants to," Richard sneered. "You know, I pegged you straight off as the soft sort—no stomach for the messy stuff. Perhaps you'd best get your folksy sensibilities back to St. Louis then, or, better yet, back to

Yale. Hasn't anyone told you that the frontier is a place for men?"

Chip laughed.

"You call yourself a man? You're a goddamn joke is what you are, all recycled prose and listless bluster."

Richard seethed.

"Son, I was writing for the biggest outfits in the land before your daddy had even set eyes on your mamma, let alone gave thought to bring you into this here world."

"That's right," said Chip. "You were, and look at you now, a scared old man running a second-rate, yellow rag. One knee bowing to the bank, the other to the Klan."

Richard's face went red.

"You look here, I bow to no man. Scared? Me?"

Richard put his arms out to the side and turned in each direction, then picked up a copy of a Tribune from a desk nearby, holding it up.

"I speak my mind right out in the open," he said, waving the paper. "And I'm the easiest man in town to come and find."

Chip laughed.

"Like that's some sort of courageous act in this place? Fear mongering and race-baiting in Tulsa is like playing chess against yourself, you damned fool. You're a scared, washed up has been using this pathetic platform to distract you from reality and make you feel important once in a while."

Richard let go of a sinister chuckle.

"Is that right? They teach you that up there at that Ivy League school daddy sent you to, you spoiled little shit? Who's self-righteous now? You practically begged for this job. Came out to our second-rate, yellow rag on your own goddamn dime—or your daddy's most likely. I only know I didn't send you no ticket."

"Well, you take this job and stick it..." Chip paused as he glanced to Amy then back to Richard. "Well, I'm sure you can find an appropriate place."

Richard leaped toward him, but two reporters managed to get between the men.

"Best to the wife and family," Chip sneered, as he swaggered off, Richard pushing the others away from him.

Gary chuckled.

"You know what," he said, looking to Richard. "I think I'm done too."

The publisher's jaw dropped.

"You walk out that door, Kale, you best believe you don't ever work for me again."

Gary stopped and looked him in the eye.

"I can live with that," he said, picking up a copy of a paper, "but I can't be a part of this."

"I'd think twice, young man," Richard screamed. "Because I'm good and goddamn sure you ain't got no rich daddy to fall back on."

Gary smiled and gave him the middle finger as he backed away toward the door.

"You set that camera right down too," Richard screamed.

Gary looked at it and smiled.

"This is my personal camera, Richard."

Richard fumbled for words.

"Well... that's my film then, and anything on it is the intellectual property of this here newspaper. You try and publish a single print, and I'll sue your ass off, young man, you'd better count on it."

Gary smiled again and walked off.

Moments later, Chip was inside the elevator when Gary ran into the hallway and toward the open doors. Chip put his arm out to stop them from closing.

"You think you might be able to use a freelance photographer?" he asked.

"No way! You walked out?"

Gary entered the elevator car and the doors closed.

"Yeah," he said, "fuck him, right?"

Chip nodded.

"I know, but are you sure? I mean this is your hometown."

Gary shook his head.

"Not anymore, man," he said. "Not after this. I'm out."

"I can't believe I said all that shit," Chip laughed. "I've never told someone off like that in my whole life."

"And I never saw anybody rattle his cage like that," Gary said, "ever."

"So what now?" asked Chip as the car came to a stop.

Gary shrugged.

"I was gonna ask you the same thing."

"Hell if I know," said Chip. "It's not like I came in here thinking I was gonna quit today."

The elevator doors opened and they walked into the lobby.

"In fact," Chip continued, "I thought I was gonna file a really introspective piece on the injustice of it all."

Gary raised his eyebrows.

"Really? You thought something like that would see the light of day at this place?"

They pushed open the front doors and walked into the street.

"After what happened?" Chip said. "Yeah, I guess I did. I mean, I figured there'd have to be some sort of contrition for it all."

"What, like he'd be sore about what went down, blame himself?" asked Gary. "Chip, he *wanted* it to happen. Don't you see that? In his mind, *he's* the hero in this story."

Chip was befuddled.

"But how could-"

Gary waved him off.

"Man, you will drive yourself crazy trying to make reason out of it. It's just the way he's wired, the way half the city is wired."

"Half?" said Chip.

Gary shrugged in concession, then raised the camera that was hanging from his neck.

"If you still got that piece, I've got some incredible art. Likely be a lot of national papers in town today, one of them is bound to be interested in a freelance piece, especially with a local perspective."

"Local?" said Chip. "I've been here what, a week?"

Gary laughed.

"I mean I wouldn't advertise that part."

****

Captain Jackson couldn't move fast enough when he'd gotten word that his son had been badly wounded and was being held at a Red Cross triage tent in McNulty Park. He arrived just in time to see A.C. draw his last breaths, and though the two men could not exchange words, he would be grateful for the rest of his days that he at least got the chance to squeeze his son's warm hand and look down on his handsome face before he was united with his late mother.

As he looked down on the body of his departed child, the old soldier was torn apart with emotion. Had he been wrong to give up his anger? For all of his teachings and all of his son's accomplishments, the end result was still this horrid scene that he'd become all too familiar with: the corpse of a slain Black man, cut down in the prime of his life by the very hatred and anger he had come to believe that deference and assimilation could help him avoid. Had he failed his son, or had he been doomed at birth by the world he'd brought him into?

Chapter 11

The Aftermath

In the days that followed, the city, overwhelmed by the logistics of holding the thousands upon thousands of Blacks that had been detained, began releasing them to their white employers. For nearly two months, Blacks who did not wear police-issued green cards pinned to their chest with their name and employer written on them were subject to arrest.

From coast to coast, the national press in more progressive cities wrote scathing articles about the deplorable "race riots" that had taken place in Tulsa.

"The ruthless demolition of virtually the entire Negro quarter south of the tracks is condemned as indefensible violence," read the front page of The New York Times. "The bloody scenes in Tulsa are hardly conceivable as happening in American civilization of the present day," read the front page of the Philadelphia Bulletin.

None of it mattered much, however. In less than a week, the rest of the country had moved on to stories with less complicated social subtext. In Tulsa, Richard Lloyd Jones soothed white guilt by continuing to milk the racial animosity of his white readership with explanations as to how the Blacks had brought this tragedy on themselves, scorning his colleagues in the big cities for having no understanding of the kind of "vile Negroes" the good people of Tulsa had to endure.

Subscriptions to the Tribune swelled in direct correlation with membership to the city's Klan chapter along with the Tulsa Benevolent Society. Just a year later, the latter would erect Beno Hall, ostensibly short for benevolent, though members commonly bragged that it stood for *be no niggers, be no kikes, be no Catholics* inside its walls. In perhaps the most callous example of acceptable attitudes of the time, photos of charred Black corpses and the burning Greenwood skyline became best-selling postcards, many of which were purchased by whites as commemorative memorabilia.

While thousands of Blacks who had managed to flee during the attack never returned, the city was still left with thousands more who'd lost their homes and had no servant quarters to live in. The Red Cross began erecting tents on the still smoldering plots where buildings once stood, and Greenwood soon looked like a massive refugee camp.

Booker T. Washington High School, one of the few buildings left standing in Greenwood when the burning finally subsided, never hosted its prom. The building was re-purposed as a Red Cross hospital during the summer recess to treat hundreds of Black victims still suffering from persistent wounds like gunshots and infections.

For their part, the stain on the city's reputation was the only matter that the elders of Tulsa's economic elite cared to address. The Tulsa Chamber of Commerce formed a committee to "lead recovery efforts," which promised to raise the funding to pay for every burned building's reconstruction, though nothing ever came of it.

From a legal standpoint, little was also achieved. Embarrassed by the bad press, Governor James Robertson ordered a grand jury investigation. The all-white panel returned 88-indictments. However, because almost no whites came forward with information on others who'd played a role and few Blacks could identify individual white mobsters, the results were predictable, including an attempted rape indictment for Dick Rowland. While some notorious whites like Cowboy Long were also indicted, along with Chief Gustafson, who was not only found to have shirked his duties but to have been involved with a car-theft-ring (he'd be fired and forced to pay a fine), the majority of blame was still shifted on Black "agitators," and in a pathetically predictable outcome, there were more Blacks than whites charged for crimes related to the massacre.

The official story had three-ring leaders responsible for the horrible massacre, and they were all Black: J.B. Stradford and Andrew Smitherman were said to be directing the leader of the armed Blacks, Obie Mann. These words came from the mouth of the grand jury's star witness, Otto Gurley. Gurley left town after the events, settling in California. He was branded a traitor to his people and never returned.

Neither Smitherman nor Stradford ever returned to Greenwood after taking flight that evening, and though Stradford had been briefly detained in Kansas, he made bail and slipped away to Chicago before he could be extradited. Smitherman wound up in Buffalo, where he founded another Black newspaper.

Obie Mann went on the lamb for about six months, hiding out in Canada until McKinley let him know that the heat had died down enough for him to come back. He eventually returned but was never the same, forever bitter at the way the events of that night played out and the fact that the people of Tulsa—both Black and white—seemed to have eventually contented themselves to silently agree to sweep it under the rug of the city's history.

Without men like Stradford and Smitherman leading the charge for equality, and with the rest of the prosperous having suffered the losses of that night, Greenwood's citizens had been broken like an angry dog who'd suffered too many kicks at the hands of an infinitely stronger force.

There is no official record of what happened to Dick Rowland after being shuttled by deputies to Kansas City to prevent him from being lynched, perhaps because he assumed yet another name when he left. All that is known is that he was still in Kansas City when the charges were dropped and that he never moved back to Greenwood.

Damie Rowland did, however, reveal in an interview several decades later that she saw Dick one more time, that he woke her in the early morning hours several months after the events and told her that he had stayed in Kansas City, where Sarah Page had also returned. Damie said that her adopted son was racked with guilt over the outcome of his ordeal and that both realized he'd never be safe in Tulsa. She said that he continued to write her from Kansas City and would regularly mention Sarah. The implication that they still communicated has led some to conclude that the two did know each other and possibly even had a relationship prior to the events at the Drexal building, though no definitive proof exists.

Damie said that Dick eventually stopped mentioning her and ultimately moved on to Oregon where he found work on the loading docks of a shipyard. The last communication she said she had received was a letter from a roommate there in the 1960s, informing her that Dick had been killed in a dock accident.

In perhaps the boldest move of all, Tulsa's power brokers immediately sought to forever ensure that Greenwood would not return by passing a fire ordinance so restrictive that it would have proved prohibitive for anyone without considerable financial resources. Intending to capitalize on the holocaust by developing an industrial/commercial zone, they mandated that replacement buildings in Greenwood be constructed only of brick, concrete, or steel, meaning that no one could build a wooden house or business.

However, in perhaps the only bright spot amid this wretched tale, a group of Black attorneys led by Buck Franklin and Isaiah Spears waged a legal battle that went all the way to the Oklahoma Supreme Court, where they had the ordinance struck down as unconstitutional. That victory saw the resurgence of Greenwood with everything from the Dreamland Theater to the Williams Confectionary and Mt. Zion church rebuilt beyond even their former glory.

Indeed, the community of Greenwood rose from the ashes like a Phoenix, eventually growing to a size and level of prosperity that eclipsed the peak of its high times before the massacre. But as those who survived and those who perished in those dark days of 1921 would surely attest, there is no prosperity worth the heinous crimes that were committed against innocent people.

Afterword & Acknowledgments

Like so many others, when I first heard of the events in this book, I found it difficult to believe that such a profoundly horrible crime against humanity could have somehow escaped the annals of mainstream American history. How could so many otherwise astute Americans remain unaware of such a grotesque massacre? After all, as noted in the final chapter, it's not as if the events had been ignored by the national press at the time.

However, the outside outrage seems to have dissipated at an alarmingly brisk pace. In Tulsa, it was almost as if the sides ultimately made a silent pact to never publicly speak of the burning of Black Wall Street and, for the better part of a century, the history of Greenwood was deliberately kept from history textbooks throughout the state.

An integral figure in bringing the story back to life has been Don Ross, who served in the Oklahoma State Legislature from 1983-2003. Ross grew up in Tulsa and, like most children who grew up in the generations following the events, knew nothing of them having had taken place. That is, he knew nothing until high school, at which point he met none other than Bill Williams, the son of John and Loula Williams, who is depicted as a teenager in this book.

Williams became a history teacher at Booker T. Washington High School, and Ross credits the impact of

Williams' telling of the events with inspiring his lifelong dedication to sharing the story of his native Greenwood community with others, while fighting for racial justice in the state, at large. Among Ross's accomplishments was convincing the legislature to commission a study on the events that would stand as a much more accurate official account, the results of which were published in 2001 and were a help in writing this book.

Buck Franklin's son, Dr. John Hope Franklin, became one of the top American historians of his time and has given much to what we know today of the events. The younger Franklin, who passed away in 2009, contributed to the landmark Brown vs. the Board of Education case, participated in the 1965 Selma march, and was later awarded the Presidential Medal of Freedom. He also saw to the completion and publication of his father's autobiography decades after Buck passed away in 1960 with his memoir unpublished.

Buck's account of the events were one of the primary source materials for this book, including a long-lost, handwritten, 10-page manuscript discovered in 2016, in which the elder Franklin details his eyewitness account of the use of airplanes to bomb Greenwood—a facet of the story that had been debated in terms of its veracity until that time. A scan of the manuscript is available on Smithsonian Magazine's website. A park developed in the Greenwood area in 2010 as a memorial to victims of the riot is named in his honor.

There have been a number of other academic, non-fiction accounts of the events that were extremely helpful in my effort to be as historically accurate as possible in their depiction. First among them, were the works of Ruth Sigler Avery, a Tulsa native and local historian who had the foresight to document the events by conducting extensive interviews with as many survivors as she could find. The resulting first-person accounts remain an invaluable tool in terms of understanding not only the events but the time and place in which they occurred.

Another fertile source of first-person descriptions came from the court transcripts of a lawsuit filed by a white businessman, William Redfearn, who'd owned property that had burned down in Greenwood and sued an insurance company that refused to pay out his claim. The case, which went all the way to the Oklahoma Supreme Court, included a number of depositions and testimony transcripts that have helped historians gain an accurate understanding of the events.

Ed Wheeler, a Tulsa talk-radio host, began working on an extensive, long-form journalism piece on the events in the late 1960s. However, Wheeler, who'd been threatened with violence while researching the still taboo subject, couldn't find a major newspaper or magazine willing to publish it. It ultimately appeared in *Impact Magazine,* a fledgling publication that had a pretty much exclusively-Black readership. But while the piece failed to reach the larger audience it deserved when it was written, the work it contained provided another very useful tool for future historians.

A 2000 documentary titled, *The Tulsa Lynching of 1921: A Hidden Story*, which was first released on Cinemax and is currently available on YouTube, offered insight from both historians and survivors.

Two works of exhaustive non-fiction were particularly enlightening in tying together a coherent narrative of the events, and I highly recommend both to anyone interested in further reading on the subject. The first is *Death in the Promised Land: The Tulsa Race Riots of 1921* by Scott Ellsworth, which, for many years, stood as the seminal historical account of what happened on that fateful day. The second is *The Burning: The Tulsa Race Massacre of 1921* by Tim Madigan, which built on Ellsworth's work with the help of not only exhaustive additional research but key interviews with figures such as Bill Williams and descendants of Obie Mann.

My ethos in approaching this work of historical fiction was always to keep the emphasis on *historical*. To make the book work as an accurately-dramatized account of actual historical events, it was of course necessary to take certain liberties. The vast majority of characters are real people, and their depictions are based whenever possible on their own first-person accounts, as well as those of their descendants, along with depositions and witness testimony. Historical fiction inherently requires the author to imagine conversations that cannot possibly be known, though I can assure readers that in each character's instance, tremendous effort went into capturing a persona that would reflect the historical figure as accurately as possible.

One of the challenges in creating the characters through which the story could be told was owed to the very injustices that make it such a compelling and worthy subject of study to begin with. Because so few of the whites were ever held accountable in any way for their actions, there simply was not enough source information available to depict some of the worst offenders. As a result, I used first-hand accounts of the atrocities to create characters that could be depicted as perpetrating them. The character of Lawton was inspired by a famous photograph of a menacing young man in a flat cap wielding a shotgun just after the events. Because there had been considerable tension among returning white vets who had not enjoyed as much of the city's new prosperity while serving abroad in World War I and the suddenly thriving Blacks of Greenwood, I chose to make his crew—Horse, Willie, and Red—frustrated veterans as well. While the characters may be fictional, I can assure readers that the acts of violence they and other unnamed assailants are depicted committing all come straight from first-person accounts and in no way whatsoever sensationalize the level of atrocities that are known to have occurred.

Annie Shepton was a fictional character created to give additional depth to Sheriff McCullough, an important historical figure for whom there simply was not enough available information to bring to life in a way that I felt respected his seminal role in the story. The account of the old Black man reporting having been robbed by a Tulsa police officer was one of the few instances in the entire book when such an event was purely fictionalized. This was done for the purpose of establishing the sheriff's character in a way that coincided with historical accounts, and I felt very comfortable in my research that such an event was extremely likely to have happened in that time and place. Except for the historical character of Deputy Barney Clever, the other deputies were fictionalized for the sake of storytelling.

Richard Lloyd Jones was indeed a very real historical character for whom there existed an enormous amount of biographical material that made him one of the easiest characters to effectively fictionalize. However, except for Amy Comstock, the rest of the Tribune's staff was fictionalized for the purpose of creating a historically-accurate account of the paper's role in the events.

The book also ignores, for the sake of a streamlined story, that there was a second and larger Tulsa daily called the Tulsa World, which ultimately absorbed the Tribune and still exists today with most of the Tribune articles related to the events archived on its website. While Jones' notorious editorial that is credited for inciting the attempted lynching of Dick Rowland was removed from the paper's archives not long after the events and seems to be lost to history beyond second-hand descriptions, the portions depicted in this book draw on the large body of his writing that relates to the subject. While I obviously cannot know exactly what he would have written, I feel very confident that my depiction is not materially different or overly-dramatized in a way that would not be congruent with the most probable history.

The O'Dell family, along with Miss Annie and Kelly Ann's classmates, were fictional characters whose purpose was to give life to the first-hand accounts of whites who were not directly involved in the atrocities but did not feel empowered to stand up to those who perpetrated them. This was tricky business, as I wanted to be very careful not to seem as though I was creating sympathetic white characters for the sake of making the story more palatable to white audiences.

In reality, while the Tulsa of 1921 was unquestionably one of the most systemically-racist places in the entire United States at the time, there were nevertheless whites who held disdain for that reality even if they ultimately accepted and even ignored it. I also found it useful to examine the degrees of *whiteness* that existed at the time with groups like Irish Catholics, Jews, and Italians largely excluded from the definition and regarded as barely above the Blacks by groups like the KKK.

In depicting such a family, I also intended to speak to the manner in which those just above the waterline of society can often be silenced into complicity by the mere replacement of violence toward their class with simple disdain. *We might not yet be accepted by the more powerful and privileged, but at least we're not being beaten and killed. What power do we have to stop them, and what will come of it if we try beyond the same violence at our expense?* Some of mankind's most embarrassing history seems owed to this very dynamic and later first-person accounts from both death-bed confessions and those who were only children when the events occurred confirm that it played a role in this tragedy as well.

There is also the matter of unknown or less than fully-verified history. It is unknown what exactly transpired in the elevator between Dick Rowland and Sarah Page. We do know that McCullough and others thought little of the evidence presented and that Page ultimately recanted her (possibly coerced) claim that she'd been attacked and even dropped the charges. Those familiar with the building did claim that the elevator had some sort of defect that often caused it to jolt when stopping just as it reached a floor, which supports Rowland's own account, given the next day. Also, as I noted in the final chapter, the possibility that they'd been intimately familiar with each other prior to the event and were perhaps engaged in consensual affection when spotted by the clerk cannot be ignored.

Finally, it was with careful consideration that I chose the words and language of this book. There was no way to accurately portray the perspectives of those involved or the extent to which systemic racism in the city existed without having characters casually, and with great frequency, toss out abhorrent racial slurs. As much discomfort as it caused to type such atrociously-vile language (to say nothing of having to read it for the audio version of this book), I felt very strongly that censoring or otherwise watering-down the degree to which such language was used would have ultimately been a greater disservice than any offense readers may have to endure in absorbing it.

There was also a great degree of disparity among the Blacks who are depicted in terms of their education and literacy. From highly-educated professionals with advanced degrees from respected institutions such as Stradford, Smitherman, Gurley, Buck, and Isaiah, to non-educated and likely illiterate characters in Greenwood, I relied on written communications and other accounts from that time and place to craft slang and other colloquialisms that would ring true.

In the end, I feel very strongly that I have told the story in a way that respects the factual events as we best understand them and have used language and storytelling devices to dramatize a historical event in a way that is both engaging and accurate with the emphasis always remaining on the latter. My intent in writing this book, which may well have been the most gruelingly-difficult project of my career, was always to try and bring long-denied attention to a horrific tragedy for the sake of not only honoring its victims but, more importantly, better informing people of our own time, in the hope that such perspective might contribute in some small way to our collective struggle to overcome the sins of our nation's past and build a better future.

Also by Dennis Mitch Maley:

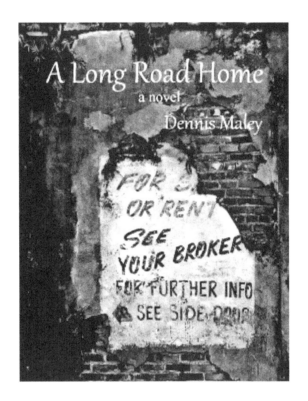

A Long Road Home

Available in hardcover, paperback and Kindle at Amazon.com.

"A coming of age story for all ages"

Charles Clappsadle, Up Close

"A great book that truly captures the spirit of New Orleans"

Dominique Espinosa, NOLA Matters

Also available at Amazon.com

Casting Shadows: Short Stories by Dennis Mitch Maley

Also available at Amazon.com

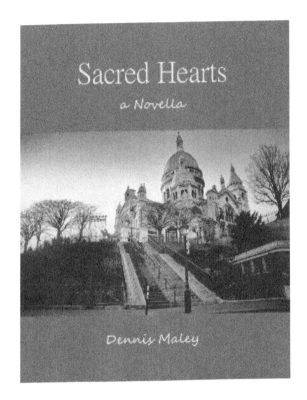

Sacred Hearts by Dennis Mitch Maley

Made in the USA
Coppell, TX
03 August 2024

35526528R00298